THE TAKING . . .

To those who would listen, Blount would have sworn that a wolf had come howling into the room and leapt at the girl. The muzzle hovered between man and beast as the wolf struck the child, and the force of the impact should have propelled her through the far window, but didn't. Instead, it looked as though the creature was thrust into her. Not *through,* but *into* her, as if she absorbed the other's body, and the two became one. There was another blinding flash, and for a split second Alan thought that both animal and child had exploded. When Blount was able to see again, the animal was gone. Only the girl remained.

Stunned, Blount lowered the shotgun. . . .

Books by Jessica Palmer

Dark Lullaby
Cradlesong
Shadow Dance

Published by POCKET BOOKS

JESSICA PALMER

POCKET BOOKS

New York   London   Toronto   Sydney   Tokyo   Singapore

An *Original* Publication of POCKET BOOKS

POCKET BOOKS, a division of Simon & Schuster Inc.
1230 Avenue of the Americas, New York, NY 10020

ISBN: 0-671-78715-2

First Pocket Books printing March 1994

10 9 8 7 6 5 4 3 2 1

POCKET and colophon are registered trademarks of
Simon & Schuster Inc.

Cover art by Jim Warren

Printed in the U.S.A.

For Maggie
In loving memory . . .

Acknowledgments

*With special thanks to Ray Miller,
without whose support this book
would never have been completed.*

Author's Note

To the people of Stockton Springs:

Let it be noted, the people in this book in no way resemble the people I knew in the lovely little community in which I lived. I have tried whenever possible to be true to the geography of the location. I may, however, have taken certain liberties for reasons of plot. Some authors would claim "poetic license."

All I ask is a learner's permit.

Prologue

A tower of darkness loomed over the bed. Tall, lean . . . scary. Like the lady in the Bible story that his momma sometimes read to him, the one who had looked at the "bad place" and turned into a pillar of salt. The family Bible had a picture in it; and this fluttering shadow looked just like it. Only this pillar was black.

A warning voice. A sharp prick of pain. And a blade was withdrawn from the little boy's throat. The knife gleamed as it caught the pale reflection of the moonlight streaming in the window. The child's gaze followed the mean curve to its scarlet-stained tip. A single bead of red quivered there before falling to the floor with a faint plop.

Then the child's eyes were drawn upward—following a ghost of a hand up to the wrist, from the wrist to the forearm, then from the forearm to the upper arm, and finally from the shoulder to the deep curve of the neck where they froze—as if the boy was afraid of what he might find if he should gaze openly upon this dark countenance. But the temptation was too great, and spellbound, he continued the upward sweep until he reached the face.

Familiar lips twisted into a sneer. The boy's mind retreated in gibbering terror, and the image was transformed. And the creature had no face. No features besides glittering eyes, sharp teeth, and a blackness, a blankness where the face should be.

The little boy wormed his way farther under the covers, shaking. *It was a dream. It had to be.* Any minute now his mother would come rushing into the room—all loving and concerned, smelling of soap and talc—to chase the nightmare away.

But no mother arrived in a flurry of flannel. The shadow beside the bed moved with a soft *swoosh*. The child screwed his eyes shut tight. Maybe if he pretended he was asleep, the figure would go away. There was another whisper of cloth, and the child braved a peek at the space above his bed.

Nothing, no shadow flittered there, just a faded cardboard mobile of butterflies and bees that swung languidly overhead.

Suddenly the boy realized that he had to *go*. If he didn't go soon, he'd pee in his pants. He scooted to the edge of the bed and scuttled across the floor to the hall. His scurrying progress was arrested by the blazing lights. He hurried for the bathroom, past his parents' bedroom door. It was ajar. He gawped. His parents were creatures of habit. They had regular hours and repeated rituals, and normally at this time of night they would be in bed, their door prudently closed against a child's prying eyes. A shudder rippled throughout his tiny frame, and a small amount of urine dribbled down his leg. The inky black line pulled at him, and he walked jerkily toward the door, slipping soundlessly through the crack into the room.

His sphincter muscles let go completely, and the wet warmth spread across his crotch, soaking his pajama bottoms. There was red, everywhere. Red discoloring the sheets, drenching the bed, splattered against the walls, and splashed upon the floor. So much red that he barely noticed his parents' lumpy shapes upon the bed.

Then he saw them. The child ran toward the bed until he was parallel to its head, and he halted. His mind recoiled from a sight too gruesome to comprehend. He whined, and backed toward the door toward the stairs to the first floor. And the red, the room, his parents' figures, all faded away, and the bed was empty.

Chattering mindlessly, the child crept to the top of the stairs. "Mom?"

The back door clicked.

"Dad?"

His foot slid down to the first step, and it screeched loudly. The boy cringed, waiting for his father to come charging up the stairs, demanding his immediate return to bed. When neither father nor mother appeared, the child tested the next step, and the next.

"Mom? Dad?"

No answer.

His foot plunked leadenly onto the next.

"Mom? Dad?" His voice took on a quavering note. "Mom, Dad?"

He reached the first floor and hesitated, blinking in the bright light. Did he really want to go on?

But he couldn't stop himself. His feet and body carried him forward where his mind refused to go. Woodenly he moved toward the kitchen. He faltered before the door, and his mind shrieked at him to turn back, back up the stairs and into bed. Tomorrow he'd wake to his mother's warm kisses and hot oatmeal sweetened with swirls of brown sugar and honey.

But if he opened this door . . .

His hand inched forward, and the slight body leaned against the door. It swung silently open to reveal . . .

His mother's head upon a platter. Her eyes protruded in horror, and her mouth was open wide, blue-white lips pulled taut over tooth and gum. His father's sat at the head of the table directly opposite his mother's. It wore an expression of shock and betrayal.

The little boy let go of the door, and it closed upon the ghastly apparitions. The child slid down the wall with a choked, mewling noise.

And his mind exploded . . .

1

"I don't know if I should believe you." Ten-year-old Tiffany Blair squatted next to the hole she had dug. Shielding her eyes from the blinding sun, she turned to her brother. "If this is a burial ground, then how come I never heard of it before from the other kids?"

Her older brother, Sam, looked down upon her with sad resignation and didn't state the obvious—that if she had been told she probably wouldn't remember. That's just the way she was. She had a mind like a sieve.

"I don't know," he said. "I heard it from Grandpa Blair, and when I looked I found this." Sam pulled an arrowhead from his pocket. Tiffany examined his find.

"How do you know it wasn't just an old village or a camp?"

"I don't," he said, shrugging and pocketing the small gray triangle. "You don't have to look if you don't want to."

"Naw." She hunched, elbows out and knees splayed in a position that would have been thought ungainly except that

5

she held it with an easy grace. The girl leaned against a branch almost as large as herself, using it to score the stony soil. Her forehead creased in concentration.

The young man settled against an old elm. Fifteen years her senior, Sam Blair spent three-quarters of the year working as a teacher, and he despised the confines of the school as much as his students did. He hated wearing a suit with its constricting belt and tie. He usually shed the coat and loosened the tie as soon as he walked in the classroom door.

During the summer months, Sam made his living as a house painter. Today, on the last official day of summer, Sam had opted for his painter's garb and the freedom it represented—wearing his spotted overalls and no shirt. Pink flab rolled out from either side of the constraining cloth.

He was a whale of a man. Towheaded and pale like his mother, Sam bore a striking resemblance to the Pillsbury Doughboy. Once he had been slim. The army made him that way, but since he'd gotten out, onetime muscle had gone all soft and mushy, and Sam's body had turned to fat.

Sam swayed from side to side to scratch his back against the rough bark of the tree. Had it not been for his precarious perch against the tree, he could have easily dozed. Golden light bathed the small glen in softly caressing rays. Cedar, spruces, and pines towered overhead, framing a sky that was the deep royal blue of early autumn.

The girl's look was intense as she tore at the unyielding earth beneath her feet. The limb snapped in her hands.

"Darn!" She stood up and wiped her palms on tattered jeans.

"Why don't you try over there where the ground isn't as hard?" Sam handed her another branch.

Through half-closed eyes, he studied Tiffany's delicate features. Dappled sunlight lit Tiffany's hair, turning it into a fiery blaze. Their now dead father had named her. With her florid coloring, red hair, and bright blue eyes, she gleamed like a jewel. But the gem was flawed, as if the seed—the child conceived even as the cancer ate away at his father's flesh—had also been flawed.

She was in special ed, not because she wasn't bright. Tiffany learned easily enough—she seemed thirsty for knowledge—but she had absolutely no retention. Sam could tell her something, ask her to repeat it, and she would; but fifteen minutes later he would ask her the same thing, and she couldn't remember what he had said. Information slipped through her, leaving her empty and waiting to be filled again. Yet she had infinite curiosity, infinite interest. Perhaps if someone kept after her, Tiffany could retain what she had been taught. But who was there to do that? Certainly his mother wouldn't.

Sam cursed his mother under his breath. He loved his little sister with a fierce protective instinct that went far beyond sibling affection. He knew their mother could do better by her. Leah Blair could afford better clothes. Tiffany's once-white blouse was gray with age. An appliquéd balloon, lost in one too many washings, was revealed only as a lighter shade of gray, and Sam wondered how many generations of children had worn that particular blouse.

Sam *knew* where his father's meager pension and the welfare checks went—to that drunken asshole Jimmy Sheridon. The only thing Sheridon didn't walk off with was the food stamps. He couldn't buy beer with those.

Around their mother, Tiffany became a chameleon, blending into the background and adapting its colors. In the violent environment that was her home, it was a matter of survival, so she attracted as little attention to herself as possible.

Sam grimaced. Tiffany avoided the house whenever Jimmy was in town, and Sam couldn't blame her. The small trailer was a battleground. He worried that the violence would spill over onto her, and Sam swore that if Jimmy ever raised a hand to Tiffany, he, soft and flabby as he was, would gleefully tear the man's lungs out.

Sam would have liked to kidnap her away. Tiffany was far too precious to leave to his mother's less-than-tender ministrations. Sam doubted his mother would have noticed the loss. Leah Blair hadn't been available for her daughter for years, ever since their father died.

Often, Sam dreamed of moving farther south—someplace civilized, someplace warm. Someplace where people couldn't trace his history back generations or know every member of his family twice-removed, like they did here in Sandypoint.

In the back of his mind he would imagine himself—slim, trim, lounging on a Florida beach during spring break and summer vacations as Tiffany played happily in the sand. Real sand, not this pebbly shit they euphemistically called sand—Pebblypoint would have been a better name. Somewhere by the sea, for Sam loved the water.

Beyond the far ridge the Penobscot Bay churned in restless and perpetual motion. It was hidden from view by the rocky cliff and a stand of trees. Voices from the beach below carried far along the ridge. The local populace celebrated Labor Day noisily, marking the season's turning and the end of the all-too-short Maine summer. In a final frenetic blast they commemorated the transition from summer's mad rush to winter's hibernation. The mouth-watering aroma of charbroiled burgers wafted to him from the beach.

Sam let the holiday sounds wash over him, listening to the soporific hum of the end of the season's tourist traffic along the distant Highway One. He took another swallow of his Molson and closed his eyes. As he did, the air around him became charged with electricity. His scalp tingled. In that single interminable moment, the atmosphere had changed and darkened, as if a cloud obscured the sun.

Sam bolted upright and opened his eyes. A puzzled expression flitted across his face as he noted the sun was still burning brightly high in the heavens. He glanced around him. Every needle, every leaf, each blade of grass stood out in stark relief, separated from its companions with crystalline clarity.

The leaves moved, rustling softly, and it felt as though a million tiny eyes stared at him from under their cover while faces formed in the writhing limbs. Sound—from both the beach and the highway—receded, and a preternatural silence descended. Insects flew in circular spires, dancing in the light, like a sparkling cyclone of fairy dust.

Tiffany gave a sharp cry and straightened. She spun to face him. "I've found something."

She held out her right hand. An arrowhead was nestled in her palm. Then she grinned impishly, dropping her right hand and extending her left, in which she held twin ivory cylinders, joined at one end.

A human finger!

Her jaw went slack, and her mouth drooped. Color drained from her face, her freckles becoming bloodred stains against blue-white skin.

Sam was physically wrenched from his lethargy as he levered his reluctant body away from the tree. He lurched forward, lumbering across the clearing like a bear. His movements slowed, becoming sluggish and torpid, as though he were moving through thick molasses and something external resisted his impetus. He railed at the unseen obstacle. His leg muscles bunched in eternal slow motion, and Sam hurtled through space to slap into something as cold, hard, and unyielding as a wall. His head snapped back—and his body followed, spinning. His brain slowed to a crawl as this wave, as clammy and oppressive as autumn fog, washed over him.

From somewhere behind him there came a muffled growl, and a blinding light speared across the small glade to strike Tiffany right between the eyes. Sam blinked, the ghostly afterimage of her puzzled expression seared across his retinas.

Then as quickly as it came, the sensation was gone, and Sam, carried by his own weight, crashed down beside his sister. His teeth closed with a sharp clack, and for a moment he sat there stunned.

Tiffany thrashed wildly. Spittle drained from her mouth. Her legs twitched and her teeth clicked like castanets. Sam tried to reach her through a maelstrom of arms and legs—it looked to Sam as though she had sprouted a couple of extra appendages just for the occasion—getting clouted on the ear for his trouble. A shiver ran through her. She flailed weakly. Then with a shuddering whimper, she went limp.

Sam lifted her head to rest on his opulent lap and cradled it in the crook of his arm, crooning soothingly, as he examined the fair skin for bruises or marks.

The wolf lifted a grizzled muzzle from his paws and peered at the playful pack. Six-week-old pups nipped at the larger yearlings. The pack's leader was separated from the rest—by rank, size, and position. He stood a full eleven hands tall, two hands larger than the next largest pack member. While his reign was as yet unrivaled, his time drew to a close. He could sense the change upon the wind. Time rested heavily upon the hunched shoulders. His joints ached, and though his size remained undiminished, the beast had grown surly with age.

The lupine snout was scarred, and one ear hung limp. The light film of cataracts clouded his eyes, giving them an eerie cast, especially in the full sun. His sight had dimmed, but his sense of smell was acute. More than a millennium had elapsed in which this highly tuned instinct had developed, and it was not dulled by time.

A rollicking pair of pups tumbled into his sacred citadel, and the pack leader snarled and snapped at them. A bitch rounded up the litter mates and herded them away from his sanctuary.

The predator sniffed the air with its sharp tang of coming winter, which arrived early in this far northern tundra in the area humans called Hudson Bay. Something had disturbed his slumber—not the pups' antics nor the den's drowsy activity—but something else again. Something which no other member of the pack had noticed. The gray beast sensed the change in the air that went unnoticed by the others, as faint as the autumn breeze.

Something stirred within his breast—recalling the image of the upstart man, a creature of two legs, who had placed his soul within the gray wolf's ancient form ages ago when the predator was young.

The spirit had awakened.

10

The wolf cocked his head, emitted an uncharacteristic whine, and then rose arthritically. A younger wolf—large but by no means approaching the height of the elder—cowered, tail tucked between his legs in token respect. No fight marked the transfer of leadership. The older wolf nuzzled the younger with true affection. The younger wolf inclined its head respectfully. Then the beasts turned right and left, nose to tail in ritual greeting.

The ancient wolf leader cocked his leg and sprayed the smaller beast with urine. The new leader accepted this complacently, standing erect and proud. The old leader bent his head to indicate the abdication of his power, and the smaller wolf received the other's acknowledgment calmly, as was his due.

Resigned, the predator slunk through the door into the crisp air of autumn as the new leader howled his farewell, and the pack added its mournful voice to his sonorous song.

The sun was suspended in the sky, lending no warmth, but beneath the chill the wolf sensed heat that rose from the earth itself. It seemed patterned, throbbing in the same rhythm as the gentle puffs of warmth that came to him from the south. The wolf bounded through crackling brush, matching his stride to the rhythm, and the pulsing eased.

The long-awaited call had come.

Loping along the path, the wolf knew that before his shadow had faded from the walls of the cave, the new leader would erase all trace of his existence, and he would be forgotten. Such was the way of things. Throughout time the need to leave had overtaken him periodically. His mate would die, and he would move on—to different packs and different mates—and all the seasons of his life merged into one.

The wolf paused, howled, and the pack answered hollowly. With a final shake of shaggy head, the wolf strode across the northern tundra wastes already hardening toward winter's freeze. Then he swerved heading south and east, in the direction he knew he must follow.

The distance was great, and the wolf had not much time, counted only in the number of suns, to return to a place that had once been home—a home he had left far behind and now resided someplace deep in his memory. The time had come to satisfy the covenant that had been placed upon him eons before.

As Tiffany showed her prize to Sam, she sensed something approaching out of the corner of her eye. Something big. She turned her head, catching sight of a dog. A great big dog. It paced, snuffling, through deep woods. It swiveled to face her. Sinewy muscles of shoulder and haunch rippled, and it launched straight at her, lips curled in a silent snarl. Color drained from her face. Her mouth dropped open as she prepared to scream. Too late, the creature connected with her flesh.

Then the next thing she knew she was floating far above the bay, drifting in a haze over the dense treetops. She felt a sudden surge of triumph and joy. For that split second *she knew.* Tiffany—the dummy—understood all that went on all around her as she had never done before. Tiffany drifted, content in her newfound completion.

Below her, her body hung limp in Sam's arms, and she perceived a stain, a blight, that spiraled above them. The shadow spread outward, stretching dark talons across the land. In it, Tiffany grasped other things. Ominous and evil. Too much to assimilate, for already the sense of impending peril was drawing her consciousness back into her twitching body.

Tiffany jolted awake. For an instant all that had gone before remained clear. The understanding, the knowledge, and the klaxon of alarm at the swarming dark cloud. She remembered it, and she knew what she should do.

The hubbub of the merrymakers came to her, unconcerned, static, only interrupted by an occasional shout or a few strident giggles. Tiffany struggled to sit up. She jumped to her feet and plunged through the tangle of branches to the ridge. Sam followed at her heels, trying to restrain her. She stopped at the cliff's edge to survey the scene below. Brilliant sun glinted off the gently rolling breakers. No animal disturbed the peaceful scene. No angry dog capered through the crowd. No one ran for life or limb. Tiffany held her breath, dimly aware as understanding receded and the knowledge she had so recently discovered vanished, leaving her empty and confused.

A boat roared past, its waves lapping vigorously against the shore. Children scrambled along the pebbly beach, and a girl squealed as a young boy pushed her into the ice-cold bay. The feeling of danger evaporated, and Tiffany couldn't remember what she was looking for anymore.

Hands clenched protectively over her head, Leah Blair leaned against the kitchen door. Her world had shrunk to a tight circle of pain and flailing fists. She was vaguely aware of the door against her back and knew some small measure of relief that Sam had taken Tiffany to the beach, thus sparing her daughter this violence.

No blow fell, and Leah risked lifting her head from the defensive hamper she had created with her arms to stare at two splayed legs. She looked up farther, and her heart contracted. Jimmy stared at her with that crazy smile of his, more of a sneer really, and that strange glint to his eye that he always got when he was ready to explode. As if to say that he'd been waiting for her to look at him just so he could smash her face in.

Her gaze drifted to his upraised fist. She watched it apathetically, struck by the unreality of it all.

He laughed, and the fist swooped down upon her face. A part of her brain detached itself, and she concentrated on the creases between his fingers and the folds of bunched flesh. The fist swelled, filling her horizon, and she noted the fine down of hair and the tiny pores as it crashed into her eye.

Pain exploded across her face, and this time she was sure bones were breaking, driving shards into her skull. Leah wanted to scream for help or cry, but she did nothing. She knew that so much as a peep from her now would unleash a new torrent of fury.

No sane man would do this to me, Leah thought wildly as his fist hovered over her, quaking with repressed energy.

Mute, she watched as it rose and fell, shrank and swelled, in the space of a few seconds. Over and over and over again he rained blows upon her head and shoulders, until she thought she could stand no more.

"Come on, squirt, we're going home," Sam said as he put his hand protectively over her shoulder and steered her away from the cliff's edge.

"No." She stuck her lip out. "I don't want to."

"Look, I want to talk to Mom," he said, propelling her into the small woods that separated the ridge from the road. This was no little fainting "spell," as his mother so quaintly put it. Sam had long suspected that his sister suffered from epilepsy, *petit mal* seizures that drained her of life and left her dazed, but this had been *grand mal* if he'd ever seen it.

"What about?"

"Never you mind," he said. "Besides, I think you should have a little something to eat."

"Me, hah! You, you mean," she said as she poked his flabby side. "You don't need it. You could live off of this for a month."

"Whoa, runt. Show a little respect for your elders," he said.

The canopy of leaves closed overhead, blocking out the sun, and Sam shivered. They went down the small dip and up again to emerge from the trees upon the gravel road. He turned left and started a slow trot toward the Four Corners.

A car roared down from the Point. The driver flashed his lights at them. The sudden light, in the tree-lined tunnel, dazzled them. Tiffany hesitated, stepping aside as the car raced through the intersection, rocketing forward along the road which wound beside the bay to the village of Sandypoint.

In the stunned stillness that followed, Sam would have sworn he saw two gleaming scarlet eyes. He glanced apprehensively over his shoulder into the shaded forest. "Come on, let's go."

They turned the corner leading up the steep hill that led to the trailer and trudged wearily up the sharp incline. Sam's face became flushed with the exertion, and he wheezed. To their right a twig snapped. They stopped. Sam turned in the direction of the sound and waited. There was a crackle of leaves and twigs, then nothing. They moved on. A soft rustle, and the shrubs chattered with a wooden rattle. He halted and peered into the dark tangle of trees. He strained to hear the soft swish of branch or twig.

Sam grabbed Tiffany's shoulder and pointed toward the trailer. "Race you!"

"Sure." She ran ahead of him, and Sam shuffled along behind, the cooler banging against his thigh. The swoosh of cloth and his own labored breath drowned out all other sounds.

Tiffany turned into the drive, and he ambled after her. She bounced past the kennel, a dirty gray concrete block building, and scrambled over a pile of wood just outside the trailer door to the rickety metal stairs. "Beat ya! Beat ya! Slowpoke!"

He motioned for her to go inside. Behind them the dogs began to howl, their mournful yelps filling the air. Sam hefted the cooler, steeling himself for battle. Sam strode through the door as Leah Blair uncoiled from the floor, her face flushed and a bruise already starting to form upon her cheek. Jimmy stood triumphantly behind her. Sam's anger at his mother dissipated, and he decided to postpone the discussion about Tiffany's seizure until another day.

The forest around him was clothed in summer greens. He tracked the young man and his little sister, not exactly sure what drew him.

The small meadow beyond the drive rippled in row upon row of golden waves. Blackberry bushes spilled down the ditch, cascading across the clearing. The man had to crawl through the tangles of wild roses to follow them. The plants sported a few late blossoms of tired, ragged pink. The branches slivered the fluffy white clouds that floated across the sky, and the prickers caught at his shirt.

He reached the clearing. The environment around the turquoise trailer had been raped—the dooryard was littered with debris and beer cans. The man settled on his haunches with loose-limbed ease. He stared at the door, his expression blank.

He listened to the dogs and tried to remember why he was here. He picked at a spot of mustard on his jeans. It fell away in a shower of yellow flakes. Then the man unfolded and took off through the short stretch of woods that led to Highway One.

2

The dread and gnawing hunger he would never forget. The child had lived with the bodies of his parents for a week—although he had no way to measure time's passage. Day blended into night, blended into day, as his parents' bodies grew ripe in the bedroom. His mind refused to acknowledge their presence, but he could not deny the smell. So the boy was forced to bypass both bedroom and kitchen, sticking to the living room whenever he could.

The detached heads guarded the kitchen, gazing down from the table with wide and accusing eyes. Their skin was snow white, bleached of the rosy hue of life. A puddle of deep purpling blue gathered on the floor beneath the table, and as the week progressed it darkened from purple to black, then to a cracked, scabrous brown. Flies crawled like a hankie of writhing black around their noses and mouths, and at the base of their stubby necks.

At first he had tried to avoid the kitchen, unable to stand their questing gaze, for the eyes followed him everywhere, but eventually hunger drove him into their dominion and under their sights. The flies rose like a black cloud at his entrance, and he'd slink, back pressed against the wall, groping his way to the pantry to forage for food.

Without supervision, he ate as he pleased. The cookies went first, followed by the Frosted Flakes. Sitting on the pantry floor with the door closed to keep out the flies and his parents' lidless stares, he munched sugar by the fistful. Later he ate his way through the Fritos and the Saltines. Then the bread, which by now had a light coating of green fuzz. It tasted funny, making him sick to his tummy.

When he was feeling particularly brave, he'd creep to the refrigerator to dig out jelly or jam, or drink milk that was so lumpy and sour. It made him wanna puke. As the child crept about the room, the blank eyes followed him.

When the cereal was gone—even the nasty-tasting bread eaten and the jar of peanut butter licked clean—the child found himself staring longingly at the pictures on boxes and cans. Roast beef hash. Bright red circles of spaghetti dripping with sauce. The yellow-orange temptation of macaroni and cheese. The pink luxury of ham.

Real food.

He cried and he banged the cans against the wall, even went to the drawer and got the hammer. He hurt his finger and his thumb, trying to open the intractable cans as they rolled away from his blows. Finally he tore into the box and ate the macaroni dry.

The lights burned as his parents had left them. Unable to reach the switches, he was compelled to stay within the narrow band of light from kitchen to hall. Eventually the downstairs hall light burned out, and he had to dart through the darkened corridor from one pool of light to another.

During the day the TV rattled and buzzed with the hum of human voices. At night he watched it snow—staying within the protection of its blue-white glow. He watched Lucy and Beaver, "The Edge of Night," "As the World Turns," and "Password" on Stockton Springs' two stations. Only when his bladder screamed at him to be empty did he go upstairs to use the toilet or drink water from the tap in the tub—the one faucet in the house he could reach. Perhaps he could have dragged a chair to the kitchen sink, but he didn't want to get that close to the table.

Sometime around the fourth day a neighbor knocked, made curious by the ever-glowing light in the kitchen and upper hall. The door boomed. The neighbor shouted, her voice muffled by the wood, and the child slouched next to the door, weeping silently. He wanted to open the door to let her in. Maybe Mrs. Jenkins had brought some food. But the boy couldn't disobey the parental injunction never to open the door to anyone if he was alone.

Hovering between window and door, he debated with himself, reasoning that he could open the door, should open the door. His parents *were* home. But with remarkable insight he realized that the lifeless masses of bone and flesh were not *really* his parents. They resembled his parents less and less as the days progressed. The eyes drooped and oozed, and the skin had begun to peel as flies collected to deposit eggs and filth. A verdigris growth had formed on their cheeks and noses. The child squeezed his eyes shut and moaned.

He was alone, and he mustn't open the door. His parents had said. So instead he cried and cried, unable to move, unable to do anything to save himself.

And the lady went away.

On the seventh day, when the little boy was picking green olives from the broken glass jar on the kitchen floor, a policeman broke down the door to find the child, dirty, hungry, and babbling incoherently.

The ghostly gray beast rested on the edge of the clearing beyond the human settlement. The beast slept poorly within sight of man's road. As the dawn came, the aged predator lay in his makeshift summer den and dreamed uneasily of its former occupant.

An eighteen-wheeler roared by, and the wolf leapt to his feet with lightning reflexes, his eyes glowing like twin moons. The lupine brain whirred, tormented, tortured by the continuous sensory input—of cars, of people, of all the sleepy villages and towns through which it had journeyed. The varied scents created a miasma, a stench, which threatened to overwhelm the animal. Stoic and silent like a god, the wolf raised its head high, listening.

His travels had transformed him, and the wolf had lost some of his lanky, gaunt look as muscle filled in the space between ancient ribs. The fur smoothed and the scars that marred the gray coat shrank. The aches of battles melted away to become little more than vague memories of ancient triumph.

The animal fought against the instinct to run, sorting through smells and sounds to isolate one. The predator seeking his quarry, seeking the spirit of "the man." Here, the man-scent was strong, and it was difficult to differentiate one from another.

Cloaked in straggly spring growth, his lair remained unobserved, as did the wolf. To the human eye the beast appeared nothing more than a ghostly apparition, a presence felt rather than seen, as an unexplained chill or a presentiment of danger. Rarely did this animal deign to reveal himself to modern man. The predator instilled an atavistic terror in the European mind. Lesser wolves had succumbed to the ways of the white man, using his roads and eating from his dumps, but not this wolf.

Older than the oldest legends, the predator had, years ago, lived beyond the average life span of its species. The wolf had been a part of the land since its creation. For the natives of the continent, the predator was a protector, a god and totem for its strongest clan—secure in nature's pantheon.

Instead, the beast ranged from one pack to another—one life to another. In many, the leader would yield, acknowledging the newcomer's divinity. The natural order imposed respect, even reverence. In other packs, where white man's influence was strong, the wolf had had to rip and tear his way to the top of the heap.

Inevitably, though, the wolf would be forced to leave, knowing his time was through by the aches in his body and the number of challenges from his bustling young. Or when the blood of his body flowed too potently in the veins of a single pack. Often his departure was hastened by the loss of his mate. Each parting brought pain, and each was necessary, as the time of rebirth and renewal is necessary—when spring follows winter and summer follows spring.

Forests had replaced the rolling tundra as the beast invaded the sparsely populated realm of man. He could feel the hostility that the earth had absorbed from humanity, for humankind bent everything to its collective will, and the land itself had become saturated with enmity toward wolf and all wild things.

The unwelcome visitor did not mark this new territory or leave his scent to note his passing. With a patience and sapient intelligence beyond the inborn abilities of the species, he followed the call without stopping unless hunger and fatigue forced him to. Dawn came and he arose, leaving his temporary den behind, and he slithered over the blacktop into the woods beyond. The wolf trotted cautiously forward a few paces, only to halt. The great lupine muzzle lifted to the sky and sniffed. His head ducked and he sniffed again. He could smell distant rain and the salt tang of the sea.

Some primordial part of his being, some ancient wisdom, told him which direction to go, told him he must follow the scent of sea and man. An ear pricked at the distant bay of hounds, like some far-off dream. He cocked his gray head and moved in that direction.

The jarring jangle of the telephone was incorporated into his dream where Alan Blount slogged through a seaside marsh he knew did not exist upon the Point. The Retreat, atop the promontory of Sandypoint, jutted into the sea across the small cove, and here, where he should have stood upon dry land, his feet were sucked into a deep black mire. It clung to his boots, his legs, dragging him down.

His pheasant gun was cradled in his arms, and Alan Blount struggled to reach . . .

The telephone.

His arm lashed out to bash at the alarm. It crashed to the floor.

Opening one eye, he sat up. Yesterday's beer sloshed sickeningly around in his stomach.

Brrring!

He brought the receiver to his ear and croaked into the phone.

"Hello." He paused. "Sheila? What's wrong?"

His wife, looking rumpled, threw off the comforter and yawned. Scratching her ribs, she slipped to the edge of the bed and padded softly toward the bathroom. Alan watched her sleepy-eyed. He listened for a few moments and then spoke into the phone.

"Calm down, Sheila. Something's happened to Andrew? I'll be over as soon as I can."

The toilet flushed, and Ginny returned. "What's up? Do you have time for coffee?"

"Sure. That was Sheila Erhart. Something's wrong with Andrew. I think he's dead, probably got hit by a car or something. Don't know why the hell she called me."

Ginny shouted over her shoulder as she moved toward the kitchen. "Because you are the local fuzz, my dear, and you know how she feels about that dog. Andrew is all she's got."

"Well, I'm not rushing over without coffee. Besides, I gotta dress. What time is it?"

"Seven."

"Great, on a day when I could have slept in. Christ, a damn dog."

"Come on, honey, she's just a lonely, little old lady."

He paused over his uniform—it was too soon for work— and then shrugged. Sheila would expect it.

Ginny filled a thermos with coffee and poured a separate cup for him to drink on the way. He gave her a hurried peck on the cheek and walked out to the squad car, not quite ready to begin the day.

No putting it off, he thought, and he slid behind the wheel and turned on the squawking radio out of habit.

Normally, Alan Blount worked out of the modern

Bucksport police station. By rights, he shouldn't be answering this call. Stockton Springs was not within Bucksport's jurisdiction. It belonged to Belfast some seven miles southeast of here.

But then by rights, Sheila shouldn't have called him. Unfortunately, most of his neighbors didn't give a hoot about jurisdiction or care which station Blount was attached to. He was local, someone who knew the area and the people. When something happened in Sandypoint or Stockton Springs, they didn't waste time calling one department or another, they called him—exhibiting total disregard for the pleasantries of police protocol.

Generally he didn't mind, except on days like today. The day after Labor Day when he'd drank too much, eaten too much, and gotten too little sleep. He was working evenings this week and would have preferred to sleep in. One thing he didn't want to be doing was starting his day so early in the day. Blount stuck his finger inside his collar and gave a little tug before pulling onto Highway One.

Unofficially, at least, Blount *was* the Stockton Springs police department, and he was often pulled from his duties to deal with minor matters here or at the Point. Belfast PD never objected. Why should they? It lessened their work load and saved them a long drive for no better reason than to break up a family squabble, which could probably be handled with more tact by a local.

Stockton Springs, with its one-man de facto police department, was a nightmare of overlapping jurisdictions. It had absorbed the smaller village of Sandypoint, despite the fact that the two communities were detached by landmass and geography. In every way the two were divided. Sandypoint commanded a separate dot on AAA roadmaps and even had its own post office, open all of two hours a day. Yet by arbitrary ruling in far-off Augusta, the two communities had become one. The boundaries were redrawn, and Sandypoint was assimilated into the Stockton Springs township.

Although the people of Sandypoint shrilly decried their status as a separate village, when trouble came, such points of contention were forgotten, and the citizens of Sandypoint and Stockton Springs both called Alan—as one of their own—in preference to far-flung Belfast.

Generally speaking, he didn't mind. But sometimes the officer wished his neighbors would follow the normal line of command.

Alan turned right off Highway One heading toward the Four Corners. At this time of day Verona Island across the bay remained shrouded in mist. The dark blue-green line of pines formed an indistinct picket, marking the area where the water, land, and sky met. The sky above was the crystal, pristine blue of a late summer. Already the heat was oppressive, and Blount paused to wipe the sweat from his brow before turning at the Four Corners.

The village of Sandypoint lay to the left, in the cleft near the small inlet which separated the town from the beach. The area along the blacktop leading from the Four Corners to the post office was also populated while the area toward the Point itself was reserved for summer camps.

The cruiser swung from the blacktop onto the gravel road leading away from the village and toward the Point, where Sheila lived. She was the only full-time resident on the Point proper, and sometimes Alan worried about the older woman living out here all alone.

Branches twined overhead, and Alan blinked as his eyes adjusted to the sudden change in illumination. The squad car followed the bend in the gravel road, turning again as he reached the long drive.

Blount parked next to the garage and stepped from his car. His heart skipped a beat. Sheila Erhart stood next to the house atop the hill, in the midst of the normally well-kept flowerbed. The roses had been flattened, and the many red blossoms were strewn across the lawn.

No, not blossoms, something else again. Pieces of flesh and tufts of gray, white, black, and tan fur that had once been Andrew were scattered around Sheila's feet.

Swallowing hard, Alan froze, stunned, not wanting to believe his eyes. Sheila's seamed, tear-stained face swung on him as a large crow landed a hundred yards away to carry off some juicy morsel. He felt ill. Sheila screamed, lunged forward to chase the bird away with the broom, looking for all the world like a witch in a storybook. Her foot skidded in something pink—in what Alan recognized, with a second glance, as intestines—and she fell facedown in the muck.

It was too much. Alan vomited up this morning's half-drunk cup of coffee and a few stringy remains of last night's supper.

Two peas in a pod, that's what they look like, Blount thought a few hours later as the Fletcher boys confronted each other, eyes sparking. Only these "peas" fended each other off with pitchforks clenched in white-knuckled grips.

First the damn dog and now this!

It seemed as if Alan had already done a full day's work, and he hadn't even made it into the station yet. Despite the early start, he was going to be late clocking in.

The boys stood with legs spread wide for balance on the opposite sides of the large barn. Heads of identical curly hair, the deep tan of oak leaves in autumn, moved in unison, dodging this way and that, miming the other's movements, as though each twin knew and could predict the other's maneuver before he made it.

Few people could tell Terry from Eddie. Closer than close, they liked the same things, played on the same teams, even wore the same clothes, enjoying people's confusion.

Terry—at least Blount thought it was Terry—took a swing at his brother.

Both were football heroes. In this fight they were well matched, and if Blount had had to bet on one or the other, he didn't know which he would have chosen.

The officer regarded them dryly, as far removed from the action as possible. He knew better than to try and drag the two of them apart. Blessedly they were tiring of the sport, and their swipes were less vicious, cutting a broad swathe that hadn't a snowball's chance in hell of connecting. The way Blount figured it, sooner or later one of them would give up. He couldn't imagine either boy staying angry with the other for long.

The officer heard a hissed name, but the word was lost in

the swoosh of a pitchfork as it swept through the dead space between them.

A girl. That was what this whole thing was about. Some girl.

He chuckled softly. Puppy love. It hadn't been all that long ago when he was young, and he remembered how damned important everything had seemed. Especially his first love. Blount probably would have gleefully taken after his brother with a pitchfork if the elder boy had started fooling around with Alan's girl.

The susurrating sounds of the slashing fork brought him from his reverie. Eddie sagged against the side of the barn, and Blount sprung before Terry could take advantage of his brother's lapse. The officer yanked the pitchfork from Eddie's limp grasp and then spun to disarm his brother, only to be met by dirt-clotted tines pointed right at his gut.

3

For Tiffany, school was exquisite torture, especially the first day. Even the thrill of new schoolbooks—with their bright pictures and their pages still smelling of ink and feeling cool and moist, as if they were still damp and fresh from the presses—palled as soon as Tiffany's teacher gave her her first assignment. The image of the previous year's agony would surface from a vague and hazy past. Time stretched menacingly before her, and the school year yawned like a black abyss into which her future fell.

First, there was the bus ride, which she faced alone each day. The other children of her age went to a different school while she, the dummy, rode with the high school students to the special class in Searsport. The seats around her were always empty, and Tiffany was isolated from the others by more than physical distance—she was segregated by the rift of years and a gulf of human intelligence.

For the most part the other riders on the bus ignored her—except when John Simpson, the bus bully, deigned to heap his scorn upon her. Then she'd retreat into her special place where they couldn't find her, and the John Simpsons of the world couldn't bother her.

This sense of difference carried over to the hours after school, when the other kids in town would gather in a tight knot from which she was inevitably excluded. As if what was wrong with her was catching.

School recess was a unique punishment designed by someone, Tiffany had decided, who hated kids in general and her class in particular. The school board had decided, with infinite wisdom, that the other children would be more understanding of, or less frightened by, Tiffany and her classmates if they associated with them on a daily basis. In reality the other students raised cruelty, embarrassment, and shame to new heights, or depths. Perhaps if the board had ever seen the resulting debacle, or listened to the taunts and jeers, they would have revised their estimation, but they did not notice or even seem to care.

Often Tiffany wished it would rain, and keep on raining *forever,* so they wouldn't have to go outside and face the other kids. The special ed students were something of a captive audience. There was Gerry, with his hearing aid, bigger than a Sony Walkman, but at least he couldn't hear their derision. And Heather, with her white stick and milk-white eyes that seemed to look every place and no place all at the same time. And Wally, with his continuously moving body strapped to his wheelchair. Luckily, the other kids left Tiffany alone. She, at least, *looked* normal.

Class wouldn't have been half bad if it weren't for the lessons. Tiffany liked Miss Grant, her special education teacher. In the child's eyes, the woman was young and pretty—because anyone who treated Tiffany tenderly became beautiful. The teacher was, in fact, quite plain. Tall and thin to the point of being gangly, she walked with a loose-limbed gait as if her joints weren't quite strung together properly.

Tiffany turned from her contemplation of the clouds forming to the north and stared owlishly at her book. She was vaguely aware of Miss Grant's presence behind her as the teacher ambled from student to student. Tiffany glared at the miscellaneous squiggles that graced the page, trying to make sense of them. She knew they meant *something*. She squinted. Her fingers traced the figures. Two lines joined at the top like a cub scout tent or a tepee with a line drawn through it. A round thing like an incomplete circle, also with a line drawn through it. A line with a dot, like a hat or a head on top. Another circle. A horseshoe.

Frustrated, Tiffany glanced up from the primary reader, stared outside, and then back at the board. Miss Grant was bent almost double over Wally. His body writhed like a snake as he batted at the computer keyboard that allowed him to communicate with both teacher and classmates. The activity distracted Tiffany, and she turned quite happily away from the confusion of black hashmarks and mysterious curlicues in the book. Only action could hold her attention for long. Something that flitted and moved. Otherwise the world dwindled and faded into a gray nothingness until something else stirred, capturing her interest. The flicker of a fly's wing or whirl of dust along the road.

People also could seize her attention. Sam often did this, directing her energies. Occasionally he would have to remind her of what she was doing, for Tiffany was prone to getting caught in a motion, performing repetitive tasks until she was told to stop.

The computer screen flashed, and the computer beeped as Wally hit the wrong key. The computer had been Miss Grant's idea, and when the school board had not been willing to cough up the money, the teacher had bought a cheap, second-hand Commodore and brought it into class.

It had worked. Everybody but Heather enjoyed the thing —she couldn't see the lights—and Tiffany eyed the computer wondering when it would be her turn to play with it. Miss Grant noticed her watching them and grimaced her disapproval, indicating Tiffany's open reader with a jut of her chin.

Torture. Absolute torture. Boredom, beyond boredom. Beyond tears.

Two lines joined at the top. A round thing like a circle,

with a line drawn through it. A line with a dot, like a hat or a head perched on top. Another circle. A horseshoe. Tiffany had seen all these things before. She saw them nearly every day, or whenever her mom would let her watch "Sesame Street." Tiffany tapped her lower lip contemplatively.

They were . . . letters!

And Tiffany tried to remember what Big Bird, Bert, Kermit, or Grover had to say about letters, but it eluded her. Tears of rage squeezed out from under her lids. She and Sam had recited them together, and he had explained them to her. She *knew* what they were. She knew that she knew, but whenever she got close to the idea, the meanings ran skittering away from her.

A shadow fell over Tiffany's book as the teacher paused behind the student, clearing her throat. "How are we doing, Tiffany?"

The child lifted shining eyes to peer at Miss Grant, and the woman sighed.

"Can't remember them?" She stooped over the book, placing a finger on the tent-thing. "This is an *A.*"

Her finger moved over to hover above the circle thing. "This is an *E,* and this is an . . ."

The dawning light of realization flashed in the girl's eyes. *"I!"*

Tiffany's smaller index finger took over where the teacher's had halted.

"O and . . ." The girl's voice faltered.

"U," Miss Grant prompted. "And they are all called . . ."

A bewildered expression crossed Tiffany's face.

"Letters?" she said hopefully.

"Yes, and vowels," Miss Grant corrected her gently, and Tiffany's face fell.

"Let's try it again. This is . . ."

Tiffany stared at the page as all the letters dissolved into a bunch of meaningless squiggles and lines, and she burst into tears.

Gideon Sheridon sat in the crotch of an old apple tree. Shielded from casual view by a large sign on his left and by twisted limbs on his right, it was his favorite roost. From here he could survey the entire village, what there was of it, like a king viewing his domain. He could watch all, and no one could see him. Sheltered by the branches, Gideon was protected from prying eyes and unmolested by the taunts of children, adolescents, and adults.

Across the street a single solar starburst glinted off the plate-glass window of the new post office. Built two or three years ago, the post office had been transferred from an old clapboard house farther up the street to its current domicile, a modern glass and steel affair that was still new by the town's standards. Behind the shiny edifice they kept the trucks owned by the township, and Gideon could observe the town's custodian as he rambled back and forth between machinery.

Gideon wriggled deeper into his seat, molding his body to the bough's bends. His age was difficult to gauge. His skin was florid and greasy, covered with acne, which gave the illusion of youth. Yet silver streaked his hair. His expression was guileless, and when caught by the young man's vapid, vacuous gaze, the observer soon realized that his mind was likewise empty of thought or reason.

Life appeared to Gideon as snapshots. Like those he found pasted in the scrapbook his Gran had given him so he wouldn't forget his parents. For some reason the photos filled him with disquiet, and he had burned the book years ago, one night when he'd run low on fuel in the shed he had called a home.

Family meant little to him. He missed his grandmother, whom he thought of only as the nice lady who had taken care of him—once. The village idiot, he was tolerated by the citizens. After his grandmother died, the townspeople looked after him, after their fashion. He was, after all, one of their own. They gave him food and odd jobs. During the summer, Gideon cut people's lawns, and in the winter, he shoveled snow.

Gideon missed the nice, cozy little house where he had once lived—that had been taken away years ago to pay for back taxes—but he still had the shed, where he kept his torn sleeping bag and a camp stove for cooking, and a small woodstove that a neighbor had donated, so the outbuilding behind his former house had become home.

He didn't miss the older brother who used to beat him, who made the children's jibes and jeers and the teenagers' stinging rocks seem small things. These days his brother studiously ignored Gideon, but Gideon didn't care. In fact, he preferred it that way. The man touched his misshapen nose broken by his brother in years past, then let his hands drop to rest lightly upon his thighs. He rocked back and forth, moaning—a single monosyllable of lament for remembered pain.

Below, people scurried to and fro between Stockton Springs' little grocery and the post office unaware of his presence. Bored, Gideon turned away from the bustle and activity. His neck and jaw relaxed, and his head rolled to one side. From this strange posture, the idiot examined the sky. It had changed. The blue of autumn had turned to an unnatural purple as if a hole had opened over the town. It was surrounded by cloud, like a giant smoke ring. The gap resembled a hungry mouth that seemed to suck in all sunshine and the surrounding light. Gideon glanced nervously down at the ground, half expecting the townspeople to pause and point at the turbulent sky, but they hustled with the same ceaseless motion—into the post office and back to cars without a moment's notice.

Scowling, Gideon wondered why no one else besides himself saw it. Often in the past he had discovered that he saw a great many things that other people never took time to notice.

But this . . . this was big. This was huge! Something was eating the sky.

His scowl turned to a frown, and the crease between his brows deepened to a fissure.

Something bad was happening here. The gap threatened to let in the immense unknown. Something that had started . . . *How long ago now?*

His brows dipped as he concentrated, trying to find some measure, but he had no concept of time. The thought fluttered away as the surrounding branches were tormented by a monstrous wind that affected none of the other trees around him.

Black clouds that no one else could see billowed overhead, hurtling east toward the gray waters of the bay. A large droplet of rain splashed against his face. The earth beneath him rumbled. Thunder crashed, and lightning snaked from the opening as the sky split with a blinding flash. It burned its afterimage onto his lids.

In his mind's eye the clouds ruptured, releasing a silver deluge.

It had begun. The words echoed inside his head, as if put there by someone else. He shivered, realizing that soon even this haven would be safe no more.

Gideon opened his eyes, gazed at the inky spot that no one else observed, and waited for the storm to enter from this hole where sky, land, and sea fell in upon one another.

"Ptchsh. Ptchsh. Ptchsh. Ptchsh." The sound of machine-gun fire spewed from puffed cheeks.

"Eh-eh-eh-eh-eh," Tiffany responded, making machine-gun noises—like a *girl*—in the back of her throat.

The clouds that had gathered during the day churned threateningly overhead. Wind whipped through the trees as Jonathan's flight was arrested by a spray of imaginary bullets.

"Got'cha!" one of their opponents yelled jubilantly.

Jonathan's head-butting charge dissolved. He flung his head back, his spine arched, and he spun in a stiff pirouette before nose-diving forward, his hands clutching his chest.

Dead.

"Pssst," another one of Tiffany's playmates hailed her from behind a clump of bushes. The five-year-old Freddie Archibald motioned for her to enter their hideout. With another rattled splash of gunfire, Tiffany lunged through the underbrush.

"Have they got you yet?" Freddie asked, eyeing the officially dead Jonathan as he sat up to brush dust from his pants.

"Uh-uh," she said. "Or would I still be walking around?"

"Good. Find Tommy and meet me up at the Point," Freddie hissed, and then he burst from their hiding place with a loud sputtering of lethal bullets. Tiffany watched the younger boy as he bounded away.

Tiffany usually played with the younger boys, five-year-old Jonathan and his friends. Their games always required action, and their attention span was about the same as hers. Together they'd play catch, or baseball, tag, or tackle and war. King of the mountain. Like perpetual motion machines, there was always some sort of game going.

She almost never played with girls. A game of dolls left her cold, soon bored, and groping in perpetual fog or mist, which seemed to settle between her and an immobile world. She had a few dolls, which she rarely touched. Most of them were broken, sacrificial victims to the games she played with the boys.

Because of her size, Tiffany was their leader. Through her association with them, she was invited to join in the games of the older boys, as they had today, adding a whole gang of kids to swell their ranks. Or sometimes the older boys sided together against their younger brothers, allowing them to play because it was an easy win. Their games tended to be more involved, with elaborate plans and discussion, and Tiffany was easily lost.

As soon as Freddie withdrew from her line of vision, the girl's face went lax. The world faded out until a butterfly flickered across her view, and Jonathan broke into the bushes. Her eyes sparked and lit upon her younger cousin. His T-shirt was dirty, smudged from where he'd done his death-defying plummet into extinction.

"Wha'cha s'posed to do?" Jonathan asked.

"Uh"—she scowled, fishing around in a fuzzy brain for the recent discussion—"find Tommy and meet Freddie at the Point."

"I'll go, too."

"But you're dead," she protested.

"So? Doesn't mean I can't tag along. I just won't shoot anybody," he added reasonably.

Satisfied with this logic, Tiffany shook her head in assent. "Okay, let's go."

They erupted from the bushes just as a large group of enemy soldiers stumbled upon them. Both were treated to a barrage of clattering bullets, from chest and throat, at point-blank range, and disregarding an obvious hit, Tiffany ran on.

"Hey," said Royce to the retreating pair, "you've been hit. You're dead."

Jonathan swung around, hopping on one foot backward, arms extended in an indifferent shrug. "You can't kill me; I'm already dead."

And he pursued Tiffany into the stand of trees, screaming after her, "Hey, Tiff, they hit you. You're dead. . . ."

The sticks, which they had once cradled as guns, swung free as the older boys careered after the duo, descending upon the Retreat beach en masse.

"Hey," hollered Royce, self-nominated spokesman. "Come on out. Game's over if you can't play fair."

Crouching beside Tiffany, Freddie shouted back at them, "Wha'd'ya mean?"

"That dummy Tiffany can't play anymore; she's dead."

"Am not!" she said.

"Are, too! I shot you myself," Royce said.

"Me, too," said another boy.

"And we're not going to play with you unless you play fair, and that means"—he paused for effect—"you lay down and die when you're shot. Anybody but a dummy would know that."

Hiding behind a rock, Tiffany's face melted, and her cousin Jonathan looked from her to Freddie Archibald. Tiffany stood, crying.

"Dummy!" the boys shouted.

Tiffany wished she could crawl between the rocks and die for real.

"Dummy!" Alex Fletcher shrieked. And a rock thunked somewhere between her feet.

"Hey, dummy, don'cha know when to lie down and die?" Andy Harmon mocked.

"You're so *stoopit* you don't even know when you been shot," said Steve Smith.

Royce Brennigan and his buddies leapt in a ring around her. "Dummy, dummy, dummy," they chanted.

There was the echo of thunder in the distance.

"Whad'ya learn in school today?" said Royce, "Did ya learn how to spell ya name?"

Pulling her shoulders back, Tiffany stepped from the protective shade into the sunlight.

Her tormentor noted a tear in her jacket and guffawed. "Don't even have any decent clothes? Ya' motha' too busy fucking Jimmy Sheridon to look after you, huh?"

He made a circle of thumb and forefinger and proceeded to probe the circle with his forefinger. She launched at him, arms swinging. The children jeered as her fist connected with the side of his head, and then fell silent as their hero wailed, one hand clasped to his ear.

"Take it back!" she screamed.

He glowered at her from his little piggie eyes before catapulting forward to land on top of her, and they dropped in a tangle of arms and legs. Tiffany grunted as the air was forced out of her, squished from her lungs in a noisy rush. Her arms and legs splayed, Royce's larger body covered hers, and they faced each other, nose-tip to nose-tip.

"Fuckin' bitch," he said, and Royce stuck his hand up her shirt to squeeze an undeveloped tit.

A shadow darkened the sky, and a large hand grasped the boy's shoulder. Tiffany looked up at the silhouette. Royce sputtered and turned. He stilled, and Tiffany squinted her eyes so she could see her savior, who was backlit by the harsh glare of sunlight.

Two huge hands hefted Royce from her body and tossed him aside as if he were nothing. One of these hands—which Tiffany noticed were dirty, the folds lined with mud—reached out to offer her his assistance.

Tiffany peered into the face of Gideon Sheridon, Jimmy's younger brother. She swallowed a few times before she took the proffered assistance. All the children, except Tiffany, scattered. When she had righted herself, Gideon clumsily

36

tried to pat the dirt from her clothing, and his touch was surprisingly gentle. He released her, and she debated whether or not she, too, should bolt and run. He made no threatening moves, so she stayed put, taking the time to examine his features.

Everybody knew the village idiot, but Tiffany had never seen him up close. He kept to himself, skulking in the shadows, slinking away at the approach of another human being.

He stared at her with infinite sadness.

She put her hands in her pockets and studied her feet for a minute, thinking that there was something she should say. After all, they were almost related, and Tiffany realized that he had probably saved her from a darn good thrashing. When she raised her head to thank him, he was gone, hardly a leaf disturbed by his exit.

Thunder exploded overhead with an ear-splitting crack. The first fat raindrops splashed against the ground, and the wind whirled, picking up her hair and blowing it in her face.

Sam's car pulled up. "Hi, squirt, I was just on my way over to the trailer. Can I offer you a lift, kid?"

With a glance at the vibrating foliage, she said yes and climbed into the passenger seat.

As Sam and his mom fought in the other room, Tiffany crawled on her hands and knees to the bed, where she dug her Wonder Woman lunch box from the rubble of unmated shoes, dirty socks, and dust bunnies that had found permanent residence there. Her battered treasure chest contained everything she thought worth keeping. Her favorite stones —smaller pebbles and big, black stones striped with the purest white and deep ruby red. Little pieces of Maine's rocky coastline. Broken pieces of jewelry and shiny baubles. Here was her baby ring, the one her father had given her just before he died. Tiffany couldn't remember him, but her mother had told Tiffany about him often enough that he had become larger than life.

She poured the contents onto the floor and stopped to examine a mollusk shell with its milky mother-of-pearl interior. Her finger circled and darted over the heap. With a slight hesitation her hand hovered over the item she sought. It trembled slightly before dipping to grasp the human bone. She lifted it gingerly and stared at the smooth ivory. It felt silky to the touch and lighter than the many rocks she collected.

In the living room Sam's voice rose in anger. "Don't you understand what I'm trying to tell you? We're not talking about fainting spells. What happened on Labor Day was a full-blown seizure. She should be tested for epilepsy. If she does have it, there's medicine she could be taking."

"And where do you expect the money to come from? These tests cost money, you know," Leah said.

"If money's the problem, I'll pay for it."

Tiffany listened as her mother paced in the living room. Then she brought her knees to her breast and tried to make herself as small as possible. She did not like being a subject of contention. Her eyes glazed slightly, and she hardly seemed to breathe, blending into the wall.

"No, money's not the problem. You are. I wish you would get off my back and leave Tiffany and me alone. She's"—her mother paused for a moment—"a good girl."

"Don't you think I know that, Mother?"

"Then why are you and everyone else always trying to tell me that something's wrong with her? They've got her in special ed, fer chrissake. Get off my back. Get off *her* back. There's nothing wrong with Tiffany."

The girl squirmed, ill at ease. She wished Sam wouldn't worry. He had never really understood. There was nothing to worry about. During her spells, as her mother called them, Tiffany went away to a place where she was protected. She was pulled out of herself and transported away like in her dreams, when she would fly high above life to watch the world below, detached from all that happened.

"You weren't there! How the hell would you know?" Sam said.

Tiffany ran the bone through her fingers, like a thread through the eye of a needle, until she reached the slight bulge of the joint. Then she flagged, slumping against the wall to retreat once more into her nowhere place. The bone dropped from her flaccid fingers and rolled to her feet.

And Tiffany was in a shadowy world, a place gone gray and devoid of all color. The woods that surrounded her were not her woods. They looked subtly different, somehow altered and changed. Sounds around her were amplified, and her ears detected much, much more. She sensed the movement of grouse before it took flight, the screech of the hawk as it was borne on the wind, and she understood them, knowing the meaning of each. Tiffany could hear the cricket as it trudged wearily through the grass, and she noted new trills in the whippoorwill's song. Its warbling descant carried a different message than she had known in the past, and Tiffany realized that the bird's refrain was neither sweet nor melodious, but harsh, the avian cry of territorial imperative.

And smells. In this place that was no place, Tiffany was surrounded by a universe of odors. The familiar fragrance of leaf and fern, pungent pine, and crisp grass became almost overpowering, and there were other smells she had never noticed before. The boundary markers of wolf and deer. The faint tang of urine or the more ephemeral aroma of a rutting buck's tears. Without knowing how she did so, Tiffany sorted and identified each according to its nature.

Soft fur brushed her cheek, and Tiffany recognized the dog that had come to her upon the ridge. Only this time she knew it for what it was—*a wolf*. But she felt no fear. Inside the trailer her hand reached out to stroke an unseen head while in this land of dreams Tiffany mounted the beast's broad back. She clutched the shaggy pelt, knowing at long last she was safe.

Something hit the ground beyond her window with a soft thud and the rattle of scratchy twigs. A shadow disconnected itself from the trailer, head bent against the steady rain. The loping figure dodged into the trees to be swallowed by shivering trees of the forest.

4

Fall began with a punitive blast, and the fine weather of
Labor Day was replaced by rain. The storm displayed none
of the characteristics of typical autumn rains—a slow,
steady drizzle that cooled. Instead, it came with all the
turbulence of the summer tempest, with lightning flashes
and thunder strikes. It dampened, with scalding pelletlike
drops, as though the sun still beat with a vengeance somewhere beyond the clouds, and the air became oppressive.
Neither did the storm retreat after unloading its burden of
rain, as summer storms often do. Instead, it lingered, as
though it played a cat-and-mouse game with the inhabitants.
Centered precisely over Stockton Springs and Sandypoint, it
left the surrounding communities untouched.

Robert Schoenwald grunted and moved with purpose
between the huge machines that had become his family—
the township's large Cat, the snowplow, and the old Chevy
truck. As Bob watched, someone darted across the post
office parking lot, a newspaper draped over her head.

Anyone with a lick of sense had stayed indoors today. Not Bob. His job demanded his attendance—something like the mail—neither rain, nor snow . . .

Picking up a wrench, he shambled back over to the truck and gave the radiator a ruddy great whack. Then he swore as he eyed the jumbled pile of barricades in the bed of the truck. People depended on him to keep the roads clear, to grease the physical machinery that kept the township functioning, but the rains were gaining on him. He should have had these barricades up an hour ago. The dead battery didn't help. Normally, Bob liked his job—he believed it commanded a certain amount of respect—but today he wasn't so sure.

Not an ambitious man, Schoenwald had never had big dreams. He didn't ask for wealth. His goals had been the same ever since he was a kid. He wanted to work out-of-doors, using his hands rather than his mind, and in that, he had been successful. Bob had wanted to stay in the same town that he had grown up in, with his wife—who, when he spared time for daydreaming, always wore the same face—and his kids. Although he wasn't always so sure about the latter.

Through the years—with his head stuck inside the guts of the township's antiquated Caterpillar coercing and cajoling it with threats, sweat, and labor into operating for just one more season—Bob could almost forget that he had been carrying a torch for Aggie McKenzie since high school. He had stayed single long after she had wed, and when her husband died, he'd waited quietly at the sidelines, hoping she would notice him.

Bob and Aggie had grown up together, and she was still to Schoenwald's thinking a mighty fine looking woman. If Stockton Springs had had a Rotary, Aggie McKenzie—as the owner of the primary local business, a gas-station-*cum*-grocery-store—would have been its premier member. Bob took every opportunity to court her, after his fashion, and each coffee break was spent lounging around the store, leaning on the counter, exchanging bits of information and idle gossip.

Schoenwald had once believed that with so few ambitions, he couldn't possibly fail. He didn't ask for much, and at times like this, when the sky spit rain and he was up to his armpits in work, Bob was forced to acknowledge—with a thirsty look at the gray storefront—how far down along the social scale he was and just how far away his dreams were.

His desire for children was gone. It was one ambition he didn't mind botching. He didn't understand them. Bob was one of the few to breathe a sigh of relief at the start of the school year. The past week had been one of peace. Even the weekend had been quiet, the rains forcing parents to keep their children at home. Kids had changed since he was a child. Gotten mean. Bob had tried to get along with them. He even coached Little League one summer, but Bob had found them intolerable, and he had been the butt of more than one child's joke, which always seemed to take a physical form. They threw stones at him in the summer as he mowed the grass around the schoolyard and snowballs as he plowed the streets in winter. And they called him names. *"Weirdo, queer, homo."* Probably in reference to his single status, but how could you explain to kids nowadays, when marriages were as quickly cast off as yesterday's clothes, the concepts of devotion, love, and loyalty to a single woman.

Schoenwald banged on the battery and inhaled deeply, relishing the assorted smells of tar, gas, grease, and motor oil, which he found somehow reassuring. Making a disgusted noise, he set to work, removing the battery from its position and hauling it inside the shed where he could replace it with the one he had just charged. He placed the dead battery in the charger, cradled the live one against his gut, and shuffled back to the truck.

Then he climbed into the pickup and tried it. It started with a growl. He got out to lock the shed. A door slammed, and he turned toward the store, wishing he could stop and take a break—maybe visit with Aggie—but thunder rolled across the sky, reminding him of his duty. The roads back toward the lighthouse were flooded. All it would take was a couple of citizens plowing through the water and killing their engines, and Bob would have to deal with that effete little prick Bruce Maxwell who would tell Bob, with a superior smirk, that he wasn't doing his job properly.

Schoenwald stamped his feet before entering the store. His yellow slicker ran with rain, and his dull black boots were coated with mud and slime. The slicker's hood covered his forehead and eyes, revealing only a pinched mouth surrounded by a full beard and reddened nose. Schoenwald shook himself, and droplets cascaded from his arms, sparkling like diamonds under the fluorescent lights.

Stockton Springs' excuse for a grocery store was a cluttered affair, stuffed full to the brim, providing staples for an unimaginative town populace—Chef Boyardee ravioli, Oreo cookies, Jell-O, marshmallows. Fan belts hung next to extension cords. Things were stored without apparent rhyme or reason. Motor oil graced the same shelves as potato chips. Crates of apples, bananas, and oranges were stacked on the floor near the kitty litter and rock salt. The entire place smelled faintly of rotting food, which his nose was too numb to detect.

Bob slapped his leg, unleashing another small shower of droplets. "Hi, Aggie, how's things?"

She shrugged. "About the same."

"Nice weather we're havin'."

"Muggy," Aggie commented.

"Doesn't feel too bad in here, though," Bob said as he stripped his hood from his head.

"The air conditioner is working overtime. Poor thing. I think it's developed a wheeze." She paused. "Figures. I had it put in after that horrendously hot summer in 1988, and the five-year warranty's up."

"Yeah, fine weather for ducks," Bob said.

"It's sure playin' havoc with business. Nobody in their right mind's gonna be out today. So how come you're out and about?"

"Work, what else? It's floodin' toward the end of School Street. Had to put up signs," Bob said as he pulled the hood from his head. "Got any coffee left?"

"Does the pope shit in the woods? Is a bear Catholic?" she quipped, and Schoenwald chuckled at the well-worn response.

She bustled around the crowded counter, returning to hand him coffee just the way he liked it with a bit of sugar and a generous dollop of cream. He took it and blew across the steamy surface.

"Well, another tourist season ends. Business is dead, and the rain's not helping." Aggie gazed forlornly out the window. "I hope this winter's better than last."

"Yes, me, too, but it ain't lookin' good. What with the rains coming too soon and all the weird things that have been happening lately."

Aggie nodded absently. "Poor Sheila. She's gonna miss that dog of hers."

"That's not all. Haven't you heard? A lot of strange shit's going on," he said, took a sip of his coffee, and did a quick mental tally. "If you count Mrs. Jenkins's chickens, some ten animals have died in the last week."

"Oh, them. Weasel probably got 'em."

He shook his head. "I don't know."

They lapsed into silence as they paused to consider the recent events.

"More likely it's kids," he said. "A friend of mine in Bucksport says there's been odd stuff going on there, too. Says some teenagers got arrested for witchcraft the first week of school—some weird ritual where they slaughtered a cat and splashed blood all over the walls of the gymnasium."

Aggie peered at him over her glasses. "Witchcraft?" She tisked. "What are things coming to?"

The bell rang over the door, and as one, they turned to look at the entrance. Jimmy Sheridon walked into the store.

"G'day. Some coffee, Aggie." He leaned against the wall, whistling breezily. "Mighty pretty day. Specially after you had a great night." Sheridon rubbed his crotch and elbowed the older man, giving him a conspiratorial wink.

Disgusted, Bob grimaced and moved slightly away from Jimmy.

A strange expression flitted across Aggie's face, a mixture

of admiration and revulsion. Like other women in the community, she was not immune to the man's strange attraction. He exuded sexuality of the most animal nature. She'd even succumbed to his attentions, once right after her husband had died. Knowing full well that he had had nearly every woman in town, he had seemed a secure way of getting sex without involvement. But Jimmy Sheridon, Aggie discovered, was anything but safe; he was a jerk of the first order. She had almost been relieved when he had moved in with Leah Blair and her daughter, Tiffany, although the older woman questioned Leah's sanity for letting him into her home.

Aggie passed a Styrofoam cup to Sheridon and pointed at the pot. "Go ahead and fill 'er up. We was just talkin' about all the pets that have been dying around here lately."

Sheridon chortled, and as if on cue, Stockton Springs' token police officer, Alan Blount, pulled in. He sprinted across the parking lot. Despite the short distance between car and store, the cloth of his uniform was soaked clear through before he entered the door.

"Jesus Christ, it's colder than a witch's tit in here," Blount said, shaking himself like a dog. "What are you trying to do, Aggie, refrigerate the place?"

Aggie opened her mouth to answer, but the officer wasn't listening as he headed for the cooler and grabbed a six-pack. Blount slammed the beer on the counter. "Ring it up!" Alan said as he took a can from the plastic rings, popped the top, and toasted them.

"It's a little early for that, isn't it?" Aggie said.

Blount regarded her over the can. "Look, I'm sicka' this shit. Animals bein' torn up right and left. As far as I'm concerned, they can take this job and shove it."

Aggie rang up the beer without further comment.

Blount burped. "No, not early at all. Not after what I just seen." He winced. "It don't make sense. This used to be a nice quiet little town. Now everything's going crazy. I've spent more time with the goddamn veterinarian in the last few days than I have with my wife."

Aggie and Bob perked up. "Something else happen?"

"I'll say. Marc Simpson's horse got it last night. I mean *got it*." He made a slicing gesture across his throat and wrinkled his nose in distaste. "Fuckin' blood all over the place. Windpipe's torn out, fuckin' legs ripped off."

"Big news in town, eh?" Jimmy Sheridon snickered. "Horses! Hot shit!" He put the empty cup on the counter, tossed a couple of quarters to Aggie. "See ya!"

"Asshole," Bob muttered under his breath.

"Yeah, of the first degree." Alan ducked his head in assent. "He treats Leah and her little girl like crap."

Aggie agreed. "I don't see why Leah doesn't dump him."

Blount crumpled the can and bounced it off the lip of the trash can and onto the floor with a strident clang. The officer grinned sheepishly.

"Sorry. I guess I'd better go home; Ginny'll be waiting lunch for me."

He turned to go. Aggie stopped him. "Your beer."

"Oh, yeah, I forgot." He picked up the six-pack.

The telephone pealed in the background, and Aggie went to answer it. Her eyes followed Alan out the door and to the squad car. He walked with a weighted, sagging gait. Then she listened to the excited voice on the other end of the line.

"Well, I'll be . . . Bob, run out and get Alan. It's for him. Hurry!"

Schoenwald burst from the store and ran to the cruiser. Aggie viewed the pantomimed conversation and spoke into the phone. "Bob caught him. You're kidding? The Brauns' goat? Alan's not gonna be pleased."

The overhead bell rang as he entered again. She handed him the receiver, ducking under the cord.

"Blount here. Christ, you're kidding. You're not kidding, are you? Have you called the vet?" He paused. "Okay, I'll radio it in. Then I'm on my way."

He held the receiver distastefully away from his body. Aggie took it from his hand.

"Well, I'll be a son of a bitch," Blount said. He took his cap off, pushed a few wisps of salt-and-pepper hair from his eyes, and repeated himself. "Son of a bitch."

"You said that already," Aggie said.

He ignored her and slouched out the door, leaving the six-pack on the counter a second time.

Bob began to follow him. "Hey, Alan, you for—"

Aggie shook her head no. Bob's mouth snapped shut. She waited until Alan got into the car.

"He's got enough on his mind right now. He'll never remember it. You take it, and I'll give him a fresh six-pack next time he comes in."

His eyes lit up. "Gee, Aggie, thanks."

"No problem. Now, why don't you go get some work done? I'm a taxpayer, you know, and don't want to be payin' for you to stand around in here and gab all the time."

Bob laughed. "I guess I'd better. Thanks again, Aggie." He waved the six-pack at her. "Want to come over to my place tonight and share this?"

"Naw, I never get out'a here before midnight. By then it's too late to do anything."

The earth churned under the continuing torrent, and the nearby ditch was flooded and choked with fallen branches and debris. Droplets, like hard pellets, splashed into the surging surface of water to create a strip of whipping frantic mist—a band of silver froth. The sky was watery gray and without warmth. The temperature had plummeted during the night, and the morning brought rain mixed with hail. It was falling still. The branches dipped, bending under the combined weight, looking as dreary, sodden, and depressing as the heavens above as the patrol car inched along the road toward the lighthouse.

Alan steered carefully around the barrier that Schoenwald had put up. Even with expensive radial tires, the going was treacherous. Twice the vehicle had gone into a stomach-wrenching skid. Blasted by gale-force winds, the rain fell horizontally, raking his windshield, and his wipers strove valiantly to keep up with it, creating a strobe effect. The view alternated between a rain-washed soft focus and split-second clarity.

Whoosh, splash! Whoosh, splash!

A bolt of lightning ripped through the heavens, followed

rapidly by a clack of thunder so loud that Alan jumped. His eye was drawn to the old Cape house, with its peeling paint and sagging foundation. The image lasted no more than a second as the wipers cleared the view.

Drooping house and white blur.

A thin ribbon of gray smoke curled tenuously from the Brauns' chimney only to be whipped and scattered by the gusting wind. And the image was erased again, washed out by the pounding rain on his windshield.

Drooping house and white blur.

And the house reappeared again. Blount gaped, and it took a moment before he realized what it was that had caught his attention. A scarlet stain extended across the crest of the hill above the sagging barn. *Blood?* His mind refused to comprehend the incongruous stain, which should have been washed away by the relentless rain.

"Well, I'll be a son of a bitch," he said.

This really was too much.

A branch crashed to the ground in front of his car. Alan jammed on the brakes. The cruiser fishtailed, and he fought to regain control. The car slid in graceful, nauseating motion toward the ditch. Blount yanked at the wheel, and the car wove drunkenly toward the other side of the road.

He whispered a quick prayer, closed his eyes, and pressed steadily on the brake. The cruiser lurched to a stop. The engine died as the car shuddered and settled in the soft mud.

He slumped over the steering wheel, tired. His gaze returned to the crimson smudge upon the hill.

"Shit." He started the engine, rocking the vehicle back and forth gently until it was free of the mud. Then he swerved cautiously around the limb and crept the rest of the way down the street to the Brauns' dooryard.

Les Braun, bundled against the penetrating damp, joined him on the stoop. "It's up there."

"I noticed."

"I reckoned you did. Look, Alan, this is gettin' a little out of hand. That's my best nanny—good breeder and good producer, too."

"Sorry, Les. There's not much I can do. Was she okay last

night? I mean, I assume that's the last time you checked her." Blount began to climb toward the shredded corpse.

"Sure, I checked her last night. I was a little late getting out this morning. I noticed her missing when I went in to feed 'em. I didn't notice that"—he pointed at the splotch—"until later."

"About when?"

"Noon, mebbe."

The officer glanced at his watch. Less than half an hour ago. "Did you hear anything last night? Any strange noises?"

"Nope, can't say that I did."

They had drawn closer to the remains. Now Alan could make out recognizable pieces of goat—a hoof, two. The head had been gnawed off, separated from the gutted torso.

"Crap." Blount beat a tattoo against a meaty thigh.

"Don't you have any idea who's doin' all this?"

He shook his head. "Not a clue. Look, why don't you go back to the house? I can tell you've already been up there once. No need to go back. Besides, if there's any tracks, I don't want them wiped out."

"Nope, no tracks. That's the first thing I looked for."

"Figures." Alan turned to Les and tried to give him what he thought was a severe look. "If there were tracks, they're gone now. Well, I've radioed into the station, and they've contacted the vet. He should be along any minute. It's damn wet. Let's wait inside. Does Hedda have a pot of coffee going?"

"I would 'spect she does," Less said. "What the hell is the vet coming out here for? It's a little late, isn't it?"

"Cause of death, and all that bullshit."

"Cause of death! I'd say that was obvious."

"I know, Les, it's silly; but I'm just going by the book, that's all."

Hedda Braun emerged from the house to follow the well-beaten path to the barn and the pen. She tried to ignore the scarlet flower of death two hundred yards to her left, but it pulled at her. Despite herself, she looked. The goat had been removed. Only a few pieces of scattered fur remained as an ominous reminder.

Les had gone with Blount and the vet, leaving her to do the unfinished chores. His anger was a still palpable energy which circulated about the house. It had driven her outside despite her fear.

Unlike her husband, she felt no outrage over the loss of the goat, only terror—terror that came to her in the night, terror that whispered in the back of her mind, terror that told her the floodgates of hell were about to be opened.

She shivered.

Punishment. That's what it was. Divine punishment. The thought rose, bringing with it her mother's face—and *the spatula,* the one that her mother had used on Hedda to mete out punishment with divinely inspired strength.

Raised a Jehovah's Witness, even now Hedda would neither dance nor sing—except a discreet hymn or two. She and her churchgoing husband formed a bland pair, childless and unobtrusive. Who would possibly want to hurt them, or their livestock? She didn't know.

Hedda turned to face the barn. A lightning bolt hit a nearby tree, and it splintered. She threw her hands over her face. The wind let out a screech that loosened the windows in their sashes. Pellet-size drops sounded like stones thrown against the many diamond panes.

The fear amplified and multiplied, and Hedda began to run as though pursued, scrambling over twisted clumps of grass and wading through puddles.

The ground erupted beneath her feet, and she stumbled. For a moment she remained where she lay, sprawled, cheek against the wet grass. Then she forced herself to sit up. The house, the barn, the hillside faded, and her vision blurred. Images began to take shape upon her retinas, dim flitting figures—shapeless shadows within shadows. Hedda had the impression of drifting, floating, and she dug her heels into the mud, a reflex action.

Water soaked through the seat of her pants. The wind rumbled through the trees. It roared, and the thrashing twigs sizzled like hissing snow on the television set. Hedda sensed words beneath the crackling static, a message meant just for her, and it said: *Satan has come to Stockton Springs.*

Somewhere not far away, in the wilderness between the rocky gateway to the Penobscot Bay and man's feeble civilizing influence of Stockton Springs, floodwaters surged and boiled over once-dry land.

While Hedda sought to maintain balance, the world belched and groaned. Its stony soil crumpled, sucked inward through granite sphincter, and then it ruptured to eject a piece of a poisonous waste from its belly, farting and shitting out the bilious taint.

The parting waters revealed an ancient cemetery, of a town long-forgotten in written histories of the region. A ruffed grouse flapped noisily from her nest with a hooting protest as a tombstone exploded with a sickening slurp nearby. The worn marker wavered a bit before falling silently to waterlogged soil, and the bird settled again upon this new perch.

5

It was pissing rain. Again. Still!

Bruce Maxwell, Stockton Springs' only full-time paid administrative employee, chuffed as he contemplated the scene outside the steamy office window. The old post office building was empty, and he found it hard to believe the town was even deader on a Sunday than it was during the week.

To Maxwell's mind, Stockton Springs had long surpassed the stage of rigor mortis, only it and the townspeople weren't smart enough to lay down and die yet.

Once downtown had supported two small grocery stores. Now there was only the one, and *that* functioned as gas station, hardware store, and automotive center as well. The small gift shop directly across the street never opened—at least Bruce couldn't remember the last time that he'd seen it open. A used-book store was advertised on the street coming into town, but Bruce had never figured out where it was. Someone's home, he surmised.

A pickup truck, complete with fog lights, roll bar, and Yosemite Sam mudflaps, splashed through town and splattered into the parking lot down at the store. Bruce Maxwell blew loudly through his lips and turned back to the boxes on his desk. He was trying to be methodical about this, but he couldn't fight the overwhelming sense of panic.

The rains, which had lasted for nearly two weeks, had ruined everything, and there was no hope of letup. Bruce had had a good thing going. The city fathers paid him reasonable money, and he made sure that he didn't have to live in this godfersaken berg. Instead he drove in from Belfast every day.

And Maxwell had stolen them blind. Recently he had gotten greedy and skimmed more than a little off the top—juggling the books and fiddling accounts. He had all the codes and the account numbers that he needed. He was privy to the "state secrets." He had to be; he was a trusted employee. He had the modem and the skill he needed. Any excess funds neatly disappeared into the netherworld of computerdom.

The budget had been stretched to the limit, operating in the black only by the narrowest and flimsiest of margins. As long as nothing went wrong—no pipes burst, no roads needed sudden unscheduled repair, no one put in for overtime—Maxwell could cover operating expenses. He could pay their one street cleaner, Robert Schoenwald. He could pay the part-time clerk. Now, as if a wrathful God had discovered his petty thievery and was determined to reveal it, the sky was rent asunder. Waters rose, and Schoenwald, the stupid idiot, spent hours and hours arranging and rearranging too few barricades so some moron yokel wouldn't drive through the overflow that any fool should see was too deep.

It seemed that God had sent a whole series of natural disasters bound to expose his crime. Electrical storms and power outages that saw monies lost during the delicate transfer of funds from his accounts back into the city's, and they were lost forever. The continued flooding caused further damage to the roads, and Schoenwald put in more overtime as he raced like a rat on a wheel, going on the assumption that more activity would eventually mean that he'd get farther ahead. Sewers backed up as the township sunk into the encompassing swamp.

Snarling, Bruce grabbed one set of ledgers and stuffed it in a box.

Generally speaking, Maxwell was not a religious man, but he had found himself thinking a lot about God, justice, and divine retribution lately as he watched the deluge. The rain was enough to convince him.

Each day as he drove into work his mind remained clear until he passed some invisible boundary into Stockton Springs. Then a hum commenced, which blended with the patter of the rain, and his brain was assaulted by static, and his mind turned again to thoughts of God.

"Maybe I should build an ark," he said aloud, and the sound of his own voice was enough to remind him why he was here on this rain-soaked Sunday.

Maxwell picked up a handful of pencils, considered them a moment, and returned them to the drawer. He didn't particularly care about divine retribution, but he knew when a place was bad news. Stockton Springs was getting unhealthy, for him personally, and time was running out.

This month when Bob Schoenwald deposited his check into his account, it would bounce clear to the next county, and Bruce Maxwell decided he wasn't going to hang around long enough to write the check, much less wait for Schoenwald to cash it.

He did another hurried rummage through the drawers, checked the street for pedestrians, and then scuttled out to his car. He put the car in gear and let it roll down the hill without starting the engine—not sure why he practiced such stealth. Studying the rearview mirror closely, he popped the clutch, and the old buggy chugged to life.

At the stop sign Maxwell contemplated his options. He should move from his apartment. Fast! He hadn't expected this, and he cursed himself for his greed.

As he drove under the overpass that marked the edge of town, Maxwell's head began to clear.

Maxwell laughed. On second thought maybe there wasn't

a real reason to rush. The way things were going in town, it might be a few days before they noticed he was missing. What with the weather they were having, who was to say he hadn't gotten a particularly nasty cold? And who really did he report in to at work, except himself? He only spoke to the officials at occasional meetings where he gave a slightly censored "State of the Town" address.

Settling comfortably back into his seat, he whistled and made a mental note to leave a suitable message on the answering machine complete with hoots, sneezes, and howls. That should keep the wolves at bay for a little while.

Forestville, Quebec—The long-silenced howl of wolves has been heard along Highway 138 for the last three nights. This coincides with a sighting in Forestville proper. Mr. Gerald Jardin, 155 West Maple and owner of the local hardware store, was among the first to report the wolf's appearance in the center of town.

"I was just getting ready to sweep sidewalks in front of the store, and it just appeared out of nowhere," said Jardin. "It was about 7 a.m., and not many people were around at that time of day, but others saw it."

"It was huge," said another eyewitness, Miss Marie LaJeune, 152-A Maple. "I haven't seen a wolf in a long time, not since I was a kid, and none that I remember were that big."

Wolves are rare in the area. They normally stand about three feet at the shoulder, but both LaJeune and Jardin insist that their specimen stood at least four feet tall.

The wolf was first spotted in the area by a young couple who had parked along the hill road, known locally as "lover's leap." The following day the wolf was observed inside the village proper.

No more than one has been reported, although many of the townspeople fear the arrival of a pack. A meeting of concerned citizens will take place on Tuesday to discuss its extermination. . . .

The tempest raged outside the bedroom where Tiffany and her cousin played, its noise competing with the monotonous thud of rain on the metal roof. The internal squall was underscored by shouts and punctuated by crashes as something somewhere rebounded off the wall and onto the floor.

The master bedroom was as drab as the rest of the trailer. A floral sheet replaced the door that once separated the closet from the room. The blond particle-board paneling had grayed from accumulated layers of dust and ground-in dirt, and here and there its surface was pockmarked by gaping holes where Jimmy Sheridon had once planted his fist.

Tiffany and her cousin Jonathan stood before a full-length mirror. It reflected a cracked image of a king-size bed covered with a worn orange comforter and flanked by an unfinished pine dresser heaped with old clothes.

The television in the living room blared loudly, and the dogs in the kennel yapped as if they had caught the fever that radiated from the home. Five-year-old Jonathan glared at Tiffany. He would have preferred to watch afternoon cartoons but remained in the bedroom partly out of loyalty to his cousin and partly because of the ruckus in the kitchen.

Patiently Tiffany explained for the third time what she wanted him to do. "You stand behind me, see. Then you follow my movements. If I put my arms up, you put your arms down. And if I put my arms down, you put your arms up. Like this, see. If you do it right, it'll look like I've got four arms, and we can . . ." She leaned over and whispered in his ear.

"Yeah!" The little boy's eyes glinted as he thought of himself and Tiffany scaring Jimmy with their homemade bogey. Happily he took his place behind her, and they practiced waving their arms. Jonathan mewed and growled in his best imitation of a monster. He stuck his head out from behind her. "No fair. I can't see."

"Of course not. I'm bigger than you."

"I wanna see. I WANNA SEE!" he shrieked.

In the kitchen something clanged.

Tiffany winced and then scratched her head.

"Here, you stand in front of me, and we'll do it again."

They switched positions before the mirror and flapped their arms—his up, hers down, and vice versa.

"It doesn't look like no monster," he said critically.

"Of course not—you can see both of us if you stand in front." She pointed at the opposite wall. "Look at the shadow. See how it dances?"

They repeated the motion. Jonathan was not impressed.

"This is a stupid game," he said and darted out the door. "Stupid!" Jonathan yelled back over his shoulder for emphasis. He opened his mouth ready to launch into a diatribe against "dumb games" when a pan hit the living room wall and bounced into the hall, clanging to a halt at his feet.

Jonathan stared, and speaking to Tiffany from the corner of his mouth, he whispered, "Ah, I think it's about time I go home. Lunch and all."

He gave her an apologetic shrug and scrambled for the door. Tiffany scooted into the living room to stand before the picture window and watch her cousin as he escaped up the tree-lined drive to the road.

This close to the kitchen the sounds became clear, and Tiffany stuck her thumb in her mouth and curled up in a ball on the couch, staring with empty eyes at the television set where some football hero hawked breakfast cereal.

Jimmy Sheridon burst into the living room. Tiffany's mother's lover was a small, wiry man. He had a hard, muscled physique. With high cheekbones and jet-black hair, he had the kind of dark, exotic good looks that even Tiffany, at her tender age, realized turned women's heads. His chest heaved, and Sheridon loomed over her mother as she tumbled into the room after him. Leah looked up, and Tiffany saw that her right eye was already turning purple.

"... but, Jimmy," Leah pleaded, "I already got the kennel to keep 'n' the books. When do I have time for a job?"

"I told ya, babe, this is at nights. It's CD's, fer shit's sake.

Just a pissant little café. The old choke and puke, not the Waldorf-Astoria. The only thing you're likely to get there is gangrene."

"Ptomaine," she corrected, and Jimmy grabbed her by the throat, pushing her against the wall.

"Ptomaine, gangrene, what's the difference?" he snarled. "You're gonna do what you're told. I ain't that faggot son of yours." Sheridon hit his chest for emphasis. "Fuckin' queer as a three-dollar bill."

She swallowed her reply, and he released her.

"Look, it won't be hard. That place is slow and is probably gonna go under, so ya won't be workin' there long. Besides, we need the money now."

"But my benefits . . ." Leah whined.

"That's what's so great about this. They pay ya under the table, ya see. You ain't gonna lose a thing."

"When am I gonna sleep?"

"Sleep, hell. All you do all day long is sit on your duff anyway. The kennel's no big thing. Wha'cha gotta do there? Feed a few dogs, let 'em run, clean out stalls every once 'n' a while. I don't believe you could be so selfish. You know we need money. You're always bitchin' about our not having enough, and what with my bad back . . ."

Leah plucked at his shirt. "I'm sorry, honey. I'll take the job."

He snorted and turned a baleful eye to Tiffany. She pressed against the back of the couch, trying to make herself small as her mother slumped against the wall, crying. Tiffany glanced from Jimmy to her mother, slid from the couch, and walked softly over to Leah to place a gentle hand on her mother's arm.

"Mama?"

Leah jerked her arm away. "Go on, leave me alone!" She stumbled back into the kitchen.

"Look, kid, get lost for a bit," Jimmy said. "Me and your mom got a few things to talk about."

Tiffany peered at him distrustfully. A small line formed on her forehead.

Sheridon fumbled in her mother's purse and pulled out a dollar bill.

"Here's a buck." He leered and winked at her. "I guarantee she'll be smiling when you come home. Now, go walk the dogs, okay?"

All small towns have their characters, all across the broad expanse of America. They are its aching, groaning back. Such individuals, with personal peculiarities and idiosyncrasies, can also be found in urban America, too—lining the entrances to the subways or lying in pools of their own puke—but in cities they are numbered, without faces or names.

Only in rural America do characters have names, faces, and personal histories, and Stockton Springs had more than its share. There was Duke Defleurieu, with a disfiguring wen that stuck out the side of his head, smooth and round, and the size of a small baseball; Granny Simpson, with her bouts of depression and well-advanced senile dementia, who wandered the streets looking for someone to talk to each day; and Gideon, with his head filled with stuffed cotton. They had their old, comfortable sheriff in the person of Blount—even if that wasn't his official title, it amounted to the same thing—and, of course, the town bully in James Sheridon.

Stockton Springs could lay claim to a clubfoot, a poet, a hermit, a schizophrenic, a self-professed psychic who did horoscopes and tarot readings, and a nymphomaniac. And even if a native couldn't claim to be a particular type, each individual's idiosyncrasies were known. So-and-so was a randy sombitch, and so-and-so-else's granddaddy was illegitimate. Whether due to the coldness of the climate or the harshness of the landscape, no Mainer could be moved to the passion of Appalachian-style feuds; but old grievances were remembered and nurtured, and certain families shunned others because of a spat that was several generations old.

Here, as elsewhere, the characters were created by the

land. The people were as harsh and hard as the rocky soil and as intemperate as the climate. For Maine shaped its people in its own image and likeness. It shaped them as much as it was shaped by them. The rocky, boulder-strewn earth was ill-suited to farming, so its people had adapted. Most earned their living from the lumber trade, or from the frothy sea. The lucky ones had jobs that allowed them to escape Maine's confines, hauling goods from here to there and back again.

June Gascon was not one of the lucky ones. As usual, she was stationed in a shaded area near a bend, one of the few places where the road widened enough to permit parking and as far from sight of houses as it could be along this curving strip between the Sandypoint post office and the Four Corners.

Each day she could be found here—or a little up the road next to the field. As regular as clockwork, for the last three years, until she was something of a fixture. Most people ignored her presence. They didn't care. They reckoned that she needed to get away from her husband, Rich. And she did.

Last night there'd been another blowup in what seemed an unending conflict, and Rich had come upon her not with his typical savagery, but stealthily.

Strange that. With Rich, yelling was something like the seasons. Inevitable, just as inevitable as the Mordens calling the cops when he got too wild. Things with Rich, like things in Stockton Springs, were predictable. You could almost set a clock to the daily rhythms.

School would be out soon. The bus would drop the school kids at the post office, and the boys would have to pass this way on their way home. The boys ignored her collectively, but their sidelong glances at their peers indicated their awareness. By common consent, no one remarked upon her presence, but their amble slowed to a crawl as they passed, and they'd dawdle, looking to see if anyone would try to slip away unnoticed.

Probably every male child between the ages of thirteen and twenty had discarded his unwanted virginity either in the back seat of June's Toyota Corona or on the moth-eaten blanket she kept in her trunk. She was one of Stockton Springs' best-kept secrets. She was reasonably sure that the boys didn't even talk among themselves. She played upon their sympathy, pointing to her bruises and indicating either directly or indirectly that she would see more of the same if they breathed so much as a word. She didn't even have to mention what might happen to *them* if Rich found out. So the secret held, and as far as each was concerned, he was the only one.

Not even Blount knew, although he was probably aware of her peculiar habit of parking along the side of the road. But no male-child who hoped to find solace in her arms would have risked the loss that even the merest slip of a lip may have occasioned.

It had become something of a hobby of hers. June's way of keeping sane and getting even. She was still young yet, and she remembered vaguely that she was good looking, if you ignored the bruises and the broken front tooth. For every slap, every wallop Rich had given her, one boy had found manhood—in her mouth or between her thighs.

June did not analyze her actions, nor question the need that drove her. Her introduction to love, at the hands of James Sheridon and his friends, had been anything but gentle. When Rich had asked her to marry him, she, the despoiled virgin, had accepted gladly, foolishly confiding her past. Years of accusations had followed, and June had decided that if she was going to be convicted of the infidelity, she might as well enjoy it. So day after day she came out when he was away at work. Rain or shiner—and June chortled mirthlessly at her wit—she'd come; she'd watch; she'd wait.

The boys didn't always come right away. Sometimes they didn't come at all. There'd be Scouts or something going on at school like football. Usually they walked in a group. She just left them alone. She'd follow them with her eyes.

Eventually, though, someone would come home alone, and she'd stop him. If it was raining, she'd offer him a lift. She'd offer him other things. She'd offer him herself. . . .

Who it was didn't matter. A precocious ten-year-old who was just starting to feel the first stirring of adult desire could entertain her as easily as a fifteen-year-old. Perhaps better. Their inexperience often aroused her more than the more adept caresses of their older brothers.

She shifted in her seat. Not one but two figures appeared in the mist beyond the car. The Fletcher twins. The voice of unreason whispered to her, and she decided to break her steadfast rule. What the hell. She had had one or another of the boys before. What was a little tumble among friends?

June rolled down the window and called them over to the car. Twin heads turtled under twin hoods in the rain. They turned to her. Both blushed right down to their roots as she nodded at the empty garage across the road.

A bemused expression passed over Eddie's face, and he looked horrified when he realized what she intended while a wild light gleamed in Terry's eyes. The latter gave a sharp tug on Eddie's jacket, pulling him toward the dilapidated building. With a quick glance over her shoulder to make sure no one was watching, June emerged from the car and meandered innocently across the blacktop to disappear into the garage.

Tiffany pocketed the money and picked up her filthy, ragged sneakers, stuffing her bare feet into them. She wiggled her toes through the holes in the worn cloth and peered out the window at the rain, considering. Then she grabbed her bright red boots and torn windbreaker. She fingered the loose flap of cloth and shrugged, slipping it on before going out into the sodden afternoon.

Fight forgotten, Tiffany skipped down to the littered dooryard and slogged through the mud to the kennel. The population varied, growing frantic in mid-summer, but once school started, it had dwindled until only two dogs remained.

A whimper greeted her as she walked in the door.

"Coming, Goliath," Tiffany said as she reached for the leash.

She went into the first fenced stall, bent absently to pet the beagle and hook the leash to his collar. After looping the handle over a doorknob to hold him, she moved to the wire mesh gate two stalls down, where a German shepherd barked excitedly.

Tiffany grabbed the second leash; she'd walk them both at the same time.

"Good boy, Goliath." She spoke quietly, soothingly, and slid inside the pen. "Okay, Goliath, we're going to try something new."

She pushed the gate open, and the dog bounded out, freezing when it saw the tiny beagle where it cringed next to the door, hackles raised.

"Goliath, meet Bilbo."

Goliath growled. Bilbo cowered harder.

"Goliath, no!" The shepherd stopped and turned to look at her, inquiringly. She anchored him and went to pick up Bilbo. She brought them nose to nose. They snuffled. Goliath let out another throaty rumble, and Bilbo mewled pitifully. Supremacy established, Goliath wagged his tail in welcome.

Tiffany put Bilbo down, and they greeted each other snout to rump, circling. The shepherd had the advantage—longer legs and greater height. The beagle scampered comically to keep up with its larger cousin. Tiffany giggled.

She opened the outside door, and the two animals exploded past her—one to either side. She leapt aside to avoid getting tangled in their leashes, already regretting her experiment as they yanked her out the door. Her legs tensed, and Tiffany slalomed along behind them as they dragged her through the mud like a couple of sled dogs.

"Whoa!"

The shepherd halted, but the beagle kept running until it was brought to a jolting stop by the leash.

"Okay, fellas, let's get organized." She stepped cautiously forward and unsnarled the leads. "Okay. It's okay; let's go."

They rushed forward, and Tiffany had to run to keep her feet underneath her. The wind whistled through her hair. They crashed through the brush, beside the drive, their tongues lolling happily.

They turned the corner from the drive to the gravel road, and she strove to bring the animals under control. Her foot hit something hard, a small boulder completely covered over with brambles, and Tiffany went flying, losing her grip on both dogs. Free, at last, they bolted ahead. She groaned as they romped blithely down the street toward the bay.

Only a few isolated stars penetrated the thick cloud cover to twinkle in a sky made of deep, dark velvet. Over an hour ago Tiffany had wished: *Starlight, star bright, first star I see tonight* . . . But Goliath had not returned, and she didn't expect her wish to come true. She huddled next to the kennels, clinging to Bilbo. Her clothes were soaked. She was covered with mud, and the shepherd was gone, long gone— off chasing deer or whatever dogs do once freed from the restraints of the master and hall. And soon she'd have to go inside and face the music.

Already, Tiffany could hear the shouting through the thin walls of the mobile home. Their voices carried over traffic noises of people returning from work, even over Bilbo's wheezing pant.

"Well, where the fuck is she, then?" Jimmy's deep voice boomed.

"I don't know," came her mother's softer tones, "but I'm worried."

"Worried, hell! I can tell you where the fuck she is. She's hiding. She lost the fucking dogs and she's hiding. How could you be so fucking stupid as to let her . . ."

Tiffany cringed. She was in trouble. Big Trouble. Even if she hadn't been late for supper, even if she hadn't gotten dirty, she knew she'd get what-for as soon as she slipped into the house. So instead, she leaned against the concrete block kennel out of sight from the trailer, molded her body around the small beagle, and buried her face in Bilbo's soft coat.

Sometime later she dried her eyes and turned to face the house. *It wasn't going to get any better,* she thought.

Tiffany returned Bilbo to the kennel, placing him in the first stall, and scooped dried food into his bowl almost as an afterthought. She slid out the door, moved silently over to the trailer, where she tried to slip unnoticed into the living room.

Her mother and Jimmy spun on her. He was on top of the girl in two strides.

"Where the fuck have you been?" he yelled as he picked her up and threw her onto the couch. "And where are the fucking dogs?"

Drawing her legs up to her chest, Tiffany tried to dig into the crease between the sofa's back and its arm. Sheridon pinned her down, raising his fist. "WELL!"

"Jimmy, please?" Leah took a step toward them.

He shot her a warning look. "You better shut the fuck up."

Leah withdrew to a safe corner, and Sheridon turned his attention to Tiffany.

"Bah-Bilbo's in the kennel."

"Bilbo, who the fuck's Bilbo?"

"The beagle."

"And the shepherd?"

Tiffany tried to extricate herself from his grasp. She glimpsed mutely at her mother, who turned away.

Half lifting her off the sofa, Jim shook Tiffany hard. Her head hit the wall with a loud crack.

"Where's the fucking shepherd?" He growled through clenched teeth.

"I—uh—I dunno," she sobbed.

Sheridon shoved Tiffany against the wall, slapped her, and wagged his finger at her. "You are gonna go look for the damn dog, and if you don't find him, I can tell you there's gonna be hell to pay."

"But it's dark out," Leah protested.

"I don't care. I'm going out, and that dog had better be here when I get back." He yanked Tiffany up by the arm and pushed her toward her mother. "Or you know who's going to get it."

He slammed out of the house. Tiffany whimpered and wiped her nose on her sleeve. She gazed shyly up at her mother.

"Don't expect sympathy from me. You asked for it. From now on the kennel is your responsibility. Do you understand? You're old enough to start helping out." Leah loomed above Tiffany—arms crossed, her face red—and tapped her foot impatiently, waiting for an argument which was not forthcoming. "Soon I'm gonna be working at night, and I'm not gonna have time."

Tiffany tried to smile. "Sure, Mom, I like taking care of the dogs."

Leah continued angrily, ignoring her daughter's quiet acquiescence. "I'm tired of this crap. Stuck takin' care of you, that damn man, and the dogs. Well, I'm tired of it, tired of the whole goddamn thing. So I ain't gonna take no shit from you."

"Yes'm."

"And don't give me any lip about this. I won't take it, you hear?"

Tiffany nodded, aware that her mom was too far gone to listen to anything her daughter said.

Leah grabbed Tiffany's arm roughly, swung her around to face the door, and pushed. "Now, you get out there and find that dog, and don't come back until you do."

The young man plastered himself against the side of the mobile home as the little girl appeared. She stood confused for a moment, staring at the closed door behind her. His Adam's apple bobbed up and down convulsively in his throat. He wanted to go to her, to comfort her, but he was afraid.

His body moved sinuously, reflecting this inner debate. His twisting shadow blended with the writhing limbs of the trees. The rain had abated to a steady drizzle. His gaze was drawn away from her toward the apparition that stood beside her. Without substance, the shrouded shape wavered. Gideon gulped as the pointed snout dipped to touch the child's shoulder.

With a single sideways glance at the trailer, Gideon melted back into the trees.

6

Sheridon propelled Leah across the gravel parking lot toward the restaurant, half steering and half shoving her up the short wooden ramp. Knowing when Jimmy had reached the end of his limited patience, Leah complied meekly— putting on her best dress and leaving Tiffany at home alone. Better not to have the child witness her mother's humiliation.

Leah huddled under the eaves, away from the driving rain, as Jimmy grappled with the door that was made balky by the blustering wind. It surrendered suddenly, blowing open with a bang, and he tottered back a few steps. The sound of laughter tumbled out the open door, followed by the smell of coffee left in the pot too long, stale cigarettes, and over-worked grease.

CD's, Stockton Springs' excuse of a restaurant, was a single room with food stains that graced the walls almost as old as the building itself. It was the one place where the people of the village could congregate, a tradition as sacred and profound as church, but more hallowed. For here they could be themselves without God's puritanical eye gazing down upon them. The café moved in its own time and its own rhythm, matching the slow, sleepy rhythms of the community. Here lives intersected; people met to gossip about some particularly juicy tidbit and later withdrew to chew over its meat. On a Friday it was crowded with those people too broke or too lazy to drive to Bangor for a little fun.

As the door crashed against the outer wall, the dialogue inside faltered. Several sets of curious eyes turned to regard the arrivals, waiting to see if conversations would need to be altered with its subject newly appeared on the scene.

Fuming, Jimmy stormed into the restaurant, and all discussion fizzled and died.

"Should get that goddamn door fixed," he grumbled. Leah entered behind him. Conversation resumed. Grabbing her arm, Sheridon led her to the counter and plunked her down on a stool. He pounded the cracked linoleum countertop.

"Barkeep! Barkeep! How about some service here?"

A group of men gathered in the corner frowned their disapproval. Betty Young got out of her seat at a nearby table where she had joined a neighbor over coffee.

"Keep yer shirt on," she growled as she shuffled around the counter.

"How about a little coffee for me and my lady?"

"Sure. Cream, Leah?" she said.

Leah Blair slouched lower on the ripped vinyl stool and nodded a mute yes.

"I heard you needed another waitress." Sheridon seized Leah and hauled her to her feet, presenting her for inspection. "I've got the perfect girl for you. Right, Leah?"

"Is that what you want, Leah? You want a job?" Betty said, handing Leah her cup with a small smile of encouragement.

"Where's your better half?" Sheridon interrupted Betty.

"He's out back doing the books."

"Can I talk to him?" Jimmy said, thrusting his face between hers and Leah's, demanding her attention.

Betty set his coffee down in front of him so hard that it sloshed over the sides and onto the saucer. *"Leah can talk to me* if she really wants the job," she informed him coldly.

Jimmy stiffened and his eyes narrowed as he considered arguing with her. Then he brightened.

"No matter, you two ladies can gab, but Betty . . ." His eyes sparked a challenge. "You wouldn't mind if I went out back so we menfolk can jaw over the important things, like pay and hours."

"Anything to get you out of my hair," Betty said as she walked back around the counter to sit next to Leah.

"Great. You two girls chat." He patted Betty on her rather ample ass as she tried to slither past and said: "I love a woman with meat on her bones, don't you?"

Deeming her duly chastened, Sheridon marched through the door into the kitchen. The buzz of conversation, which had ceased altogether as the café patrons watched the confrontation, escalated.

Betty threw a towel at the closed door, then turned to Leah.

"Do ya wanna work? It seems like you have enough to do with the kennels and Tiffany."

Leah shredded her napkin. "Well, I can manage a few hours if that would help out, and a little extra cash never hurts."

"You're crazy, girl. Get rid of the lazy, good-fer-nuthing."

Leah shrugged again and reached for another napkin to rend. The younger woman contemplated Leah and nodded abruptly. "I think I understand. The job's yours if you want it."

The door burst open and Jimmy emerged. "That's great, Tom; she'll start Monday."

Someone chose that inopportune time to voice his opinion. "Poor bitch, she ain't the one that needs the job, if you ask me."

Sheridon's grin slid off his face, and his back went rigid as he swung slowly around, fists clenched. His jaw began to work rapidly from side to side as he considered the group of men in the far corner. The hush that descended was underscored by the steady drip of coffee in the coffeemaker.

"What was that?" Jimmy said as he took two menacing strides toward the table.

No one replied.

"Who said it?"

"Calm down, Jimmy, we wasn't talkin' about you. Was we fellas?" One of the younger men looked around the table for confirmation. There was a ripple of assent.

Sheridon began to circle the table, like an animal around its prey. He thumped the back of each chair as he passed, paused, and spun to reverse the circuit.

"Come on, man, it wasn't nothing." The same man spoke again for himself and his cohorts. "Just one man's opinion, and this *is* still a free country, isn't it?"

Sheridon clutched the speaker by the collar and lifted him from his chair. His face turned red, and he gagged and choked, hands struggling feebly with the cloth.

"Says who?"

"Leave him alone. He didn't say nothing. I did," said Duke Defleurieu. His lip trembled slightly and his voice shook. The older man hooked buck teeth over his lip to control its tremor and sat a bit taller in his chair.

Sheridon turned to appraise the offender, loosening his hold on the other man's collar. Duke Defleurieu's expression hardened as he returned Sheridon's stare. Old Duke had been the butt of many of Jimmy's poorer attempts at humor. An ugly son of a bitch, if there ever was one, with the tumor the size of a fist that grew in the center of a balding scalp, as if the head could support either hair or disfiguring growth but not both.

Sheridon pushed the first man down and snatched at Defleurieu, hoisting him easily from the chair. The man was probably old enough to be Jimmy's father, but that didn't faze Sheridon. Democratic with his wrath, he did not care. The way he figured it, he'd be doing the man a favor if he rearranged Defleurieu's features a bit.

Jimmy slapped the older man. The wisps of graying hair Duke used unsuccessfully to cover his bald scalp and wen fluttered, and his head rolled with the blow. A maniacal gleam lit the man's eyes, and Jimmy knew the old fart was gonna fight.

Giving the other no opportunity for thought, Jimmy rammed Duke face first into the wall. Blood oozed from his nose and dribbled, mingling with the grease stains. The stunned Defleurieu drooped slightly, and Sheridon spun him around, bringing his knee into the other man's groin. Defleurieu doubled over groaning. Sheridon seized Duke by the collar and pulled him upright. He scrutinized the old man's agonized expression with satisfaction. Then Jimmy shoved Defleurieu's face into the laden table. The heavy mugs skittered away unscathed, but one of the water glasses shattered. Sheridon yanked the misshapen head up by a few straggly wisps of hair, peered into his eyes, then smashed him against the table again. Old Duke howled as one of the ragged ends of the water glass pierced his eye, driving its point through iris and lens into the vitreous humor and the optic nerve. Its liquid center, the consistency of an egg white, oozed soupily from the bleeding socket.

Sheridon rammed the man's head against the table one last time just to make sure he had gotten his point across, then dropped Defleurieu to wipe his hands almost delicately against his shirt.

He was shaking with laughter when he peeled out of the parking lot, gravel flying. Inside the steamy windows Leah stood at the cash register dutifully paying for their coffee.

Stupid cunt! he thought as he turned onto the highway heading for Bangor.

Late-night stars had begun to fade, and Venus hovered on the horizon. The air near Greely's Landing was crisp, cool, and clean. Here the seasons seemed to be following their normal progression, moving from the green of late summer to the first coppery kiss of early autumn, without a hint of the rains that had plagued Stockton Springs since Labor Day.

It was sometime near dawn when Sheridon parked his truck on a grassy knoll not far from the road that led to his property. He opened the door and was greeted by the joyous, bubbling, tumbling cry of a bobolink while a yellow-throated warbler called to its mate with a thin, lowering trill. Jimmy grinned, savoring the sound.

He tugged a small roll from behind the seat and slammed the door, frightening a woodcock. It zigzagged off through the underbrush with a whir of wings. Its sudden movement dislodged a grouse, which squawked raucously and sprung skyward. Sheridon grimaced, hefted the package over his shoulder, and made his way toward the forest.

He maneuvered with a sinuous, lissome gait, tucking his feet under lush growth with each step so that nothing was disturbed by his passage. So light was his tread that not even the grass bent underfoot. Those that knew him best as a lumbering drunk and blustering bully would have been astounded to see him now. Few would have heard Sheridon, much less recognized him, as he moved through dense foliage with animal instinct and grace.

Fewer still knew about his land—himself, a single lawyer, and a country clerk to be precise—and even fewer knew that *this* is where he came during his long forays away from Stockton Springs. Most people simply assumed that he was out carousing—his reputation took care of that—and even Leah would have been surprised to discover his secret.

For here, Sheridon was in his element. When the chips were down, when he needed to lay low for a while, or needed just plain solitude, he came to the peace and serenity of his small undeveloped tract of land near Sebec Lake. In truth, he had no taste for cities. They might be okay for an occasional blowout, but Sheridon did not like it anyplace where the natives did not cower upon demand. Jimmy *was* a territorial animal, and his territory was Sandypoint and Stockton Springs.

Sheridon had acquired his woodcraft from his Indian ancestors. Only a thin trickle of native blood ran in his veins, coming to him from his great-grandmother. Unlike the rest of his family, who all had the blond hair and the light skin of the European, his Native American heritage was revealed in his dark coloring and his exotic bone structure. Some sort of throwback, Jimmy Sheridon had managed to inherit the worst characteristics of each—and the savagery of both—carrying within him the deceit of the whites and the anger of the Indian.

True to his nature, in all the years Jimmy had owned this land, he had never built a permanent structure upon it, preferring to pit himself against elements—surviving as his forebears had once done with no more than a knife, an ax, and a single blanket—and he had never gone hungry. Had Jimmy been like other men, indeed like his Indian ancestors, he might have taken pride in this skill, but Sheridon took no pride in something that did not carry with it the outer trappings of white man's power.

Still, when Jimmy finally returned to Stockton Springs, he would be invigorated and renewed, ready to force others to his will or face his most recent transgression.

Sheridon glided noiselessly like a bird of prey into the clearing, then paused under a paper birch to consider his options. He rolled a cigarette, lit it, and fished a stray piece of tobacco from his mouth. He wondered how long he'd have to stay lost this time. Usually, all he had to do was wait until tempers had cooled. Then he could go home and his victim could be induced, by persuasion or coercion, to drop any charges that might have been pending. Every once in a while some "upstanding citizen" wouldn't be swayed, and Jimmy had had to do a little time, but never more than thirty days.

This time, though, Sheridon had a feeling that it might take just a little bit longer for memories to pale and tempers to dwindle. He'd really cut that poor bastard up, and Jimmy reckoned that no amount of coaxing would dissuade Defleurieu from filing a complaint. Perhaps Jimmy *had* gotten a little bit carried away, and this time he reckoned he'd end up with more than the usual thirty days in the clink.

"Asshole deserved it," Jimmy muttered under his breath. That guy had no right to be stickin' his nose into Jimmy's business. No fuckin' right. After all, the way Sheridon treated Leah was nobody else's concern.

He took a deep breath, enjoying the fresh, clean smell, and then turned to study the small hollow before him. Black spruce, balsam fir, and eastern white pine crowded around the combe, but its center was clear enough of undergrowth to permit a fire. His hand caressed the white trunk of a birch, fingers followed the serrated horizontal lines. The tree, with its thin, drooping crown, would provide limited cover. The deadfall would provide him with kindling. The papery bark peeled away in a curl to reveal the tender orange inner bark. He tore a strip from the tree and proceeded to clear a place for the campfire.

Two hours later a lean-to graced the side of the clearing, and Jimmy squatted before a roaring fire. A rabbit skin had been tacked down to dry, and its stripped body was sizzling over the fire. Jimmy gathered mushrooms and a few roots. These he cleaned and wrapped in leaves and set to roast among the coals.

The sun had risen above the treeline as Sheridon pulled a long straight stick from the pile beside him and began to file at it, sharpening one end to a point. He dozed intermittently, awoke to continue his work creating the tools he needed to survive, only to drift off again in contented slumber.

A few hours later the fire had dimmed to coals. The trees around him spoke in seductive whispers. The boughs wove mysteries of light and dark. Sheridon gnawed on the red and white cap of a mushroom. His pupils had grown large and dark, so huge that they completely swallowed the irises, turning brown eyes a shiny black that reflected redly under the late afternoon sun. Sheridon examined the crimson speckled skin of the mushroom, then popped it into his mouth.

God, he was stoned!

He stirred the fire, adding a few more sticks, and then slumped against a log, letting the forest sing to him. A slight breeze blew through the clearing, raising a spiral of sparks that glowed so brightly that even the sunlight could not compete with it. Sheridon gaped at the spinning cyclone of amber and gold. He reached out tentatively to touch it, but common sense prevailed and he drew his hand back before he was burned.

The scene shifted subtly around him. The crisp air, if anything, became more clear. Power resonated through the ground, up through the soles of his feet into his legs and thighs. Vibrating life rippled through his body from the land. It was a peculiar sensation he had noted in the past when he passed over sacred soil, and Jimmy knew this to be a place empowered by the old gods of beaver, wolf, and deer. Sheridon had happened upon these spots before, areas consecrated by deities far older than the God of Jehovah, and that was why he had bought this piece of land.

The skin on his scalp rose, and Jimmy cast an anxious glimpse over his shoulder. For some reason he was not surprised when he saw the familiar timberline of Verona and the flash of the Penobscot Bay, as if he were standing on the ridge over Sandypoint. Time and place merged, and the tingling on the back of his neck intensified.

Something moved among the trees behind him, and his heart skipped a beat.

Someone had followed him here!

An old man entered the clearing, and for a second Jimmy thought it was Defleurieu. His face was seamed, the left side drooped where he had apparently lost an eye.

Jimmy raised his hands in a placatory gesture. "Hey, look, man, I'm sorry. I got a little carried away."

The old man didn't seem to notice Jimmy, walking *through* him, and younger man yelped, whirling to watch this apparition as it moved through the fire to squat down beside it. Then the old fart began to rock back and forth, moaning. Jimmy's gaze took in the vest of fur and the robes of a shaman.

The medicine man continued to keen, the wail starting deep within the bony chest. It climbed higher, and higher, carrying Sheridon with it. A chill rocketed up Jimmy's spine, and incredible sorrow welled within his breast. The skin on the back of Jimmy's neck began a slow creep. The hair on his back and arms stood on end in quivering gooseflesh, and even his scrotum shriveled.

Eieeyee!

A sense of loss and responsibility enveloped Sheridon.

Eieeyee!

Doleful, mourning. Images of another time and an ancient tribe who had given their name to the river and the bay.

Eieeyee!

The screeching lament swelled like a wave that threatened to engulf the younger man. Jimmy touched his cheek and realized that it was wet with tears.

The old man grasped his shirt of leather and beads and ripped it from his body with surprising strength. He pulled a knife from his belt. Jimmy half rose from his place on the opposite side of the fire, as if he knew what would happen next.

With deliberate movements the Indian began to slash at his forearm, making short, diagonal cuts across wrinkled skin. Across the fire searing pain shot up Jimmy's arms, and he looked down to see blood seep from gashes that had opened spontaneously between elbow and wrist, like stigmata.

Sheridon ground his teeth, collecting himself to spring and disarm the man whose image wavered beyond the flames. The old man's hand moved to his exposed chest. The knife scraped the withered breast, and in turn, Jimmy's chest stung. Sheridon glanced down it as the ghostly old man drew his knife from left to right with a sweeping sluggish motion, and blood oozed from cuts that sprouted magically across the younger man's pectorals.

One slice.

Jimmy swore.

Two slices.

He bellowed.

Three.

He collapsed in a heap on the ground.

The old man didn't seem to notice Jimmy or his distress. He persisted in making diagonal cuts across his chest, without a sound. As if he felt no pain, and perhaps he didn't—Jimmy was feeling it for him.

Sheridon pinched himself, trying to draw himself from this hallucination, while the bony hand holding the dagger rose and hovered next to the wizened face. And the strange mourning chant began anew.

"No," whimpered Jimmy. The warmth of blood flowed down runnels in the younger man's cheeks. Sheridon licked his lips to taste the coppery saltiness of his own blood. He had to stop this guy—whoever he was, whatever he was—somehow.

For the first time the old man's gaze caught Jimmy's and held it. Something passed between the two of them in that brief contact. A roar filled Jimmy's head. Hatred unfolded within his breast, and hubris bloated his spirit. Suddenly Sheridon realized that his hand also held a knife.

The ululation increased to a shriek, and the old Indian raised his blade—Jimmy did the same—and the shaman brought it down with extraordinary force upon the gnarled hand to hack off the knotted little finger. Paroxysms of agony shot up Sheridon's arm, so intense that he blotted it out, detaching himself from the pain. Dazed, Jimmy looked down to see his own knife sawing at his finger. He pressed the flat of the blade against the stump to stanch the flow of blood and felt a slight grinding sensation as metal grated against exposed bone.

The apparition stood and started to chant, waving the finger above his head like a crazy man. The Indian's song pounded through Jimmy, matching the beat of his heart, and he thought he heard drums throbbing away in the background. The shaman began a shuffling dance around the fire, passing in and out of flames as though unaware of their presence. The next thing Sheridon knew, he, too, was standing. His feet moved of their own volition, and he found himself mirroring the old man's movements and following him around the fire.

The shaman screwed up his face to shout, and Jimmy's face contorted, inadvertently mimicking the medicine man's expression, flicker for flicker, twitch for twitch.

The old man hopped on one foot and then the other. Jimmy jumped, left, then right. The man took a step forward and then back. Jimmy did also so that they were moving in unison. They continued, revolving, faster and faster and *faster* around the fire. The old Indian spun, this way and that, pointing the bloody finger at the four winds— the ground at his feet stained crimson. The shaman cavorted like some kind of lunatic. Jimmy's body swayed in time with the cadence and the rhythm of the old man's dance, matching the shaman beat for beat. Pictures flashed in Jimmy's mind. He saw phantom people, milling in the background, and yet another image of the strange shaman bending over sick and ailing natives. The second medicine man gesticulated, waving demons away. The prostrate form below the shaman stiffened and sighed. *The death rattle.* The old man wailed.

Still the shaman across the fire moved, oblivious to this ghostly double. The throb of drums reverberated inside Sheridon's head, the pulse seeming to radiate from the earth itself.

Then, as abruptly as it had begun, the medicine man's capering halted. The Indian stared at Jimmy, the severed finger pointed directly at him. And Jimmy knew that he and the old man were bound. Jimmy could feel his anger; he could feel his pain. The man's hatred pulsated through Sheridon, drummed through him as had each thumping stamp and each intoned syllable.

Belatedly Jimmy realized without understanding the words that the old man had cursed someone, and Sheridon would not have wanted to be the recipient of that curse for anything in the world. He pitied the poor sucker who was.

Slimed by blood, the knife twisted in Sheridon's grip, and he dropped it as the Indian hunkered down to bury the bleeding finger in the soil while the spectral bay seethed in the background. When the last of the dirt had been tapped back into place, the shaman withered into the dust, and Jimmy stood alone in the clearing once more.

But the shaman's malice remained. It coursed through Sheridon in waves. Jimmy absorbed it, was empowered by it. It became his, and he knew without knowing how that the curse had been released and even now was working upon the world.

And he, James Sheridon, was its vehicle.

Veiled by the undergrowth, Gideon stooped over a large limb. Putting all his weight into it, he carved a deep gash in the moist earth. He mumbled as he worked. Nonsense syllables that seemed to make some sort of strange sense as he muttered them.

The curved ditch formed a perfect circle some ten feet around the mobile home at its closest point. Its line never varied or wavered, even though he had worked his way through dense brush.

Straightening, Gideon surveyed his work. The trench was already filling with rainwater. He looked warily at the mobile home. It was time to join the ends, and that meant exposing himself to view.

Spurred by fear, Gideon gouged the last fifteen feet rapidly, moving crabwise across the dooryard. He was sweating by the time he had retreated back into the trees. With another askance glance at the trailer, Gideon leaned into the last few inches, and the limb twisted with mindless perversity in his hands.

Blood welled from a cut on his finger, and Gideon stared at it spellbound as a long-dead memory reached skeletal arms toward him. He crouched down in the protective shelter of the grove and let his arms dangle uselessly between his legs—his forehead becoming seamed with concentration, and his expression absorbed as it always was whenever he tried to follow the gnarled skein of thought.

Blood. Blood from a finger.

Something soft brushed his cheek, warm fur, hot breath, the wet tongue of greeting. He leaned against the ephemeral touch. Somehow comforting. Like a friend. Like a . . . like a . . . pet.

The word came with difficulty, and Gideon tried to remember why. He sucked in his cheeks and squinted. He had had a pet once. Something small, soft, and warm that would wiggle in his arms and nibble on his nose. His scowl deepened.

A pet. A pet.

Blood dripping from a cut.

A gerbil. The word brought recollection—and a name, Wuffles—and Gideon recalled soft brown fur, two rounded ears, and a nose that never seemed to stop moving. A smile burst across his face, followed by a small cry of joy at recaptured memory.

Then the image of a gerbil was replaced by another, his big brother, Jimmy—his face a dark oval of rage, lip pursed cruelly, and the gently slanting eyes gone to the flat black of hatred.

He held out a finger from which blood dripped, and . . .

"It bit me," this younger version of his brother spoke, "the sonofabitching little rodent bit me!"

The child Gideon cradled his pet next to his chest and threw a desperate look at the door, hoping his parents would miraculously appear.

"He didn't mean to!"

Jimmy roughly extracted Wuffles from Gideon's embrace, and the creature tried to bite him again. Shaking the terrified animal, Jimmy stormed into the kitchen. His head pivoted on his neck as he searched the room, looking for something that would provide adequate punishment. His gaze landed on the steaming deepfat fryer, still hot from dinner. A lazy curl of vapor rose above the silver lip.

Gideon followed his eyes and screamed. He threw himself at his older brother, clutching at his arm as Jimmy switched the fryer on to high.

Jimmy held the writhing gerbil only inches from his face and said: "You hurt me, and now I'm gonna show you what it's like to hurt, really hurt!"

"No!" wailed Gideon. He jumped, arms waving frantically

*as he tried to extricate his pet from Jimmy's grasp. With a
look of triumph at his younger brother, Jimmy Sheridon
lowered Wuffles into the hot grease, and the gerbil, too, began
to scream.*

Weeping, Gideon stood up, returning to his ditch and
completing the circle's ends. As the two lines met, it began
to gleam with a subdued light. Gideon slumped against the
tree, relieved.

He had drawn the circle in such a way that the trench
encompassed the home itself, but fell outside the bounds of
the drive, where it would have to compete with the many tire
tracks. The line immediately over the path would be tram-
pled soon enough, he knew, and he would have to come back
to renew it.

But for now, the trailer and its occupants were protected
from harm.

7

The squad nosed slowly out onto Highway One. Blount craned his neck, looking left and right, trying to locate another vehicle in the roiling mixture of rain and fog before committing himself to the road. Nothing. He pressed gently on the gas and steered on to the highway, north toward Bucksport.

Out of the corner of his eye he could barely perceive the trees by the side of the road as they drooped forlornly— their boughs dripping dully during this lull in the rain—and the mist was so thick he could see only a few feet beyond the hood of the car. Blount leaned forward, his chin just above the steering wheel, and squinted, concentrating on the gray strip of road before him.

The deluge had continued—for one week, two weeks, three going on four—coming down in sheets, and he wondered how much longer it would last. Water collected in little gullies and ran down the hillside in streams. The roads down by the lighthouse were a washout; only people with four-wheel drive got in and out of the area. The lighthouse itself was purely decorative, for the bay was up and the rocky shoals of which it warned no longer existed. The creek down by the Point, usually little more than a trickle, was no longer contained by the pipe that ran under the gravel road. It had turned into a raging river that cut the camps from Sheila's place south off from the outside world.

The officer tapped irritably on the dashboard. The seasons were all screwed up. It was too soon for autumn rains. September usually was a continuation of August, minus the tourists. September's warmth and sunny days would tempt even the most dedicated worker to delinquency. Its crisp nights burnished the leaves for October's dispersal. The rains, when they came, normally arrived later to strip dull brown leaves from gnarled branches.

This year, though, the trees that should have begun to change to autumn dress were still cloaked in an unnatural green. Their boughs clung stubbornly to their summer coat while late fall's weather hurried autumn along its relentless course to winter. September, it seemed, hadn't existed. Instead, August's heat had been superimposed on October's rains.

A native, Blount wouldn't have dreamt of moving anywhere else. Still, as far as he was concerned, autumn with its tumult of bright yellows, livid scarlets, deep maroons, and blazing oranges was the only redeeming factor to living in this state. As if nature had given the Maine fall a splendor and a grace unrivaled elsewhere on God's green earth as an apology for the hard winter she forced the inhabitants to endure. Maine was in Alan's blood, and he felt this strange juxtaposition of seasons acutely. He felt cheated. More than cheated, he felt dispirited, disheartened—*doomed*—by time's apparent suspension.

The forest dropped away to his right, and he caught a glimpse of slate where water-laden sky, river, and bay had converged to become a uniform gray sheet.

The police officer frowned. No wonder cabin fever was striking early this year. With everything that had been happening recently in Stockton Springs, Blount seldom made it into the Bucksport station, and the officer was surprised to discover that he actually missed the bullpen-type office and the casual banter with his fellow officers as they dallied over reports and forms. He missed the mundane routine of picking up drunks, breaking up fights, or stopping an occasional marital dispute. Or the long hours of cruising around his set route—which began with the station, swung past the cemetery, made a long meandering trot around the perimeter of Bucksport, and returned to town again, past the cemetery—with its bleeding-heart monument—and the supermarket back to the station. He even missed the paperwork.

Inside his car Blount kneaded the taut muscles of his neck as a semi appeared and disappeared into the fog, grinding past as the trucker changed gears. The driver was traveling far too fast for the road conditions. Blount thought briefly of flipping on his sirens, swinging round, and giving chase, but decided against it. He wasn't feeling particularly suicidal today. Let the sucker wrap himself and his vehicle around some tree somewhere if that's what he wanted to do.

The fog ended abruptly, and Blount found himself blinking in the bright sun. His spirit soared as if some damp hand had released its grip upon his heart, for it seemed that only when he got away from the suffocating band of mist and cloud that shrouded Stockton Springs could he think. The officer relaxed against the seat and began to whistle a cheery little ditty.

Before him stretched the spectacular vista of Bucksport, framed by steep rocky cliffs, blue water and a bridge painted an unobtrusive green. The town shone like a white jewel, although living and working here all these years. Blount had grown immune to the view. Like the rest of the citizenry, the officer was more concerned about the potholes on Bucksport's Main Street than the picture-postcard scenery.

His heart quickened as he approached the suspension bridge that straddled the gorge between Verona Island and the mainland. He dreaded this part of the trip. Each time he drove across the bridge, his stomach gave a gut-wrenching twist and his mouth went dry, and Blount was glad that the railing hid the sheer drop to the water below where the Penobscot River scudded into the surging bay.

Once over the bridge, Highway One touched briefly upon Verona. The sharp bend led to a second bridge—this one built low over the surface of the water—that took him back to the mainland and into Bucksport proper. The rabbit warren of detours had been removed after the completion of the new bridge, and it was always a shock to turn from its smooth pavement onto Main Street. Blount skirted the many ruts and craters—his hands steering automatically. People hustled between Tru Value and the five-and-dime, looking nervously at the boiling cloud bank beyond the bridge.

At the last minute Blount turned left instead of right to park in front of the coffee shop. He wasn't quite ready for the office or the reports he'd have to fill out for each one of the innumerable incidents. The thought brought the frown back to his face as he hoisted himself from the driver's seat with a groan. Inside the restaurant the waitress greeted him like the prodigal son.

"Where ya been, stranger?" she said as she handed him his cup.

"Stuck in that," he replied, and Blount thumbed at the wall of mist visible through the picture window, where the coast beyond the bridge vanished, taking Stockton Springs with it.

"Yeah, what's going on over there?"

Blount exhaled loudly through loose lips, making a sputtering noise into his cup that echoed back at him mockingly. "Dogged if I know. Ever since the rains began, it seems like everyone in Stockton Springs has gone nuts."

She nodded. In an area this small, this close knit, this was not news. The waitress waited for further illumination. Alan Blount stared gloomily at her over the rim of his coffee cup. When no additional information was forthcoming, she shrugged and returned to refilling the salt shakers.

Blount sighed. He would have to recount events soon enough in the myriad forms he faced back at the office. He didn't want to tell his tale twice. Someone else could explain it to her. If they knew how.

The fact was that the whole fucking town was going crazy, and living there, Blount bore the brunt of it. Marital disputes were up—with ominous rumbles between normally peaceful couples—like a dress rehearsal for winter, when cabin fever would strike everyone with a wicked one-two punch. Twice this week Blount had been called by the Mordens to break up a fight between June and Rich Gascon. Alan sensed another blowup in the offing. They usually happened in threes, like death. He chortled hollowly into his empty cup, set it down on the counter, and, catching the waitress's eye, pointed at it.

There was the Fletcher twins' fight, and that still shocked him. It was something he never thought he'd live to see, the two were so close. Blount wasn't particularly surprised that they had fallen for the same girl. After all, they shared everything else. Was it all that illogical that they would have similar taste in women? Once he'd disarmed the brothers, more of a fight than he expected, he'd given each a stern talking-to and for the first time discovered a difference between the twins. Terry was the more volatile, his attitude defiant, while Eddie was much more sensitive. The latter boy seemed genuinely disturbed by the fight, crushed by the open antagonism and hurt about the girl. Terry, however, had revealed a much more cynical approach to their sharing a single female, as if it were amusing and something of no great import. After their discussion, Blount decided that he would never have trouble telling the two apart again.

Then there had been the ruckus at the café. A humdinger. Jimmy Sheridon cut up Duke Defleurieu real bad and then conveniently disappeared as he always did when things got too hot. Blount swore that Sheridon would not get away with it this time. Jimmy Sheridon was one mean son of a bitch, dangerous when riled, and Blount would just love to see that bastard behind bars. He planned to arrest Sheridon as soon as he showed his face in Stockton Springs. With this in mind he'd spent more time on Leah Blair's doorstep in the last week than his own.

On top of it all, the "city fathers" had discovered an embezzler in their midst. The entire township of Stockton Springs hovered on the edge of bankruptcy. That, blessedly, wasn't his case. Belfast took it. Alan wouldn't have had the objectivity. As a private citizen, Blount would have gleefully rung the sucker's neck. As an officer, he could not.

Sitting down to write a report on Les Braun's goat—the officer blinked; was he really that far behind?—seemed like comic relief. What with everything else that was going on, the butchering of a few animals was small potatoes. The police here had caught a bunch of kids doing some kind of satanic thing, and the mystery was solved. Case closed, except, of course, for the paperwork.

Blount blew gently at the steamy surface, relishing the taste of real coffee that Bucksport's restaurant served. It in no way resembled the burnt umber they served in CD's café. It came in real cups, unlike the reconstituted bullshit of McDonald's, with its Styrofoam mug with twin arches or leering clown face. That was enough to put any man off his oats.

"Hey, stranger, mind if I join you?" a voice interrupted his reverie. Blount turned to regard the fellow officer, Evan Duffy.

"You look as if your dog died," Evan said.

"I don't have a dog, thank God," Blount said. "Sure as shit if I did someone would have its balls floating in a jar somewhere."

Evan nodded. "Heard you had trouble at CD's the other night. That Jimmy Sheridon's bad news. Stockton Springs' own mini-Mafia."

The waitress walked up with a coffee for Evan and paused to top up Blount's cup.

"Wait a second. Wasn't it Sheridon who led the manhunt some fifteen years back? He may be bad news, but it seems he was on the right side of the law that time," the woman interjected. "Besides, he's kinda sexy. Don't you think?" She gave them a sly smile.

Both officers rolled their eyes to the ceiling and snorted.

"Women!" said Evan.

"Yes. And look what happened," Blount said. "Nothing. Turned the countryside upside-down, and what did they find? A few kids making out in cars."

"Besides, you can't go taking the law into your own hands like that," Evan added sagely.

"Can you blame him?" she asked.

Both men fell into a sour, disapproving silence. Neither wanted to be reminded of the time when Jimmy had turned vigilante after the death of his parents. Two men had been injured in the ensuing witch-hunt, one girl prematurely wed as a result. The waitress examined their churlish expressions and retreated, shaking her head in bewilderment.

"So what're you in town for?" Evan asked.

"Paperwork, piles of it!" Blount turned his back on the fog and glowered out of the front window toward the unseen police station just as a van pulled up before the coffee shop bearing the familiar logo of Channel 12, one of two Bangor television stations. A long-haired man with a heavy belt and a videocam slung casually over his shoulder emerged from behind the van. A pretty young woman followed, clutching a microphone.

"Must be a slow Saturday if they're coming here to look for news," Blount said, indicating the pair who huddled in conference next to the police cars. The woman looked in through the steamy windows, waved at Blount, and smiled as if she knew him, and the officer had to admire her style.

The waitress chuffed. "Yer caught now."

She scuttled off to pick up an order from the kitchen.

The café doors swung wide, and the reporter wound her way up the aisle toward them. She walked with the mincing gait of someone wearing impractically high heels. The cameraman slouched disdainfully behind. His eyes darted about the room.

"Sheriff."

Evan looked bored and concentrated on his coffee while Blount gave her his correct rank. She fidgeted impatiently, not listening.

"Sheriff," she repeated and Blount swallowed the retort that came to his lips. "I'm Jennifer Collins with—"

"Yes, I see," he interrupted, "it's stamped all over the equipment."

"We've come over to cover the rain."

Blount made a rude noise, and the cameraman's disinterested stare came to rest upon the officer.

"What, nothing happening in Bangor? You gotta come here?" Blount said.

"Well, we have reports of flooding, although there doesn't even seem to be much rain here."

"Not much rain here, or even on Verona. It's all over at the Point, and the flooding, well, that's not news. Been that way fer a while."

"Could you direct us there?"

"I can, but you won't find much. If you didn't know that the little stream had been dried up for years, you wouldn't even know what you were looking at."

The cameraman wandered off and started to talk to one of the younger waitresses. She watched him goo-goo-eyed and giggled.

"Well, isn't this weather a little unusual for this time of year?" the woman asked.

"I s'pose, but who kin predict the weather. Certainly, not that turkey you call a weatherman."

The woman laughed, a little too loud, as if she had been expecting his comment.

"The only thing that's odd about it," Evan mused, joining the conversation for the first time, "is it's so isolated. Like Stockton Springs sprouted its own special cloud, like that fellow in 'Li'l Abner.'"

The woman looked baffled.

"You don't remember it?" he said.

"Can't say that I do," she said.

"Look," Blount said, "if you really want to go wander around in the fog, come over here. I'll draw you a map." Alan sketched a rough map on a napkin, a squiggly line representing Highway One over the bridge through Verona and up the coast. He placed a large *X* next to the turnoff.

"There's a motel there," Blount explained. "You can't miss it. Unless the fog's so thick you can't see it," he added.

The cameraman ambled back to the counter, and they conferred briefly. The reporter wheeled on Blount, pivoting on a stiletto heel. She opened her mouth to speak, but Blount deflected her question before she could even begin it.

"So I understand there's been an arrest on that witchcraft case," he said to Evan, his voice lowered conspiratorially.

"What was that?" She thrust her face between the two officers.

"Some sort of black-magic rituals," he said nonchalantly.

"What can you tell me about that?"

Blount chuckled. "Not my case, sister. You'll have to go up to the station for that one."

The two heads bent together for another mumbled conference.

"Ah, thank you." She tapped the rolled-up napkin against the palm of her hand. They turned in unison and headed for the door while Blount swung to glare at the young waitress. She busied herself, spilling the catsup she poured from one container into another, and Blount's attention went back to the television crew.

If the lady had been a little nicer—had even listened when he gave her his correct rank and name—Blount could have bent her ear about the goings-on in Stockton Springs, but she hadn't, and he fully hoped she'd get lost in the mist or stranded in the flood. He stared out the window and was pleased to note that the van had turned toward the police station instead of heading up Main toward Stockton Springs. She had taken the bait, deciding that witchcraft was more interesting than water.

Evan elbowed him. "Why'd you tell her that?"

"What?"

"About the witchcraft. You know that's nothing more than some childish prank," Duffy said.

Blount pulled at his lip. "Dunno. Who needs her poking around Stockton Springs anyway?"

"The boss ain't gonna like it."

"He'll get over it," Blount said.

* * *

Ann Blisson swore as she moved the pan to catch another drip that had sprouted in the ceiling. She cursed her husband, who had decided to postpone having the roof fixed in favor of a new hunting rifle, and she cursed herself for letting him talk her into it.

Ping, pong, splatter, ping. The water dripping into the pans set up a dissonant refrain to which she provided counterpoint with her sharp invectives.

The lazy bastard had been putting off clearing the gutters because of the rain, and now they were getting the backwash. She peered disconsolately at a puddle on the living room floor. That was the problem about good old New England homes. Too many dormers, gables, and additions that left odd nooks and crannies, where the runoff pooled.

The monotonous thrum of rain, the buzzing in her brain, and the constant drip was driving her nuts. She couldn't stand listening to much more of this. Eyeing the stained ceiling, Ann decided that one problem, at least, she could solve if she cleaned the gutters herself.

Once outside, Ann hesitated questioning the wisdom of her decision. The eaves loomed dizzily overhead, and rain beat in her eyes and face. The sixteen-foot ladder weighed heavily against her shoulder. Ann thought of going back into the plink of water in buckets and pails, pots and pans, and she sighed, propping the ladder against the wall and adjusting its position. Again, she pondered the far-off roof versus the lowering sky. She would be all right, if she was *real* careful. . . .

Lorraine Garreth pulled a batch of cookies from the oven and slipped them onto the rack to cool. Then she brushed the crumbs from the cookie sheet and spooned small mounds of fresh dough onto the clean surface. Toll House cookies. David's favorite. He would be pleased when he came home tonight. Then the young woman scowled, trying to remember if he would be home tonight. She shoved the cookies in the oven.

The day was dreary. The gloom and depression had

seeped into her soul the same way the damp seeped into her bones. The baby was down for her nap, and Lorraine was bored and restless. She strode from room to room, looking for something to do. She progressed sporadically, with no set purpose. Movement for movement's sake. Anything just to keep active. She missed David, and she was as horny as a two-peckered billy goat. That was the problem. She was screaming, raving horny, and David, of course, was gone. As always. Off on a run, hauling livestock, lumber, or who knows what to God knows where, and she was sick of it.

Lorraine had not expected this when she had said "I do." Oh, she had known that he was a truck driver, but she hadn't realized precisely what that would mean. He was gone *all* the time, and she was left alone.

The rain thrummed steadily against the pane. The ceaseless sound was soft, caressing, and Lorraine ran a sensuous hand underneath her frayed bathrobe. Her eyes fell upon the plastic crucifix hanging upon the wall, and she looked guiltily away to stalk through the house yet again. In the living room she paused, studying it critically, searching for any stray dust or child's toy that might have escaped her notice. The room was spotless. She had cleaned the house thoroughly twice this week.

Turning her nose up on this week's project, a paint-by-number picture of a tiger on velvet, Lorraine gazed dejectedly at the already completed Elvis and heaved a great sigh.

She felt wet and wiggly all over. She giggled. Pretty soon she'd start backing into doorknobs.

The timer buzzed and she slunk back into the kitchen, thinking about David, wishing he were home. She scraped another batch of cookies from the sheet. He was probably humping some other broad right now.

Lorraine began whacking big balls of dough back on to the sheet. If he didn't hurry home soon, she was going to get fat. She rammed the cookie sheet back into the oven and went to the bedroom.

This was ridiculous. She slid from her robe and stood before the full-length mirror. Her stomach had flattened out nicely since the baby, although her waist still looked a little too thick. She'd have to start exercising. She turned sideways and inspected her profile. Not bad.

But there wasn't a man around to enjoy it.

The drone of a car engine penetrated the patter of raindrops. Curious, Lorraine walked to the front of the house to see who was fool enough to be out in weather like this.

Lenny Walsh adjusted the hood of his raincoat so water didn't run into his eyes and shoved a bunch of letters marked Occupant into the mailbox. That the hood obscured his view didn't matter. He'd done these same postal rounds for the last twenty years and could have delivered the mail in his sleep. Lenny knew all his neighbors, had known them for years, and he figured he would know which box was which just by counting.

His stomach grumbled, gaseous after last night's repast of corned beef and cabbage, and he farted. Every week the same thing. Meatloaf on Monday. Pork chops on Tuesday. Corned beef on Wednesday. Chicken on Thursday, and so on. And every Thursday, during the day, he could count on indigestion.

Walsh coughed, sputtered, and rolled down the window to let the trapped air in the car out. Just once he'd like to have gas on Fridays. Or Tuesday. Just for a change of pace. His life was boring, like his route, this town, and his neighbors.

Oh, there were a few outsiders in Stockton Springs, seduced by the idea of life in the country, but they never lasted long. A year, two, maybe three. Eventually, though, terminal tedium drove them away, and Lenny envied them.

But could he get Joyce to move? Even consider the idea? What the hell, he could transfer anywhere in the country if he wanted to. Go to Florida or Texas. Someplace warm. But no, Joyce had grown up here, and she wouldn't leave the secure confines of Stockton Springs for *anything*.

Walsh pulled the hood down further and slumped against the rain as he reached from the car to cram the usual assortment of junk mail—flyers, circulars, and bills—in the box labeled "Garreth." The rain was falling so hard that he almost didn't hear the gentle knocking on the glass. He glanced up. Mrs. Garreth rapped against the pane a second time, and he gaped at her from beneath the plastic hood. The young woman stood in the picture window. Stark naked.

His mouth dropped open.

She smiled at him and waved, casual-like, as though nothing were remiss with her standin' there in her altogether. She was pretty—twenty years old at the most. Her body shapely, lovely, and firm.

The Garreths were newcomers. Outsiders, and he knew next to nothing about them. Lenny vaguely recollected that the husband was a trucker, and Walsh wondered if the man was home. Unlikely, considering the state his wife was in.

Mrs. Garreth beckoned to him. Lenny pointed at himself and mouthed the word: *Me?* She nodded yes. He swallowed hard, and his pecker gave a weak twitch.

"Jesus Christ." He didn't need this shit. He put the car in gear, took one last admiring glance at the window. She bent her index finger slowly, indicating that he should come in. Her other hand fondled her breast.

His gaze swept up and down the street.

"Son of a bitch," he muttered. Putting the car in park, Lenny yanked her mail from the box to take it to her door. This would be something of a special delivery, a public service, courtesy of the post office.

The alarm of reason klaxoned futilely in his brain. *This is nuts,* it said. *This is crazy. You're gonna get yourself killed. Get back in your car and drive away.*

But his gonads were thinking for him now.

Jimmy contemplated a world made of layers—where clearing and wood were one, and the Penobscot surged over Lake Sebec. Where rain fell from a clear sky, and Stockton Springs and its satellite Sandypoint were superimposed over the adjacent wilderness. Where time and space had become one, and where flame and air met with the shimmering heat inside his fevered brain.

Not so much as an eyelash flickered when a detached

hand reached across an ocean of time and expanse of space to dump a dozen hard-shelled seedpods into Sheridon's lap. The impression of weight drew his gaze downward, and he plucked one of the spiny spheres from his lap, its many spikes drawing blood from his fingertips.

Without a second thought Sheridon cracked the shell, emptied the tiny black seeds into his hand, and began to eat, mumbling. As he spoke, pips spewed from his cracked, dry lips. His injured hand lay forgotten in his lap. His clothes were crusted with dirt and the salt of perspiration. The cuts on his face, chest and arms had hardened to thin-razor black lines that cracked and bled again whenever his face contorted with psychotic animation.

Sheridon slumped, half dead, next to the fire. He saw nothing, and he saw everything—through fever's agitated veil—and he knew better than to trust anything he saw. Trees formed in mist and vanished as soon as he put out his hands to touch them. People appeared to him. His parents' disapproving faces surfaced from the flames, and Jimmy chased them away with a wave of dismissal. They were quickly replaced by others—living people who moved against the familiar backdrop of Stockton Springs.

Faces he had known for years, and faces Sheridon could barely identify, features dimly recalled from a trip to Aggie's store or over a cup of that crap they called coffee at the café. As if the entire population of Stockton Springs were intent on parading through his waking dreams.

And Sheridon cursed them, touching each, giving them some small darkness of his own. He sent to them echoes of the fell voices that played within his head, to wheedle and cajole.

Even now he observed not one but two images in the sheets of flame. A glittering Ann Blisson struggled up a shaking ladder next to a picture of a young woman and an old man fucking in some dark, anonymous hallway.

Lenny Walsh! Jimmy wouldn't have thought the old fart could get his pecker up, but perhaps with a little help from his friend James Sheridon . . . Shoveling more of the tiny black pips in his mouth, he stroked the air before him, and

Lenny climaxed with an arching of his back and an unheard groan. Sheridon snickered, closing his eyes to project the vision elsewhere. Lids still shut, he brought his hand down hard, and the table beneath the couple crumpled.

Extending his injured hand, Jimmy gave something invisible to the normal eye a tweak, and the woman on the ladder was sent spinning into space, mouth open in an unvoiced screech.

David Garreth was on the bridge in Augusta along the route that led from I-95 to Highway 3 when the vision struck him. That fat slug of a mailman screwing Lorraine right there in the front hallway. The prick had her stretched out over the telephone table, and Garreth could see it was ready to crumble under their combined weight. He hollered a warning as the table splintered soundlessly beneath them. Acting on reflex, the startled man slammed on the brakes, and the semi folded like a child's toy, taking every other car in both lanes with it.

His climax was so intense Lenny was sure he had died and gone to heaven. The table shattered beneath them with a loud bang. It, and they, fell crashing to the floor, and somewhere toward the back of the house the baby began to cry.

For a moment Mrs. Garreth stared at him in stunned silence, and then she started to batter at him with both fists.

"Get off. Get off!" she screamed.

"Hey!"

Her fingers curved into tight little claws, and she gouged at his eyes.

"What the—" he said, capturing both hands and holding them away from his face.

"Look, you called me in here," he snarled. "Don't tell me that you didn't want it. You was hot to trot."

She deflated.

"He knows, he knows," Lorraine said into her clenched fists. "My David saw us. He knows."

"Where is he?" Lenny said, scrambling to his feet as he pulled on his pants and zipped them. His head swiveled, and Lenny looked this way and that for her husband to materialize out of nowhere, shotgun in his hand.

"Gone, all gone." She motioned at the front door.

"You're nuts," he said as he eyed her. Despite himself, Walsh was moved by the sight of her lying so helpless and miserable among the splinters. The baby howled.

"Look, I'm sorry, let me help you up."

The woman swung on him. "Get the fuck out of here."

She grabbed a table leg, raised it above her head to heave it at him as Lenny ducked out the front door.

The moist air hit him like a wet fist. Lenny gasped. His balls shriveled to the size of peanuts, and his penis retreated protectively into his groin. He heard a dull thud as something—a table leg, most likely—hit the other side of the door, and Lenny scuttled across the porch and down the short steps, running blindly for the car. Thin wisps of vapor drifted across the road, cloaking his movements.

Only when he was safe within its confines did he permit himself to inspect the windows of the neighboring houses, looking for the telltale smear of ghostly white or flick of ruffled curtains. Nothing stirred, and Lenny sighed. The widow Mrs. Jones would probably be watching her favorite game show. The Franks would both be working, and blessedly, Mrs. Armand's car was missing from the drive.

The adrenaline that had been pouring into his veins decreased infinitesimally. Lenny straightened his shoulders, looked casually around one last time, and started the motor. He stared at the now empty picture window and shook his head.

Had he really done that? He, Lenny Walsh, of the protruding paunch, receding hairline, and Thursday gas brigade. Had he really just gone inside a neighbor's home and played hide the salami with a woman thirty years his junior? He must be out of his mind.

His hand shook, and he ground the gears.

This town was much too small. All it would have taken was one face at the window, the Avon representative of the week at the door, or hubby arriving home early . . .

What was that the woman had said? He'd seen? Holy shit. What the hell was he doing hanging around here?

Lenny tromped on the gas. The wheels spun, and he had a moment of panic when he thought he was stuck. He let up on the accelerator slightly, and the vehicle's wheels caught. The car veered ahead, and he steered it back onto the blacktop.

The heater turned the water on his raincoat to steam, and even with the defroster going full blast, Lenny had to stop and wipe the windshield clear at every other mailbox. His progress was slow, and he was running late. He'd only made it halfway to the end of School Street when he noticed Ann Blisson's body.

At first it appeared nothing more than a crumpled heap of clothing until he noticed the foot sticking out. His gaze followed the foot to the knee and realized it was bent the wrong way, backward.

Groaning, he got out of the car and paced up the stone walkway until he was almost on top of her. The corned beef and cabbage rolled in his stomach as he stared. Her spine was twisted, inverted, and her head faced the wrong direction. Her eyes were wide open and staring blankly at him.

Last night's dinner churned some more, and suddenly Lenny, who only an hour ago had been cursing the boredom, found himself wishing that he had a little less excitement in his life right now.

Alan Blount let the blanket drop over Ann Blisson's bulging eyes and moaned as he heaved himself from the ground. He had been called from his paperwork, and he could see the forms mounting as he walked to his car to radio for State Police. As a "suspicious death," this was their bailiwick.

Lenny Walsh skulked in the background. Head cocked to one side, Blount considered the man. His gaze darted to and fro, and Blount thought Lenny was acting as culpable as any criminal Alan had ever seen.

"Looks like an accident to me," Blount said, and Walsh relaxed visibly.

Alan craned his neck to examine the ladder, took off his cap, and scratched his head. "What the hell did she think she was doing climbing up to the roof in weather like this?"

The officer scanned the scene around him as though he could divine the answer in the water-laden air. He half expected Jennifer Collins and her trained cameraman to materialize like vultures. This was just the kind of thing the media loved, and he was glad that he had fielded her questions. If Stockton Springs was going to get into the news, this was not the image he wanted the world to see. Blount was pretty sure she had gone off to hunt witches, and he wished her luck.

"It doesn't make any sense," Alan said, adding under his breath, "nothing makes any sense anymore."

Next to him Walsh cradled his scrotum, unconscious of the officer's scrutiny, and spoke for the first time since Blount's arrival.

"That's for sure."

8

Shielded from the driving rain by the overhang of tin roof, Gideon hunched between a fifty-gallon can of heavy-grade motor oil and the gas tank used to fill the township's "fleet" of vehicles.

His expression was peaceful, and his face was haloed by a beatific glow. A radiance and soft inner light surrounded him that belied and defied the storm-swept sky above his head. From his position, protected and hidden from view, Gideon turned to regard the figure struggling over the crest of the hill. He recognized Tiffany Blair immediately. He peered at the animal at her side, did a quick mental shuffle, and labeled it: dog. It loped, head down as though tracking a scent. Intermittently its step would falter, and it would look over the massive shoulder, pausing as though it waited for her to catch up.

Lightning sliced like a jagged knife, cutting through the rain. The girl's shadow leapt before her, creating a black slash against a bleached-white background. Another flash, and Gideon noticed that the second figure cast no shadow.

His jaws clenched as Gideon tried to force his reluctant brain to work. No shadow. The young man didn't know why this bothered him, but it did. He scrunched up his eyes real tight so he could see better, but it was too much effort, and he gave up. Dazzled gloom replaced the scintillating light, and neither figure cast a shadow. The thought, whatever it was, darted away.

His eyes followed the halting progress of girl and dog as they drew near to the shed. The child leaned into the wind, but the animal did not appear to be troubled by it. Not a hair stirred in the thick gray coat. And again Gideon frowned, disturbed by the discrepancy. His head rotated creakily on his neck as he followed their erratic movement up the street until they turned toward the general store and disappeared from sight.

Junk was stacked everywhere, but Tiffany quickly zeroed in on the snacks. Cookies and cakes were stationed directly across from assorted chips and nuts. Finger in her mouth, the girl lingered before bright packages of candies, meditating on her mother's instructions.

Lunch, lunch.

Lunch meant it was supposed to be healthy, and healthy meant it couldn't be sweet. She made a wry face and turned her back on the candy.

The girl eyed the dollar bill in her hand, all her mother had given her, grabbed a bag of potato chips, and then paused to ponder the fruit. An image of some cartoon character sprang to mind, saying that fruit was good for you.

Tiffany pictured her mother asking her what she had eaten, in her familiar arms-crossed, toe-tapping posture, and picked up an apple from the stack.

Maybe if Tiffany stayed out long enough, her mother would forget all about her. The child was not particularly eager to go home. Her mother had been in a foul temper ever since Jimmy left. She waffled between hollering words of defiance at the wall and weeping.

Tiffany's gaze flitted briefly to the candy, and for a moment she was lost, forgetting why she had come.

"You okay, kiddo?" Aggie's voice roused her. "If I know your ma, you'd better not bring home M&Ms when you were supposed to get milk."

"Nah," Tiffany mumbled to herself. "Lunch."

She moved up to the counter and hopped from one foot to the other as Aggie stared down at her purchases, her eyes taking in the potato chips and apples.

"Lunch? Where's your protein?"

"Wha'd'ya mean?" Tiffany looked genuinely bemused.

"Meat, cheese, milk," she explained to the child with a brow raised in disapproval.

"She only gave me this." Tiffany squirmed, uncomfortable under the woman's scrutiny.

Aggie clicked her tongue a few times. "If I had a lovely little girl like you, I would make sure you had a proper lunch." Aggie swung away from Tiffany. "Some people don't deserve the children they got."

"No, ma'am," Tiffany said.

Aggie glanced back at Tiffany, wondering if the child were mocking her, and the girl shrank away. Aggie gave Tiffany a reassuring smile.

"Pearls among swine," she muttered, and Tiffany stared at the woman, perplexed.

"How about a hot dog?" Aggie asked.

Tiffany opened her fist to reveal the crumpled dollar bill in her hand.

"Don't worry about it." Aggie waved the money away. "It's on the house."

She rung up the chips and weighed the apple. "Honestly, between you and Bob Schoenwald I'm gonna go broke." She hastened over to the rotisserie, where hot dogs gleamed and spun lazily under the heatlamp.

"I always was a sucker for a hard-luck case," she said as she extracted a hot dog and plopped it into a bun. Aggie returned to the counter, passed it to Tiffany with one hand, and pointed at a small tray with catsup, mustard, and relish.

"Go ahead, fix it up the way you'd like, and eat it here. It'll stay hot that way, and it ain't like we're real busy." Aggie indicated the empty store with a sweeping gesture.

"So how's your mom?" she asked. "I heard that she was working nights at the café."

"Mrmph," Tiffany said around a mouthful of hot dog.

"What was that?"

"Tired," Tiffany said.

"I'm not surprised. I don't know why she took the job. I'd think she'd be busy enough with the kennel and everything else. Should make that lazy good-fer-nuthing Jimmy go to work, if you ask me."

Tiffany applied herself to her hot dog with renewed fervor at the mention of Jimmy's name as Aggie went on to catalog Sheridon's faults, dating back to grade school. As she talked, the woman moved from one end of the store to the other, shifting this piece, straightening that, and was still speaking when Tiffany got up to go.

". . . surprised all of us, though. He turned out looking like a real hero." Aggie paused to peer out at the waterlogged landscape.

"Scuse me, ma'am, I gotta go."

"Oh, yes, well, it looks like the rain has let up a bit. Here, take this." Aggie selected a piece of fudge from the basket on the counter and handed it to Tiffany.

"Gee, thanks!" she said, stuffing it in her pocket.

"And say hello to your mom for me."

"Sure and thanks, again." Tiffany gave a huge smile and fled.

Aggie muttered to herself as the door closed behind the girl. "Poor child."

Satan moved abroad. The voices told her so. Although whether they spoke with a divine tongue or demonic, Hedda could no longer tell, only that they drove her to guard her premises against the coming horde. The mist curled like writhing snakes around her, brushing against cheek and breast. Her breath came in ragged little gasps, and she crossed herself.

The first of his minions glared at her with eyes like red lanterns; teeth lined a slobbering mouth which extended from the snarling snout of a wolf. It raised its head to howl silently at an unseen moon and then vanished.

Unwilling to go inside, Hedda prowled the boundaries of their small yard. Her husband, Les, was in there, and she didn't want to face him, for he was one of the damned, just as she was damned, and their marriage was damned. Hedda tried to remember what had attracted her to him in the first place. He had offered her freedom. A way out, an escape from her stilted and stultifying home.

Foolish youth. She shook her head sadly.

To this day, Hedda could still conjure the image of her mother standing outside the house, shrieking contempt and scorn after the car as Hedda and Les drove away.

Harlot of Babylon! Whore!

Hedda's worst fears were confirmed when they discovered she was sterile. Their marriage had been corrupt from the start. Her ardor cooled, but Les's had not, and she was ensnared by her husband's coarse needs. She hadn't hope of redemption.

To outsiders they looked like a good God-fearing couple. Staunch Lutherans. They went to church each week. She participated in the church bake sale, and she collected for the auxiliary. And Hedda ached to do more as penance for her downfall, her sin, for Hedda knew the truth of it. Their marriage had been steeped in sin, immoral from the start. The serpent of lust had laid its dark seeds in their marriage bed. The first time he'd placed his man's hands upon her and his maleness inside her, she had enjoyed it, like the harlot she was. In those first days his touch had awakened fires in her that she hadn't known existed, and Hedda realized her mother spoke the truth.

Hedda shuddered and marched along the fence, stopping every few feet, quoting broken fragments of Bible verse, snippets from Psalms to Revelations, casting them into the fog like the ingredients of a spell.

The Lord is my Shepherd.

She had sinned.

I shall not want.

Sinned when she'd married.

It profiteth a man nothing . . .

Sinned when she succumbed to Les's attentions. Sinned when she continued to allow him to indulge his profane passion upon her person.

For once the truth had been revealed to her, Hedda never enjoyed sex again, never let herself. Through the years, though, Hedda had been forced to suffer her husband's attentions, lying dutifully, as stiff and still as a board until Les would roll away in disgust.

'Twas woman's curse to bear a man's caresses as she bore his children. In pain. A curse brought upon a woman by the wily serpent of Satan. Her mother had discussed it with her—surprisingly liberal for a Witness—painting it in the worst possible colors to dissuade Hedda from this marriage.

In marrying Les, she effectively divorced herself from the church that had formed her world view. Lutheranism had offered an escape from the restraints of the Witness Hall, but underneath it all, Hedda retained her original beliefs. These had evolved slowly, becoming more colorful as the years progressed. Until it had become ornamented with all the fervor of the hopping-hallelujah, Bible-thumping, born-again Christian. Her belief system now was a mishmash of spartan Witness Hall mingled with the idolatry of Catholicism and the ritual of the Lutheran church. Added to this was a dash of brass-plated television ministry, with its Hollywood pomp and neon verity.

Hedda had spurned the church that gave her faith, and that church, in turn, had spurned her. Her house was one of the few in the area that never received visitors brandishing copies of *The Watchtower* and *The Word.* But she did not forget the church's teachings. Each year she kept one eye on the calendar and another on the book of Revelations.

The apocalypse drew ever closer, and Satan had come to Stockton Springs. She could feel it. Hadn't she received divine confirmation when they arrested those teenagers at their unholy rituals? Satan was nigh. So she stalked ahead, flung an epistle at the wind, and continued along the fence, a sentry against demonic intrusion as her mind whirled in a series of confused religious images.

Rapture, she thought as she hurled another parable at the mist. *No, not rapture. Eternal life for the chosen!*

During those rare times they traveled to stock the small antique store they ran out of their shed, Hedda would go to the local Witness Hall and garner whatever books, leaflets, and pamphlets she could find. She recalled the simple childlike drawings of men and women working the fields side-by-side while round-cheeked and industrious children hauled wood from shed to house. This picture was superimposed with a silver-white light like the haloed glow of a streetlamp in the rain. In the picture the streets were paved with gold and their clothes were white.

Some would call it heaven, but not a Witness, for they knew the secret: that the chosen, the select few—*the Witnesses*—would survive beyond the apocalypse, becoming immortal at last.

Outwardly Hedda had rejected those beliefs for the Lutheran image of Armageddon, and to this she added the lurid narrative and fiery depiction of the television preacher, who told her she could dig into her pockets and buy redemption for a nominal fee, and much of her money was spent there—or as much as Les would allow. Hedda did not want to die in an unshriven state.

The woman shot a glance at the house, reminding herself that she was not among God's chosen anymore, and the devil roamed in the woods in the form of a wolf. Hedda hesitated at the next fence post, spun in confusion, before casting a disjointed proverb at the rain.

Behold, God exalteth by his powers; who teacheth like him.

And she shivered despite the oppressive heat of the muggy, rain-soaked summer that nature, or God, had extended far too long.

Outside the store Stockton Springs' main drag was a whirling, white wall of fog, but the rain had slowed to a drizzle. Looking up and down the street, Tiffany wondered what she should do next. Nothing came to her, few opportunities for fun presented themselves on a rainy Saturday afternoon, but she didn't want to go home. Not yet.

Mom would probably be mad, with Jimmy and with the world. Or she'd be cleaning, and that was worse. For then she'd shout at Tiffany for getting in the way because no amount of shrinking could hide Tiffany from her mother when she was on a cleaning binge.

The girl shrugged and stared up at the sky. It seemed lighter, a cream color instead of its usual dull gray. Tiffany scampered across Main, making her way up the short hill toward School Street and the playground. Houses lined both sides of the road, some neat, some not so neat. She ignored them, and they were absorbed back into the fog as she passed.

Beyond the school the line of houses thinned. The land to her right opened into a field which had been turned into a swamp. Tiffany passed the turnoff which would eventually lead back to town, heading instead for the lighthouse.

Dawdling, killing time, she rounded the bend, and the town behind her vanished.

The gray beast followed the route of least resistance, the road that had been cut by man through the woods and hills. The wolf was led by scent that wasn't scent, and sound that wasn't sound, steering toward a feeble glow that grew stronger as he approached it.

Around him the language spoken changed from the fluid, lilting French to the more guttural English. The switch registered subliminally somewhere in the complex brain, and in his sleep, the significance was recognized. He drew closer to his goal.

His feet crunched in the gravel along the shoulder, and late at night, when the wolf was sure that it was safe, his long nails would clack along the concrete.

Click. Click. Click. Click.

The wolf passed human settlements in the stillness of the night, sleeping by day in borrowed dens. Night and day, waking and sleeping, merged. Each evening the ancient predator greeted the gloaming silently, listening to the whisper on the wind and scent on a breath of breeze.

Click. Click. Click. Click.

The wolf loped along, steadily, rapidly, his pace never flagging.

Click. Click. Click. Click.

With each step the wolf's appearance altered, shifting subtly, as he grew younger. Under the limited light of the stars, his once-frayed ears straightened until at last they stood erect and proud, quivering forward and back at each buzz of motor or slamming of car door. Even as he stalked, legs stiff, along the human highway, his fur smoothed here and there. The old scars that once adorned the neck and snout had healed. His toughened frame, with its sinewy lines of muscle and rib, filled out, and he no longer had the gaunt moth-eaten look of the creature that had left the pack just a short while ago.

The time of renewal was upon him, and he was rejuvenated, revitalized. The journey strengthened him, was strengthening him, and he hadn't felt this way since the world was young.

The wolf snuffled, noting the acrimonious odor of gasoline-tinged exhaust. Light flickered. Twin beams of cold white light, like stars, appeared on the horizon. The predator slunk into the brush, growling deep with his chest as a car rumbled past.

The yellow-gold of dawn stained the horizon, and the wolf pushed deeper into the undergrowth—turned once, twice, three times in the tall grass before settling with a canine sigh. The predator fell immediately into a writhing slumber. In his dreams he traveled still. The great beast whined, his feet twitching as he glided in and out of the phantom forests of his youth.

The flare of dawn throbbed the dull ochre of evil, and superimposed over this glow was the face of the old shaman, his expression distorted by rage. Then the features shifted, the skin smoothed, and the wolf was confronted by a young

man. The beast's muscles contracted, and he sprung upon
. . . the enemy.

Despite the brisk night air of Maine's inland, Jimmy
Sheridon felt no chill. His eyes shone with the lunatic glint
of delirium. Sweat stood out on his forehead, neck, and face,
and his cheeks were streaked with soot. His stump wept
thick, creamy liquid the color of butter, and throbbed
incessantly.

Babbling meaningless gibberish, Sheridon stared into the
fire, and his muttered drone blended with the crackle of the
flames. He blinked, and Hedda Braun peered at him from
within the blaze. Her plain face, so haggard, worn, and gray
that it seemed to negate the ruddy glow of the fire. This
mini-Hedda marched back and forth across the coals, and
Jimmy could, by reaching into the smoke and giving it a
little twirl, deflect her from her current course and send her
scurrying back the way she came. Another twitch and she
would stop.

Chuckling, Jimmy extended his arm over the fire and gave
a quick stir, and on cue Hedda made an abrupt about-face to
hurry back along the distant Stockton Springs fence line.
Pus from the infected stump dripped into the coals with a
hissing noise. She halted. Her eyes started out of her
simpering face, and Hedda glanced both ways, as if she had
heard something scrabbling in the brush.

Jimmy twittered, manically, clapping his hands together
and wincing when a piercing pain raced up his arm to his
shoulder. When he grew bored with this sport, Jimmy
dismissed her visage—flinging his hands out and up as if
shooing away a child. She vanished with a poof.

Sweat dripped from his brow as he tried to call up another
image. Sheridon glowered at the embers. The fire guttered
and dwindled, as if its flames cooled. No matter how hard he
tried, he could not call Leah's likeness to the fire. When he
did, all he managed to summon was a strange blue-white
iridescence that surrounded the blurred mental picture of
the trailer, and his head would ache. Sheridon released the

fluttering image and slumped against the tree, exhausted. And Hedda's thin face materialized again in the fire.

Jimmy lifted a shaky hand to wipe his ash-smeared brow. White drainage trickled down his cheek unnoticed. It washed away the soot that darkened his features to expose thin red scabs. Stigmata raised by the Indian's dance. Jimmy fingered the cuts.

A shudder rocked his body, moving from his crown to his feet. His face, already red, became even more flushed under its coating of ash as he was taken by uncontrollable shivering. Hedda's floating face wavered, dissipating in tattered shreds, and the smoke before him began to take on another shape, approximating that of a bent, wizened old man.

The Indian!

The figure solidified, but even as it did it began to mutate and change. Its forehead collapsed and flattened while the old man's nose stretched, growing longer and longer until it formed a snout. That's when the pain hit Jimmy, hard, forcing him down to the ground. It started at the top of his head, and it felt as if some giant hand were crushing Jimmy's skull, driving bone into a depressed brain pan. Simultaneously something yanked at his nose, and it felt as if it were being ripped from his face.

Shimmering in the flames, the old shaman's ears started to shift, drifting upward along the skull. And the same inhuman hand that had battered Sheridon's skull and tugged at his nose now wrenched at his ears.

Jimmy cringed, whimpering like a dog.

The old man's wrinkled skin grew fuzzy, and through the haze Jimmy noted fine hairs as they sprouted along the old man's cheek and jowl. Sheridon's flesh began to creep, and the skin around his mouth and jaw tingled. Jimmy froze, unwilling to bring his hand up to touch his face, afraid what he would find.

As he watched, the medicine man's jaw stretched and thinned.

"No," Jimmy wailed, but all that came out was a choked growl.

The peach-fuzz on the old man's face thickened into fur

while Jimmy tried to crawl away from the fire to hide behind the paper birch, only to find that his limbs were not his to command. He swayed and lurched on all fours, falling facedown in the dirt.

Helpless, Jimmy watched as the old man's human body continued its grotesque transformation. The back stooped and then bent while his torso was compressed, becoming more compact. The legs shrank, a portion retracting into the body, as did the arms which drew into the old shaman's shoulders.

Jimmy flopped uselessly on the ground, unable to tear his eyes away. In what remained of the reasoning part of his brain, Sheridon recognized the transformation. It was familiar enough to anyone who'd ever watched a Grade-B horror flick. But that was in the safety of his living room on a little gray box, with a woman to fondle and popcorn to fling derisively at the screen. Living through it, feeling it, was something else again.

Before his startled eyes, the old man's fingers were absorbed into his palms, and what remained of the human hands shrank. The nails, lined and thickened by age, extended from the old man's palmar stub and curled to claws, and Jimmy shrieked as someone put red hot slivers under each one of his nails.

The metamorphosis complete, the old man was replaced by a slavering wolf. At that moment Jimmy's body was released from its thrall. He scrambled to his knees, anxiously looking at his hands. He half expected them to be covered with fur and to have sprouted doglike talons. Relief washed over him as he saw simple, human flesh. He laughed, throwing them up toward the heavens, rejoicing.

A deep rumbling rose from the embers. The wolf peered at him from the flames. Jimmy scrabbled backward, digging his heels into the earth to give him impetus.

The creature leapt, and before Jimmy could fully react, he felt hot breath on his cheek that reeked with the sweet-and-sour scent of carrion. The wolf nipped and bit, toying with Jimmy, playing with him the way a cat would a mouse. Arms extended before him, elbows locked, Jimmy tried to hold the ephemeral jaws away. Snapping ivory teeth descended on his throat. He wrestled with the image, but his hands would not find purchase on anything more substantial than smoke.

Alone in the clearing Jimmy flailed, slashing at the empty air. The smoke above his head whipped and eddied. Yet the teeth that clamped around his throat felt all-too-real, and Jimmy clawed at the specter, using both hands and feet. Kicking at it, biting, scratching like any animal. To no avail, for sharp canines sank into his flesh.

Agony worse than anything that had preceded it ripped through him as the wolf tore his esophagus from his neck, unleashing arteries and veins with a spray of blood. And Jimmy folded in upon himself to twitch and jerk convulsively upon the ground. The cloud of billowing smoke hovered above him for a moment, detached itself, and slowly drifted away.

Miles from his camp, the wolf's body stilled, and it slid from disturbed sleep into peaceful slumber.

9

The Brauns' house appeared as if from nowhere. The chimney weighed down the center of the building and the foundation sagged, but the fog softened it, and one almost didn't notice the peeling paint or its bowed, drooping aspect.

A dark figure emerged from a stand of trees near the fenceline, and Tiffany recognized Hedda. She raised her hand to wave, but the woman turned away to swing at the air as if batting away invisible flies. Every few steps she would halt and peer intently through the swirling vapor. Her lips moved constantly, as though she spoke with someone. Tiffany squinted. Someone Tiffany could not see. Tiffany watched amazed, and Hedda spun to face the child and waved her hands wildly outward, banishing the girl to the mists.

The agitated woman shrieked, "Go away! Begone! I'll not let thee on my land."

Tiffany gaped. The woman was staring straight at her, and

113

yet didn't seem to see her at all. The girl swallowed and glanced anxiously over her shoulder at the mist-shrouded forest.

"Go!"

Taking a big bite of her apple, Tiffany swerved to give the house wide berth and hurried around the curve in the road, and the house was lost from view. The fog crowded around her, enveloping her in a white blanket. Somewhere she heard the steady *drip, drip, drip* of water from branches on trees she could not see.

The crunch of gravel beneath her feet turned squishy. She stared down and stopped. She lifted one foot and then the other, amazed at the sight of soggy grass beneath her feet. It had been battered flat by the rain, and even the bracken was so drenched that it had a sickly-yellow appearance. Tiffany scanned the area around her, searching for blacktop, and saw nothing. The road was gone. She moved on.

Squish. Squish. Squish. Her footsteps squelched wetly across the ground, and the cloud bank surged mindlessly around her. Opening before her and closing in behind her, the mist clung to her clothes with clammy hands that seemed to propel her further forward. She walked for what seemed like hours. Occasionally the vapors would part to regurgitate a tree, never more than one, although Tiffany knew that an entire wood encircled her. Eventually the unseen forest disgorged a large boulder from the mist, and the girl flopped down on top of it, exhausted, reluctantly admitting that she was lost.

Tiffany closed her eyes and mentally tried to retrace her steps. She knew she couldn't be far from town. She had to be on the triangle of land that jutted into the bay. If she kept going straight eventually she'd come to the coast or to the road.

But how could she be sure if she was going straight? With the fog she could easily wander in circles for hours, tumble blindly into the floodwaters or trip gaily over some rocky cliff into the Penobscot before she even saw it.

Tiffany shifted uncomfortably on her stony perch. Anything was better than sitting still. Her windbreaker was soaked through. It stuck to her arms, and where it was ripped, her T-shirt was wet and the dampness was starting to spread. Despite the unseasonable warmth of this late September, she was chilled. Tiffany tilted her head to listen to the monotonous drip of water before sliding from her seat.

Eyes glued to the ground, she let the fairy wisps of fog steer her, sure that soon she'd find some sort of landmark. She slogged on. Stuffing her hands into her pockets, Tiffany fingered the bone and, discovering the fudge Aggie had given her, munched on it absently.

A misstep, and she was up to her ankles in mud. Holding on to a branch for balance, she tugged. The muck held her fast. She pulled again and it released her with a loud sucking noise. Her bright red boot stuck. She grabbed for it, but it sank. She gazed at the torn tennis shoe, wiggled the exposed toe, and sighed.

Her foot, which she had raised for another experimental step, halted, hovered for a moment, and came down hard with a spongy splat. Tiffany paused to survey the area around her, wondering how soon she'd reach the road, the coast, a house, something she might recognize. It seemed as if ages passed as the girl trudged through the saturated grass.

The white vapors whirled, and on every side, she was greeted by plump hillocks of marshgrass.

Tussocks of grass? Salt marsh?

The mounds formed regular round pillows, which were deceptively solid-looking. Unlike the lawns in town, which had turned a jaundiced green, this grass was thick and lush—thriving in the ceaseless rain. Tiffany felt drowsy and tired. She longed to plop down on one of the soft cushions. They looked so fat and inviting.

She stood, head tucked between hunched shoulders, too afraid to move. The salt marshes were notoriously dangerous, and all children were warned to avoid them at all costs. Then she straightened.

What salt marsh?

Tiffany had lived in Stockton Springs all her life. She had crawled through, walked around, or raced across every inch of land from Sandypoint to the lighthouse, and between Highway One and the ragged coastline, there weren't any marshes.

Sam had taken her on a tour of the salt marsh further along 1A, on the way to Bangor, and he had given her a stern lecture about its many hazards; but she couldn't possibly have crossed the highway without noticing it, or made it so far afield.

Tiffany took another cautious step back and hit water. She yanked her foot out and poked the grass to the side. Marsh water ran into her shoe. She tried to the other side. The ground was solid, and Tiffany sidled that way a bit, before testing the ground in front of her.

Solid.

Treading carefully, Tiffany moved forward, now and then poking at the grass searching for compacted dirt. The only trail led forward. Surely she would hit the shore soon, but she wondered where she would eventually emerge.

Her gait slowed to a crawl. She fingered the bone she kept in her pocket. The vapors retreated before her, and Tiffany found herself on the top of a small mound of what appeared to be good, solid earth. She stamped and turned to inspect the scene around her. A sharp breath whistled through her teeth, for Tiffany found herself in a cemetery. One she had never seen before in any of her explorations, and one she knew for a fact didn't exist, couldn't exist.

It was a small one with only a few stones. The modest monuments listed to one side or another. Some canted crazily, leaning against a neighbor for support. A couple had fallen over completely to rest facedown on the ground, and some of the still-standing slabs were broken so that they resembled jagged teeth. Beyond this were several shallow mounds unmarked by stones. As if the survivors had opened the earth and dumped bodies in without ceremony, although someone had tried. A few had two sticks twined together. The fragile twigs had broken, leaving a sharp point protruding from the ground. The cord had disintegrated and the wood had warped, but laying against the wet earth they still retained enough configuration for her to recognize the twisted symbol of the Christian cross.

Tiffany shuffled over to the nearest stone and peered dully at the letters. Lichen-encrusted, they would have been difficult to decipher at the best of times. Water ran from the windbreaker's hood down her nose, and she squinted at the squiggly lines. She clenched the bone in her hand until her fingernail dug into the fleshy palm and words began to take shape in her mind.

Normally she would have felt a thrill of triumph at her mastery, but something about the place thwarted glee. The area breathed despair. Tiffany shivered.

She leaned forward, face only a few inches from the stone to read: *Ruth _____ beloved wife of _____* and part of a date: *1656.*

Wow! That was old!

Tiffany moved on to the next marker, and the next, catching snippets of names, dates. She stopped short, ambled from one grave to another and then back again to the first. All the people had died in the same year, some within days of each other. Whole families. Mothers and fathers followed their children into the grave or sometimes preceded them.

The mist advanced, closing off the small circle, and Tiffany stared at the haze as though it held the secret to their deaths. Valiantly she tried to remember her history. She liked history, with its talk of kings, queens, and dazzling courts, but could remember none of it.

Tiffany stared at the next stone and saw three names. Mother, daughter, and son were all contained within the same grave.

A whole town must have died. Centuries swirled around her. And she felt overwhelmed by the miasma of decay. Her throat tightened. Tears threatened to fall as she strove against emotions that didn't seem to be her own, but came from the earth itself as if the land had digested the pain of death and it held it to its breast.

Tiffany clung to the bone, holding it tightly in her fist like a talisman. The mist swooped in, oddly consoling, blurring the outlines of the stones and muffling all sound. Even the closest monument became nothing more than a dark shade in a world of clouds.

Something moved, and Tiffany stared at a thicker patch of cloud which rippled in defiance of the subtle currents of breeze. She rubbed her eyes and blinked her disbelief. Someone was there!

A cry of joy escaped her lips, and she tensed, ready to dart forward to greet her invisible rescuer as soon as he appeared. The fog parted to reveal a few miserable shanties, made of mud and logs. Tiffany rubbed her eyes, wondering how they had got there. She glanced at her feet, blinked in shock as she realized that the soil was dry. The green grass had turned a dull brown, which crackled when she stirred.

Thunderstruck, Tiffany stumbled forward. A hand clutched her ankle and she screamed, kicking it away.

A voice wailed in the distance, and the girl recoiled from the sound until she had backed into a flimsy wooden shed. "Help," a voice whispered, and a spectral hand fluttered in the mist.

Tiffany's eye swept up the arm to the throat flanked by blackened swellings. She glimpsed a haggard face above the dusky goiter, and she reeled.

Squeezing her eyes shut, Tiffany willed herself away from there, trying unsuccessfully to flee to the gray, secure world of her dreams. She opened them to find the same waking nightmare where dead people walked abroad in a cemetery that didn't exist in a marshy bog that had never been.

Again she scanned her surroundings, hoping for the sanity of woods or bay, and found instead more rough structures made of wood and mud. A breeze wound through the waving crops of rattling corn that hadn't been there only a moment before.

Tiffany teetered backward, tripping over someone else. She lurched to the side to find another person lying in the dirt and then another. They were all dressed in funny old-fashioned clothes like the . . . like the . . . Pilgrims. Her mind latched on to the word.

Their upturned faces and the exposed portions of their bodies were covered with sores, red spots, and weird, weeping bubbles. A thick discharge ran from each and every living nose and mouth. Wherever Tiffany looked she saw more people dying. Some gave a small cry as their souls were loosed to the heavens and they breathed no more.

A light flickered to her left, and Tiffany bolted. It flickered again farther away, dipped, and dived. Tiffany shouted and ran after it, forgetting all the tales Sam had ever told her about will-o'-the-wisps and marsh gas.

Dank day turned into evening's gloaming, and darkness descended, wiping out nearly everything. The fog became little more than small pyramids of white under the radiance of the streetlight.

Still naked, Lorraine curled in a corner of the front hall. The baby's once-lusty wails had become hoarse and apathetic. The skriegh of the phone, left off the hook for too long, died. Lorraine's whimper twined with the infant's thready cry.

As she wept, she tried to reassemble the telephone table, fitting splintered piece with splintered piece while a videocam image of a truck folding like a paper toy played over and over again in her mind. Like an instant replay on "Monday Night Football."

With amazing forbearance, Lorraine took two of the larger pieces of a fractured leg and rotated them until they clicked and locked into place. Like putting together a jigsaw puzzle. Her index finger revolved slowly over the many slivers. She selected two and lovingly replaced them, as if she could—in repairing the table—re-create her broken marriage vows.

The last piece fit into place, and she propped the table against the wall. Then she lifted the phone, wincing as she positioned it. The table wobbled. Finally Lorraine picked up the receiver. The hand that held it hesitated before restoring it to the cradle, reflecting some sort of inner debate. It shook and Lorraine had to steady her right hand with her left, lowering the receiver gently into place.

As soon as the receiver was back in position, the telephone rang.

She jumped. The table collapsed. The telephone was overturned, and the receiver toppled from its place.

"Hello? Hello?" said an anonymous voice from the other end of the line.

A small sob escaped her throat, and she sunk back against the wall, covering her mouth with a quivering hand.

The baby, hearing some sound of life, renewed its cries with gusto. Cautiously Lorraine reached for the receiver, picked it up, and held it to her ear as though it were made of glass.

"Hello?"

A voice buzzed, and Mrs. David Garreth closed her eyes and sighed as some state trooper, whose name she'd already forgotten, informed her in subdued tones that she was a widow.

Gerald Thompson switched off the television with a grunt. Wolves in Armstrong. Hah! He tried to remember when was the last time a wolf had been sighted in the neighborhood and could not. More likely a local prank or a report made by someone who had had a few too many the night before.

A loud squawk came from the chicken coop. Not a squawk, a scream! The caterwauling of hens.

Thompson's head pivoted toward the sound.

Weasel!

Thompson leapt from his chair, made a beeline for his hunting rifle, and grabbed it. He cocked it, checking it as he rushed out the front door and raced across the porch.

He raised the gun to his shoulder, squeezing his left eye shut and peering down its sights. His finger quivered on the trigger and his grip loosened.

Opening his left, Thompson stared, wide-eyed, at the wolf. A magnificent creature. Beautiful.

The reports had not lied. It was huge.

The gun drooped down to his side, useless. The beast stared at him, the dead bird dangling from its mouth.

Thompson watched it as it turned away. At the edge of the drive the animal paused, dropped the bird, and howled mournfully at the moon.

Thompson's fingers itched. If he was going to shoot it, then this was the perfect opportunity. Its hide would make a damn fine trophy, and the esteem it would win him at the local bar would keep him in beer for a year. Thompson shouldered his gun, stared down its barrel, and then sagged.

He could not shoot this creature, so rare to this region, any more than he could have shot at God.

Driving as if pursued by demons, Leah jammed the gas pedal to the floor and managed little more than a rattle and a burp of exhaust from the clattertrap Ford.

Accusations flew inside her head. Hissing voices screeched recriminations. *Unfit mother,* they said. *You have no right to such a daughter.*

Leah wanted to evade the grim indictments all the more because she believed them to be true. She put more pressure on the accelerator before realizing she already had it to the floor.

The car shimmied drunkenly south toward Searsport, sputtering and choking in complaint. The village lights faded from view behind her. The turmoil inside her mind receded a bit, and by the time the shade of the ice cream stand was swallowed by the fog, Leah felt she could think clearly again.

A few minutes later when she passed the monument sales office well on the way to Searsport, the fog had cleared and her mind was as lucid as the sky above her head. And Leah knew her decision was a sound one, no matter what guilt may have prompted it. She needed help. She couldn't continue looking for Tiffany alone; she needed Sam even though she would rather not face his silent reproach.

Leah had been worried when Tiffany hadn't returned home by five. It was another dismal day in a series of dismal days. Not the type of day a child would want to play in. She called Tiffany's friends and came up with a blank. Unsure of what to do next, Leah had fixed up a plate and gone on to work at the café, thinking that Tiffany must surely return for dinner. Leah's shift had ended at eleven, and when she returned home, Tiffany still was not there. Worry dissolved into panic.

Spying the gray clapboard seafood restaurant on the edge of Searsport, Leah swung onto the first side street and parked in front of Sam's small bungalow.

The Ford chugged to a jittering halt. Leah switched off the engine, and it wheezed wearily. She listened to it ticking and cooling and watched steam rising off the hood. She wasn't looking forward to this. She sighed. It wouldn't get any easier.

Opening the door, Leah heaved herself from the seat into the crisp, clear night air. Again, her brain made a final shuffle, trying to unearth an excuse, some excuse—any excuse—not to face Sam. Finding none, Leah trudged to the porch, her body feeling heavier with each step she took. She knocked on the door and waited.

She knocked a second time.

"Just a minute!"

The door swung inward to reveal Sam standing there in sagging pajamas, his pudgy feet protruding from frayed slippers.

"What th—" He didn't get a chance to finish.

Leah launched right in. "Tiffany's missing. I sent her to the store for lunch, and she didn't come home. She hadn't returned by the time I left for work, so I left her dinner out. I tried looking for her. I called her friends, but I couldn't find her." She paused for a breath. Sam's expression hardened. She forged on. "I couldn't be late for work. Besides I figured she'd come back when she was hungry. But when I got home, she still wasn't there. I got real worried. I've been all up and down the streets between Sandypoint and Stockton Springs, at least all those that aren't flooded, and I haven't been able to find her. I'm worried sick."

The words that spilled out of her dried up, and she was willing to peek meekly at her son, seeking his solace. He glowered at her.

Leah winced. "Look." Her voice became cutting. He was her son after all. "I need your help. I can't get to the Point or anywhere around Hershey's Retreat except on foot, and then there's the whole area beyond the Brauns' farm toward the lighthouse. Could you . . ."

Before she could finish, Sam was stamping down the hall and pushing through the beaded curtain into his bedroom. Leah paused to marshal her resources.

"Could you search around the woods near Stockton Springs while I check at the Retreat?" she finished lamely as Sam returned, wearing a wrinkled flannel shirt and a pair of blue jeans, his shoes and socks tucked under his arm.

He leaned against the wall for balance and tugged on his socks. "Where'd you say you looked again?"

Gideon had no reason to love the night. In his childlike mind, nighttime shut out the sun, covering the sky with the big, black lid—like that off a cast-iron skillet. But for Gideon, there was little to differentiate between waking and sleeping states. Both were clothed in the air of unreality. Yet night brought dark, grim and frightening, and darkness carried with it its sinister companion, fear—fear that never visited Gideon in the daylight hours when the sky was a great big, bright blue ball he could see, before the black lid of night closed out the light.

Night brought dreams that were peopled with things even stranger than those that appeared to him in the daylight hours. The crowded shadow chattered at him. Faces surfaced from the water-stained ceiling of his shed while disembodied heads and monsters came at him from the murky tank of his subconscious.

Gideon writhed on the mattress of straw and old clothes he had made into a bed. He turned on his side, and his legs moved in short, sweeping motions like a dog running in his sleep. His head jerked back, as though he cast a hurried glance over his shoulder, and inside the place of dreams the sleeping Gideon shot a terrified look backward.

His parents stalked him.

He saw the long black shadows. Behind them another figure pursued them both. Faceless, nameless, and this figure frightened him more. He didn't want to know its name.

A shadow flitted by. The familiar child was engulfed by the cloud bank, and the Gideon in his dream ran after her.

The young man woke, a dark stain spread at the crotch of his pants. He'd peed himself. Blushing, Gideon looked around, expecting to see the glowing blue-white light of the streetlamp filtering through filthy window and thick fog. He swayed and the ground squelched wetly underfoot.

His flush retreated, color draining to his neck, and his skin blanched. He was outdoors!

Somewhere to his right a child was crying. His ears pricked, zooming in on the sound.

The young man started forward, picking his way carefully through tortured marsh grass. His feet moved soundlessly, using naive instinct.

The wind blew fanlike tendril mist across his path, and there was another muffled sob. Gideon spun, trying to locate the source of the sound. The weeping stretched and thinned like the surrounding vapors—its noise stunted and stymied by the water-laden air.

"Hey?" he yelled, and the fog digested his voice.

The stump of his little finger had closed an angry red, but the fiery crimson stripes that ran up Jimmy's hand and arm to his shoulder were fading. His fever had abated slightly, or did at intervals.

In moments of clearheadedness, everything stood out with a simple clarity he had never known before, and Sheridon felt he was a part of every blade of grass, every tree, even the land itself reaching from here to the sea.

Also during those brief periods of lucidity, Sheridon would awaken and discover something he had done in his fevered state. His hand went out to the wall of papery bark, and he shook it, testing its strength. Jimmy had broken his longtime prohibition and built something more elaborate than a lean-to, although he couldn't remember doing it. He recognized a sweat lodge from a picture he had once seen in a book. It was solidly built, and he was pleased with the result, although he wondered where he had gotten the skill.

In his waking moments Sheridon split his time between hot house and open fire. When he had the strength, Jimmy gathered what food he could from within the confines of the small clearing—trusting to luck, or some ancient god, to guide his hand as his mind wandered. With innate wisdom Sheridon plucked the dried, dead heads of the daisylike flowers feverfew and chamomile—adding to that mixture something green, a plant with saw-toothed leaves and fat, spiny seed pods. He'd eaten them before, and Jimmy seemed to remember some large hand dispensing the pods and their seeds like medicine.

For the most part his meals were unpalatable and unappetizing. This night's repast looked positively nauseating. Sheridon stewed the entire mess, softening the pods and releasing their black seeds. Now he stared at the green and yellow slime at the bottom of the handmade bowl. Pieces clung to his lips. He winced and spat, wiping his mouth on his sleeve.

Then Jimmy stared into the fire as the hallucinogenic properties of the jimsonweed took effect, and he was transported back to the cold storm-swept village of Sandypoint. Sheila Erhart appeared in the flames, and Jimmy gave the fire a little stir to see what it would whip up.

10

Few would have recognized the old woman, usually so neat and tidy. Sheila stood uncertainly before the mirror and stared at herself in shock. Her nightie was dirty, stained with coffee, butter, and jam. The unplucked bristles on her chin were crusted with crumbs. Her hair was matted and unkempt. It rose from her head, sticking out, askew, in tangled snarls. Her eyes stared out of her sockets like a crazy woman's. Sheila Erhart noted the haunted expression and the deranged leer and raised an arthritic shoulder in a desultory shrug.

What did it matter what she looked like?

Nothing really mattered anymore.

A single tear spilled onto her cheek, and Sheila fled the lunatic reflection in the mirror to pace through the house, fidgety. Her footsteps echoed hollowly in the hall, and the cottage seemed so empty and large with Andrew gone.

So empty, and so alone.

The flood had cut her off from town, and nobody had

thought to stop and check on her. *Empty and alone.* Her solitude and isolation covered her like a shroud.

And nobody cared. Sheila could die here, and nobody would know until the stench got too bad, which considering the season wouldn't happen for some months yet. A chill reached through her stained flannel nightgown, and Sheila hugged herself as she paused in the guest room, trying to remember why she was here.

Who'd know? Who'd care? Not her daughter. Sheila Erhart hadn't talked to Elisabeth in six months. Not a single phone call. Elisabeth didn't even know that Andrew was dead.

Another tear traced a path down the crease between her nose and her lip. Sheila drifted down the stairs, not sure where she was going, but anxious to be away from her lonely bedroom with its litter of open boxes and cans. In the living room she found Andrew's carpet. So filthy it was just begging to be washed, but she couldn't touch it.

It seemed somehow a sacrilege to remove the tattered remnant from its sacred place next to the door where it had lain for so many years—profane to wash away the doggie odors so soon.

And Sheila supposed that in her heart of hearts she kept hoping that someday she'd peer at it and find Andrew's mangy body there, snorting and snoring away, and she'd discover all that had happened had been a dream.

Her foot caught on an old chew bone, gliding dangerously out from under her. Sheila clawed at a table, upsetting it, reeled, and sprawled over the back of an overstuffed chair, her feet scrabbling underneath her. Panting and blinking, she lay there, realizing how close she had come to breaking a hip.

And nobody cared, an incessant voice said inside her head. The tears were flowing freely now.

Andrew had cared once. But Andrew was only a dog and Andrew was gone, she reminded herself. Sheila rearranged her feet underneath her, righted herself, and continued toward the kitchen.

Only a dog. Not a big dog, just a terrier, but big in heart and love. The only living being that had cared about her, loved her, relied on her.

And she had failed him. Unwanted memory took her back. Sheila had put him on his leash for his late-night piddle, and she was supposed to have let him back in that night, but she hadn't. Instead, Sheila had fallen asleep in her chair, leaving little Andrew on his chain to fend for himself and deal with whatever demon hell had sent their way.

Sheila slumped against the wall. Her head rolled forward; her shoulders slouched and heaved. If only she hadn't decided to watch the news, then she wouldn't have fallen asleep in the chair. If only she'd remembered to let him in before the news had started. If only she hadn't slept so soundly . . .

She didn't like to think of what his last few moments must have been like. Tied to that stake, cowering away from whatever fiend had approached, held firm and fast. Unable to run. Unable to hide.

Why hadn't he yelped? Or howled? Or something?

She would have come to him, better that they had gone together than this. Sheila surveyed the littered kitchen. Dirty dishes were stacked next to the sink, garbage sacks heaped next to the door. Empty cartons and cans were strewn across the counter. The cupboard was bare.

She was starving to death slowly. Dying by inches. And forgotten by everyone.

Now Sheila recalled why she had come down here. She was hungry, but it was a fruitless journey, a vain hope. The pantry was picked clean. She hadn't been shopping since the rains came, and she had eaten everything in the house. Still no one had come. No one cared.

Distracted, she scooped a handful of dog food from the sack and shoveled it in her mouth. Her eyes swept the messy counter and then lit on the dog bowls, and she sobbed, gagging on the hard pellets in her mouth.

Then Sheila spied the clothesline, coiled like a snake next to the stove. She had taken it down only yesterday. She scowled, trying to remember why she had done that. Looking at the rain-spattered glass, Sheila decided she probably wouldn't be needing it for a while.

Her hand grazed it, and it twisted, snaking to the floor with a thud, and suddenly Sheila remembered why she had brought it into the house in the first place.

Filled with purpose, the old woman hastened through the dining room to the living room, where her husband Pete kept his books on sailing. She extracted one text from the rest and rifled through the pages. Her knobby fingers moved with amazing agility through the complicated knot, and she'd pause to peer at the illustration.

It wasn't perfect, but it would do.

Next she studied the room, and the hall. Her gaze went to the staircase, and Sheila smiled.

Tiffany stopped again as soon as her feet found solid ground. Away from people with their funny clothes, their groping hands, and their weeping sores. The stench of death and decay still clung to her. She plopped leadenly to the ground and pulled her knees to her chest, her back against a sturdy trunk. Tiffany *refused* to move another inch even if she had to stay here—FOREVER—even if she turned into a skeleton herself, and the swamp came up and ate her.

Who knew what else she might find if she kept wandering around like this?

Tiffany stared at the enveloping fog, and she retreated, drawing deep within herself to the world of sound, of scent, of muted vision. Warm, moist breath blew against her face, and Tiffany winced, brought from her place of dreams to stare into blank space. She heard a snuffling and a soft *swoosh* as if something walked through high grass, and Tiffany listened intently. She tensed, breathless, waiting. It moved away, and taut muscles loosened.

Occasionally a parting of the gauzy veil revealed misshapen oaks and a black blanket of pine. Her stomach gnawed at her. Tiffany was cold, hungry, and scared. She began to cry. The murk absorbed the sound, digesting it.

There was another whisper of sound, and her heart leapt into her throat. A soft squishy noise, a whistle as soaked pant legs brushed against each other and a wet *whoosh* as those legs pushed marshgrass aside.

Footsteps!

Tiffany was weeping in earnest now, unable to choke back the sobs as she waited for some gibbering apparition to appear, dressed in knee breeches and frock coat.

"Hey!"

A piece of night detached itself from the darker line of trees, moving toward her, and a recognizable figure began to take shape.

The idiot Gideon towered over her, grinning, and Tiffany gazed up at him relieved, realizing for the first time that when he smiled, his whole face lit up and a certain dull intelligence glinted in his normally empty eyes.

The amber bug-light burned outside of Sheila Erhart's home, and in the fog the entire house seemed to glow. As Leah came closer, the pale illumination became more defined, forming a yellow oblong upon the inky waters behind the house. Leah waded through Sheila's dooryard toward the front door. In places the water came up to her knees, but Leah forced herself to continue, struggling up the hill to the front of the house.

Leah had already been up and down the road and had searched every inch of the camp between here and the Retreat. The late-staying summer people, who usually lingered until the end of October to enjoy Maine's fall face, had left their camps early, returning to Bangor or Portland, or wherever they had hailed from. Deserted the Point, like rats from a sinking ship. The area had an empty, desolate look.

Still Leah had pounded on doors of obviously empty summer homes, checking to make sure they were locked. Then she clambered down to peer under each home— examining the dank crawl space.

She'd found nothing, and this was the only place left along this stretch of land. If Tiffany had gotten lost, or decided that she couldn't make it home, she would have known to stop here at the only occupied house on the Point.

Stamping to return the circulation to her feet, frozen by the floodwaters, Leah knocked on Sheila's door. She jogged back and forth along the small platform. No answer. She knocked harder.

The bay side of the building was all windows. She moved around the side of the house to press her nose against the glass and peeked inside. The stairwell was only half-lit. All else was dark. Nothing appeared amiss, and surely, if Tiffany was here, she would have heard the knocking even if Sheila could not.

Just as Leah turned to leave, something eclipsed the fragile half-light. She stepped back. A shadow passed to and fro, as though someone were upstairs pacing from one end of the hall to the other.

Leah regarded the sweeping shade for a moment. Slow, inexorable. Back and forth. Back and forth. Like a pendulum. She banged on the window, backing away from the house to stare at the second-floor windows. She would have sworn that Sheila's pale face had passed next to the window on the landing. Again Leah stationed herself next to the door and waited for Sheila to descend the stairs and let her in. Nothing. No footsteps resounded in the hall. No figure appeared to be silhouetted by the light.

That had been Sheila, Leah was sure of it. She had looked right down at Leah and ignored her.

"Fucking bitch," Leah said. She turned her back on the residence and stomped down the hill toward the road.

Sam cruised through the streets of Stockton Springs one last time, getting angrier by the minute. The yellow fog lights sliced through the haze. It had been a long night, and he was sure that he sensed a growing band of gray on the horizon that heralded another dismal dawn.

The Isuzu had barely made it across the flowing river that blocked the road to the lighthouse, and he cursed himself for not getting four-wheel drive. Not much of an outdoorsy type himself, it had seemed a needless expense at the time. He could have used it now.

He had driven all the way around, or as much of it as the Isuzu could ford, and when he could get no farther, he got out and searched on foot. Sometimes Sam would have sworn that he heard something, and he followed the noise, marking his path with twine; but Sam found nothing but more mist, dripping branches, and chuckling brooks—where before there had been none. They mumbled and murmured, seeming to laugh at him.

Even now he could hear their relentless babble like the voices that had started whispering to him as soon as he had driven into the wall of mist that surrounded Stockton Springs. The longer he stayed, the louder they got, increasing in crescendo until his brain was filled with static.

His anger grew with the voices, swelling and enlarging, until he was spitting mad and spewing a continuous string of swear words.

How could she? How could his mother have sent Tiffany to the store for lunch? Sent her out on a walk of over a mile in the rain and forgotten about her until suppertime? It was a damned dangerous walk if Tiff chose the route along the highway—what with the rain and the fog. Even if she had avoided the highway, the flooded woods were filled with traps—gnarled roots and potholes that would have been hidden by the rising water.

All because his mother was too goddamn lazy to cook! Too damn lazy and too damned distraught because that prick Sheridon had left her. His mother should be counting her blessings and not weeping over her loss.

"That bastard is wanted by the police for chrissake," he said to the empty car.

The stupid crotch hadn't even gotten worried about Tiffany until five o'clock. Five hours wandering around in the rain.

And then she goes to work!

She could have called him, then. Should have called him. Sam could have looked for Tiffany while it was still somewhat light out.

"But no! She's gotta wait until eleven o'clock. Eleven—hell, fucking midnight!" Sam said with uncharacteristic rancor. He spoke out loud as if someone were in the car with him, pausing intermittently to listen and respond.

"Stupid fucking bitch!" he shouted at the dashboard.

The Pillsbury Doughboy image had vanished to be replaced by bug-eyed flush, which was growing deeper by the minute, and by the time Sam had finished scouring those upland roads, he was ready to kill her—finally convinced that in at least this one thing Jimmy was right: His mother was the kind of person who you had to knock sense into.

Gideon found Tiffany in a clearing within a few hundred feet of the blacktop, leaning against a tree. Her face was tear-stained and muddy, and she was soaked. He took off his flannel shirt and wrapped her in it. It covered her like a blanket.

Gently he lifted her, and she clung to him. He smelled the sweet, baby-soft smell of her hair and relished the feel of delicate arms clasped around his neck. He didn't even mind that she was almost cutting off his oxygen supply. Trying to find his way back, he wasn't quite sure how he had gotten here.

Stumbling and tripping, he clutched his precious burden to his chest. His arms ached and even her slight weight grew heavy. Every once in a while she would lift sleep-fogged eyes to his face and smile at him. Buoyed by her acceptance of him, he'd tightened his grip, straightened his back and marched on. Resolute, carrying her all the way back to town, and from town through the woods back to the familiar trailer.

Wet and miserable, Leah slogged through the mud to the trailer and started divesting herself of her wet clothes as soon as she got in the door.

"Sam? Tiff?" she shouted.

"Damn," she muttered, peeling off her socks. Leah trudged down the dark corridor to the master bedroom. She paused before the mirror.

Its reflection was less than reassuring. She was skin and bone—her breasts two deflated sacks. Her legs had no shape to them. Her rear was so fleshless that sitting for any protracted time made her uncomfortable.

And she was losing more weight.

Nerves. She slipped into a lumpy sweatsuit, disheartened.

Time and Maine's harsh weather had not been kind to Leah. Her face was lined; wrinkles of worry stretched from nose to mouth, making her look older than her actual forty-six years. Her pale, almost colorless hair was cropped short. Her skin was similarly light, translucent, nearly transparent.

Her eyes fell on the photocube she kept on the dresser. Jimmy grinned back at her. Ten years her junior and young-looking for his age, he was a handsome man with dark brown eyes and thick luxurious black hair. His skin was a deep coppery color, and for someone who avoided all physical labor, he still had the body of an athlete.

Disgusted, Leah turned the picture so that it faced the wall. She wasn't even sure why she stayed with him. Some sort of penance—punishment—for taking up with him before her husband had died. If it hadn't been for Tiffany's physical resemblance to her dead husband—the red hair and pale skin—Leah couldn't have said for sure who Tiffany's father was.

As she remembered those first brief meetings, her expression softened. Leah had been afraid, terrified even. Afraid of being left alone, and she had been tired, tired of death and disease. And Jimmy had been there, when no one else had.

So Leah had found her way into his arms, just like a dozen other women had, and now she was paying for it. Leah knew she couldn't hope to compete with the myriad other women who were more than willing to spread their legs for him. She had to offer something more—cook for him, clean for him, take care of the kennels. She had to be a workhorse to keep him, and she lost her looks and her youth in the process.

Running her fingers through her hair, she made a choked noise in the back of her throat. Then she switched off the overhead light and returned to the kitchen to fix herself a drink. She had just lowered herself gingerly to the chair to nurse her gin and tonic when Sam burst through the door, wild-eyed.

Leah half-rose from her cushion. "Did you . . ."

He advanced upon her menacingly. He stood, thick trunklike legs splayed, chubby chin quivering, and Leah couldn't help but think how ridiculous he looked.

"You threw her out of the house. You were too goddamn lazy to make her lunch, so you gave her money to buy something and sent her to the store."

"Yes, so what of it?"

"You bitch, too goddamn lazy to feed your own daughter." He seized her by both arms, flattened them against her sides, and hauled her the rest of the way up from the chair. Her drink clattered to the floor. Air rattled in and out of his chest. His face was purple with rage, and Leah peered into his glinting eyes and was afraid. She'd never seen him like this.

Sam sensed her rising terror, and it seemed to release the repressed fury, for he slammed her against the wall.

"You fucking bitch!" he screeched at her, spittle flying from his lips. The veins on his neck stood out, and for a moment it looked as though he were going to explode.

He struck her backhand. Stunned, she crumpled to the floor at his feet.

He stood over her, chest heaving, and Leah was sure that he was going to kick her.

A tired litany played inside her brain. *You asked for this. You deserve this.*

There was a quiet rapping on the door. Sam spun, and Leah lifted her head tiredly from the floor to stare.

Tap, tap, tap.

"Ca-ca-come in," she called.

The door crept open slowly, tentatively, to reveal Jimmy's younger brother, Gideon, holding a sleepy-eyed Tiffany in his arms. Leah's jaw unhinged, and vaguely she noticed that above her, Sam's did the same.

Both stared at the strange apparition. Tall, thin almost to the point of emaciation, Gideon stood like a ghost against a backdrop of fog. His expression empty and eyes blank. Stringy blond hair slicked against his head and neck.

The sleeping girl nestled deeper into Gideon's embrace. The movement seemed to awaken something in him. Light flooded into his eyes and life into his face.

"She's here," he announced. He stooped to put her down. She stretched and yawned.

Sam moved swiftly to Tiffany's side, scooping her into a great big bear hug.

"Are you okay?" Sam said.

Tiffany wriggled in his arms, embarrassed. Leah pulled herself from the floor. Tiffany's gaze went to her mother, and then she pushed away from Sam to peer intently into his eyes.

Sam shifted and then swung to thank Gideon, but the young man was gone, disappearing like a specter in the mist.

Sam released Tiffany.

"Is everything all right, Sam?" she asked.

"Yes, now that you're back, everything is okay. Go pack a few of your things. You're coming to my place for a visit."

He spun on Leah. "You don't mind, do you? You won't have to worry about fixing her dinner, or breakfast for that matter. Tiffany can stay with me for the rest of the weekend."

"Can I, Mom?"

Leah glanced from her daughter to her son and grimaced. "Sure, why not."

The girl scurried to her bedroom, and Sam, placid again for Tiffany's sake, turned to glower at the solid bank of mist that enveloped the dooryard.

Tiffany returned carrying her overnight case.

"Come give Mommy a kiss," Leah said, squatting down.

Again the child peeped at Sam over her mother's shoulder, sensing the tension that surged between them. He ducked his head in assent, and Tiffany complied.

Sam picked up her suitcase and herded her out the door.

As the door slammed shut on the two of them, Leah collapsed into the chair, curling up and wrapping her arms around her legs. She watched, mesmerized, as a bracelet of livid blue appeared on her wrists where he had clenched them tightly in his fists. Leah wouldn't have believed Sam had it in him.

She rubbed the bruises gingerly. Then Leah snatched the glass from the floor, raising it above her head to throw it at the door, hesitated and thought a moment before putting it down upon the table.

"Bastard." She lay a weary head on her knees.

It had been one helluva day—with Blount landing on her doorstep sometime after noon to ask if she had heard from Jimmy and then Tiffany getting lost.

Blount was an idiot. As if Jimmy would be fool enough to contact her when he was in trouble, knowing that this was the first place the local fuzz would look.

"Bastards!" Leah was sick of it. All of it! First Jimmy, now Sam. Her own son treating her like dirt. He acted as if he hated her. And for what?

The kid was okay. Leah had sent her to the store for lunch. So! What was wrong with that? It wasn't as if it happened every day, and besides, millions of children all over the country bought their lunches while their parents worked. It didn't kill 'em.

No one had told Tiffany to go wandering off in the fog. The kid should have more sense than that.

Sam didn't have the slightest concept of what it was like raising a child alone. She'd done it twice, what with his father being sick and all when Sam was a kid, then dying not long after Tiffany was born.

Well, fuck 'em. Fuck 'em both.

A dog's plaintive yelp penetrated the thin walls of the mobile home, mocking, and Leah unfolded from her fetal position, getting up from the chair, shouting for the dog to shut up.

Then she went back to the kitchen to fix herself another drink. Screw the goddamn dogs. Screw Blount. Screw Jimmy. Screw her son. Screw them all.

* * *

Gideon watched as the little girl and her brother drove away. A light went on in the kitchen and then went out. The mournful strains of Tammy Wynette started up in the living room. He waited a while longer before he emerged from shadows to stand outside the mobile home. He examined the blurred line next to the steps before he grabbed a stick, gouging quickly in the earth across the path. And the circle, complete once more, began to glow feebly in the darkness.

In Searsport the bay widened. The view to the sea was uninterrupted unlike the stretch of beach along Sandypoint. There, the Penobscot was little more than a stone's throw across, assuming a sturdy arm, and Verona Island loomed, dark with pine, over the village, giving it a claustrophobic feel.

Sam preferred Searsport with its illusion of space and its bright big sky. There was a feeling of freedom and light that he had never known in Stockton Springs. He had chosen this town deliberately for several reasons. He wanted to get the hell away from Sandypoint, and Stockton Springs, where everyone knew everyone else's business down to the most intimate details. He hated the pitying looks that had grown all too familiar as his father lay dying. He hated the scorn they heaped upon Tiffany and—if he hadn't been too angry to admit it—his mother. Yet he couldn't find it in himself to move too far afield. Tiffany needed him.

The Sunday paper forgotten, he turned to study Tiffany where she sat at the kitchen table drawing. She seemed none the worse for her experience. Indeed, she hadn't mentioned it at all this morning, as if it had never happened, and he wondered if she even remembered. She sat hunched over her artwork. Her tongue stuck out of the corner of her mouth.

Sam stirred himself away from the window and its spectacular view. Time to fix breakfast. He pulled a frying pan out of the cupboard, and eggs and bacon from the fridge.

"How about one of Sam's special superduper fry-ups?"

"With waffles?" she said hopefully.

"Waffles? Eggs and bacon, and waffles!" He paused and smiled. "Sure, why not. Waffles it is."

He dug through the cabinets, getting the rest of the ingredients out, and then had to make a concentrated search for the waffle iron. Behind him he heard the reassuring scratch, scratch, scratch of the pencil.

The sun sparkled in the choppy waters of the bay—like brittle diamonds that burned upon the retina, then sizzled and burst inside the brain. The colors and the light hypnotized her and the pencil fell away from her hand. Water and the dancing glimmer were replaced by woods deep and dark, the sharp smell of pine, and the gentler aroma of grass and fern and underlying odor of gasoline-powered engines.

A hand touched Tiffany's shoulder, shaking her, and sun capered on waves once more.

She peered at the bay, unresponsive when he called her name. Sam walked around the table to face her. Her jaw was slack, her eyes empty and dull. She stared at, but did not see, the dancing waters.

"Tiff?"

He reached over and touched her, and she didn't move. Sam shook her shoulder. She blinked and grinned at him.

"Are you all right?" he said.

"Sure. Why shouldn't I be?"

Sam pointed at the picture of a wolf. "That's good."

Tiffany looked down at it blankly as if she didn't recognize it. "Ah, yeah. I guess it's okay."

"No, I mean it is *really* good. Can I keep it?"

"Go ahead." She pushed it toward him and turned back to the bay.

"Funny, it has been sunny like this most of the time it's been raining in Sandypoint," she commented, shielding her eyes from the glare of the sun.

"No, not all the time. We've had a few gray days, but no

rain, though. As a matter of fact, they're talking drought. Listening to the farmers around here talk, you'd think Stockton Springs was stealing all the water away."

"Weird." She turned to gaze at him. "It's almost as if God was trying to wash Stockton Springs and Sandypoint away."

11

Hedda's step was listless and torpid, as though she were moving with the sluggish fatigue of maple sap after winter's freeze. For four days and four nights she hadn't slept as she maintained her solitary vigil. She had little strength left, and only willpower permitted her to raise her foot and set it down again.

The words of benediction and curse came with difficulty, now, eradicated by the other, louder voices. And when the words came, they were jumbled, tumbling out one on top of the other, becoming mystifying and meaningless.

Leaning against a fence post, Hedda fished around in her listless brain for suitable gospel or pertinent passage from the most recent *Watchtower,* but divine inspiration fled fitfully away from her.

" 'Babylon the great is fallen and become the habitation of devils and the hold of foul spirits . . .' " She faltered. " 'And the kings of the earth who have committed fornication, have lived deliciously, shall bewail her.' " No, that wasn't right.

Starting over again, Hedda quoted an even less seemly verse. "'His eyes are as the eyes of doves, by the rivers of waters, washed with milk, and fitly set. His cheeks are as a bed of spices, as flowers; his lips like lilies, dropping sweet-smelling myrrh. His hands are as gold rings set with the beryl; his belly is as bright as ivory overlaid with sapphires. His legs are as pillars of marble, set upon sockets of fine gold; his countenance is as Lebanon, excellent as the cedars.'"

Something stirred in her groin, and Hedda grew hot despite the damp air that caressed her neck and the clammy cloth of her dress that stuck to her sides.

She raised her fingers to her lips. No, something was wrong with the verse. *But it was from the Bible,* she thought. *How could it be wrong?*

Disjointed words flapped around irreverently in her disheveled mind. The text of the Good Book had become confused, a hodgepodge, as confused as her images of God and man.

"'. . . a beast rose up from the sea, with seven heads . . . and upon each head the name of blasphemy,'" she whispered, terrified at the direction God's word was taking her.

The time of destruction is nigh, a voice muttered inside her head. And the chosen would live on in a world reborn. Life everlasting, for the few.

Hedda sought redemption, lest she be condemned to live through the apocalypse drawn in her brain with all the lurid images of television ministry. But Hedda had no hope to see the other side. No hope at all. Her marriage had been sterile, barren of fruit, and she could see no better proof of God's disfavor than this. Hedda placed a protective hand over her belly as snippets of lascivious verse floated around inside her brain.

His cheeks are as a bed of spices, as flowers; his lips like lilies, dropping sweet-smelling myrrh . . .

Her fingers drummed against her stomach where *he* had placed his burning seed, and she gave the house a sideways glance. *He* had condemned her to this. Death and damnation. Hellfire and brimstone.

Had she not married Les, she would be safe, integrated into her family and welcome in the Witness Hall, and preparing for the life beyond the world's end with a joyous heart.

Instead, Hedda trotted next to the fence like a hound attempting to keep Lucifer at bay.

. . . *His legs are as pillars of marble, set upon sockets of fine gold. . . . His mouth is most sweet.*

Hedda moaned as Les materialized before her—with his sweating body, pulsing penis, and groping hands—and Hedda averted her eyes.

Evil man.

"Get thee behind me," she muttered, and he was revealed for the demon he was, transformed first into a snarling, snapping wolf and then into Beelzebub, Baal. His legions came writhing at her out of the mist.

"Honey?" Her husband's inquiring voice penetrated the fog inside her mind.

His face swam before her, and she spat at him. He grabbed her shoulders and shook them. Hedda swatted at him. Then he took her hands, clenched them tightly between his, and pulled her into an embrace. She stood rigid, her nose pressed into the scratchy wool of his lumber jacket with its faint whiff of goat and manure.

His breath brushed her cheek, and it was as if he was violating her. Hedda yanked her hands from his grasp.

Les pleaded with her. "Hedda, you've been out here four nights now. Are you coming in?"

Her vision cleared and his face came into focus. Tired. Confused. Her face burned, and she glared at him. He dropped his hands uselessly to his side, mortified.

"I'm, uh, sorry. Look, I'm going to bed now," he mumbled. "I'll leave the door open for you."

Her eyes glinting unpleasantly, Hedda watched him weave his way up the path, as if he could, by his motion, evade the raindrops.

The door opened and closed.

Hedda spun and headed for the shed, grabbing the old oil lamp that hung just inside the door. Hedda felt for the kitchen matches that they kept on a ledge and then lit the lantern. Little-used tools were arranged neatly on hooks while their more often employed comrades were heaped haphazardly next to the door. She sorted through the pile with a clatter and a clang.

A rake, shovel, pitchfork—and her hand hovered over the latter for a moment before it moved on to—the hoe.

A light went on in the bathroom. Her fingers clenched the staff so tightly that her knuckles turned an unearthly white.

I'm doing this for you, too, she thought as she bent and checked the pitted blade.

Wheezing and choking within a cloud of whirling smoke, Jimmy threw a little more moss on the fire. It burned badly, or not at all, damping the flames and creating more smoke. His eyes smarted and tears ran down his face.

If anyone could have seen him now, he would not have recognized him. Sheridon looked like he was either dead or dying. Terminally ill from some strange form of cancer that devoured his body from the inside out.

Jimmy peered myopically into the smoky fire at a distant display. Like June sitting at the side of the road or Sheila alone in her home. The scenes, Jimmy could, with almost negligible motion, manipulate and change so that the Sheila in the fire was sent scuttling into the rain to bring in the clothesline or the sister image of June started masturbating in the front seat of her car.

Jimmy's stomach grumbled, and Sheridon responded by crawling to the hollow's edge and plucking some of the mushrooms from a dancing fairy ring that had erupted overnight. He wasn't quite sure what kind they were, but they hadn't made him sick or, at least, any sicker than he already was, and in his weakened state it was the only edible thing left within reach. His digestion mutinied at the thought of the green slime that still adhered to the bottom of the clay bowl.

He scooped a few from the soil and, without pausing to brush the dirt from their bases, shoved them in his mouth.

Smoke eddied around him. A figure stalked inside the undulating plumes. Hedda again!

Leering, he blew the smoke toward her, reached forward, and chuckled as Hedda bolted up an unseen path into a shed.

Whispering to himself as his hands began to mime short swiping movements. His smile widened as the figure in the fire did the same.

Scalding tears formed in her eyes as Hedda took the hoe over to the workbench to remove heavy clumps of mud and clay from the blade. She ran her finger over the metal; it was dull and nicked. With a practiced motion she sharpened the blade, bringing it, with short, sharp swipes, against the whetstone Les had mounted in a vise on the workbench.

Les's voice drifted down to her from the house where he sang lustily in the shower. It was the only time he ever sang. She smiled a little sadly, and melancholy settled upon her thin shoulders.

"For him," she said to the empty shed.

Gripping the hoe tightly, Hedda marched toward the front door and let herself into the house. She was arrested by the commonplace sights and smells of the home and the life they had made together. The heady scent of last Sunday's roast pork mingled with the residual aroma of home-baked bread. The antique coat tree they had bought for the shop and decided instead to keep for themselves. The needlepoint stand, with its half-finished homily.

And the still-reasoning portion of her brain gibbered at her to drop the hoe, or go back to the shed. There were other ways to salvation.

She felt a breath of breeze—as though someone had given the air in the living room a twirl, or blew softly against her cheek—and overhead, Les bellowed some degenerate ditty, popular on the radio now. Her resolve strengthened. Hoe held before her like a lance, Hedda slunk toward the stairs, following a crazy zigzag course to avoid the house's many creaks.

"I"—grunt . . . splash—"love . . . YOUUUUU . . ." Les bawled.

Tensed outside the open bathroom door, she flattened herself against the wood and listened.

The water stopped. The rings clattered against the rod as Les flung the shower curtain wide. The door swung open.

Hedda stared at him, and he gaped back at her and the hoe in her hand, its newly sharpened blade shimmering and deadly. His jaw drooped. His evil member shriveled, retreating into his scrotum, only to jerk to life when his gaze returned to her impassioned face.

This more than anything else enraged her, and she swung at him in a deadly arc.

Humming softly to herself, Hedda polished a small square of the tile in the shower stall. She finished with a flourish, her hand descending swiftly in a deft downward sweep. Her head canted slightly to the left as she appraised her work. The bathroom was spotless—every surface sparkled and shone.

She stooped to pick up Les's shoes and clothes from the pile where he'd left them before taking his shower. The television blared. Some evangelist—whose pristine good looks and straight nose had more to do with the skill of the plastic surgeon than the blessed touch of God's hand—exhorted his congregation to dig deep into hearts and pockets for some holy cause.

Hedda ignored his message, heading for the basement stairs. Cobwebs grew in profusion and spiders moved sleepily, made slow and lethargic by the cellar's unnatural chill. She dumped Les's clothes in the washing machine and started it. Then she filled a bucket with water and began to scrub each and every surface.

When she had finished washing the floor, Hedda strolled over to the large chest freezer. Her hands stroked its lid, and she smiled. Her ears attuned to the stillness of a dawning day detected the insignificant crunch of gravel. It sounded like gunshot in her ears.

She swung guiltily from the freezer.

Insipid morning light filtered through the windows. Above her head someone banged loudly on the front door, and Hedda jumped, bumping into the freezer.

Another knock, and she covered the metal chest defensively with her body.

"Hedda? Les? It's Alan Blount."

She looked down at her hands, then at her smock. The apron was clean, donned fresh this morning. Anxiously she smoothed it, patting some nonexistent wrinkle into place, and headed for the stairs.

Blount cradled his head in both hands and inspected the immaculate kitchen. He was tired. With Ginny gone out of town on church business, he'd been able to work until late last night, catching up on reports. Or almost. The end was in sight. He'd only stopped when the words began to blur and Blount realized that he was putting the wrong information in the wrong blanks.

Then there'd been another blowup at the Gascons'. Explosion number three. Alan had been expecting it, and he'd been up most of the night trying to reason with Rich, trying to explain to him that his jealousy, if nothing else, would drive June away. Already she floated around the town like a wraith, sitting in her car with a beleaguered, hunted expression. But some sixth sense prevented Blount from mentioning that to Rich, who would have viewed such behavior in the worst possible light.

In the end it had taken several hours of cajoling and no few threats to get the knife from the younger man. Alan couldn't understand why June didn't hightail it away, and he wondered how long it would be before Rich carved his wife up for real.

In the small hours before dawn Alan had finally placed his head upon the pillow, and his night had been plagued by dark dreams and even darker voices that sizzled like summer rain on a tin roof, or grease dripping on a fire. Finally Blount relented, getting up, making himself a solitary cup of coffee, and preparing to greet another day. As an after-thought, he'd grabbed the vet's report to take to the Brauns, sure that they would be up despite the early hour.

And he had been right. Hedda was fully dressed in an overwashed and faded housedress, cardigan, and smock-type apron. She bustled around the kitchen, pulling a fresh loaf of banana-nut bread from the oven.

Carrying the coffeepot in one hand and her mug in the other, she hastened back to the table. Hedda cleared her throat, and he looked up and smiled wanly at her.

The smile she returned was strained, but Hedda always looked that way. Edgy and uptight, as if she had a corncob up her butt.

"Would you like a slice?" she said with forced cheer.

"No, thanks, just coffee." Blount examined her gaunt features as he offered her his cup for a refill.

A muscle under her eye twitched. She appeared to be running on adrenaline. Something was wrong, although Blount couldn't have said what. Hedda returned to marking a carefully wrapped loaf of bread, with label and date.

Noticing his curious gaze upon her, she spoke harshly. "Well, Alan, that's really all I can tell you, and as you can see I'm kind of busy right now."

Her strident voice interrupted further speculation as she gathered a roll of Saran Wrap and some freezer bags and shoveled them into a drawer. Then she picked up white paper, string, and scissors from the counter and put them away.

"Like I told you, Les went to some antique auction in Boston, I don't remember which one. We were getting low on stock."

She indicated the garage that had been converted into an antique shop with a vague gesture.

The Brauns were real believers in the work ethic. They kept bees, raised goats, and turned their hand to any number of financial endeavors, and it seemed to have paid off. The shop did modestly good business during the tourist season.

"Don't you know when he'll be back?"

"A week." Hedda found something of immense interest on the floor and stared at it. "Mebbe," she added.

"Don't you know?"

"Course I know," she snapped at him, "but things happen. He could stumble across an estate sale and need to transport more than a few pieces. He may need to arrange shipping. Who knows? He could be delayed a day or two."

"Don't you normally go on these trips together?"

Hedda glared at him. "Why all these questions? Am I in trouble or something?"

"No, of course not, I was just trying to make conversation. Look, it's no big deal. Les said he wanted to see the reports on the goat when they came through, although I don't know why. I've been so busy I haven't had time to drop them by before, and I thought as long as I was in the neighborhood—" Alan said.

"Well, if you don't mind, I've got things to do. The goats need tending, and soon people will be coming by to pick up their milk."

"I'm sorry, Hedda, I'm not being obtuse," Alan said. "I'm not really with-it today. I didn't get much sleep last night."

"If you want to leave the report, I'll give it to him," she said.

"No, I'd better not. This has to be filed with the other reports." He shrugged. "Why don't you have him contact me when he gets home, okay?"

Blount unfolded his massive bulk from the spindly Shaker chairs. He despised those things. They always looked so delicate he was afraid to put all his weight on them. His legs wobbled underneath him from the effort of keeping himself at least partially aloft.

"Ayah, will do," Hedda said as she trailed after him through the door and up the path to his car. He glanced at the garage, saw the family car, and scowled. He glanced from the old Volvo to her. Her back went rigid, and she examined her hands.

Blount climbed into the squad, and she exhaled slowly. He leaned out the window and shooed her toward the house.

"Remember to have Les call me when he gets back if he's still interested in seeing the report," he said.

Hedda took a few tentative steps toward the front door and then rotated on the ball of her foot to watch Alan Blount back down the drive. He steered carefully across the moat created by the drainage ditch and onto the street. She waited till he was lost in the curling vapors and then hurried up the walk. When the front door had whispered shut behind her, she darted up the stairs to pack.

Driving away from Les's place, Blount couldn't shake the feeling of unease. His mind kept returning to the car parked next to the shed. If Les had gone on a buying trip, how had he gotten there? Wouldn't Les need a car?

Hedda had said something about Boston—a damned expensive place to go looking for antiques. Usually people from Boston came here to the boonies to search for obscure family treasures and forgotten heirlooms, not the other way round. Or so Alan thought, but he had to admit that he knew next to nothing about the antique trade.

Perhaps Les had flown down, but Alan couldn't imagine the frugal Les springing for a bus ticket, much less a plane, as long as he had a car.

Questions circulated inside his head in a steady buzz. He was almost ready to turn and go back when an animal bounded out in front of him. A large gray blur in the mist. He swerved to miss it and swerved again to avoid settling in the ditch.

Heart pounding, Blount slammed on the brakes—glowering at the woods where he would have sworn the animal had disappeared. Nothing moved, neither branch nor twig. He rubbed his eyes with his hand and pinched his nose between thumb and forefinger. His eyes felt like two hot coals.

Blinking, Blount looked again.

From its size he would have said it was a dog, but the dull gray implied jackrabbit.

A jackrabbit? The size of a German shepherd?

Alan snorted. The whole town was going nuts, and now *he* was seeing things. Blount slumped in the car seat, feeling somehow inadequate. Unending rains. Roads torn to wrack and ruin. Old friends were being carved up, and the perpetrator, that bastard James Sheridon, was still running around loose somewhere. Ann Blisson and young David Garreth dead, both killed in senseless accidents. It was getting to be too much.

He rubbed his eyes with the heels of his hands. Accelerating gently, he let the car inch toward town, too exhausted and too distracted to turn back.

So Les hadn't taken the car? What of it? That was their business. Maybe she meant to meet him down in Bean Town later this week. No point in looking for trouble where there was none; he had enough to worry about right now.

He drove on, listening to the steady hiss which sounded so much like sizzling drizzle that he was too bemused and self-absorbed to realize that it had stopped raining yesterday.

His head beat with the all too familiar throb of a hangover, and Bob Schoenwald groaned as he thought of his mounting debt down at Aggie's store. He flopped bonelessly onto the kitchen chair and peered out the window at fog so thick that he couldn't see the Penobscot even though it was less than one hundred yards away from his door.

Unvoiced accusations hung around his head—accusations that wore his parents' faces—reminding him that he was broke; that he was living, and eating, on his onetime heartthrob's good graces; that he was a failure.

He batted at the pyramid of empties he had built on the kitchen table in a bout of intoxicated creativity and winced when they came clattering down. Granny Simpson, Sandypoint's one certifiable loony, wandered down the road, talking to herself.

Bob got up and started pacing. He needed something to do; this being unemployed was driving him nuts. With a critical eye he surveyed the room. There were plenty of things that needed doing around the old homestead, and

Schoenwald felt a little embarrassed that he had let the house his parents had left to him get into such a state. The faucets dripped constantly. A large bloodred rust stain spread across the pitted porcelain. And the entire place needed a coat of paint.

But all those things took money, and money was not something he had in great abundance right now.

Loser!

He slumped against the counter, wondering how things could have gotten so bad. He hadn't wanted much, and Bob would have thought his job was secure. Who else could they find to do it? Who else would want to go slogging around in the town's muck? The job sure as hell didn't pay much.

But he had been wrong. Dead wrong.

While the city fathers dealt with lawyers and bankers, Robert Schoenwald was going under emotionally and financially. And what the fuck did they care?

Mad now, he slammed out of the house, sprinted to his car, and roared onto the road, gravel flying. He hit a pothole and started to swear at it as if it were some kind of personal insult.

12

The rains dwindled and the fog faded, giving up their death grip on the land. The sun came out with a vengeance —as if it wanted to dry the town in a single day, or hell were trying to break through the surface of the earth—and the village was transformed into a steam bath. The heat, once dampened by rain, was blistering at a time when autumn's chill should have nipped at the air.

The sun dawdled and stretched, moving through the woods next to the trailer like a great tabby and coloring it with stripes of black, gray, and orange. Stripped to the waist, Tiffany played hide-and-seek in the cluttered dooryard. Her imaginary adversary, who also happened to be "it," would never think to find her here, and Tiffany squirmed into the cavity created by four bald tires Jimmy had stacked next to the kennel door.

Her brother and mother had watched her do this on more than one occasion, and they never had been able to understand what she was doing.

"How can you hide," they'd ask, "from yourself?"

Or: "Why don't you go get young Jonathan? He'll play with you."

Tiffany couldn't seem to explain to them that hide-and-seek against a pretend playmate meant you always won. It was like trying to explain where she went when she went away. Eventually she stopped trying. *Grown-ups never understood anything anyway.*

Tiffany giggled to herself, relishing the aroma of damp earth, rubber, and tar.

"Found ya," a deep male voice said, and Tiffany leapt straight up, erupting from the central cavity like human magma, and found herself face to face with Gideon. They stared at each other eyeball to eyeball. He gazed upon her without blinking.

"Neat game," he said.

"Yeah," she said, not surprised that he of all adults understood.

"How'd you find me?" Tiffany said as she slithered from the safe haven of tires.

A smile spread across his face, and he was positively beaming. "Been watchin'."

He sidled over to the trailer's stairs, glowered at the ground, and started digging at the soft earth with his toe.

Tiffany joined him without comment. She gave him a sidelong glance, appraising him. Stockton Springs' resident dummy. Here was someone who had faced what she faced every day. No, worse than her, 'cuz he'd been around here *forever,* and few children could resist the impulse to throw a taunt or a stone in his direction, although Tiffany had never been among their number.

No child, however, harassed Gideon in front of his parents. Gideon's history was well known, and Stockton Springs took care of its own. Any child caught pulling such a stunt would have got a good hiding. This didn't mean the behavior ceased, only that it remained unobserved and was a little more vehement when vented belatedly on its target. Her they saw every day, familiarity providing some sort of safety valve, but he skulked in the background, slinking around like a whipped puppy. His behavior elicited abuse.

Tiffany turned to him and said: "Sorry about your parents."

Gideon came to an abrupt halt. All color drained from his face, expression blank, and all animation left his body.

Parents. Gideon knew about parents. Everybody had parents. He had had parents—once. He could almost bring their images to mind. Like snapshots curling in the pages of a book. Except they had no faces, as if someone had erased them as one did the letters on a Big Chief pad, leaving their features blank.

His gaze fell on her and he brightened. "Sorry about Jimmy," he replied.

Tiffany looked up at him and heaved a great sigh. "Yeah, me, too."

In complete accord, they walked on.

"Nice dog?" He pointed at a spot somewhere behind her.

Tiffany checked over her shoulder, wondering suddenly if he was speaking to someone else.

"I like dogs," Gideon observed.

The only remaining dog in the kennel began to yelp. Its master would come later that day to retrieve it, and then the place would be empty of all life. She would miss it. Sometimes she asked her mom for a dog of her own, but her mother wouldn't give in, saying they had enough dogs with the kennel.

"Me, too," Tiffany said. She reached into her pocket for the bones and her hand came out empty. She shivered. Her lucky piece was gone. Her pace faltered, and Gideon halted beside her, waiting patiently. She had carried it with her religiously, until recently, although she couldn't have said why. She only knew that no one was supposed to know about the bones, except Gideon. She figured Gideon was okay. Now her onetime lucky piece was lost, and Tiffany couldn't recall the last time she had seen it.

Gideon touched her shoulder, bringing her from her reverie, and she dismissed the thought. If Tiffany didn't know where it was, no one else did, either. It was safe, hidden, out of sight and out of mind.

The pair meandered in comfortable silence toward the

Point. They had spent a great deal of time together since he had found her in the marsh. Gideon had never been able to explain how he had come across her there, or where "there" had been. Tiffany did not question him too much. After all, she forgot stuff, too.

Tiffany liked Gideon. He was one of the few people who didn't treat her like a dummy. Of course, Tiffany didn't think of herself as dumb, but even Sam with his exaggerated patience made her feel small. She couldn't explain to him, a teacher, that words, and their meanings, sometimes ran away from her, and she from them.

The constant companions soon learned that when the two of them—slow child and vacuous adult—were together, the other kids left them alone, as if they formed two halves of a whole, and that whole was acceptable to and accepted by the children of the village with hardly a second glance.

The way she figured it, Gideon himself couldn't be all that stupid. He knew stuff, lots of neat junk, like what was good to eat and what was not. Tiffany had discovered a whole spectrum of new taste sensations with Gideon as they set about digging up acorns and tuberous wild garlic or chomping autumn-hardened berries, sweet as raisins.

No dummy knew that kind of stuff.

He could find a grouse's nest or entice a chipmunk from its hole. One day last week they had observed the burrow for four hours, watching the chipmunks come and go, and Tiffany had been content. With Gideon she felt no competition; they would sit side-by-side, lost in a lethargy of choices, and never move.

Once Gideon had caught a mole by hand. Now *that* was a neat trick. He had just started digging, and the poor creature was exposed, right there, where it delved in the stony earth. Gideon had plucked it up and showed it to her proudly, holding it for her to pet.

Another time they had startled a woodchuck in the brush and chased it into its den. It was fat and sluggish, its internal clock set for hibernation while the weird autumn, which had never quite begun, defied its instincts. It had lurched through the undergrowth, its fur mottled and moth-eaten.

156

Back in its burrow, the woodchuck had swung around to peep out and chatter its teeth at them when they didn't leave immediately. It had been fun.

Today they went down to the beach, skirting the little car that was parked there. Gideon took her to explore the smugglers' cave he had discovered. One, he insisted, that no one else knew about. Its mouth was well hidden behind an outcropping of rock and woven net of brambles and stickers. Indifferent to the pain, he lifted the prickly curtain for her to enter. Tiffany slithered through the crevice, and she staggered a bit when the room widened before her. The air around her came alive with sound, a rustling, a whispering.

"Gideon?" she said, searching blindly for his big, warm hand.

And the noise began to take shape. Squeaks, almost beyond the range of human hearing, a chirping, and the heavy beat of leathered wings. She had disturbed a colony of bats. Gideon burst into the room behind her, talking loudly, and the place exploded.

The bats swarmed, diving this way and that, and Tiffany felt the flap of a wing against her face, and the soft breath of wind in her hair. Around and around they careered—the noise intensifying as Tiffany screamed and screamed—until they found the exit.

Then there was silence almost more frightening than the susurrating sound. The hairs on the back of Tiffany's neck stood on end, and Gideon held her, making comforting little cooing noises before leading her home.

"Where the hell have you been?" her mother said as they walked into the dooryard. "You should have been home hours ago."

Tiffany halted abruptly at the base of the rickety stairs. She peeked timidly at Leah. The girl's eyes took in the impatiently tapping toe, the crossed arms, and Tiffany blenched.

Gideon materialized from behind the woodpile, where he had been studying the circle that he had drawn into the ground around the trailer, and Leah relaxed—the lecture abandoned before it had begun. Tiffany grinned happily. As far as her mother was concerned, Gideon was okay. The young man seemed to like Leah, too, and had taken it upon himself to guard them both. He hung around the house and patrolled the woods beyond their dooryard. He even helped Tiffany with the kennels and started doing little odd jobs for Leah. The girl had watched as her mom had, with amazing forbearance, explained to him several times how to hang a picture.

"Oh, you're here, too," Leah said. "I suppose you've both missed lunch. Just a second, I'll go get sandwiches." Leah disappeared back inside the door.

Gideon motioned to Tiffany, and she clambered around the woodpile. He pointed at the smudged line and then made a broad circle with his arms that encompassed the mobile home.

"You wanna do it over again?" she asked.

He ducked his head in assent.

"Tiffany!" Her mother's voice drifted to them from the other side of the trailer. "Now, where has that girl got to?"

Tiffany took Gideon's hand. "Okay, we'll do it after lunch."

Leah had just opened her mouth to yell again when the two ambled into view. "Oh, there you are. Here." She shoved two sandwiches and a couple of bags of potato chips at them. "You two stay outside. I'm trying to get a little housework done."

And Leah ducked inside the door, whistling. Her mother was happier now than Tiffany could ever remember her being. She seemed glad to have Gideon to help around the house, and her mood seemed to improve the longer Jimmy stayed away. She listened to music more, drank less, and the dingy mobile home was really starting to sparkle and shine.

Tiffany perched on the top step, sitting sideways. Gideon followed, flopping down to face the road. The stairs groaned under his weight. Tiffany leaned back against his arm. He didn't complain, switching hands so he could eat without disturbing her.

They sat in quiet communion. Tiffany nestled against

Gideon, delighted with the warmth of human contact. Particularly now that she had finally convinced him to take a bath.

Her mother hadn't known quite what to make of that when she'd come home from work one day to find the two of them inside the bathroom. Tiffany was shoving towels, soap, a bath brush, and her favorite rubber frog into the poor man's hands. Leah hadn't been real sure she wanted Jimmy's kid brother taking a bath in her tub. She'd put a quick stop to it when Tiffany began to help Gideon to undress. Her mom had chased Tiffany from the room, leaving him alone. But Gideon had just stood there, next to the tub, as if he didn't know what to do, and Leah had finally acquiesced, stepping into the room and filling the tub, testing it, and then tolerantly demonstrating with a few mimed motions what needed to be done.

Her mother had even gone into her bedroom and dug out a pair of Jimmy's faded blue jeans and a flannel shirt, cussing the entire time. ". . . son of a bitch isn't here anyway . . . why should I keep his fucking junk . . ."

Gideon, Tiffany decided, had cleaned up nicely. After that first time, Gideon's bath had become a weekly ritual for all of them, with her mother stationed outside the bathroom door to accept the dirty clothes from Gideon's hands and handing him something else of Jimmy's to wear.

Once Gideon was washed, Tiffany had discovered that his hair was as much silver as it was blond, and she wondered idly how old he was. She had thought of him as young, for his face was seamless, devoid of the lines or wrinkles usually caused by the animation of human expression. Tiffany knew that he was younger than Jimmy, but something had turned most of his hair to white.

Sometimes Tiffany stole food from the table to give to him, and he was starting to fill out. Tiffany was pretty sure her mom knew what she was doing, but Leah hadn't said anything. So Tiffany kept stuffing an extra dinner roll into her pocket or an extra sandwich into her lunch bag, giving the food to him each morning as he walked her to the bus. Even school didn't seem nearly so bad now that she was spared the scorn of the other kids as she loped to the bus stop with Gideon trailing behind her like a faithful dog. He stayed with her and guarded her until the bus arrived, and he'd stand and watch until it disappeared from sight.

Still musing, Tiffany shoved the last potato chip into her mouth. Gideon jostled her, plucking at her sleeve. He pointed. Her gaze strayed to the drying moat just inside the stand of trees.

"Okay." Tiffany glanced over her shoulder at her mother, who was still whistling happily as she attacked a spot on the wall with her sponge. "We can do it now."

They moved off to the side of the trailer. Gideon grabbed his branch, dragging it through the still soft earth and mumbling something about protection. She regarded him as he scraped out the sections of the trench that had collapsed and wondered again what sort of defense he thought the small ditch gave them. With a perplexed shake of her head, Tiffany shrugged and followed along behind to pat the dirt more firmly into place. Renewing the line had become a ritual, like his baths.

Gideon started to chant. Nonsense words, but she had memorized them, and she added her trebling voice to his deeper bass. Carefully he traced the line around the trailer. When he was done, Gideon dropped his stick and began to cavort outside the circle, following the curving line. Some kind of silly dance he had made up. She danced with him, and whenever they did this, she would have sworn that the circle flickered an iridescent blue.

Sometimes at night Tiffany noticed this sparkling light if she happened to be looking at the drying moat out of the corner of her eye or screwed up her eyes just right. But then she'd turn her head or unscrunch her eyes because her face was starting to ache, and the glow would be gone.

The dance completed, Gideon crouched down. Tiffany almost tripped over him. He yanked a section of Indian reed-pipe from the ground and blew through it with a hollow whistle. Tiffany did the same.

"Tiffany, time to come in now." Leah stood just inside the door.

Tiffany tossed the reed aside and squeezed the young man hard until all his breath ran out of him with an *ooph*. He leered at her. She stood, dug her toe into the line, reluctant to go inside.

"Gideon can come, too," Leah added.

"Oh, good," Tiffany said. She reached up to take him by the hand, noticed the mud on hers, and shoved them into her pockets so her mother wouldn't see. They headed for the door, and Tiffany realized that she was happier than she could remember being in a very long time.

Blessedly, the waters were beginning to subside, but the Bay remained high, and tidal pools remained lagoons where the seals played unconcerned, or perhaps delighted, by the extended summer. The roads were dry for the first time in weeks, although pitted and damaged from nature's rough wash. Oblivious to the season, clouds of mosquitoes swarmed about the unwary heads of the town's inhabitants foolish enough to tarry in any one spot for too long.

Aggie and Bob leaned listlessly against their opposite sides of the counter. They had the hollow-eyed look of sleeplessness.

Swatting at the insects buzzing around his head, Blount replaced the nozzle in the gas pump and raced for the shop. Aggie watched him indifferently. He boomed through the door, wallet in his hand.

"That'll be ten dollars for gas, Alan," she said.

"How about some lunch?"

Aggie pushed away from the counter. "What about Ginny? Ain't she cookin' fa' ya anymore?"

"She's gone out of town, some meeting or another. Church auxiliary, or something."

"She's the lucky one," Aggie snorted.

"What do you mean? You aren't glad to see me?" Blount said.

"Sorry, Alan, you've been bad news lately. Every time you come in, something else has happened." She appraised the bearer of ill tidings as though considering lopping off his head. "Oh, well, seein' how you're here, I might as well feed

161

you. Wouldn't want Stockton Springs' finest falling over in a faint, now would I?" she said.

Schoenwald belched, closed one eye, and placed the other over the hole in the top of his beer can. "All gone," Bob said despondently into the can with a tinny echo.

Blount turned to scrutinize the other man's stooped posture and gaunt features and patted him on the back. "I'll buy you another one, how's that?"

Aggie rolled her eyes toward the ceiling and grimaced.

"Things are sure going to hell in a handbasket, around here," she said. "Hey, Bob, you're falling asleep on my counter." Aggie tugged the can from his hand, and he glanced blearily at her. "Why don't you go sleep in back?"

He muttered something incoherent and teetered away, heading toward the storeroom.

"Poor bastard," she said as she watched his staggering retreat.

"How's he holding up?" Blount asked.

"As you can see, not good. It was bad enough when his pay was late, but when the check bounced, he hit the ceiling. Never seen him so mad or so drunk. And it hasn't gotten any better since he discovered that he might be unemployed for a little while yet until the government can get the township's finances straightened out," Aggie said. "So name your poison."

"A hot dog and popcorn, seeing how that's all that's on the menu."

"Not so! We've got coffee and doughnuts, and there's some of those premade frozen hamburgers you can heat up in the microwave and submarine sandwiches in back."

"Made of Styrofoam," said Blount disparagingly.

"Look, if you're going to bitch about the menu, why don't you just go up to the café?"

"Naw." Ever since the incident with Defleurieu, Blount found the place depressing. The fresh coat of paint covering only one of the grease-splattered walls stuck out like a sore thumb. Most of those stains had been there as long as he could remember. They had become old friends, as familiar as his wife's face. The change was an unhealthy reminder of what had gone before, and often Blount imagined he could still see Duke's blood seeping through.

Usually CD's could boast one or two customers an hour, but now the café had become crowded, what with the weather so uncooperative and so much news to exchange. People spoke in soft murmurs, regarding their neighbors guardedly. The mutter of human voices would join the drone inside his head, and Blount found that he couldn't think.

"You just want to see me hustle," she complained loudly.

"Sure, why not? It's good for you." Blount took off his cap and wiped his forehead. "If you think you've got the energy in this heat."

"Too bad about David Garreth," she said as she tucked the hot dog in the bun. "And Ann Blisson. When two young people die like that on the same day, it sort of makes you stop and think."

Taking the wrapped hot dog from her, Blount exhaled from puffed cheeks. "I'll say, and I've had a little too much to think about lately."

"You and everybody else," Aggie commented dryly. "It also makes you start counting noses."

"Noses? What do you mean?" Alan peered at her over the bun and took a big bite. Catsup and relish squirted from the end and dripped onto the counter.

"Slob," she said as she went to grab a rag and wiped up the mess. "Noses. You know. What with Maxwell disappearing, and Ann Blisson and David Garreth getting killed, I've sort of been noticing who's coming in here and who's not."

He chewed and considered her silently.

"Oh," Aggie continued, "I know that most people do most of their shopping at the big supermarkets in Belfast or Bucksport, but everybody runs out of something now and then between times, and they don't always feel like going all the way over to Bucksport for a roll of toilet paper. So they stop in here. I suppose I see damned near everybody in town at least once a week."

Blount swallowed. "Well, is anybody missing?"

163

"Sheila Erhart."

He thought of Sheila's dog, Andrew, and his stomach soured.

"Although I don't see Sheila all that often. She usually does her shopping in Bangor. Her sister comes down to pick her up, but with all the flooding, her sister wouldn't have been able to get through. You'd think being cut off like that and all, she'd have run out of something."

"Yes, but the flooding down by the Point would have made it a little bit difficult for her to make it in here, too," Blount pointed out.

"What about since then? The waters are down, from what I hear," Aggie said.

"Surely her sister would have picked her up first thing if Sheila were strapped for supplies and taken her to Bangor."

"Yes, I suppose," Aggie said.

"I haven't gotten any calls from her, and Sheila would have called if she needed help. I could have taken her supplies if she had needed them, even if I had to walk."

"She'd've called if her phone was working, but what happens if the lines went down? No one else is out there now that summer's over, and if something had happened, she couldn't call for help."

"That's easy enough to check. Can I use your phone, Aggie?"

"Is this official? If it is, I'm gonna bill the city."

"Yeah, you and everybody else, but I wouldn't hold my breath while you're waiting to get paid."

His hot dog forgotten now, Blount dialed the operator, speaking in hushed tones. A few minutes later he hung up and wheeled on Aggie.

"Well, doesn't appear to be anyone home, but the line seems to be working. Exactly how long has it been since you saw Sheila?" he asked.

"Way before the rains came."

His appetite vanished as a hard knot of gloom settled in his stomach and the roaring buzz of premonition sizzled in his ears. Blount pushed the half-eaten hot dog back at her and fished in his pockets for a cigarette.

"There's Sheila, and there's the Brauns," she added. "I haven't seen either Hedda or Les for several days. I'm all out of eggs."

"Oh, I talked to Hedda just the other day, and she said Les had gone on a buying trip."

"When the season's over? Who's he gonna sell antiques to at this time of year?"

"Maybe he's outta stock. How do I know?"

"I hate to tell you this, but most of the dealers around here are just as happy to have sold their stock off by wintertime. And most don't bother to replenish it until spring, just as glad to have the space for storage, I 'spect." Aggie paused for a moment. "Besides, Hedda's gone, too. Just the other day one of the neighbors was in here and complaining that the Brauns' goats have gone wild, broken into her garden, and torn up the shrubs. They're all over the place."

"Why didn't you tell me?"

"It seemed like you had other things on your mind. Who knows, maybe Hedda and Les both went on the buying trip."

"Nope, when I spoke to her, she didn't mention anything about joining him." He tapped his tooth, trying to recall exactly when he had talked to her. "Perhaps, I should check it out."

Aggie shrugged. "I'm probably worrying about nothing. Still, with everything that's happened . . ." She made an expansive gesture and let the sentence dangle unfinished.

Jimmy squatted naked inside the sweat lodge. He stirred the embers in the shallow pit, not quite sure when he'd made the transition from outdoors to in. He wasn't even sure if it was night or day, for the woven roof blocked out all light.

A flame shot from the glowing coals, capturing his attention. He tossed some powder, which he recalled vaguely as dried coltsfoot and angelica, on the fire and then rocked back on his heels.

Each pore was open and sweat poured from his body.

He'd beat this fever yet. Smoke wafted around the small, enclosed cubicle, and Jimmy began to hum in a tuneless monotone. Selecting a thin pliable twig, he began to beat himself across the shoulders, back and neck.

The gray clouds caught the fire's burnished glow and sent it whirling as another, in a seemingly endless parade of figures, started to form.

The tempo of flagellation increased, and Jimmy began to hum.

Flickering before him now was the ghostlike form of June Gascon, a woman Jimmy had introduced to sex many long years ago. None too gently, if he remembered correctly, but it didn't seem to have inhibited her too greatly. A sneer ran fleetingly across his face.

His tone rose to a shriek, and his motions became more frenzied as he watched her. June peered with slightly parted lips and drooping eyes, not at him but at something or someone beyond his ken. Jimmy's fingers twitched in his lap, and he began to whisper words of passion in the spectral ear.

June plucked at her blouse and wriggled on the front seat, delighting in an unexpected Saturday of freedom. With the weather so fine, Rich and the rest of the fishing crew were working, making up for lost time. It was hot—and sticky. She unbuttoned the top few buttons, pulling her shirt open to reveal a dingy bra held together by a safety pin. She rolled down the window, letting the cool air of Sandypoint beach glide over her exposed chest.

Her nipples stiffened and it felt as if someone were stroking her breasts, her thighs. June swiveled toward the caress, and there were voices, lovely voices telling her to do deliciously naughty things.

Images rose in her mind of her last time with the Fletcher twins—both of them. Poor Eddie, the more soft-spoken of the two, had been horrified at what she proposed, and she could still recall their peals of laughter, Terry's and hers, at the younger twin's delicacy. Then they had fought over her. Silly boys. Until she threatened never to see either of them

166

again. That had shut them up quick, and from there, all she could remember was their hands, their mouths, as they both played with her body.

June hitched her skirt above her knees and closed her eyes. Suddenly Rich's disapproving face rose to the surface, glaring at her in her mind's eye. She jolted upright in the car seat to stare out the window, petrified, looking nervously behind her to see if he was there.

Last night's fight had been bad, *real* bad. She hadn't even known Rich was home. He'd just snuck up on her and was on top of her before she had noticed. Quiet-like. He'd knocked her around good without making so much as a sound. And June knew why, too. It was so old Mr. and Mrs. Morden wouldn't hear. They were the ones who kept callin' Blount, but not last night.

Yup, last night Rich'd been slick. Not even satisfied with beating the tar outta her, he'd held her at gunpoint for *hours* and told her what he'd do to her if he ever caught her screwing around.

Feeling suddenly exposed here on the beach, June experienced one of her brief moments of terror when she was sure that he *knew*, but the feeling was swiftly suppressed. It was a concept too frightening to bear.

A breeze rippled through the car, blowing sensuously into her ear, speaking to her in words that she couldn't quite understand. And June wriggled farther down into her seat. Her hand fell into her lap; her fingers searched for the moist cleft between her legs.

She moaned, twisting languidly. Her eyes fell upon the rearview mirror where a lone figure appeared in the road that led to the beach. June froze. Her hand flapped guiltily and then rose to clutch her throat as she gasped. The gasp turned into a sigh of relief. It was one of the Fletcher twins—only one—and she felt a fleeting moment of disappointment before she opened the car door. Terry Fletcher leered at her, his gaze taking in the open blouse and the car before he scrambled up the sheer ridge to the woods with June hot on his heels.

13

His nerves jangling in rising alarm, Blount drove to Sheila's house. His eyes flitted here and there, unwilling to light on any one place. As he turned the Four Corners, he noted June's empty car parked down by the beach with a certain measure of surprise. Her haunting the area around Sandypoint was usually a weekday activity. Rich must be working this Saturday.

The stream by Sheila's house had shrunk, no longer a raging torrent, but it could still lay claim to being a respectable river that lapped over the road in some places. Alan took his foot off the gas and lingered for a few moments to scan the woods. No gay colors of magenta and orange clothed the trees this year. The surrounding forest remained a greenish-yellow hue which was both unhealthy and bilious. He was procrastinating, he knew, but Alan tarried a little longer to let his eyes take in the curl of fern, and the drooping boughs of willow, cedar and pine that were creepy and somehow menacing.

"Come on, man, what are you waiting for?" he murmured to himself. "It's only a little old lady."

Only a little old lady, he chided himself. A little old lady who hadn't been seen in weeks. Missing during a flood. Missing in an area where animals were being slaughtered for fun and the local school kids were performing satanic rituals. Missing where people were disappearing right and left, and where the young were dropping like flies. Only a little old lady who could easily fall and break a hip even in the best of times, and in times like these, would most likely starve to death before someone had noticed the loss.

And Blount cursed himself for not being more observant.

The squad car was now abreast her mailbox. It was crammed full of circulars, papers, bills. So full, in fact, that much of it had spilled to the ground where it had been drowned in rain and driven into the mud.

Lenny Walsh evidently had made it through. That son of a bitch should have noticed that something was amiss. Then Blount thought of the last time they had met over Ann Blisson's staring corpse and starting eyes, and he recapitulated; the man had had other things on his mind.

The drive was slick with mud, and Blount's eye, trained by years of habit, noted that no other car had driven up this road recently. The theory that her sister had come to take her shopping as soon as the waters had abated crumbled, and Alan searched frantically for some other explanation besides the dire one, hoping that Sheila had had the good sense to go to her sister's in Bangor when the last of the summer people had evacuated the area.

But that meant that she had not returned yet, and *that* didn't sound like Sheila, who was something of a homebody.

The black and white crept up the drive until it got to the marshy remains of the dooryard. His eyes scanned the yard, looking for footprints or some other sign of recent activity. He let up on the gas. The car rattled and died. Blount winced. The old buggy needed a tune-up, the regular maintenance check long overdue, and Blount toted up another thing on the growing list of "things to do" . . . someday when things settled down. Assuming they ever did.

With the fan off, the car seemed to absorb the heat. He chuffed and rolled down his window. A faint sour aroma tainted the heavy air. Blount wrinkled his nose and stuck his tongue out, quickly retracting it. The air even tasted bad, and the hissing portent inside his head rose to a shriek.

Blount got out of the car, reluctantly. He sloshed across the deep bowl that formed her dooryard. The house, itself, was on top of the ridge that overlooked the bay, but here in the depression behind it no breeze stirred a limb or lifted so much as a leaf. Blount hesitated, then disregarding the back door, headed for the front.

Sniffing, he ascended the hill. The reek became worse the closer he came to the house, and his brain shut off, his mind unwilling to concede what the olfactories recorded. His jaw was working convulsively by the time he reached the front door, and the half a hot dog he had consumed at Aggie's was doing little loop-de-loops in his gut.

Blount retrieved his handkerchief from his pocket, shook it out to cover his nose and mouth. He didn't even bother to knock. Instead, he clasped the doorknob and twisted it.

It resisted. Locked.

"Damn," he mumbled through his kerchief.

Then Alan pounded on the door and bellowed, "Sheila?"

Backing away from the cottage, Blount examined the many windows. Sunlight glittered off the panes. He thought he saw a shadow flit past the window in the stairwell, and Blount shaded his eyes so he could see better.

"Mrs. Erhart? Sheila? It's Alan Blount."

He waited for a few moments, and he would have sworn again that something moved.

"All right, enough is enough," he muttered. Blount returned to the door and broke the window with one of the small rocks Sheila used to line her flowerbed. The stink surged through the gap, and Alan stumbled back a step.

Steeling himself, Blount tapped the rest of the glass from the frame, picking at the remaining slivers before reaching through to unlock the door. He jumped back to let the hot, still air swoosh past him, and the fetor engulfed him. The smell of soured flesh, not the semisweet aroma of recent death, but the vile stench of rotting meats.

"Christ!" Alan recoiled.

The stink was so intense it coated the inside of his mouth and the back of his throat with a revolting paste, and he hadn't even walked in the door yet!

Had it been summer, there's no way this stench would have gone unreported. Somebody would have stumbled by on his way to the beach or dropped in for a coffee and a gab.

Alan withdrew, examined the tops of his shoes, and concentrated on keeping his lunch down.

Once the front room had aired slightly, Blount marched rigidly through the door, the cloth crammed hard against his nose and mouth. Without a second glimpse around the room he hurried over to the east wall to open one window after another.

Only when all the windows were flung wide did he allow himself to breathe, plunging his head out of doors, so that he dangled across the sill, half in and half out of the house. Gulping a large lungful of fresh air, Blount drew his head back inside the house. He inhaled experimentally before shielding his nose with his handkerchief again.

He studied the front room. A pile of knitting was draped neatly over the arm of the chair. A book, some torrid romance, was placed, open and facedown, upon the end table. Everything seemed normal enough. A coffee cup sat next to it. Blount stepped forward and glowered at the thick layer of green mold that had grown in the bottom of the cup.

Nothing had been disturbed, not even the film of dust that coated every piece of furniture. Alan moved through the living room toward the dining room, flinching as he stepped through the interconnecting door.

The wall at the base of the stairs was splattered with gore.

And his mind switched into autopilot, official mode, suppressing revulsion with the iron will and control he had learned to exert as an officer. As long as Alan was forewarned, he could shift into cop-gear and not embarrass himself.

This was an investigation, and this was his job. At that moment Sheila ceased to be a person, an acquaintance, or a friend and became a case. Clinically Blount studied what appeared to be stomach contents. These too had grown a fine down of mold. Then he moved over to the stairwell and peered up at the woman's gruesome remains.

Despite his control, his gut tried to explode out his throat, and he clamped his jaw fiercely shut. Time, dampness, and heat had taken their toll. The corpse was in an advanced state of decomposition. Pocketing the handkerchief—nothing would get rid of this stench short of a bath, and Blount had his doubts about that—he moved up the stairs.

She hung from the hall light, her toes barely brushing the floor of the landing. Alan marveled that the spindly lamp had held her weight. Sheila had been no small woman.

The skin on her legs exhibited the mottled blue-gray color of hypostasis. Blount bent closer and noted that the normal pooling was already starting to dissipate. Mentally he fixed a time, or day, of death in his head.

Mounting the next step and the next, he avoided looking at her gaping torso and the abdominal cavity, whose contents adorned the far wall, and skipped to the face and neck.

If it hadn't been her house, he probably wouldn't have recognized her. Her features were swollen and distorted. Her skin a purply-black and slick. In areas it had split. Maggots teemed over the slippery surface, congregating most around her lips, nose, and eyes.

Bluebottle larvae, he noted, with a known time of larval development, and further confirmation of how long she must have hung there.

Then Blount examined the rope. It had sunk deep into the skin. The rope had cut into her horizontally, and he blinked, dredging up information from one of the courses he had taken on accumulating evidence, which of necessity included forensic pathology, recalling vaguely that when the point of suspension was not clear—in other words, the cut of the rope was not slanted—it might indicate murder, as though someone had come up from behind. His gaze fell to her toes. No, the feet were touching the ground, which could also result in a horizontal ligature.

Gratefully Blount propelled himself away from the landing and down the stairs. This was a job for the State Police, and he didn't mind handing this one over to the State boys. Personally, he didn't have the stomach for it.

Better them than me, he thought as he left to radio his report into Bucksport.

Sheridon had the biggest fuckin' boner he had ever seen. It vibrated as he regarded the tiny image of June Gascon, with her legs wrapped around the Fletcher boy's waist, undulating in the fire. Jimmy grinned; he'd taught her well. The couple writhed and grunted and groaned upon the ground as if there were no tomorrow. Sheridon stretched, touching his own throbbing penis, and when he did, June's back arched and she climaxed.

Jimmy got down on his knees and started rocking. June jerked upright to straddle the boy, imitating Jimmy's posture. Then she took the Fletcher kid's penis into her mouth and tried to coax his now-limp dick into another erection.

Jimmy's smile widened.

This *was* too good to be true, and Sheridon let his mind wander until it found the raging chaos of Rich's. The smell of sea salt and dead fish wafted through the sweat lodge. With the first tenuous touch, Sheridon sent Gascon a vision of June and her young lover, letting him look through Jimmy's all-seeing eyes.

His mind filled with loathing and horror, and Jimmy knew that he had made contact.

He fondled himself, and somewhere miles away Jimmy felt Rich stiffen.

Suddenly the wolf surfaced in the smoky haze, and Sheridon cringed away from the fire and thrashed at the smoke's flimsy screen. The picture fluttered. He threw water on the coals, and the image, projected upon both smoke and steam, strengthened. He squinted, becoming aware of the creature's surroundings.

It was coming. It was almost there, and Jimmy fretted at

his confinement. Somehow, Sheridon must free himself of
his fever and vacate this place, fast.

The big boys were in town. At least that's the way it felt
whenever the State Police arrived. They always operated in
a tight-knit little group, treating local officers like some
yokels with the approximate IQ of a turnip caused by too
many years of inbreeding. Squawks of numerous car radios
tore through the hush of evening, and bright yellow ribbon,
like bizarre birthday decorations, cordoned off the area
around Sheila Erhart's dooryard.

They worked with crisp, detached efficiency that he found
somehow disquieting, but this was the kind of stuff they
faced every day. Alan whispered a small prayer of thanks for
that decision which he had made so many years ago to stay
with the local force rather than advance up the ladder to the
state level. It could have been him that was stuck scraping
gunk off the walls and taking larvae samples.

The media arrived. Blount recognized Jennifer Collins
but managed to slip away before she caught up with him.
Stockton Springs had become a hot little news item, and he
was determined not to participate in the media circus.

Twilight had fallen like a wet blanket across the land as he
drove away, with the windows open wide, trying to get rid of
the stench. It clung to his hair, his clothes, and lined his
throat. He swore to himself that he wasn't going to be able to
eat meat for a month.

His brain working overtime, Blount coaxed a little more
speed out of the car as he headed back to town to check on
the Brauns. After what he had already found, Alan thought
to flip on his sirens and decided against it. If Les and Hedda
were off on a visit or newly returned to collect recalcitrant
chickens and goats, they would not thank him for thundering into their place with sirens blasting.

Blount took the fork leading to Stockton Springs and
turned up School Street, maneuvering carefully past broken
sections of road until he had reached the Brauns' farm.
Again he paused at the mailbox. It, too, was crammed full,

and he had cause to curse Walsh for the second time that day.

The house was obviously empty. No lights burned anywhere within. No smoke poured from the chimney. Where had he been, Alan wondered, while all of his neighbors had slipped away? They couldn't have all disappeared in the last few days' reprieve when he'd caught up on his paperwork at the Bucksport station.

Alan pulled up outside the garage. The Volvo was gone, and he tried to remember the last time he had seen it around the village. An antique, with the rounded lines of a tortoise or an old DeSoto, it was a difficult vehicle to miss.

Aggie had been right. The yard was a mess. The goats had done a number on it. Areas of the lawn had been dug up and the shrubs stripped of leaves and bark. Large sections of the fence around the pens were down.

His foot hit something, and he stooped to inspect it. Claws, a beak, and some feathers. They had lost at least one chicken, maybe more. Blount straightened, advanced to the doorstep, and banged on the door.

It boomed hollowly.

He tested the lock, and the knob turned easily in his hand. A single brow rose up in query, and he hesitated a moment before advancing into the darkened house.

"Hedda? Les?"

His hand found the switch and flipped on the light. Illumination flooded the room, chasing the shadows away. Blount rotated slowly, taking in the entire living room. The needlepoint stand, the magazine rack with its assortment of *Reader's Digest, Woman's Day,* and *The Farmer's Almanac.*

He headed down the hall to the dining room, where he found a pile of *Watchtower*s. The second batch of magazines stopped him. The Brauns were, as far as Blount knew, staunch Lutherans, and Les too much of a skinflint to buy these rags out of charity. Withered flowers draped over the sides of a vase on the sideboard.

Alan continued, going from room to room until he stood in the bedroom. Judging by the gaps in the closets, some clothes were missing, although he was not familiar enough with their wardrobe to be sure. There were no suitcases, but not everybody kept suitcases in the bedroom.

Returning to the front hall, Alan faltered. His hand fluttered over the knob to the hall closet as he thought inanely of family skeletons.

His mind went back to the last time he'd seen Hedda. Something then had seemed wrong. What had it been?

This was ridiculous. He opened the closet to find the typical assortment of junk, an empty clothes hamper, mud-caked boots, a vacuum, an ironing board, but no suitcases. His mood began to lighten. Maybe they *were* off on another buying trip. It didn't have to be the same one that had taken Les away more than a week ago.

Except for a molding loaf of bread in the bread box and something unidentifiable in the refrigerator, the place was as spotless as he would have expected it to be, knowing Hedda. He puzzled over the food for a minute, wondering why the normally antiseptic Hedda would have left it there to rot.

Maybe they had expected to be back sooner.

He had found nothing so far. Some *Watchtowers*. Some withered flowers. No suitcases. Maybe they had gone on a vacation, but he couldn't imagine the dour Les springing for a vacation.

Blount moved to stand before the basement door. A screeching voice inside his head told him to quit while he was ahead. It had already been a rough enough day. He swerved from his purpose, making another complete circuit of the first floor before he again found himself by the cellar.

With a sigh, Blount descended the stairs.

The basement was immaculate.

That was Hedda for you.

Other people cleaned only the parts of the house you saw, but not Hedda. Every work surface was clean. He couldn't even find the normal accumulation of lint around the washer and dryer, and the floor even had a freshly washed appearance.

Blount bent down to take a closer look at the washer. It

176

smelled musty. He lifted the lid to find a load of mildewed laundry twisted around the agitator.

Odd. It was beginning to look like they had left in some kind of hurry.

Again Alan spun and surveyed the room until he faced the freezer. A twenty-four-cubic-foot chest-type, it was long and narrow, reminding him of a coffin. Another picture popped into his overworked brain. An apprehensive Hedda surreptitiously, almost guiltily, scooping white paper, string, scissors, and cellophane into a drawer.

No, this was Stockton Springs, where the most exciting thing that ever happened was an occasional potluck supper —at least until recently. People like Hedda didn't just take it into their minds to put hubby in cold storage, did they? Alan tried to envision the diminutive Hedda hauling Les's bulky body and dumping it in the freezer. The officer shook his head. He'd seen one too many late-night movies, read one too many worn-out mystery novels. Blount thought of the blackened corpse hanging from a clothesline, Mrs. Blisson's broken body at the bottom of a ladder, and animals torn to pieces and strewn across the countryside. And he *had* to look.

His movements were saltatorial, and he was drawn like a puppet on a string toward the freezer. His hand fell on the cold lid, and it tingled, sending a charge like an electric shock up his arm. His breath went out in a whistling rush when Blount opened the heavy lid and saw . . .

Neat packages, wrapped in white paper. Each was dated in Hedda's cramped script. Dated the same day he had been here, and he thought of Hedda preparing a loaf of bread for the freezer.

He let the lid drop and sniggered scornfully at himself. What had he expected?

A blue Les stretched out like an archaeological find some scientist had gouged out of an ancient glacier? Or better still, with an apple stuffed in his mouth?

All the exhaustion of the previous few days caught up with him, and Alan began to twitter at himself as he thought of

Les trussed up like a Christmas turkey. Mindless mirth welled up inside of him, and he laughed out loud in a flood of relief. Until he began to hiccup, his sides hurt and hysterical tears rolled down his cheek.

Still chortling, Blount checked his watch. Too late to go in to the office. He decided to stop off at Aggie's and tell her the gruesome results of her speculation—as if she wouldn't have already heard.

Then it was home to an empty house, for Ginny's work for Saint Margaret's would keep her out of town all weekend, and perhaps that was for the best. Right now he was glad she was gone. Blount didn't figure he'd feel like talking much tonight.

His wife was something of a rare commodity, an Episcopalian in Puritan New England, as rare as a temperance lady in a brothel. It had been the English church that the original settlers had come here to avoid. Most Anglican parishes were large, encompassing huge areas of land, and their churches only sparsely attended. With the considerable French population, even Catholics were more common than Anglicans. The French and the English still didn't get along particularly well. One got the impression that the populace was still fighting the French and Indian War, only the Indians had had the good sense—a couple of centuries ago—to step out of the conflict.

Not a religious man himself, Blount supported Ginny's church work because he was a firm believer that there could be just a little too much closeness in marriage. Her volunteer work got her out of the house, just as fishing and hunting gave him time away from home. Right now she was someplace cheery, someplace safe. Something Stockton Springs didn't seem to be anymore. An uncomfortable thought. Blount hustled toward the front door, unformed doubt still niggling at the back of his mind.

Inside the store Schoenwald sat on his usual perch near the counter.

"Here, I'll spring for a beer," she said. The bell clanged

harshly, overriding Bob's objections as Alan Blount walked in the door.

"Ah, it's you," she said. "We've been expecting you."

"I reckoned you would be. You heard about Sheila," Blount said.

"Ayah," said Aggie.

"Terrible, absolutely terrible. What would possess her to do such a thing?" Schoenwald mused.

Nobody said anything for a moment, each finding separate spots on floor, wall, and space to contemplate.

"Loneliness does strange things to people," Aggie said, and she turned to stare openly at Schoenwald. Alan watched this short interchange thoughtfully. Bob continued to ponder some far-off point.

She swung on Blount. "And what about the Brauns?"

"Oh, them. I checked on them, too."

"I figured you would. Anything?"

"Nothing really. You're right; they're gone. The house was spotless and the luggage was missing. They must'a taken a trip."

"Without telling anybody? Not the neighbors? The post office? Nobody?"

Blount shrugged. "Maybe something came up. Some kind of emergency. Hedda grew up in the south, near Portland I think."

"Sacco," Aggie corrected.

"Maybe there was some kind of family emergency."

"Don't you think they'd make some kind of arrangements for the goats?"

"Maybe they did or tried to, and something went wrong. The message got lost. Christ, where I've been today, it seems that more people's mail is ending up on the ground than in the box. Let's face it, things have not been exactly normal around here lately. Things slip people's minds. The way things have been recently, I'd forget my name if they hadn't given me this pin." He tugged at his nametag.

Schoenwald spun to face him. "You at least have a job."

"Barely," Blount muttered.

Aggie persisted. "You said the house was spotless. How'd you get in?"

"What?"

"How'd you get into the house? Our one police officer didn't do any covert breaking and entering, did he?"

"No, not there I didn't. I didn't need to. The door was unlocked."

"Don't you think *that's* odd?"

"Jesus, Aggie." Alan threw up his hands in disgust. "You want my job? 'Cuz right now I sure as hell don't."

"No, really, I mean it. Would you go off on a trip and leave your home unlocked?"

Alan cradled his head in his hands. "Aggie."

"All right, I'll drop it. Frankly I'm glad you didn't find any bodies at their house, too. I think there's been more than enough people dying lately. I certainly hope you're right. Some emergency in the family, a hasty exit, a message left and lost. Christ knows we don't need any more problems."

Blount groaned. "Okay, if you want me to, I'll go check again tomorrow."

"Really," she assured him, "you're right. I'm sure." He glared at her. "Read my lips: You are right."

"Sure."

"Can I interest you in anything, or are you just going to hang around holding my counter down?"

"Uh, Aggie?" he said, preoccupied. "Do you ever do any canning or preserving?"

"What with the store and all I don't have time for such things."

"What about freezing? You know, in quantities. Berries and things. When I've watched Ginny, that seemed simple enough."

"Not often. Why do you ask?"

"What sort of things would you be freezing at this time of year? It's a little late for berries."

"Meat most likely. Lots of people buy a side of beef and freeze it. Or some people invest in a cow and have it slaughtered right before winter."

"If you were gonna do that, wouldn't you label it? Let's

face it, once it's wrapped and frozen, it's a little hard to tell one cut of beef from another."

"Well, you're supposed to. I suppose it would depend on how rushed I was. I can usually tell one piece of meat from another once it's unwrapped. Why? You thinkin' about freezing up some of the things that you've been finding around here lately?" she quipped.

"That's a gruesome thought." Schoenwald shuddered.

"Just curious, that's all," Alan said and managed an insipid grin. "Well, I'm gonna go home before something else goes wrong. See you."

Closing the door behind him, Blount decided that he had better go back to the Brauns' house for another look around . . . tomorrow.

They watched him go, and Aggie moved around the counter to stand next to Bob, resolved.

"Another beer?" she asked. "I'm buying."

"Nah, I can't let you do that," Bob protested.

"Don't worry about it. Beer is something we've got plenty of," she said. "Come to think of it, I may just as well close up shop and join you."

"Really?" Bob perked up a bit.

"Sure, why not? It's not like the customers are beatin' the door down trying to get in. I'm just wasting time and electricity, and you're looking a little blue. I say let's go upstairs and have us a party."

"Nothing to celebrate," Bob grumbled moodily.

"What the hell, we're alive, ain't we?"

"Ayah."

"I'm sure, given enough time and enough booze, we can think of something else." She took him by the hand and led him toward the back of the store.

14

He knew.

Rich Gascon had suspected for a long time, and now he *knew*. It had been going on right under his nose, and now he had *seen* it. The vision had come to him as he worked at the docks, hauling the catch from the boat. Nothing prompted him to question its veracity. The waves were lapping against the side of the boat, the sun glinted across the water, and then nothing. Everything went black, and he *saw* her. Rich had watched *her*, panting, pawing, slobbering over one of the Fletcher twins. A clear picture—like a photograph—of June, *his June*, drooling all over that damn boy. It caught him, smacking him right between the eyes like a wet fist, as he stooped over the snagged nets.

Rich had always known, but he had tried to deny it, tried to prevent it, telling her over and over again what he would do to her if he caught her. Now he was forced to recognize that what he'd believed all along was true. He had dreaded this moment, just as much as he had expected it, but now that it was upon him, Gascon felt not the white-hot heat of passion that he had in the past, but the cold, crystalline calm of rage.

And Rich knew what he must do. He had warned her what would happen if he found out she was cheating. He'd *told* her in infinite detail what he'd do to her if he ever caught her screwing around, and as suspicion hardened into certainty, he had shown her!

The bitch sure was dumb.

Gascon was beyond roaring reprisals. There would be no threats, no screaming rebuke, not this time. His stroke would be silent, swift, sure. There was only one problem, the Mordens.

Rich would not have that big, dumb cop Blount fucking everything up. Gascon didn't want to have that bastard arrive on his doorstep just as Rich was showing June that this time he meant business.

No, sir, the Mordens must be silenced.

His mind flitted around the "how" like a moth around a flame—reluctant to acknowledge the plan that was even now forming in his head—and for an instant his determination foundered.

Rich Gascon loved June—had loved her ever since the first time he'd seen her without braces. Loved her, wanted her, needed her. It didn't even matter that Sheridon had gotten to her first. Rich even forgave her her pregnancy. She had lost that baby, and Rich gazed down at his hands, wincing.

Rich didn't believe he could live without her. He didn't want to live without her. He'd always felt that way. That's why he had always been so scared of losing her. The flitting moth of his mind lit upon the scalding notion that perhaps he had driven her to this, with his constant accusations, when another vision hit with such force that he doubled over and sobbed. A slick cod slid from his fingers.

The Fletcher kid splayed across an old blanket of theirs—a blanket he knew she kept in the trunk, he knew because he'd checked, and now he knew why she had it—while June kneeled over him, taking his limp dick in her mouth.

Someone reached out to touch his arm, and the image shattered like glass, breaking into sparkling shards of hatred.

"You all right?" Charlie Remington said.

"Fine," said Rich in a voice as hard as rock, "just fine."

"Everything okay at home?"

Rich chuckled harshly, not a pleasant sound.

"Wanna go out for a beer after we're through so we can talk?" the other man asked.

Rich thought of a million different reasons why he shouldn't—he had to get home; he had *things* to take care of, neighbors to subdue—and then Rich surprised himself by saying yes.

Five hours later, dead drunk, Rich Gascon was headed for home. He ground his teeth, his jaw working from side to side like a horse champing at the bit as he reviewed his plan. The scheme came to him in pieces like a jigsaw puzzle, always in response to something Charlie said.

Good ol' Charlie had hit the nail right on the head, and he was right. Rich loved June, perhaps a bit too much. Charlie believed that Rich needed to let go, just a little, reminding the younger man gently that Rich wouldn't even let June have kids 'cause they'd take her attention away from him.

Gascon flinched, remembering what had happened during June's two pregnancies. Neither fetus had survived the beatings he had administered when he'd learned the news. He knew then as he knew now that those kids weren't his. Behind the wheel, Gascon sputtered rudely. Nope, he'd never believed those kids were his, and now he was sure of it.

What punk kid had fathered them?

His grip on the steering wheel tightened, and Rich wanted to rip the balls off of every male over the age of thirteen in Stockton Springs and Sandypoint.

Good ol' Charlie, though, had been right on both counts. Rich loved June, and he needed to let go, but Charlie didn't know the half of it.

Rich realized that he couldn't live with June. Not now. He wouldn't be able to look at her without seeing that punk's prick in her mouth. Neither could he live without her.

Briefly he thought of cutting off those lips and ripping out the tongue and the throat that had swallowed, fucking swallowed, the kid's semen; of slicing off the nipples which had been fondled by someone else; tearing out her vagina, and carving out the uterus which he *knew* had carried another man's child.

"Later, later," he counseled himself. Rich still had the Mordens to think of. Goddamn busybodies.

He always thought that old folks were supposed to lose their hearing, but nothing was wrong with their ears, and it seemed that they had nothing better to do with their time than eavesdrop. Rich could not afford to have them bringing that goddamn cop down on his head just when he was starting to get his point across.

Stealth, that was what was called for. Stealth.

The Mordens' home was only thirty feet away from Rich's. By some fortuitous quirk the two houses, built so close together, could boast no neighbors—the nearest being more than a half-mile away.

They lived on the side of Highway One opposite the beach. No lovely sea view for the Gascons—Rich had never made enough money to get one of the places by the bay. Those were reserved for summer folk, and if a body wanted to rent one of those year-round, you had to be able to pay summer rates.

Tonight, however, Rich decided it was a convenient arrangement. He cut the engine and turned off the lights as he crested the hill that led to their shared drive. All the alcohol in his bloodstream evaporated, and his mind cleared as he coasted to a stop before the house, blocking both driveways. *She* would not escape his retribution.

No way. Nohow.

He swung around and pulled his shotgun from the rack. As soon as his fingers brushed the cool metal, the last effects of intoxication vanished. He sat, surveying the two homes, looking for signs of life. Beyond them, the hill rose into the indigo blanket of forest, and from there, up to the muted sky. His home stood out in distinct detail. The light he had meant to fix and never got around to. The chipped paint, the jumbled pile of wood that he always promised to stack. His home provided a sharp contrast to the Mordens' place, with its manicured lawn and plethora of terminally cute garden statues.

Rich jammed a bullet into the chamber and shut it with a snap, glancing nervously at the other house. Then moving like a cat, he slipped from the pickup and sprinted across his uncut grass toward the Mordens' home.

Next to the fire Sheridon fed twigs to the flames. The blaze capered and cavorted, emphasizing the sharp lines of his face. A loon laughed in the background, a mocking scornful sound, and Jimmy chanted the now-familiar tune of the medicine man. The language was still foreign to him, and the words themselves meant nothing, but they held power. Jimmy scattered a handful of dried leaves onto the fire. They gave off a sick, sweet scent which he had grown immune to.

Sheridon watched the distant scene intently as the truck ground to a halt before two houses nestled together upon a rising hill. The deeper black of the forest merged with the gray-black sky. Jimmy shifted, recognizing both, and he knew that the hand that clenched the steering wheel was his to command. It was rough, scarred, scored with tiny cuts, and callused from hard labor, yet soft from constant exposure to salt water.

Chanting still, Jimmy reached behind him, and in the truck Gascon did the same.

The phone was ringing off the hook when Blount burst through the front door to his home that night. He glared at it distrustfully before answering it. He had given his statement already to the State Police earlier that day, and right now, he didn't need any more bad news.

It rang again.

Alan shuffled forward with a sigh. Unfortunately Ginny wasn't here to field the calls he didn't want. Besides, he told himself, it was probably her, checking in. Blount lifted the receiver guardedly and said a wary hello.

"Hi, honey," Ginny's familiar voice rattled through miles of copper wires, "how are things going?"

"Don't ask," he said. His heart slowed to a trot, and Blount deflated against the wall.

"It can't be all that bad."

"Yes, it can," he said as the picture of Sheila's maggot-ridden body surfaced from the inky recesses of the day. Blount rubbed his eyes with thumb and forefinger, as if he could erase the foul image with his action.

"That sounds ominous. Should I ask?" Ginny said.

"No, you shouldn't, but you will. Let's just say it's been something of a tough day."

She prodded. "So . . ."

"I found Sheila Erhart's body today. It looks like she'd hanged herself. From the look of it, she didn't do a very good job. She probably choked to death. Christ, the stench! They think she'd been dead a couple of weeks. Is that bad enough for you?" he snapped into the phone.

Stillness reverberated frostily through the lines, followed by a small "Oh."

"I'm sorry. It's not like it's any big secret. It'll be on the news tonight," he said. "It's just that it was kind of rough finding her like that, and I feel bad. No one had seen her for a while, and I should have thought to check up on her. Damn, Ginny, I'm losing my touch."

"You can't blame yourself, Alan," she said.

"Yes, I can. I'm their neighbor, their friend. These people rely on me. They don't call Belfast or Bucksport when something's wrong. They call me! And I should have known. She's a little old lady, ferchrissakes, and she was all alone."

"A lot has been happening lately. You know that. You've been busy, tearing yourself apart trying to be everywhere at once."

"I suppose, but after a day like this, all I want to do is turn in my badge. Let some young hotblood take my place."

"It's the rains," Ginny said. "That's enough to depress anybody. I know it's been getting to me. You should take a few days off and come down here to Portland. It's beautiful, sunny. I haven't felt this clearheaded in a long time. It's like a weight has been taken off my shoulders. Why don't you join me? The conference is only a couple of days."

"No, I can't take the time off. Besides, the rains have stopped now," he said. "I'll be all right. Don't worry about me. When you coming home?"

"Monday."

"Good. Look, I'm gonna get out of this monkey suit, this uniform stinks, and fix myself something to eat. You have fun, but don't go running off with some rich parson."

"You couldn't be so lucky."

"I miss you," he whispered into the phone.

"You sure you don't want me to come back tomorrow?"

"No, I'm fine. Just beat, that's all."

"Love you," she said, and the line went dead. The empty house closed in around him, sweltering and stuffy. The smell of death still cleaved to his clothing and his hair.

Blount removed his holster and his gun and ambled upstairs to take a shower. He scrubbed and scrubbed until his skin was raw, and then he scrubbed some more. When he was sure that there was no more skin left, Alan stepped from the tub, wrapped himself in a towel, and went to put his uniform in the wash.

Ginny would kill him. It was supposed to be dry-cleaned, but Alan didn't particularly care if it was ruined as long as he got rid of the smell. He added an extra cup of soap and then went to open every window in the house.

Staring into the refrigerator, he decided he couldn't stand the thought of food. A rather doubtful-looking head of lettuce suddenly sprouted features—eyes, a nose, and a mouth around which bluebottle larvae wriggled and writhed. Swallowing hard, Blount reached in and grabbed a six-pack. He'd drink his supper tonight.

He returned to the living room. For some reason he couldn't fathom, he had left his gun and his badge out, placing them on the table next to the easy chair rather than placing them in the drawer as he normally did. Beer in his hand, Alan stared at them, and they returned his stare with silent reproof. He upended the can, guzzling the beer, finished it, and belched.

Ginny was wrong. Alan couldn't shake the feeling that he should have done something, could have done something, for Sheila, for Ann. People here depended upon him. He could have, he should have, prevented this. Sheila Erhart was the most damning indictment of all. He had known that the area around the Point was flooded; he'd known that she didn't drive. She was effectively stranded, and he hadn't even thought to look in on her. She'd just slipped his mind.

The State Police said that there hadn't been any food in the house. She could well have starved to death, except that she had taken matters into her own hands, but no doubt she had gotten damned hungry first.

She had been alone for how long? Weeks. And he never thought to call on her, to check on her. Too busy breaking up fights, looking for that good-fer-nuthing Jimmy Sheridon, chasing after dead animals, and making sure that Rich Gascon didn't throttle his poor wife. Blount grunted and pulled another beer from the six-pack, brooding.

Eventually he fell into a light doze from which he would awaken intermittently to glare at the television and growl as some "hot-shit" detective careened through another blood-curdling chase scene.

Occasionally his eyes would fall upon the forty-five. The gun's barrel pointed at him from the table, like an accusatory finger. The blue-black muzzle seemed to whisper: *You're a community joke.* Blount, the comfortable old sheriff, typecast for some sitcom or funky mystery like "Murder She Wrote," left fumbling in the dark while he was outwitted and outfoxed by a little old lady.

The credits to Roger Corman's *The Pit and the Pendulum* rolled onto the screen. The dialogue penetrated, filtering through the sleepy haze. His psyche took it and ran with it, incorporating the plot into a dream where Vincent Price was poised with pseudo-Shakespearean grandeur next to Sheila Erhart's rotting corpse, reciting her epitaph with typically overwritten oratory.

His brain picked up the images, and everything in his dream was covered with red paint, or catsup, or whatever Hollywood used as blood these days. And he floated to a place where Corman's special effects blended with the still more grisly reality he had been living recently. A world of bruised purples, fuzzy greens, and purulent yellows. Of opened mouths and bloated tongues, and gaping bellies.

The first feature ended with typical histrionics and ear-splitting harmonics. He woke up long enough to notice that the second half of the Corman double bill, *The Tell-Tale Heart*, was beginning with the usual melodramatic flair. Dimly he thought he should take himself to bed before he descended again into a fitful slumber.

Boom-BOOM, boom-BOOM.

And Blount was lost in ruby fog, hands in his pockets. He stood before the old Sheridon place. The house was empty, derelict, taken over many long years ago by the county to pay for back taxes. Gideon still lived in the shed out back, and Blount—and everybody else who knew—turned a blind eye to his presence. It was, after all, the boy's only home.

Boom-BOOM, boom-BOOM.

A swirling crimson cloud interposed itself between himself and the building. Time contracted, and the paint on the modest clapboard house was fresh and whole again. It wasn't a big place, nothing fine or grand, but the Sheridons had always kept it clean.

Boom-BOOM, boom-BOOM.

He gazed down at a body grown suddenly lean, and he scowled. Something was wrong with all this—with the flat stomach, the fresh paint—but Blount couldn't quite put his finger on it. He tried to remember why he had come here. He knew he was here for a reason, but the pounding tom-tom beat kept distracting him.

Boom-BOOM, boom-BOOM.

His fist rapped loudly on the door, and Blount realized with a shock that the thud he had been hearing was the sound of his own hand knocking on their front door.

Suddenly Alan remembered. He had been called by a neighbor, concerned by the lights left burning for too long. But that couldn't be right, could it? This place wasn't occupied anymore. Hadn't been for a long time. The electric power should have been cut ages ago.

Blount backed away from the house and studied the upstairs window. Sure enough, the light was burning brightly, and the backyard was faintly aglow as though half-lit through the kitchen window.

In this dreamworld where time had been compressed, Alan was a rookie again. He hadn't been in the force long. He saw nothing particularly sinister about lights burning in a window. Perhaps the Sheridons had gone on vacation, or maybe they were visiting their relatives in the south, and left the hall light on as a deterrent.

Scarlet mist drifted past his nose, beckoning to him. Compelled, Alan followed the curling wisp around the side of the house. The ground sloshed wetly underfoot. The illumination from the kitchen was jaundiced, weak. Perhaps he'd better take a little peek.

Boom-BOOM, boom-BOOM.

Bile rose to his throat and adrenaline pumped into his veins. The Alan Blount upon the chair moaned. He had been here before; he knew it. His mind shrieked a warning to leave this tantalizing filament of cloud, so like the cold finger of death, and return to his car at once.

On the chair in his living room, Blount loosened his robe as the young rookie in his dream loosened his tie, feeling choked and claustrophobic.

Boom-BOOM, boom-BOOM.

Only feet from the house, from this vantage point Alan could see nothing, but he heard the child's tuneless humming.

"Well, I'll be damned," he said. The place was occupied.

Alan ascended the steps to the back door and looked in the window. His eyes were drawn immediately to the small square of light cast from the open refrigerator door. A five-year-old Gideon squatted among broken glass, picking olives from a pool of oil on the floor.

"Son of a bitch."

He straightened and the shift in position revealed something that before had remained unnoticed. The Sheridons' decapitated heads placed neatly on plates. Blount gagged. His fist hovered before the glass, in frozen horror. If it hadn't been for the blood and the hair, he might have mistaken them for children's toys, or Halloween masks. He hadn't realized then that he was spared the worst of the effects of their glassy-eyed stares and their openmouthed shrieks.

In his dream Blount vomited—right there on his nicely polished shoes. And in his living room an older version of Alan Blount bolted upright and heaved about a quart of beer onto the carpet.

"Shit," he mumbled, wiping his mouth with the back of his hand. On TV some actor clawed his way through the floorboards searching for the telltale heart as Blount got up from his chair to weave his way drunkenly into the kitchen for paper towels.

That had been one hell of a dream.

Christ, he hadn't thought of that incident for years. Hadn't wanted to, really. It had been his first truly gruesome experience as an officer, and one of the few times Jimmy Sheridon had come off smelling like a rose instead of the skunk that he was.

The young Jimmy had returned two days after his parents' death, and his alibi for the time in question was iron-clad. Although Blount had had his doubts when he met the old man who vouched for Sheridon. If the old coot was sober enough to tell one day from the next, Blount would have quite happily eaten Sheridon's shorts.

But there had been no proof to the contrary, and the child, Gideon, wasn't talking. In fact, he never spoke again, except in monosyllables. His young mind forever crumbled by the experience.

Then the often-outlawed Jimmy had turned vigilante. At the time Sheridon's grief had seemed excessive. As a family they had never been all that close, and Blount couldn't help but think that Jimmy's sorrow was staged.

Sheridon had led the manhunt to find his parents' killers, and the outraged citizens had followed like sheep. Forgetting that days had passed, they tore around the countryside to no apparent purpose. Unless one considered the shotgun wedding that the manhunt had precipitated, when a couple of teenagers were surprised in the act, as an accomplishment.

No, Blount hadn't thought about that incident in years. It was one experience he preferred to forget, and he often wondered what psychologists had to say about a cop's ability to quash certain memories. Ignobly, that had been the first time Alan Blount had lost his supper in his role as a police officer, but it wasn't the last. Alan had disgorged more lunches than he cared to remember. He had never gotten used to seeing the human body dismantled and dismembered no matter how many times he had seen it. He preferred the human form with all its pieces intact and not melded to a piece of fender, impaled upon a steering wheel after a car crash, or with its head served up on a plate.

That was just the problem, he thought, gazing wearily at the badge, *no stomach for the job.*

As weak as his digestion was, it was amazing Blount had acquired a beer belly. Sometimes if he was able to prepare himself, if he was forewarned—like today at Sheila's house —he'd be okay. Otherwise, he'd tossed his cookies, his cake, his doughnuts, and his coffee enough times to be humiliating.

Coward, the voice of conscience breathed at him. Grimacing, Blount leaned over to clean up his mess, but the beer had already soaked into the carpet. Blount took a few idle swipes at it and gave up, glad that he hadn't eaten.

More credits scrolled onto the television screen. Alan frowned at it, daring it to be another in the endless creature features they seemed to play on late-night television these days. It was. Swearing, he grabbed the remote and turned it off, before dropping shakily to the couch.

Something is wrong. Alan puffed noisily. *Of course something is wrong, you idiot,* he thought. *Everything is wrong.*

And he couldn't seem to keep on top of it all. People dying, or badly hurt, while he was running around like a chicken with its head cut off. Blount flicked through everything that had happened recently, ticking names off on his fingers until he ran out of fingers.

He wasn't as young as he used to be, and quite frankly he was getting tired of it. Blount looked gloomily at the wet splotch on the carpet and thought ruefully: *I should get out of the business.*

Still, something else was bothering him, and again he sputtered out loud, with a staccato spray of saliva. *What wasn't bothering him?*

Something specific. Something that had been brought to his attention today. Something that hadn't registered at the time, forced out of his mind by other, more spectacular events. And mentally Alan reviewed his day.

His conversation with Aggie, both before and after finding Sheila. His stop at the Brauns' place. The house spotless, except for the dying flowers and a few *Watchtower*s scattered on the dining room table. The basement, the mildewing laundry. That didn't seem like Hedda. If she were going to trifle with a load of laundry before a trip, wouldn't she have put it in the dryer at least? Blount retraced his steps to the front door. The unlocked front door. Why unlocked? Most people didn't bother with locks hereabouts, not like they did in the cities, but few left their houses unlocked and unattended for days.

And the heaping stack of mail in the box. If they had made a trip, there must have been some sort of urgency to it, or they would have notified the post office of their absence, wouldn't they? At least, they would have notified their neighbors.

"Sombitch," Alan said as he hefted himself from the couch. Aggie was right. He had to go out there. Tonight. He couldn't wait until the morning. Something was definitely wrong, and he *had* to find out what it was. He wouldn't get any sleep until he did.

The wolf crouched at the edge of a clearing. He neared the end of his journey. He stood straight and proud, ears erect. All symptoms of arthritis and age had faded. His fur was smooth and unblemished. The clouds of cataracts had cleared, and his eyes gleamed green where he paused beneath a streetlamp.

The beast panted, paused, sniffed, and panted some more. The stench of man was unavoidable, but for the gray shade, it was not a disquieting smell. Man did not plant fear in the massive lupine chest as it would an ordinary animal. This wolf had known man before, had been worshipped by him. In time beyond reckoning, the Indian and his clan had claimed the wolf as their own. The sound of the veneration still rang in the peaked ears with the same cadence and chords of the chant that called him now from afar.

Indeed, as the predator moved closer to the power's source, human faces would suddenly surface in the wolf's brain. Faces of past and present. He saw a little girl, with pallid skin and glittering red hair, and sometimes he found he looked through her eyes, gazing upon a woman whose skin and face were the color of grasses bleached by the summer sun. The wolf knew that the two were linked, for he would feel the bond of love and he would feel fear as a man, whose face was dark as his spirit, would suddenly appear.

Other times as the wolf moved among the human habitations, the predator found himself drawn back in time to view a world before the advent of white man. The old shaman of his past haunted both sleeping and waking moments, coming to the wolf as he last appeared, blood dripping from the self-inflicted wounds on his arms, chest and face, life's vital fluid gushing from the missing finger.

A coppery tang would fill the air, and the wolf would whine, for the shaman had given the wolf his pain, and the memory remained clear as if it were yesterday. In those last few moments the Indian embraced the shaggy beast who housed his soul, and the animal dragged a rough tongue across the bloody cheek. A blinding flash arced between human and wolf, and in that single moment the two had become one. The memories merged and all that the Indian had known and seen became the wolf's.

And the wolf-god in the guise of red man walked among white settlers, as the Indian had once done—both beast and man baffled by these people who built their homes not of bark and twig, which could be easily dismantled and transported, but of thick trunk and sturdy stone. The white built for permanence, foolishly believing that they could own the land upon which they dwelled.

In this living memory the wolf knew that the shaman had come to the white man's village in response to a call, for the settlers suffered from some mysterious sickness. The medicine man would not listen to his people, who said that these pale men were demons. He knew this could not be true. Did not the white man bleed when wounded? Did he not ail like any other man? True to his calling, the Indian took care of them, using woodcraft and lore, ancient and wise, roots and herbs. But one by one the settlers died. With more charity than his tribe, the shaman buried the last of them, according to their curious custom—although he did not house their bodies in a wooden box, unwilling to confine their souls—but the medicine man honored at least some of their traditions even in death, putting up the rigid tree they so adored above the final graves.

Then the shaman blessed the land around them, singing a funeral dirge to commend their spirits to the gods, though he had little hope that they would be accepted, for surely they must have angered the ancient ones to be so afflicted. With this thought in mind, the shaman beseeched the gods, calling upon the wind spirits to carry the blight away. The earth beneath his feet grumbled as if in protest, the tremor extending outward. The land foundered, and the sea rushed in, submerging all trace of the settlement and cemetery.

Breathing his thanks to unseen powers, the Indian had returned to his village of tepees, not knowing that death had followed him, lapping at his heels. Like the settlers before them, one by one his people had sickened and died. His tears and entreaties were as useless as his herbs. His prayers remained unanswered. His deity had deserted him; the gods spurned him, turning away from him and taking with them his power to heal.

Only the medicine man was spared, and when the Indian laid the last member of his tribe out with honor, he put a curse upon the white man—consecrated in blood, flesh, and bone—calling upon the earth to rise up and devour him should he return to profane this sacred soil once more.

The shaman had died of his wounds, a long and lingering death, and he had had time to regret what he had done. To ponder his blasphemy. Who was he to taint the land with his hatred? If the gods were angered and wanted vengeance, they would get it. They did not need his assistance, and so he tried to undo what he had done. He called the wolf to him one last time.

Then the shaman gave the wolf his remorse, his guilt. The grizzled god had nosed the inert body. Life's warmth lingered. The wolf licked the medicine man's face, wishing he would take his memories away, but it was too late. The body was nothing more than an empty shell and the wolf was caught in the Indian's curse.

The great beast understood the old man's loss and fury, for mourning was not new to him. In his long life, the wolf had lost many a mate and cub. Once he had watched as an entire pack was wiped out by hunters and their thundering sticks. Mothers were slaughtered and their babes clubbed. The anguish the wolf had known then mirrored that of the Indian.

The old man's spirit resided within wolf's breast, still, keeping the beast here long past his time. The predator wished to be relieved of this burden. So when the call had come, the wolf came gladly. Soon human spirit would pass from lupine breast to a mortal abode, and the beast would be freed. The spirit glow guided him to the mortal body that would reclaim the Indian soul and see the old man's malediction upon the stony soil expiated.

Blount brought the mail with him as he lumbered into the Brauns' house, shuffling through assorted circulars, bills, and letters. He studied the postmarks. The earliest letter was dated a week ago. The same day, in fact, he had come here to see Les about the goat.

Which meant that no one had been home since that day, or perhaps the day after.

The plot sickens.

So why hadn't Hedda mentioned it to him then if she was going to join Les on his buying trip? Blount was starting to feel more and more uncomfortable by the minute, recollecting her stilted, almost hostile attitude toward him. But Alan had gone through the house with a fine-tooth comb already once today. He'd opened closet doors and poked into each and every nook and cranny, even in the basement.

Reluctantly Blount recalled the chill that had come over him when he had looked at the freezer and opened it. A chill which he had then associated with its proximity and the sudden blast of arctic air when he had raised its lid. He remembered his relief when he'd discovered the completely innocuous packages.

Pushing his John Deere cap back on his head, he considered.

Packages of what? Freshly wrapped what?

Bread? Surely she hadn't baked some ten or fifteen loaves of bread that morning. Besides, the sizes of the packages, except for one or two, had been all wrong.

It was too late for berries, and he hadn't heard that they had purchased a cow or a pig for slaughter. He had come here early, then, around six A.M. What would she be doing wrapping up a hog or a side of beef at such an hour? That would have meant that she had been up all night sorting, wrapping, and freezing, and that didn't make sense.

Blount didn't like the direction his thoughts were taking him. What had seemed so simple and commonplace suddenly had sinister overtones.

So what had Hedda been wrapping before he'd arrived? Why had she found it necessary to hide the evidence, scooping the Saran Wrap and white paper into the drawer when he looked at it too closely? For it did seem, now that he thought about it, that her movements had been nervous and somehow furtive.

Blount dumped the mail on the table next to the phone, picked up the receiver, listened for a minute before replacing it in the cradle.

The line was dead. His gaze fell on an open phone bill, unpaid and long overdue. He hadn't been aware that the

Brauns were having problems making ends meet. Blount glanced at the date, and his feeling of dread intensified. Alarms went off in his brain, and the clamor in his head rose to fever pitch.

Without realizing what he was doing, Blount strolled through the house to the basement stairs. He faltered before the door, unsure of what he planned to do next. Open those packages? Only to learn that they had, indeed, bought a side of beef or she *had* baked some twenty loaves?

Then he thought again of the sizes and shapes of some of the packages. Some had been long and thin, too long and thin, come to think of it, to be any cut of meat that he was aware of. Except maybe a leg of lamb or a long strip of ribs. Others had been small and square, like hamburger. Patties, maybe.

Or a human hand.

"Oh, God." Alan leaned against the door for a moment. He had to know. Alan spun and opened it and descended the stairs quietly as though he feared disturbing someone. Again his resolve wavered as he stood next to the chest freezer, and again he was struck by its size and its shape.

Coffin-shaped.

"Stop it!" he said out loud and jumped at the sound of his own voice.

Blount lifted the lid and reached inside, pulling the first package from the top. About a foot long and four inches wide and flat on one end.

Like a leg of lamb.

His gaze flickered back inside the chest and rested on a single odd-shaped parcel. Big and round, about the size of a basketball, and he remembered his dream.

Boom, BOOM!

"No," he groaned.

Alan fumbled with the tape. The package was so cold that already his fingers were going numb. It slipped from his grasp and he caught it in midair. He tore savagely at the white paper, no longer concerned over the amenities of leaving no trace for the Brauns to find later.

He had to *know.*

A small cry escaped his lips as Blount stared in stunned disbelief at grayish-blue toenails attached to frosted toes. The bundle fell from nerveless fingers. The foot clattered icily against the cement floor. His stomach lurched.

With an audible gulp, he bent again into the freezer to confirm his finding. Not that there was any doubt.

Avoiding the ball, he picked a second package, larger than the first, both longer and wider. And round, tapering. Like a leg of . . .

Les. His gibbering mind supplied the word easily.

Alan ripped the paper aside to reveal dark brown hair curling off a blue-white calf.

"Jesus, sweet Jesus," he said as he stooped to fetch another parcel and open it.

Over and over again, as if he were obliged to retrieve and examine each and every appalling piece. A big masculine thigh and its mottled partner. A hand, small snowflake crystals embedded under each fingernail. Another foot and another hand.

Every instinct he had as a policeman cried out for him to stop, to leave the crime scene undisturbed and go radio for the State boys, but he couldn't. Just couldn't.

At this moment Blount wasn't an officer. He was a man, just a man, a horrified citizen who had been pushed too far for too long.

Each piece he unwrapped completely and examined thoroughly. Each a mute rebuke. And he swore, calling himself names as each hideous part was exposed, without even realizing he had been doing it. *Fool! Idiot!*

Les had been Alan's friend. They'd played baseball on the same Little League team as kids. They'd caught their first fish together. He'd even been an usher at Les's wedding. They'd gone their separate ways since then. Hedda had never particularly approved of Blount, who enjoyed his beer as much as the next man. The feeling had been mutual. Blount found her form of Christianity too severe, and as much as he tried, he could never find it in his heart to like her.

With each piece he lifted from the freezer, he heaped more abuse on himself.

Inept. And Alan studied a baby-blue knuckle.

Incompetent. A ragged flap of skin or a protruding bit of bone.

Until he had run out of names to call himself and had disintegrated to mediocre profanities. His pulse roared in his ears.

Boom-BOOM, boom-BOOM.

Until at last Blount had retrieved the head and gazed upon the waxy features of Les's slightly bovine face. Time slipped and merged, and Les's features were replaced with those of the Sheridons, whose detached heads he had found so many years ago, their mouths open in a silent scream.

15

Gascon slipped with a grace and skill, tucking his toe under twigs and brush and melting from shadow to shadow as he rehearsed each step in his mind. He knew the floorplan of the Mordens' home well. He knew that they hadn't slept together for years, and he knew which bedroom was Lilian's and which bedroom was George's. The information had been gleaned from years of proximity, dating back to the time when Rich was a kid, and the Mordens' son Ted had been a friend, before he had been killed in Nam.

Rich knew their habits and their routine. They kept a key in the flowerpot. He made a beeline across the lawn, knowing exactly where he was going. His feet moved without his conscious thought, sidestepping dead leaves and swerving to miss a plastic flamingo, a birdbath, and the little cut-out figures of the California Raisins.

Once Rich reached the back door, he hesitated fleetingly next to the hanging pot where they hid the key. One eye on the bedroom windows, he groped through the dying fern, grimacing when it rustled. Each small crackle sounded like fireworks on the Fourth of July in the still night air.

His fingers grazed something metal, and the key seemed to leap into his hand, confirming in his own mind the righteousness of his cause. Silently he moved over to the door.

Rich reviewed the layout that he had seen during his previous visits one last time, ticking obstacles off a mental list. The kitchen table was off to the left, the wastepaper basket next to the counter, and a vegetable stand next to the door.

Reasonably sure he had everything fixed in his mind, he entered and set off on a winding path, furtively moving this way and that—without so much as a creak—as if his feet knew which boards were safe and which were not. Through the kitchen and living room to the front stairs. Ascending the steps, one at a time, his foot hovering over the next, sliding right and left until it settled without a squeak. Sometimes he skipped a step instinctively.

By the time he had reached the top of the stairs, the stealth and reserve had taken their toll, and his breathing was labored. His heart thundered in his chest, and Rich wanted to throw all discretion to the wind and go screaming down the hall to blast those bastards to kingdom come, but he didn't. Something restrained him.

Rich couldn't remember if one of those old farts had a telephone next to the bed, and if he shot the wrong one first . . . He shivered at the thought.

So Rich allowed his feet to carry him slowly, following their intuitive trail with care, and felt vindicated when he stood between the open doors on opposite sides of the hallway.

This was perfect. Both beds were occupied, and all Rich had to do was take out one before pivoting to the next.

George let out a hooting snore, and Rich almost dropped the shotgun. Lilian rolled over and opened her eyes to stare straight at him. She struggled to a sitting position, a babbling protest rising in her throat, and Rich acted immediately. Cradling the butt against his shoulder, he squeezed the trigger.

And her face was gone, along with most of her head. It sort of blossomed outward like a scarlet flower. Rich was grinning like an idiot as he spun and released the contents of the other barrel into George's inflated beer belly.

Something had awakened Aggie. Perhaps it was the heat of false summer. The night muggy, hot—oppressive. The screens, which by happy chance she had never found time to exchange for storm windows, let in air so sluggish, so weighted, that it seemed to slither through the window and fall leadenly to the floor. Aggie felt no breath of breeze against her exposed breast or upon her cheek except when the fan dipped in her direction with a mechanical whir.

Its hum merged with the sound of Bob's snoring. Aggie rolled over onto her side and gazed at him—her expression one of nostalgia combined with pity—and wondered if she had taken leave of her senses. In a town this small it didn't do for a woman of her age to take a man into her bed, particularly a local. She was marked from that moment on as an easy lay, and every disgruntled husband within a five-mile radius would probably take it as his duty to try his luck with her.

But unusual circumstances often precipitated unusual responses, and last night she had needed his comfort as much as he had needed hers. Bob wasn't a bad sort. He was, after his fashion, a gruff gentleman who had had the misfortune to fall on hard times, and Aggie wasn't exactly unaware of the fact that he had been carrying a torch for her since high school.

Schoenwald smelled faintly of beer, and man, and Aggie smiled. She breathed deeply, savoring the smell. It was an odor she often associated with her husband, when he'd arrive home all happy after a day of fishing, smelling of cedar, pine, smoke, and beer. They would make love, as she and Schoenwald had made love last night, and she would rest her head on his chest, relishing his male smell. *Cedar, pine, woodsmoke, and beer.*

The fan revolved hypnotically in the dark.

Cedar, pine, woodsmoke . . .

Had Aggie been more awake and alert, she would have probably gotten up and checked the kitchen—the smell of smoke was so strong—but she didn't. Instead Aggie slept, drifting in clouds of woodsmoke and dreaming that her husband Jack was home, boasting about his latest catch.

Smoke! And voices, bitter voices, jeering voices, that whispered and hissed. They followed him day and night.

Ssssap. Sssssssucker. Los-s-ser.

Like the mocking laughter of children who hurled snow-balls and taunts as Bob tried to clear the village streets. *"Weirdo, queer, homo."*

Not queer, he thought, *just lonely. Sssooo lonely, for such a long time.*

Waking into the breathless twilight, Schoenwald moaned and rolled over to hold Aggie close, reveling in the dream made flesh and the fantasy fulfilled, and vowing that he would never let her go again.

The first shot rang out, a deathly knell that echoed across the night, and June was catapulted from sleep—blinking wildly as a second report followed the first. June slithered to the head of the bed to huddle in a fetal position.

No doubt about it. That had been no car backfiring. It had been a gunshot blast, and it came from the Mordens' house. She slipped from the bed. The police, she thought, she must call the police. Her gaze fell on Rich's truck parked in front of the house, and she realized with a sinking feeling that it was too late.

Rich had finally flipped. The Mordens were gone, finished, and she was next.

She froze, unable to gather her muddied thoughts around her.

He knew. He knew! The words played over and over again in her head like some deadly refrain.

Her eyes darted right and left. The truck was placed across the drive, cutting off all escape except through the woods, and her gaze sought the shadowy protection of the trees as a dark figure hurtled across the lawn. The movement freed her, and she threw herself at the closet.

The front door opened, and her legs turned to butter. June melted into a little pool of quivering nerves right there in the middle of the bedroom floor. She whimpered, covering her face with her hands.

Now that his retribution was upon her, June discovered that she was glad. She deserved this; she'd asked for it, been asking for it for a long time. She had never completely reconciled her behavior with her strict Catholic upbringing. Although she had discarded the teachings of the church many years ago rather than face the austere box of confession, June knew fear and she knew shame.

When Rich came upon her, crumpled in a heap upon the bedroom floor, she was praying as she hadn't prayed in years.

Beside the fire Jimmy's hand made little slicing motions. Sheridon stabbed at the air, viciously, and then he carved, sawing roughly at invisible prey.

The lascivious smile never left his face.

Blood everywhere. On the walls. On the floor. Even on the bed where Rich sat smoking a cigarette.

And the smell of gas. Rich dimly remembered blowing out the stove's pilot light before coming up the stairs. He had taken his time with her. As far as he was concerned he had all the time in the world.

Rich didn't shoot her, in either body or head, because then there wouldn't have been enough left of her to do what he wanted. Instead he had teased her, taunted her, told her what he knew.

He had listened to her plead and let her think if she begged real pretty, that he'd let her off the hook. He even let June give him a blow job, like she'd given the kid, and then he carved her up slowly, taking her tongue, her lips, her breasts, everything he had wanted to do. Last he had cut her uterus out.

The sound of her screams had been sweet music to his ears.

Now it was done, and Rich had to face the predicament he had chosen to ignore all the way home from the bar. He had repressed it even as he cut her, and she—when she still had a tongue—promised to be good.

Rich couldn't live without her. Didn't want to live without her. He was no good without her.

Tossing his cigarette to the floor, Rich took the gun, propped it under his chin, squirmed a bit until he was in a position that enabled him to reach the trigger with his thumb, and then compressed it in a leisurely fashion.

His body jumped, thrust back by the force of the bullet, and his corpse fell over June's. In death, his body draped over hers and his blood mingled with hers. Together for all eternity.

Birds in the surrounding forest twittered in alarm and fell silent. Downstairs the refrigerator kicked on.

And the house exploded.

Duke Defleurieu pitched fitfully in his bed, mumbling to himself. He rolled away from the window, with a hissed *sh-h-h.* He was tired of arguing with the voices inside his head. Voices he'd been hearing since September. Imperceptible at first, they took over his mind, filling it with continuous chatter. Whispering voices, their words indistinguishable, but their message was understood. They prattled alarm.

These same voices had told him to speak against Jimmy Sheridon that night. How long ago was it now?

Defleurieu shook his head. They had fooled him into believing he could stand against Sheridon. They had lied.

They wouldn't fool him again.

The clock in the hall chimed midnight. He tensed. Something rustled in the bushes in back of the house. His ears strained for the sound—judging its volume and its quality. Its threat.

Just the wind. The tension in his muscles eased slightly. *Afraid of things that go bump in the night, eh?*

Yet as Defleurieu lay on his bed with his eye, or what was left of it, throbbing, he could easily imagine that crazy bastard, Sheridon, coming back to finish the job, and for the umpteenth time Duké wondered if he had been wise to let Alan talk him into signing the complaint against Jimmy.

One down, and one to go.

Chuckling softly to himself, Jimmy poked the coals. Duke tossed and turned on his bed.

"Little man," Sheridon whispered. This person, more than anyone else, was the enemy. Defleurieu kept Jimmy from his home, keeping him in exile.

Sheridon isolated a particular coal, separating it from the rest, and prodded it, pushing it around the fire. And Duke tossed some more. Absentmindedly, Sheridon tapped his belt buckle with his knife, and on the bed Duke Defleurieu sat up, good eye wide open and staring.

Outside, something fell over with a metallic clatter. Defleurieu snapped upright, and the pressure of the action made what had once been his left eye ache. Whatever it was clanged stridently. He relaxed—coons, most likely, getting into the garbage—and he settled farther down in bed, pulling the covers protectively around him.

Then the part of him that had once been a lumberjack rebelled. He, Duke Defleurieu, would not sit here quaking in his bed like some old woman. Eye or no eye. Crazy bastard or no crazy bastard.

If that sombitch Jimmy Sheridon had come back to finish the job, well, Duke Defleurieu was not going to go quietly. He'd make goddamn sure that Sheridon knew he'd been in a fight. Perhaps Duke didn't have the muscles he once had, but he had a gun.

Defleurieu got out of bed. The room swam around his head, and he waited, crouched, until he had regained his sense of balance. He cursed his injury. He had not expected this amount of debilitation. Duke absolutely *hated* the dizzy spells that left him swooning like some sissy schoolgirl.

Losing an eye, he had discovered, was like learning how to

live all over again. He couldn't even pour himself a glass of milk because his depth perception was shot. Not too long ago Duke Defleurieu had never even heard of the term *depth perception,* and now it was a factor in everything he did. The glass wasn't where it appeared to be, so he had to stick his finger in it like a blind man just to make sure he hit it.

Neither was the furniture where it was supposed to be, what with the neighbors helping out around the house, and he was tripping constantly. Even the floor couldn't be trusted. It bucked and dodged under his feet. Duke headed for the living room, where he kept his gun. He'd have to fill the gun with rock salt. He sure as shit couldn't aim at anything and expect to hit it now.

A vague shadow flitted across the square of wall, illuminated by the faint light of the unseen streetlamp on the opposite side of the street. He waited for the next sound. None came. Kids maybe. Tomorrow he'd probably find some smutty word painted on the side of the house, or the trees wrapped in toilet paper.

No, things had changed since his little run-in with that creep Sheridon. Now no sound was innocent, and the fleeing shade could just as easily hold a gun or a knife as a can of spray paint or a roll of Charmin.

His progress down the short unfinished hall to the stairs was shaky. He felt along the walls, tearing his fingers on exposed wires, and he promised himself he was gonna put the plates back on the switches just as soon as he could. Groping his way down the stairs, Duke misjudged the last step, slipped, and rebounded off of a well-known piece of furniture. He stumbled over the rug and swore vehemently.

"Goddamn, son of a bitch. I'm gonna clean this hall," he murmured to himself. He'd been meaning to do it ever since his wife had died.

Sheridon played with the single coal, batting at it, poking at it. Then he gave it a twirl or two.

"I'm coming to get you, little man." He shoved the ember across the fire and back again.

"And you"—he tapped it—"can't—*"tap"*—see"—*tap*
—"me." *THWACK!*

Intermittently Duke would pause and peer into the night
with his remaining good eye, trying to discern movement.
He flung open the door to the gun cabinet and reached for
the shotgun only to misjudge and miss it by an inch.
Defleurieu swore harder.

He should'a kept it next to the bed.

His fingers closed around the breech, and then he began to
toe the darkness. His foot hit something hard, but pliant or
slightly so. With a grunt he bent to pick up the bag of rock
salt he kept next to the front door, ready to use to clear the
stoop of snow, and then he fled as swiftly as he could back to
the bedroom.

"Shit," he said when confronted with the prospect of
loading the gun half-blind. Defleurieu pulled a *Sports Illus-
trated* from the bedside table and made a funnel. By the time
he'd finished, Duke reckoned he'd be sleeping with rock salt
for a month, or until he next changed the sheets—
whichever came first.

But the gun, at least, was loaded, and he was armed now.
Nothing, no one, could hurt him without taking a faceful of
salt for his trouble. And maybe lose an eye or two. He
laughed mirthlessly. It seemed fitting justice.

Duke started to drift, comforted by the feel of the gun at
his side. Tomorrow he would find out if his nocturnal visitor
had left any clues of his passing. He felt the soft caressing
arms of slumber. A silhouetted image played across his
eyelids. His brow furrowed and he floated somewhere
between sleep and wakefulness.

A soft step, a muffled noise. His eye popped open.
Somebody was out there, goddammit! He knew it.

Another muted rustle came to him from inside the house.
He stood, and his heart clapped against his ribs so hard that
Duke was sure he was having a heart attack. So he was
surprised that when the next pain hit it struck him right
between the eyes—or more accurately, eye—arrowing
through his hollow left socket. Searing, blinding agony—or

it would have been if Defleurieu had not already been blinded—and the older man was forced to relive that scalding torture Sheridon had inflicted on him, all over again. Only this time it didn't stop with his eye. It pierced the bony socket and ricocheted around his brain. He folded.

Defleurieu opened his mouth to speak. "Ah-ah-ah-ah-ah-ah" was all that came out.

The noise gurgled in the back of his throat as blood slammed through his body, thundered past his temples and into his skull, only to leak outward from the weakened vessel wall into his brain.

The world around him turned gray. One arm was pinned helplessly under his body, and the other hand fluttered ineffectually. Defleurieu tried to move and found he was paralyzed.

The gray faded, and his one good eye rolled around in its socket as what was left of his thinking brain sought something it could identify. The umbra swirled, and his eyeball pivoted until it found an anchor.

The last thing Duke Defleurieu saw before the world went black was Jimmy Sheridon leering at him from a sheet of flames.

THWACK! Sheridon brought the stick down on top of the glowing embers with savage fury, and a shower of sparks spiraled toward the heavens.

It was time to go home.

Whistling, Jimmy threw dirt on the fire. It smoldered, reluctant to relinquish its power. He rose and pissed on the feeble flame, and the light in Duke Defleurieu's eye guttered and went out.

16

Robert Schoenwald woke to find Aggie watching him. He reached for her sleepily, still believing this to be a dream. His hand connected with soft flesh, and he realized this phantasm was real. Playfully Aggie ran her fingers across his chest. A small voice inside his brain told him to take her while he still had a chance. He pulled her over on top of him and entered her, and she let him.

It had to be a dream.

As they made love, the voice inside his head clamored, directing him to shut down his home in Sandypoint, grab Aggie, and run as far away from Stockton Springs as he could.

The village was cursed, it said.

Aggie gazed down on him, a small smile curling her lips, and he shut out the voice. This was all that was important. This moment, here and now. For years Bob had waited, and now that he had what he wanted, he didn't want to lose it. Aggie rode him lazily, a slightly bemused expression on her face. Robert arched into her until . . . he was unable to contain himself anymore, and . . .

Kaboom!

. . . the earth moved.

The windows vibrated violently in the shutters, and the entire building shook. Little glass bric-a-brac performed a clattering jig across the dressing table. In the store below them something fell to the floor with a bang. Schoenwald twisted under her, caught in a rippling orgasm; Aggie halted, mouth agape.

"Son of a bitch," she uttered.

Bob opened his eyes to stare at her, just becoming aware that the explosion he had felt was something other than his own ejaculation.

"Wha-wha-what was that?" he said.

"I don't know." She climbed off of him and scooted over to the side of the bed, reaching for the telephone.

Schoenwald rolled over, dazed. The voices in his head, so recently silenced, were screaming at him now, and he wanted to hit the receiver out of her hands, seize her, and flee this demon-ridden place. Her fingers trembled as she stabbed at the dial, and she missed.

"Should'a gotten one of those push-button jobs when I had the chance," she grumbled.

"Who ya calling?" Schoenwald asked.

"Blount, of course," she said.

"But—" His words faltered and died as he gawped, out the window, at the aurora glowing in the western sky. "Oh, my God, look."

Receiver cradled between shoulder and ear, Aggie followed his gaze to the hillside behind the store where the horizon burned a bright orange.

"Well, I'll be damned," she muttered. She hung up the phone, picked it up again, and started to dial the number for the fire department.

Alan Blount was standing next to a neatly stacked pile of frozen body parts when a boom rattled through the house and the earth surged beneath his feet. Blount rode it as he would the crest of a wave, bending his knees for balance, and then numbly, as though surfacing from a dream, Alan glanced around the room, trying to locate the source of the disturbance.

A hand separated from the pile beside him and tumbled with a dull thud to the cellar floor. Head cocked to one side, Blount stared at it and thought idly, *He's thawing.*

With a groan Blount swung around and lumbered up the stairs to the kitchen, picked up the phone, and, finding it dead, shuffled out to the car to radio for backup.

Out in the dooryard he was confronted by a fiery sky in the west.

"Son of a bitch." Alan ducked into the driver's seat to make the call.

Highway 15 curved before him, curling and uncurling like an asphalt serpent, and the lines of yellow and white coiled in the tunnel of light created by the truck's headlights. Trees sprang from each new twist in the road. An owl frightened by the vehicle's arrival sailed before the windshield, and Sheridon swerved to avoid hitting it.

Jimmy whistled tunelessly to himself. He liked driving at night, when the traffic was nonexistent and he could get the old pickup up to speed and fly around the many twists and bends of Maine's highways.

The radio chattered, some late-night call-in program, and Jimmy turned it off and began to sing a country-and-western tune. His severed finger lay on the car seat beside him. It was wrinkled, and ripe, but he had grown oblivious to the smell. He had nurtured it, wrapping the digit in moss to keep it moist.

The highway widened, straightening as it approached Bangor. In a hurry Sheridon wanted to avoid the convoluted streets of the city—which were laid out like the spokes of a wheel, each leading to its center—driving the longer way around until he navigated the spaghetti bowl where Interstate 95 and 395 intersected above 1A. He ignored the plaster monstrosity, a huge statue of Paul Bunyan that guarded the gateway to Maine's far north, and followed the latter road, heading for the coast.

Through the sleeping burg of Hampden beyond the large supermarket, until the night swallowed him up again. Away from the towns, the stars held dominion over man's insipid light. He had just started down the steep descent into Wintersport when he detected the flush in the eastern sky too early for dawn.

His foot hovered over the gas for a minute. He laughed softly to himself as he accelerated beyond the sharp bend near Wintersport's post office onto the final stretch of road that would take him home.

The phone rang and rang. One time, two times, three times. Watching Robert, Aggie extended a single finger for each ring she heard on the other end of the line until she ran out of fingers.

"Hmm," she said as she replaced the receiver. "I guess Alan's not home."

Schoenwald reached up to stroke her back, and she smiled wanly. "Maybe he's there already," she commented. Bob cradled his head in his hands.

"You all right?"

"Fine," he said, rubbing his eyes roughly.

"How about some breakfast? I'll go down and get some eggs from the store. I don't think I'm going to be able to get any more sleep until I know what's happening." Aggie tugged at her robe. "It's too hot anyway."

Schoenwald grunted, and Aggie hesitated, gazing with concern at his troubled expression. "Are you sure you're all right?"

"Just a headache, that's all. Probably the beer." Bob grimaced. "I guess I made a real fool of myself last night."

She grinned at him. "Not at all."

He watched her as she padded across the room. His head throbbed, and the urgent voice that had been telling him to run screeched shrilly in his ear, keeping time with the pounding in his skull.

Doomed, it seemed to say, and Bob saw a narrow strip of Highway 1A unfold before him. Trouble was coming out of the west, and soon it would settle in their midst.

No more, Bob thought. He couldn't handle any more. He'd lost his job; he stood to lose his home. But last night he had found something, and Bob didn't intend to lose that, too.

Rousing himself, Schoenwald slipped into his pants, ready to go after Aggie and persuade her somehow to depart with him, leave this town, before trouble landed on their doorstep.

The wolf trotted through Bangor. He stole through yards and wound between homes like a shade. The predator loped through the park, past the tennis courts, and paused to lift his leg and urinate, signaling his disdain for man's mastery over this land that was once his.

The beast glanced up and flinched momentarily, for there stood the biggest man he had ever seen. An immense monument to human frivolity. The figure towered above the gray shadow, with legs the size of tree trunks. A giant ax rested upon its shoulder. The wolf sniffed at the concrete block upon which it stood.

The man-scent was faint, only a remnant of those who had gone before him, perhaps to pause and contemplate this folly as the wolf did. This was no living being. To emphasize his sovereignty, the predator cocked a leg one last time and squeezed out a few more drops before moving on toward the wide boulevard.

His journey had been long—too long—and the great beast wondered if he was going to be too late. The sense of urgency grew, the route had been selected for him, and, compelled, the wolf followed the designated path like a hound on the trail—sniffing out his quarry.

The great gray shade bounded across the empty main thoroughfare, past large buildings, until he reached a slight incline that led up to the twisting ramp of the interstate.

The wolf turned away from this, racing through the short tunnel east, to stalk the illumination of false dawn.

They leaned at their usual stations in uncomfortable silence. Aggie glowered over her cup at the egg carton. Schoenwald had taken leave of his senses, she was sure. Bob wanted her to pack up and go with him, now, this minute, this day, just lock up the store, abandoning both it and her home, never to return again.

Perhaps she should have been flattered, thrilled right down to her toenails—proposals of marriage didn't come all that often—but his proposal was quickly followed by this strained plea to flee, motivated not by infatuation, but by fear. She saw that in the quick darting of his eyes and in the quaver of his voice. No "let me take you away from all this"—just "we gotta run; we gotta hide."

Aggie hedged, hemming and hawing, and the rejected Schoenwald slumped over the Formica surface, mumbling to himself about curses.

There was a knock on the front door, and they both jumped. Blount's disembodied face floated next to the plate-glass window at the front of the store. Aggie hustled around the counter to let him in.

"My God, what happened?" she asked. His skin was positively green. "You look ill."

He waved her question away, headed for the refrigerator at the back, grabbed a bottle of wine, opened it, and made a good stab at draining it.

"Almost didn't recognize you in your civvies," she said.

He raised the bottle, and his throat moved up and down. Wiping his mouth with the back of his hand, Blount faced her and burped.

"Moving up from beer to wine? Soon you'll be hitting the hard stuff," Aggie reproved him gently.

Blount shot her a warning look, but she continued.

"I tried calling you earlier. What the hell was that big boom?"

Blount reached for another beer. "Dunno. Something on fire, I 'spect."

217

"Aren't you going to find out?"

"Naw, let the police take care of it," he said.

"Police?" She mouthed the word at Bob. He shrugged.

"Don't worry, I called 'em," Alan said. "Radioed it in, when I called the State boys. So the police and the fire department, whoever is needed, should be here anytime now. They'll probably be crawling all over the place by morning."

"They? Last I heard, *you* are the police," Aggie reminded him, adding with blunting humor, "or the closest we got to it."

"Not anymore, I'm not. Gonna give 'em my badge in the morning."

"What? You're kidding, aren't you?"

He peered at her with one eye closed. "Nope, never been more serious in my life. I can't handle any more of this, and I think it's time to retire. I'm gonna grab my wife in Portland and hightail it off to some place cushy and soft, like Florida. I don't want to be here when winter sets in."

Schoenwald toasted the air with his Styrofoam cup. Coffee sloshed over the sides. "I'll drink to that," he said.

Aggie disregarded him, concentrating her attention on Blount. "You can't just up and quit like that. We depend on you."

"That was a mistake," Blount said.

"Why? What happened?"

"I just found Les Braun," Alan replied.

"That's good. How is he?" She caught something in the officer's expression and ventured cautiously, "Everything's all right, isn't it?"

"Oh, everything's just dandy as long as Les don't mind being in about thirteen pieces."

Her legs gave out from under her, and she plopped, gracelessly, down on a stack of banded newspapers.

"It would appear," Alan continued, "that Hedda's a pretty dab hand with an ax."

Jimmy Sheridon was flanked by twin dawns as he drove north along Highway One. To the east, the sky blossomed the pale peach of morning. To the west, it burned yellow with incandescent heat. The once-handsome face, now lined with fine scars, contorted into a smile.

He passed the Stockton Springs turnoff and headed toward the beach road. His hand went to the gruesome package to his left, picked it up, and placed it on his lap.

The smile spread so wide that it looked like his face would crack, and the skin around his mouth *did* split, a small trickle of blood escaping from the corner of his mouth and dribbling onto his chin.

Christmas was going to come early this year, Jimmy thought, and he knew to whom he was going to present this grisly gift.

He saw the familiar hotel up ahead. Sirens wailed. A ruby-red shaft split the sky somewhere up ahead, adding to the confusion of twin dawns.

Jimmy signaled left, turning away from the little mobile home toward the leaping amber horizon, the villain come to view what he had wrought. He followed the light to the Gascons' home. He could have found it easily enough. Even if it hadn't been blazing, he knew the way blindfolded. Jimmy had, upon more than one occasion, availed himself of June's attentions if nothing better presented itself. He of all people in Stockton Springs was aware of her secret, and she *knew* what would happen if she refused.

Sheridon pulled over some distance away from the fire, parking behind a tangled clump of trees. A fire engine careened blindly by as he stepped from his truck. Jimmy noted the town's name written on the side of the vehicle: Bucksport. He slipped between the trees when a second one arrived, siren blaring. Searsport.

It must be one helluva blaze.

With practiced ease he moved from shadow to shadow, aided rather than revealed by the frenetic leaping light of the flames. The Gascons' house looked like a bomb had hit it, and the Morden home was also ablaze.

Sheridon needed no more convincing that what he had experienced up at the camp was real. Here was living proof of the destruction he had seen on the smoky screen. He had no doubts that they would find the charred bodies as he had seen them, with Rich draped over June—or at least part of her—and the Mordens, blasted in their bed.

The heat was intense. Only the wet ground, saturated still from the recent floods, prevented the woods behind the two homes from bursting into flames. The scars in Sheridon's face deepened, and the sneer turned into a scowl.

This would never do.

He closed his eyes, clenched his jaw and fists. Fine beads of sweat sprang onto his forehead as Jimmy reached into himself, through himself, to the earth below his feet. At first its cold dampness leeched him of life and drained him of warmth, but as Sheridon concentrated, his own internal temperature began to rise, until the heat inside himself was so intense it demanded outlet, and he let it go so that it radiated outward, spiraling out through the rocky soil. Soon Jimmy was hot, and had he been aware of himself and what was happening around him, he might have paused to shed his jacket. But Sheridon wasn't cognizant of his body or the perspiration that soaked through his shirt to the light denim coat. All he could feel was the grainy texture of the earth, the hardness of the granite, and the weight of ages pressing down on him.

The heat of the fire poured through him, from his feet into the ground, corkscrewing down and swirling away from him. Drying the soil between himself and the baked earth that surrounded the houses. Roots shriveled away from the heat, and trees began to roast and die. The moisture boiled, steaming and evaporating, until the land beneath his feet was as scorched and arid as a desert, and he knew he had bridged the gap between earth and flame.

Sheridon opened his eyes, pulled a handkerchief from his pocket—crusted and dirty, the same he had used to bind his hand—and grimaced. A small hawthorn next to him burst into flame, and Sheridon, seeing this small token of success, darted away from the burning bush, laughing.

* * *

The light went on in the trailer as Jimmy pulled into the drive and parked behind the old Ford. He let the truck choke, quiver, and die, and he waited.

A face appeared at the window, and Jimmy felt revulsion at the pale features and almost snow-white hair. How had he ever touched her, made love to her? She had been okay as a meal ticket, but . . .

The door swung open, and Leah stepped into full view, the rifle braced at her hip, and his brow went up, questioning. This was not the Leah he remembered, ready to defend herself against him of all people. There she stood, gun at her hip like some backwoods Annie Oakley, and Sheridon paused to wonder what had happened to her in the intervening weeks. Of all the townsfolk Leah had been one of the few he hadn't been able to reach through the flames, and with Leah glaring at him from behind a rifle, Jimmy had time to ponder the gaps in this control. He noticed a flicker of blue out of the corner of his eye. His gaze went to the circle cut into the ground around the mobile home, and he frowned.

Then Jimmy trained his features into a smile and jumped from the cab. The gun swung round to greet him, and he ducked, hands extended in a placatory gesture.

"Who the hell are you, and what the fuck are you doing with Jimmy's truck?"

For a moment his jaw moved soundlessly as Sheridon tried to comprehend what she was saying. He put his hands up and smiled harder.

"Hey, babe, it's me. It's Jimmy."

The gun wavered and then dipped.

"Jimmy?" Leah said. "Jesus Christ. You look like hell. What's happening? What are all the sirens for? Cops after you?"

"Who, me? What for?" He opened his hands to reveal empty palms. "Wha'cha holding a gun on me for, babe? Put it down."

"Maybe I don't want you here. There's a warrant out for your arrest. Defleurieu signed a complaint against you. You hurt him bad, real bad," she said. "That prick Blount's been here damned near every day, at least, when he's not busy tripping over dead bodies."

"Well, I don't think Blount's gonna be a problem anymore," Jimmy said. "Defleurieu, either," he added as an afterthought.

"Wha'd'ya mean?" And the gun's muzzle rose a few inches. "Did you do something to that poor man?"

"What, me? Naw. How? I've been out of town. What could I possibly do to him?"

"I don't know," Leah said uncertainly.

"Are ya gonna keep me out here all morning?" he said. She conceded, backing into the trailer, still gripping the gun tightly.

"What's that for?" he asked, indicating the rifle.

Leah looked at it, confused. "Oh, yeah." She gave a small nervous twitter. "Things have been kind of strange around here lately. Besides, I didn't know it was you. You look like shit."

"Been sick lately," he said as he placed his foot on the rickety metal stair. "I'd feel a lot better if you'd put that gun down."

"Ah, yeah, sure," she said, leaning it against the wall.

He emerged into the light. Leah took in the missing finger, the scarred face, and gasped. Tiffany's head appeared from behind her mother, and Jimmy swung on her. The child retreated to the far side of the room, making herself as small as possible, and Jimmy pounced—her mother forgotten. He lifted the child from the floor so that her face was only inches away from his own.

"Hi, squirt," Jimmy said in a voice oily and smooth and full of false enthusiasm. "Did ya miss me?"

The girl squirmed and glanced imploringly at her mother.

"Put her down, Jimmy. If you've been sick, what ya got might be catching."

"Catching?" Jimmy chuckled as if Leah had just said something funny. "I'll say it's catching, wouldn't you, squirt?" He deposited her on the floor.

"Look, Jimmy, I think—" Leah started.

Ignoring her, he went on, his voice taking on a menacing note. "Got a little present for you, kiddo."

Both mother and daughter looked stupefied. Jimmy dug around in his pocket. His hand surfaced, clutching a small parcel wrapped in green moss.

The aroma of rotting meat began to circulate through the mobile home. Leah gagged while Tiffany tried to push her way through the cheap paneling.

"Here." Sheridon shoved the parcel at her.

Tiffany stuck her finger in her mouth and shook her head no.

"Here!" He waved it under her nose. "Take it."

The child whimpered.

He backed off slightly and his voice softened. "It's something special, something just for you."

Glancing first at her mother, who nodded gruffly in assent, Tiffany took it. With tremulous fingers she unwrapped it, dropping it as soon as its contents were revealed.

The withered finger rolled to her feet, pointing straight at her, and she cowered against the wall, whining. Then Tiffany's face went blank, and she folded. Her limbs started to twitch and writhe in a convulsion.

For an instant neither of them moved. Leah's mind was slow to react. Jimmy saw her confusion and threw back his head and howled.

"You bastard, what have you done to her." Leah launched at him, and he belted her—good. At that moment the door in the hall opened, and Gideon stumbled, blinking sleepily, into the room. His eyes took in the child jerking pathetically in the corner and Jimmy looming over Leah.

"What the hell is *he* doing here?" Sheridon said, pointing at his brother.

Leah straightened, temper flaring. "He's been stayin' here. I told you things have been weird lately. I didn't want to be alone."

"So you're fucking my half-wit brother now?" He snorted. "Is that the best you can do?"

The younger man's eyes sparked with a twinkle of con-

sciousness, and he lunged toward his hated older brother—
arms flailing, hands balled into fists. His attack was clumsy.
His punches wild. All the more reason to avoid them,
Jimmy reasoned, and he dodged them, ducking out the front
door. Gideon swerved to continue his awkward arm-
swinging advance.

Leah edged toward Tiffany, who now lay still and lifeless
on the floor, and knelt by her side.

"Look what you've done, you son of a bitch!" Leah
screamed at him. "Stay away from us and take this with
you."

She hurled the finger at Jimmy.

"I'll be back, Tiffaneeeee!" Sheridon shouted over his
shoulder and raced for his truck.

Gideon hunched, a lump of human flesh on the torn sofa.
Leah paced back and forth, and as she walked to and fro, she
mumbled to herself, "He's nuts, absolutely nuts."

She spun and headed back the way she had come. "What
did I ever see in him?"

Stirring himself, Gideon looked around the hospital waiting room. He didn't like this place. It smelled—he wrinkled
his nose—funny. The blue-white light overhead hummed
and hummed, reminding him of someplace else, someplace
where dead people go, someplace where . . .

He shook his head. It was too much trouble; he couldn't
follow the tangled thread of thought through to its conclusion.

Leah paused in the middle of her tirade about damned
men and dreamily patted the pocket of Tiffany's frayed
sweater. The movement caught Gideon's attention, and he
leapt up, grabbing the garment from her hands, and quickly
dug in the pocket looking for the two ivory pieces, finding
nothing. Shocked, he stared at the sweater and said nothing
when Leah grabbed it back again.

A man with big floppy ears advanced upon them from the
curtained examination area. Leah turned to face the doctor.

"Is she all right?" she asked.

"Well, the EEG reading is a bit, ah, strange."

Leah dropped into a chair. "She has epilepsy, then."

"Well, I'm not really sure. I'm a GP and no expert on reading these things. It's just that the line seemed, well, a bit off; but I'm going to have to send it off to a specialist for an accurate reading. It probably wouldn't hurt if she went into the big hospital in Bangor for more tests."

"How much will that cost?"

"Cost?" The doctor looked at her as if she were a peculiar specimen. "You mean you don't have insurance?"

"No."

"Well, maybe we can try her out on a child's dose of Dilantin," he said. "Tell me, how often does this happen?"

Stockton Springs resembled a war zone, or so Aggie thought. Not that she had ever been to a war zone. The closest she had been to one was watching news clips on the late-night news. But it was how she had imagined one to be. The place was crawling with uniforms, all of them sporting guns. The air crackled with the sound of car radios, and the buzz of static was more common than human speech. The State fuzz were here, and both Belfast and Bucksport had contributed officers to help pick up the pieces. Firemen, representatives of several different departments, clumped around in slickers and boots. Vans from the two Bangor TV stations were parked off to one side, and it was rumored that another was due to arrive from Augusta or Portland, or somewhere else farther south.

Aggie noted with satisfaction that Blount had reluctantly donned his uniform and joined the general hubbub of activity, directing people this way and that.

A Sunday, the school was closed, and all those who didn't have to work a shift at the Bucksport lumber mill hung around the half-block section between store and post office, which was Stockton Springs' downtown. At first glance an outside observer might have mistaken the gathering for an old-style town meeting or a Sunday social, unless looking closely, one noticed the wearied and harried expressions of the participants.

Sales had been brisk, people stopping at the store for Coke

or beer and the latest news—Aggie being considered a reliable source. She provided what information she could, while a sullen Bob Schoenwald leered at her like a gargoyle from the back room. She couldn't seem to shake him out of his depression.

From her place behind the counter Aggie saw gaps in the crowd. People conspicuous by their absence. Ominous gaps. Sheila Erhart, Ann Blisson, David Garreth, the Brauns, the Gascons, and the Mordens. Not as haunting, but no less glaring, was the absence of the spouses—Lorraine Garreth and Timothy Blisson—and the many others who had just slipped away from Stockton Springs, having given up on the place or gotten lost in the fog.

By this time everyone knew about Les Braun, and the Gascons, and the Mordens. They collected hushed and stunned in groups. There had been too many deaths to assimilate. Occasionally one person would lean over to another and whisper something in an attentive ear. Then both heads would bend together in fruitless speculation.

Someone came in for a pack of cigarettes, and her attention was diverted from the window as the Fletcher twins separated from the assembly and started back toward the Point and home.

The boys walked away, silently, in unspoken agreement. If someone had looked close, they might have noticed something strange about their expression. But no one looked; each member of the milling crowd was caught in their own nightmare reality, trying to make sense of the senseless.

"Maybe it wasn't us," Terry said.

"You heard 'em." Eddie indicated the police with a quick dip of his head. "She was dead before the fire. He killed her." He dashed the tears away. "She said he was jealous."

"Well, maybe there was someone else."

Eddie stopped dead in his tracks and glared at his brother. "No." He shook his head. "No, I don't believe it."

"I wonder what could have set him off," Terry mused. He thought guiltily of yesterday's encounter and fell silent.

The church bells pealed, calling the congregation to

worship. Behind them, no one moved to answer the summons.

Jarred from their reverie by the clanging, the boys started, proceeding as if by common consent.

Not a single word passed between the two of them as they made their way back to the Four Corners. Neither had any words left, and both felt the weight of responsibility.

Once inside the house they halted before their father's gun cabinet. Their eyes met. The eldest by five minutes, Terry reached into the cabinet as Eddie handed him the key. Terry released the chained padlock and slid a .22 from its place while Eddie searched for the shells.

As one they moved toward the back of the house and the barn. Silently they ascended the ladder to the loft that they used as a clubhouse, which they had outgrown long ago. A poster from "Miami Vice," the red Ferrari faded to pink, peeled from the far wall.

Terry broke open the shotgun and loaded it, closing its breech with a snap. Then he handed it to Eddie who took it, looked at it, and returned it.

"I . . . I can't," Eddie said.

"You want me to go first?"

"Uh-uh."

"But?"

"You do it. I can't. I really can't."

The older boy frowned, examined the gun, and then cocked it. Eddie dropped to his knees, bowed his head as Terry brought the muzzle around, placing it next to his brother's temple, and pulled the trigger.

His brother's skull exploded, splattering the far wall, and the Ferrari was red once again. The boy's body spun a full ninety degrees, so it faced Terry before collapsing backward against an old derelict easy chair they had salvaged from someone's garbage years ago. Its two back legs missing, it formed a deep well into which Eddie's headless body sagged.

Terry had never shot something at point-blank range and had been unprepared for the bullet's impact. He stared at the gun, horrified.

What had he done?

His fingers spasmed, releasing the gun, and it banged to the floor. Terry scooped it up again and turned it so the muzzle pointed back at himself. A sidelong glance at his brother half-hanging over the arm of the chair, and his determination dissolved.

He'd promised.

Taking one hand away from the swaying gun, Terry wiped one sweaty palm against his jeans and then the other. His fingers twitched.

Another glimpse of his brother's corpse, and he faltered. Terry had thought that he could do it, but in the final analysis he was no braver than Eddie. Only he was alive, and his brother was not. But he couldn't, just couldn't. The youth let the shotgun slip to the floor with a clatter. Then wailing, he clambered over to his twin to drag the body from the chair and cradle it in his lap, rocking Eddie like a baby.

And Terry wept.

17

Leah joined the gathering throng, having returned with Tiffany from the hospital via Stockton Springs to stop at the store. Gideon rode along in the back seat, a calm presence that seemed to radiate outward, filling the car with his tranquillity, and Leah found herself reassured by his size and bulk, if nothing else. Although last night the usually placid Gideon had exhibited real anger, and Leah was glad that she had let Tiffany talk her into having him stay.

The assembly was ugly, its collective temper frayed. Leah placed the small sack of groceries in the back of the car and remained, listening eagerly to all that went on around her.

"Boo!"

Leah flinched, recognizing the voice, and whirled to gawk over the top of the station wagon at Jimmy. He had washed, changed his clothes, and now carried himself with his usual jaunty charm, and Leah felt herself weakening. His lip curled in a sardonic grin, and she realized with a shock that the lines she had thought before were wrinkles were, in fact, small scars.

Sheridon strolled around the end of the car, and Leah realized that his concentration was centered on Tiffany, rather than herself.

Leah's throat contracted and her gaze flicked to Blount's squad car. Certainly, that dumb cop had given her enough fits—coming to visit, nosing around and asking her questions—he ought to *do* something. Pick Jimmy up or something. The idiot had sat outside her drive for long enough. Leah then had greeted Blount, welcoming his spectral presence with a wave of her hand and a snicker of derision. Blount should have known better, as if Jimmy'd arrive home with a county-mountie, or whatever he was, sitting on her doorstep. Now she wished Alan would appear and lead Jimmy away.

"Hi, squirt! I've got something for you," he said. Tiffany shrank against her mother.

"Come on, Jimmy, leave the kid alone," Leah said.

"Shut up, Leah, this is between the brat and me." He turned to Tiffany. "And I understand you have something for me, too."

"Jimmy, I mean it." Leah crushed Tiffany against her side as Jimmy extracted the wrinkled finger from his pocket.

"Come on, kid, an eye for an eye," said Jimmy.

Tiffany's eyes rolled back into her head so only the whites could be seen, and Leah tried to interpose her body between Sheridon and the child. Jimmy grabbed her wrist, wrenching her aside. Gideon reacted, reaching out to seize his brother's hair and yank back.

"Ouch!" Jimmy twirled, ducking instinctively into a fighting stance. "Oh, it's you, little brother." He straightened, hooked his thumbs in his belt loop, and regarded Gideon. His eyes narrowed, glancing back to Leah.

"Okay, I'll leave it for now." Sheridon advanced toward Gideon, to thump the younger man's chest with an extended index finger. "I told you before . . ."

He let the threat hang in the air before stalking through the crowd.

A whisper started at one end of the crowd, rippling

outward. The murmur rose to a hum. People parted, falling quiet as they did, to let Jimmy Sheridon pass. With a jaunty confident wave at the townsfolk, he entered the shop.

Good riddance, Leah'd thought as the throng pulsed and parted before him, avoiding all contact as though Sheridon were tainted or carried some dread disease.

An animal rumble went through the crowd, and she realized that her voice had joined that of the mob. A grumbling growl welled deep in her chest, and her fingers squeezed Tiffany's hand reflexively. Her outrage needed an outlet, and at that moment she would have quite happily torn Sheridon limb from limb.

Tiffany squirmed. "Mom, that hurts!"

"Sorry," Leah said as she spared a look for her daughter. Her glimpse was arrested when it lit upon Gideon, for he was awake and alert. Not for the first time, Leah wondered what went on behind the normally empty blue eyes.

The store's door slammed, and the crowd outside the store breathed an audible sigh of release. Blount rambled amidst the crackle and pop of police radios and CBs, following in Sheridon's wake and elbowing his way through the crowd with a "'Scuse me" here and a "Sorry" there.

He disappeared behind the screen, and everyone found a reason to study the ground, a branch, or a twig. Looking at their toes, or anywhere rather than directly at their neighbor.

"You!" Aggie spat at Jimmy as he entered the store.

"Glad to see you, too, Aggie. You are lookin' good, woman. Been getting a little on the side lately?" Jimmy leered at her, and she looked at her feet and blushed.

"How about some coffee?" he said.

A hand fell on Jimmy's shoulder. He swung slowly to confront Blount.

"My, my. The local fuzz," Sheridon said. "How ya doin', ossifer?"

"You're under arrest," Blount growled.

"What for?"

"The assault on Duke Defleurieu."

"Oh, yeah? Did he send you after me?"

"He didn't have to; he signed a complaint a couple of weeks back."

Sheridon considered this for a moment. "Are you sure he still wants to press charges?"

"Of course he does. That man ain't no coward, and you're not gonna wiggle out of this one. No sir."

"Maybe we should go see," Jimmy said with a little too much confidence.

"Suit yourself," Blount said. "With the State boys here, I haven't got anything better to do, so why don't we drive out and ask him? Duke may not look like much, but he's no pansy. He won't back down. I can guarantee you that."

"Sure." Sheridon clapped his hands and rubbed them together gleefully, and an expression of fear flitted across Alan Blount's face before he shoved the younger man roughly out the door and manhandled him toward his squad car.

When the door exploded outward, and Jimmy was propelled through it by Blount, everyone perked up, eyes riveted to the unfolding drama. Blount couldn't help himself. He was enjoying this; he had waited for this moment for a long time. He pushed Jimmy a little harder.

"All right, punk, spread 'em," Alan said before a rapt audience. His fellow townsmen looked on implacably, chewing tobacco or lip, cherishing the spectacle of Alan Blount frisking Jimmy Sheridon. The bastard was getting his comeuppance at last. They leaned toward the squad car and Jimmy as Blount performed more than a cursory search.

A trill raced through them when Sheridon's head hit the roof of the car with an audible clack, and they almost applauded.

"Mom! Mom!" Tiffany yanked at the hem of her mother's shirt.

"What, honey?"

"Can I have my hand back now?"

Leah looked at the tiny fist she clasped in her hand. The girl's fingers were turning an angry purple.

"Ah, sure. Sure. Why don't I go get you an ice cream?"

Tiffany fixed her mother with a sidelong stare. They hadn't even eaten breakfast yet. Then the child shrugged. Who was she to refuse a treat?

"Can Gideon have one, too?" Tiffany asked slyly.

Leah turned to Gideon, quizzically. His mouth had gone slack, and his eyes were flat and empty again.

"Sure, Gideon can have one, too," Leah said.

The wolf squatted on the crest of a hill overlooking the town. The sky burned the dull red of malignancy, and bright colors, usually beyond the capacity of the lupine retinal cones, were imprinted on the primal mind, within the spirit consciousness carried by the predator. Clouds appeared, their underbelly stained peach, and birds flew as bloodred streaks across the sky.

The woodland before him was blackened and scorched. The wolf padded silently forward, skirting the burned-out area, past dry tinder and charred scrub. The devastation stopped abruptly. Across the narrow strip of tarmac, the woods in the cleft that led to Sandypoint were still soggy from the recent rains.

The spell had been loosed upon the land. The wolf perceived its action in the stiff crackle of dead grass and leaves. It oozed from the soil and ricocheted off the rocks, flowing liquidly in the teeming bay, between granite gorge and pebbled beach.

The beast snuffled, noting the redolent smoke and the sour stench of illness and decay like that which had once clung to the old Indian. And something else again. The acrid aroma of insanity, a scent too mild for human senses, and the subtle blending of chemical pheromones of mortal terror.

The predator tried to detect the curse's human carrier, but the mental message was scrambled by the sudden onslaught of other human thoughts and cumulative cognitive detritus.

An entire town grieved; the hex bounced off boulders, and the wolf was bombarded with conflicting sensations and emotions, observing the world from myriad eyes and bodies that thought now with a single animal mind.

Shutting out the din, the wolf closed his eyes, looking through the membraneous lids, seeking the soft-blue radiance that had drawn him here. He dived down into the marshy thicket beyond the road, turning left and zeroing in on Tiffany's small mobile home.

Duke Defleurieu's house wasn't far from the café—less than one hundred yards. It was set back a pace from the blacktop road that led from highway to town. With its tarpaper roof and dark green paint, it was difficult to distinguish from the surrounding spruce and pine.

Like many houses, Defleurieu's was hidden from view by a stand of trees, and when seen, it appeared as a scourge upon the landscape. For no matter how long man had managed to survive here, no human habitation thrived in this inhospitable environment. The stony soil and the harsh weather always strove to take back their own and often succeeded, as they appeared to be succeeding here. Tall weeds grew along the central track that was Duke's driveway, already taking over where few cars passed now that Duke could no longer drive.

Following its curving path, Blount rarely took his eyes from the rearview mirror, as though the cop expected Sheridon to turn into a demon, sprout wings, or develop superhuman strength and dive through the window to escape into the thicket beyond.

Jimmy Sheridon slouched against the back seat. A large lump was forming on his forehead where it had cracked against the door, and Blount couldn't deny the thrill that had run through him as he cuffed Sheridon and shoved him into the squad car.

Jimmy looked up sullenly, glaring back at the officer.

The car crunched to a stop. The house was ramshackle. Like many of the homes in town, its dooryard served as a storage area. A newly reconstructed engine hung suspended over the primer-spotted body of a '57 Chevy. There was a rusted-out hulk of a tractor next to the dead elm. Tall weeds grew through its chassis, and a dead tree added a further sinister countenance to the skeletal remains.

Active in his retirement, Defleurieu had more projects than time, and he always had something on the drawing board. Something he was going to do. The second story had been added haphazardly and contained little more than the promise of a bedroom and a bath. It was one of those things that Duke was always gonna finish . . . someday.

Alan opened the door, announcing his intentions. "I'll go get him."

Sheridon grunted.

Blount's eyes narrowed. "On second thought." He pulled his gun from his holster and opened the back door, yanking Sheridon out with him. "I think I'll keep my eye on you."

"You're enjoying this," Jimmy said, spitting at the man's feet. "Pig."

Blount resisted the impulse to wipe the crazy smile off the motherfucker's face and prodded him forward along the dirt path to the house.

"What the hell do ya need the gun fer? You afraid of me? You think I'm gonna bite ya?" Sheridon taunted, and he made little growling noises, snapping at the air.

Blount chewed on bile, not dignifying Sheridon's caustic remarks with a reply. They paused before the door. Alan knocked—no response—and Jimmy started to grin.

"Wipe that smile off a your face, boy," Blount said.

Sheridon's grin broadened.

Blount rapped louder, using the butt of his gun.

Silence billowed from the residence, and Alan noticed the buzz of traffic on the nearby highway.

"Crap. I didn't see him in town. He should be here." The officer indicated the door with a wave of the gun. "Kick it in."

"What? Me? John Q. Public and private citizen?"

"Yes, you."

Raising his cuffed hands behind his back, Jimmy said, "I'm kind'a tied up here."

"And you're staying that way."

"How do you expect me to maintain my balance?" the younger man complained.

"What'sa mattah, don't think you can do it, punk?"

"No, but—" Again he indicated his wrists with an awkward shrug.

"I don't give a tinker's damn if you fall flat on your ass, boy. Now do it."

The two stood face to face, the younger man appraising the older man, and Blount couldn't help but think as he gazed into the dark brown eyes that somewhere in the last few weeks Jimmy Sheridon had crossed that fine line from meanness to madness.

With a rude noise Jimmy stepped back and examined the door. Leaning against the porch rail, he lifted his leg, aimed, and—*Crack!*

The door crashed against the inside wall, the lock hanging uselessly, still in the frame. Jimmy tottered for a bit, righted himself and, with a smug sneer at Blount, sauntered into the living room. The house smelled of stale beer and rotting food—musty and close.

"Duke?" Blount hollered into the gloom.

"Duke?" Jimmy parroted in a tremulous falsetto.

Blount considered rearranging the younger man's orthodontia and thrust Jimmy through the door and into the kitchen instead.

"Duke?" Blount bellowed before starting an unwilling search.

Living room, kitchen, and the onetime dining room that now served as a workshop: with jumbled tools and nuts and bolts strewn all about on tables made of upraised planks set on trestles.

"Come on, Duke, get off your dead ass. The whole town's going berserk, and you're sleeping in." Blount continued talking as he dragged Jimmy up the stairs to the bedroom, where they found Defleurieu's crumpled body.

Blount's ham-hock hand rammed Jimmy against the wall, seizing his throat and squeezing his windpipe. Sheridon struggled, clawing at the restraining hands.

"You knew, you fucking bastard," he bawled. "You knew!"

Sheridon coughed and choked and finally managed to whisper, "How the hell could I have known?"

Blount lifted Jimmy by the throat, and his feet did a little dancing jig.

"Let go. What the fuck do you think you're doing?" he rasped.

Blount released him, placing the barrel of the gun next to the younger man's head.

"Yer under arrest," he said.

"Why?" Jimmy said. "It's obvious he's not gonna press assault charges."

"And *that's* why. Until we know the cause of death, let's just call it suspicion of murder."

"You'd like that, wouldn't you?" Sheridon snarled, but Blount noticed a slight tremor in his voice, and he pushed the gun's barrel against the man's skull so hard it left an impression on the temple.

"Mebbe," Blount said.

"Whatever you say." Jimmy sidled away from Alan and the gun. "But I'm gonna get you, Blount. I'm gonna get you for this."

"Yeah, but you're gonna have to get out of jail first."

The ambulance had gone roaring off up the street toward Defleurieu's house—siren ominously silent—a one-way ticket to the morgue. The more normal conveyance, the mortician's hearse, was already full. The State Police pursued it, departing en masse as if they couldn't get out of there quickly enough. The frightened population tarried, waiting for some word, some sort of official notification that never came.

Rumors flew.

Old Duke had been found horribly murdered . . . like the

Gascons and the Mordens and Les Braun . . . Jimmy was the culprit. He had rubbed them all out, picking them off, one by one. . . . No, it was animals. . . . No, kids . . . some kind of black magic thing.

Tempers wore thin as imaginations bloated with theories, and each new rumor was more gory than the next. They had found body parts strewn from one part of the house to another. . . . Some creature (a.k.a. Jimmy Sheridon) had lived in the woods outside of town, coming down at night to feed first upon animals, then on human flesh, cutting their hearts out and eating them whole.

Leah sat behind the steering wheel and cried. Tiffany and Gideon fluttered around the car anxiously. Occasionally Tiffany would cuddle her mother, trying to offer some reassurance, a few soft words of comfort that the woman did not hear.

Gideon wandered away bored.

Tiffany watched him ramble unnoticed through the crowd—sometimes he would stop and pick up a crust of bread or a few stray potato chips—until she lost him and turned her attention back to her mother, patting her arm wordlessly.

"Pssst."

Tiffany peeked under her mother's arm at the stand of trees.

"Psssssst!" Gideon motioned to her. "Come here."

"Mom?"

Leah loosed her daughter.

"Is it okay if I go for a walk with Gideon?"

Leah snuffled, wiped her nose on a tattered paper towel, and scanned the crowd. "Okay, but don't wander too far or be gone too long," Leah said.

The girl shuffled a few moments undecided, and Gideon's gesticulations became more agitated.

"PSSSSSSST!" Others looked up from muttered conversations and glared, recalling just whose brother Gideon was, and Tiffany hurried off to join him and drag him deeper into the shadows.

"What? What! Don't'cha know what's going on out there?" she asked peevishly.

He didn't answer, rather he tugged at her arm and motioned up the hill. He scrambled through the brush, crossed the road over near the old apple tree and climbed up to the summit. Tiffany chased him with difficulty, hampered by the growth as they topped the knoll and descended into a valley on the far side.

"Where we going?" she puffed, barely catching up with him when he plunged into the stretch of marshy woodland whose boundary was demarcated by the railway to the east and the highway to the west, the most direct route—if someone felt like circumnavigating the fallen logs, weed-choked boulders, and winding through dense scrub—to her house.

"Hey, wait!" She trotted after him. "Slow down."

Gideon halted, waiting impatiently for her.

"What's the rush?" Tiffany said.

"Shhh." Gideon put his finger to his lips, looked left and right, and said, "He's here."

He plucked at her sleeve and pointed ahead, urging her to hurry.

She extricated her sleeve from his grasp. "Here? Who's here?"

"Come." He lifted a low-hanging branch and waved her through. She climbed over an uprooted tree and ducked under the bough. He released it, dodging the branch as he forced his way through the gnarled limbs.

A watchful hush had fallen upon the woods as if the birds and animals resented their presence. Tiffany moved along quietly behind him. She had seen this kind of intensity before, and Tiffany knew that she would never get any sense out of him now.

By the time they had trekked through the wet trough between Stockton Springs and the next summit, Tiffany was hot and sweating. She shed her sweater, and she groused irritably when she finally realized where he was guiding her.

"We're almost home!" she exclaimed exasperated. "If

you'd just waited a bit, Mom would have driven us both, and if you were so all fired up to get there quickly, why didn't you just tell me and we could have asked for a ride?"

He pushed through the brush, ignoring her.

Finally they stood just outside the circle Gideon had drawn around the yard. The dogs were silent. Tiffany opened her mouth to scold him, but he cut her off with a swift slicing motion. Then his arm stretched out in a sweeping motion, and she followed his upraised hand and gasped.

A gray shade drifted among the shadows within the circle. Long, pointed ears ... *all the better to hear you with, my dear* ... pointed snout which opened to reveal sharp incisors ... *all the better to eat you with* ...

Tiffany broke into a smile, remembering not the animal of the fairy tale, but the creature of her dream, whose back she rode like the wind. The wolf had come.

Jimmy hunched insolently inside the cell at the Belfast police station. Once painted an industrial white, the years' accumulation of grime and nicotine had turned it a scabrous yellow.

Like baby shit, or puke, he thought sourly.

Sheridon scanned the graffiti to see if anything new or particularly diverting had been added since he'd been here last. It was, as graffiti goes, uninspired—boring. His gaze went to the barred and screened window which cast a tiger-striped shadow across the floor, the wire mesh obscuring it slightly with its own crosshatch pattern.

His confinement was more of an inconvenience than anything else. This hadn't been his first time here. It probably wouldn't be the last, and Sheridon was confident of his impending deliverance. He felt secure that whoever or whatever powered his movements would not leave him cooling his heels in the local clink too long.

Since his return he had had the opportunity to view first-hand what he had seen from afar. If Jimmy had had any doubts about the validity of his observations, they were allayed. Les Braun was dead, and Hedda suspected of his murder. Duke was dead, and that Blisson broad. All that he had witnessed had been confirmed. Confirmed in the conflagration. Confirmed in the scorched earth. Confirmed again from the charred bodies they carried from the houses' shells.

Some power moved through him, worked through him. Now Sheridon *knew* his experiences at the camp had been more than some fevered hallucination. Something linked Jimmy to the land around Sandypoint. This was no mere tingle of hallowed earth that vibrated through the soles of his feet. This resonated throughout the body and the mind.

The land was angry, aggrieved, and the people who lived upon it accursed. The very soil demanded vengeance, and its spell worked through him. Something had touched Jimmy, empowered him and bound him to his birthplace, as much as it doomed the rest of the town's inhabitants. He couldn't have explained its mechanism. He only knew it to be true. The earth would wreak its revenge, and he, James Sheridon, was the chosen instrument of destruction.

People died in sacrifice, and the earth was glutted, but not sated. This bloodthirsty land craved more. The curse charged through fields and rebounded off the granite rock. Its hatred seeped from the soil, corrupting all that it touched, and all Sheridon had to do to control it was direct it with a thought or a glance.

He heard a slight snuffling noise, and he pivoted to face the window in full. Then he climbed on the aging cot and stood on his toes, trying to look outside.

His fingers barely grazed the bottom sill, but when they touched it, he stiffened as if electrified. His eyes viewed a place far beyond the outer walls of his prison.

Next to the old dilapidated trailer, Leah's stupid daughter Tiffany, with no more sense than a two-year-old, clambered onto a huge wolf while his idiot brother smiled on beatifically. The creature's head lolled and its tongue reeled from its mouth. It looked like it was grinning, and in fact, the huge tail wagged in wide loops, like some goddamn shaggy dog.

The breath whistled shrilly through Jimmy's teeth as he strained toward the jailhouse window. His fingers twined with the mesh that bit into his flesh.

It was here!

In the land beyond his reach, but not beyond his vision, the shaggy head swung, rotating eternally on the long stem of its neck, to stare at Sheridon. His idiot brother spun, too, following the creature's troubled gaze, and Jimmy realized that Gideon was going to be a problem, a problem Sheridon must solve.

"I warned you once, little brother," he whispered. "Never again."

Metal rattled in the lock. Jimmy's fingers uncurled, releasing the mesh screen.

"Hey, you, what the hell do you think you're doing? Trying to escape?"

The voice brought him back to the grimy cell with its fat, juicy pig glowering in the doorway.

"Not really, Officer," Jimmy said with uncustomary mildness.

"Good, 'cause it's not necessary. You're free to go."

His knuckles had turned blue-white, such was the strength of his grip upon the receiver.

"He what!" Blount shouted into it. Evan Duffy winced and peered timidly at Alan over the top of a form.

"How can you know so soon? I mean we just found him."

Pale, unshaven and hollow-cheeked, Alan Blount looked like hell, and felt worse. The voice on the other end of the line droned on about pupil dilation, this, that and the other thing, all couched in tongue-twisting polysyllables.

". . . classic symptoms and no evidence of violence," it concluded.

His faith in the system, already shaken, descended another notch, sinking into the morass of growing doubts. Worse, Blount's faith in himself had been shaken to the roots, and the only thing that kept him on the job was what Aggie had said: People depended on him.

Ha! he thought, speaking into the receiver. "You'll still do a full autopsy to make sure, won't you?" His tone indicated the abandonment of all hope.

A buzz of an answer.

"I'd like to see the reports," he said.

Blount lowered his voice. "Are you sure that someone couldn't have scared the shit outta him or something? He had a gun with him, you know."

Another protracted buzz.

"Of course, of course, I understand," Blount said. "You couldn't hold him, not if there aren't any other charges, and the only man that signed the complaint is dead now."

Another pause and a murmur.

"Convenient, wouldn't you say?"

"Yeah, sure, thanks." Blount replaced the receiver. "For nothing."

People depended on him, so Alan had stuck things out, and he'd failed. He'd wanted to help, to set things right, and hope against all hope that they, at least, had gotten rid of that perennial pest, Jimmy Sheridon. Blount didn't like that smug, grinning son of a bitch. He'd hung on until this moment, when the last hope dissipated. Alan deflated as if someone had let all the air out of him.

"What happened?" said Duffy.

"They say it was a stroke."

"And Sheridon?"

"You haf'ta ask?" Blount gazed at the other man over the mounting pile of paperwork and reports.

"No, I don't suppose so," he said. "Gee, Alan, that's too bad. Maybe this would be a good time to take a vacation."

Blount pulled the badge from his pocket and tossed it onto the desk. "I was thinking of something a little more permanent."

"Quitting? Not you. You've got to be kidding."

"Uh-uh." Blount swiveled in his chair, pulled a piece of typing paper from the pile, puzzled over the typewriter a minute before feeding the sheet under the platen and aligning it, and started to type his resignation.

Mentally he made a list of what he'd need to do to get out of town—for good. Put the house on the market, sell the furniture. Maybe call one of those big auctioneers in Bangor. He decided he'd better call Ginny, and Blount frowned. He didn't like thinking of her in the house all alone. He hadn't been pleased when she arrived home early, but no amount of persuading could convince her to stay in Portland or go visit her sister in Hartford until this thing blew over, and prevailing over his objections, she had returned this morning, cutting her trip short.

Alan bashed at the keys a little bit harder, made a mistake, swore, and started looking for that correction tape the secretary hid somewhere around here. It came in small packs, and the dumb twat hoarded it like gold, doling it out accordingly, one sheet at a time.

Where the hell does she keep the stuff?

The urgency and pressure were building. Alan Blount decided as he gave up his search—*what the hell, this didn't need to be pretty*—he had to get home. He didn't care what Ginny thought. He wasn't going to leave her alone in the house for a minute.

18

The store was packed. A half-dozen people clung to the counter. Four more lounged or were draped over heaped merchandise. A few wandered up and down the aisle, looking bewildered and confused. They'd stop and peer purblind at something on the shelves, then mosey on and never did seem to find what they were looking for.

With nowhere to go, James Sheridon leaned on a six-pack—his third that evening—and one can was already missing from it. Evidently Leah had greeted Jimmy more warmly than he had expected when he'd arrived at the trailer for the second time that day—with a gun in her hand—and this time she meant business.

Aggie had to suppress a grin and tacitly cheered the younger woman. It was about time Leah Blair came to her senses. Still, Aggie wished that Sheridon could have found some other place to hang out. The café, the truck stop in Searsport, or the bar down in Bucksport. Or up to Bangor, where it was rumored he kept some other woman in style.

Aggie snorted.

She kept *him,* more likely.

"Fucking bitch, I'm gonna show her who's boss," Jimmy said.

"Shhh." Aggie indicated the children among the customers, but Sheridon persisted without noticing her reproof.

"She should know better'n that," he said, jamming his hand down on an empty can and grinding it under its heel before glaring from one member to another in his audience, defying comment.

Her gaze met that of another customer, and both rolled their eyes toward the ceiling. Aggie wouldn't want to be in Leah's shoes tonight after the sun had gone down, and Jimmy had had enough time to finish his third or maybe his fourth six-pack.

Idly Aggie considered tossing him out on his ear. Then she surveyed the loiterers, a crowd of old fogeys and old farts, and bemused women and children, and she realized with a sinking heart that they didn't have enough collective strength to throw out a spitting kitten, much less Jimmy Sheridon spitting mad.

"What Rich did to June," Jimmy continued his tirade, "is gonna look like child's play after I get through with Leah and that damn brat of hers."

Aggie's back stiffened. "How do you know what Rich did to June?"

"Didn't you hear? He carved her up good." One eye open he nodded sagely at her over his beer.

"I haven't heard anything like that. So how do *you* know that Rich did anything to June?"

"I have my ways," he said, turning to consider her with disdain as if she were a bug or a virulent virus.

"What makes you such an expert?"

"Where the fuck do you think I spent my afternoon, you stupid bitch? The cop shop. You think I didn't hear a thing or two?"

"Hey!" Bob, who had remained quiet on his newly reserved perch behind the counter, rose from his seat, and

Aggie felt a tremor of terror run through her, hoping he wouldn't foolishly decide to defend her.

"I won't hear that kind of talk," Schoenwald said. "Not to Aggie. Now, you apologize."

Sheridon pulled himself upright and appraised the older man, a brow raised in question.

"*You?*" He looked incredulous. "Who the fuck are you?" His gaze went from Bob to Aggie, and he snickered. "So you're going to defend yon fair maiden." Jimmy motioned in Aggie's direction. "You, and what army?"

He raised a threatening fist, and Bob shriveled, dropping back onto the stacked newspapers that made up his "chair."

"Come on, dumb fuck," Sheridon said, "defend the damsel in distress."

"All right!" Aggie interjected, shocking even herself with her voice so loud that no few customers jumped. "I've had it with you, James Sheridon. You can be a mean so-and-so and pick fights anywhere you want, but *not* here. You can swear like a sailor. I don't care what you do outside of this store. But this store is mine, and I say who does what and when. And you don't pick fights in this store at any time, do you hear me?"

Jimmy recoiled, his eyes seeking out those of others, and for once, Aggie noted with satisfaction, the rest stood firm. Every old fart and old fogey in Stockton Springs nodded their heads in animated agreement.

"And I think that unless you're planning on doing a little shopping, I'd just as soon you took your six-pack elsewhere."

The entire store held its breath.

Jimmy scowled at her, considered challenging her, and relented.

"Okay, what the hell do I wanna hang around with you dipshits for anyway?" Sheridon plucked his beer from the counter, peered at them, noting each and every face, before spinning and marching out the door. Aggie deflated against the counter, relieved that he hadn't called her bluff.

* * *

His six-pack tucked underneath his arm, Sheridon considered the adamant Aggie and the hunched Robert for a moment. A flush crept up the old man's throat to his cheeks. Bob sank lower on his seat, and even Aggie glanced down at her feet and cleared her throat, nonplussed.

Jimmy stormed from the building—just for effect—letting the door slam behind him, his anger feigned.

Let the dumb cunt think she's won. Let all the little assholes think they got one over on me. I'll show them.

His time was coming. Soon enough Jimmy would have every one of them dancing to his tune. He swerved, heading for his truck, let down the tailgate, and hopped inside, plunking the beer down beside him.

The door banged again, and Schoenwald raced into the street, the blush still coloring his features. He rocked back and forth in confusion, as if he didn't know what to do next.

So that's the lay of the land, Sheridon thought.

Examining the man's stooped shoulders and protruding belly, Jimmy tried to imagine the two of them making love and couldn't. It was like trying to imagine two fossils fucking.

So, he'd gotten the man by the short hairs, for sure. Embarrassed him in front of his lady love. He snickered. Perhaps Jimmy had found the form his vengeance would take.

He roared with cruel, cutting laughter. Schoenwald swung around, noticing Jimmy for the first time. He blanched and rushed up the street toward the highway.

Crimson all the way to the tips of his ears, Robert Schoenwald rushed from the store. The gathering outside had long since dispersed, everyone going to their separate homes—the excitement over for the day, and all the bodies found, or so they hoped.

Behind them, they'd left a residual trail of disorientation. Their stupefaction whispered across the pitted parking lot, reverberated against the gas pumps, and rang hollowly around the small town.

Schoenwald paused to scan the scene. The sun hovered

over the hill just above the timberline, poised. The sky was painted a rosy hue. So deceptively peaceful.

Despite the early hour, every light in town was burning, as if the townsfolk hoped to chase away whatever foul fiend had disturbed their sleepy village through sheer wattage alone.

Laughter erupted behind him, and Bob spun to confront . . . Sheridon.

Shit!

Again his flesh burned. Bob did a quick about-face, and nervous energy propelled him past the post office up the hill toward the highway.

"Chicken!" Jimmy's raucous laughter stalked Schoenwald up the street.

Turning left after the post office, Bob lingered awhile near the huge equipment which sat forgotten in the building's shadow, but he found no comfort there. Shrugging, he went toward School Street. Sprinkled here and there about the town were holes in the blaze of outdoor lamps, where shadow gobbled up all glimmer of hope and left pools of darkness, sinister and foreboding. Around the empty houses light disappeared as if devoured by some black hole. In the east not even stars dared to put in an appearance.

No illumination shone from the Brauns', or the Blissons', or the Garreths', creating a void where once had radiated the warmth of human habitation. Shades of former inhabitants collected in black pools of early evening shadows through which ghosts gamboled and spirits walked. And any who happened to glimpse them out their window would have occasion to ponder the umbra around the empty residences and contemplate what it symbolized.

Death.

As though whispered on the wind, Schoenwald heard each and every unanswered question that was now being voiced in the many hushed living rooms across Stockton Springs. Words spoken low so the children wouldn't hear. Sometimes they remained unvoiced, the query unasked as each individual retreated in silence and solitude into the uncharted realm of conjecture—wondering why, how?

A glance into someone's picture window revealed a familiar family huddled around the television set, and when they noticed Bob peering in, the father, or mother, would get up and close the drapes, shutting Schoenwald out as though each man in town feared the other. These people who had known each other for years, back several generations, suddenly afraid of their neighbors. So suspicion was heaped on suspicion; distrust upon distrust. Until no one—not even the familiar faces he had known since birth—was safe, and there was no place Bob could go where he would not confront some reminder of death.

The entire world had gone mad.

Bob strode up the street, agitated. The sound of children's shrill laughter floated to him from the schoolyard, jeering, and Bob completed the short circuit around town to pace in front of the store, wondering whether or not he should go in, but he realized that he couldn't face Aggie, not yet.

He had failed her. He had failed tonight with Sheridon. It had been *Aggie* and not him who had kicked that prick Sheridon out of the store. Tonight his woman had to come to his aid, defending him against Sheridon. Now Bob had sunk so low that he was hiding behind a woman's skirts.

And if Sheridon had decided to press the issue rather than going compliantly outside, would Bob have been man enough to protect her?

Schoenwald tried to see himself challenging an outraged Jimmy Sheridon and couldn't. Bob hadn't been at the café the night of the fight—if you could call one man tromping all over another one a fight—but he had heard enough of the stories, and they grew more gruesome with each recounting.

As if Bob's thoughts had summoned him, Sheridon emerged from the shadows to stare with those damn crazy eyes of his. Arms crossed, leaning nonchalantly against the side of the building, he watched Bob, grinning his lunatic grin. Schoenwald flinched away from the laughing specter, spun on his heel, and dashed blindly up the street, his cowardice confirmed. Bob could never face Aggie now. Never.

He had failed, failed with Aggie.

Last night he had realized his heart's desire, and today already it seemed he had lost her, and the time he spent with her was a dream fleetingly recalled, nothing more.

His feet hit the pavement with a loud, slapping noise, which throbbed in time to the litany that beat inside his brain. Hissing hard words.

Ssssap. Sssssssucker. Los-s-ser.

He had failed. Everywhere Bob looked, he saw a fallen limb here, a crater there. He had failed. He had been overwhelmed by the rains, unable to keep up, and a rift opened in the road before him in silent accusation. Every pothole was a personal insult—every crack or crevice a slap in the face.

Failure. Loser.

Schoenwald found himself walking around the back of the post office where the township kept their vehicles, and Bob ached to start up the old engines on the Cat or the snowplow. In the past few weeks he had worried about them the way a parent would a child. Schoenwald revolved slowly, surveying what he perceived to be his private domain. He inhaled deeply. The assorted smells of tar, gas, grease, and motor oil were somehow reassuring, and he realized he was more at home among the obstreperous old brutes that operated where and when they pleased than with human companionship.

Bob gripped the keys in his pocket, keys to the old Cat and the snowplow. He wasn't supposed to have the keys anymore, but no one had ever asked for them back, and he didn't volunteer them, hoping—no, presuming—that the city would sort through its financial difficulties and allow him to return to work.

Children's voices floated about him in a bloodred sky, echoing his thoughts.

Ssssap. Sssssssucker. Los-s-ser. The voice inside his head jeered as children's laughter drifted between the small knot of clustered houses and over the field to flit mockingly around the machine yard.

"Jonathan's a dummy!" someone in the schoolyard shouted.

Jonathan Blair, Tiffany's cousin.

Ssssap. Ssssssucker. Los-s-ser.

Bob couldn't understand children's cruelty. They picked on the weak, the handicapped. He had watched them, with Gideon and Leah Blair's poor daughter, Tiffany. At least Bob didn't remember being cruel. Oh, some kids had been mean back then. They were mean as kids and they were mean as adults. Like that bastard Sheridon.

And Bob had been the butt of more than one childish joke.

Weirdo, queer, homo.

Of late Schoenwald had come to realize that the children's ridicule was a reflection of their parents' attitudes. They were most likely repeating what they had heard at home. Once he thought his position had commanded a certain amount of respect. They depended on him to keep the roads clear that enabled them to go to work. Now Bob wasn't so sure.

He took the key ring out of his pocket and twirled it around his index finger, pensive. Their engines would seize up if they weren't turned over every once in a while.

The keys spun round and round his finger, jingling. While the kids' play got more wild, and he recognized a few shouted names and not so snappy retorts.

"Weirdo, queer, homo."

A strange man, a loner, a man who had never married. Perhaps Bob was the man parents warned their children about before they went to bed. Watch out or so-and-so will get you.

The keys spun round and round, faster and faster.

Ssssap. Ssssssucker. Los-s-ser. Faster and faster.

Someone only one rung above Gideon, the village idiot, and it hurt. *Is that what they really thought of him?*

The key ring came to a jangling halt.

This was the town he had been serving all these years. He paced. Inner voices whispered, the twitter of childish giggles filtering through leaden air.

Laughing at him! Laughing as their parents had been laughing at him all these years.

Queer. Homo. Failure!

He marched back and forth across the small parking area, becoming more and more upset with each step he took.

Queer. Homo. Loser!

Something hit the ground next to his feet so hard it sent sparks flashing off the concrete. Schoenwald jumped back, landing on the rusted step that led up to the cab.

Crack! Followed by the faint patter of pebbles. Schoenwald glared at the growing shadows.

Goddamn kids! Throwing rocks at him again.

He swung into the seat of the plow and revved it up. He'd show them.

Two of the old farts chattered at Sheridon, vying for his attention—*total losers, both of them*—and Jimmy let their words wash over him as he mentally traced Schoenwald's frenzied path. The man's thoughts skittered agitatedly around him, and Jimmy gave them a twitch or two, adding a few of his own.

Loser!

Predictably the man's walk took him to the yard, and Jimmy extended his hand out before him, flicked his wrist, and was satisfied to see a shower of stones descend on the hapless Schoenwald.

Sheridon chuckled at some private joke. The old men paused in their conversation to stare at Jimmy curiously.

Vroom-rooom. Vroom-rooom!

The sudden roar of the engine, reverberating inside his brain, nearly knocked Jimmy flat and sent him sprawling under the branches of the tree in the parking lot.

Head throbbing, Sheridon opened his eyes, the contact with Schoenwald broken.

Her eyes flicked from Bob Schoenwald's fleeing figure to Jimmy Sheridon and back again. She wanted to cry after Bob. She didn't want him to go. She didn't want to be left alone, although with the store full of people, it wasn't exactly like she was alone. Still, she had found comfort in Bob's stolid presence, and now he was gone.

The conversation eddied about her. The weather. Football. The upcoming hockey season. Any topic was permissible, except the most recent events. Mindless prattle, a feeble attempt at normalcy. She didn't bother to listen, only nodded when it seemed appropriate.

Sheridon lurked outside the door, and the customers who had backed her up before drifted out to him. He was evidently a better conversationalist than she was.

Stationing herself next to the window, Aggie waited until Bob had passed the place once and considered going out to call him in. He paced in front of the store a few times and was gone again before she had time to act. His retreating back was a dark smear near the monstrous machines he loved so well, and Aggie scowled, tearing her gaze away from the window.

One of the motors roared to life. So deep, so churning its timbre, that conversation faltered and, as one, those who had stayed in the store turned to face the window.

Vroom-rooom . . . followed by the sleepy, slow *chug, chug, chug* of the . . . and Aggie cocked her head, attentive . . . snowplow?

People poured out the door into the gathering twilight. Others pressed their faces against the glass. Shadows from the setting sun stretched yawningly across the street. The sky to the east was indigo, which blended into a band of deep turquoise overhead. Aggie could well imagine the horizon behind the store, the blue-green line of trees and, beyond that, the apricot and gold glow of the sun's final rays.

Vroom-rooom! Vroom-rooom!

"Bobby?" Aggie mouthed the word, sure that it was him.

Vroom-rooom! Sputter, sputter, chug.

The huge snowplow roared around the corner. Unimpeded by snow, it was moving faster than she had ever seen it move before. It ground up Main to School Street.

Aggie watched Bob fight with the gears as the vehicle disappeared between buildings, *chug-chug-chugging* toward the schoolyard where the town's children got in the last few moments of play in the light of the dying day.

After Jimmy had been released from jail, he had arrived on their doorstep in an attempt to liberally dispense his own peculiar form of insult and abuse. Once again she had convinced him to leave by waving the gun, its safety released, in his face. Then Leah had gotten sullenly drunk. One hand still rested lightly on the rifle and the other swept away the cooling plate of Rice-a-Roni and hamburger onto the floor.

Gideon regarded the gesture as an invitation, and he slipped under the table to accept the proffered meal, scraping the remains gratefully into his mouth. Grains of rice spewed from either side while he chewed happily.

"Please, Mom?" Tiffany moaned. "Pah-leease. I'll be all right. Gideon will be with me."

Gideon chose that moment to smile, and grains of rice fell from the twisted lips onto his lap.

Leah sniggered. "Great, great, you two run into that asshole Jimmy, and Gideon can spit rice at him. I love it."

"Please, Mom, nothing's going to happen to me. I got a lucky piece." Tiffany reached for her pocket to show her mother while Gideon perked up, watching intently. Tiffany's hand clenched at empty air, and she mouthed a single word. "Lost."

But already her mother was speaking, commanding the girl's attention. "That's even better. You can thrash his left kneecap with a rabbit's foot while Gideon smacks him right between the eyes with a mouthful of Rice-a-Roni.

"Aw, hell, go ahead. I'm not going to have a minute's peace until you do," Leah said as she went to the kitchen to refresh her drink.

Tiffany eyed the rifle distrustfully and grabbed it. Gideon stopped her with a shake of his head. Then he took her hand, and they escaped into the still-warm evening air.

The wolf uncoiled from his hiding place behind the stacked tires and trotted over to the man and the child, tail wagging. The beast nosed at her now-empty pocket and whined. A huge paw raked across the cloth. Then the wolf seized it between sharp teeth and pulled, nearly ripping the fabric. Giggling, she pushed the gray head away.

"Stop it," she said.

The wolf gazed on her and then licked her face—the hot-blood smell of a fresh kill still on its lips—and she giggled harder.

"That tickles!"

The wolf moved off toward the trees, and Tiffany and Gideon followed. As a group, they darted across the gravel road to the marshy woods beyond. The wolf matched its pace to the more ungainly humans, slowing slightly.

Companionably they wound through the trees, the wolf moving with silent purpose toward town. Impatiently it tugged at Tiffany's sleeve, and Gideon, catching its urgency, swept Tiffany from the ground and deposited her on the creature's back. Like her dream.

The wolf bolted, head hanging low, pacing nervously, and Gideon trailed along behind with an easy loping gait. A rattling roar and the tinny sound of screams pierced the night, and the young man halted, tumbling in a half somersault over the overturned tree that he had been vaulting, quite gracefully, only a minute before. Gideon rolled back to his feet in a single fluid motion to stand with forefinger upraised, as though requesting silence.

"Damn," Gideon muttered, and Tiffany blinked. It was the first time she'd heard him cuss.

The wolf paused, head tilted toward the sound, concentrating, and they raced, fleet as the wind, toward the village.

Screaming. Shrieking. Crying. Caterwauling that went on and on and on and on. Keening, slicing like a knife into their brains, it dissociated their thoughts from their actions so that no one inside the small store moved for an agonizing moment. Then they bolted for the door. First Roger Goodall, then Barry Frank and Tom Ditherton, then the others, until the store was empty except for Aggie. Briefly she hesitated, reluctant to leave the store unattended. Then she followed, not completely sure whether or not she wanted to see what was causing all the ruckus.

The people moved like a swarm, traipsing across Main to School Street. The roaring grumble of the plow changed in character, getting deeper, and the cries rose a notch.

Doors opened up and down School Street as the townspeople were torn from their lethargy to emerge, necks craning and hackles raised at the unearthly skreigh. There was the clatter and clash of gears, the screeching scrape of plow's blade against concrete.

Aggie and the customers jounced up the road. Aggie felt the drumbeat of her heels against irregular pavement and the staccato throb of her heart, unused to such exertion, and the sensations merged into a single *boom-boom-boom* that rocketed past her temples and jogged down the tightened muscles of calf and thigh.

The schoolyard opened before them. Aggie stopped and thought she was going to puke right then and there. The plow had beat a broad swathe through the children. Several had been injured, one crushed under the heavy wheels, and another, Jonathan Blair, mangled by the blade. His body was torn in two.

Bob climbed down from his seat, jabbering incoherently.

Astounded by the carnage, the people's pace slackened and they swayed indecisively—appalled at the bloodshed, yet unwilling to turn on one they had once called friend.

"I didn't, I didn't . . ." Bob Schoenwald stuttered.

A shadow moved beside her, and she turned to see Jimmy Sheridon kneeling next to an injured child, Tom Ditherton at his side.

Aggie hurried over to join him. Ditherton shook his head in assent at something the younger man had said.

"Right, I'll go call right away," Tom said, nodding eagerly.

Sheridon rose. "Recognize any of their parents?" he said, gesturing toward the crowd.

"No," Aggie said, embarrassed that she hadn't thought of the children first.

As if reading her thoughts, Jimmy thumbed toward Schoenwald, who even now was trying to extricate the child from the gears and swearing. "What should we do about him, do you s'pose?"

"Bob?" Her voice cracked on the single syllable.

"Yeah, Bob." Sheridon sighed. "Don't look like no one else here is man enough to handle him, not even you, eh, Aggie?"

Aggie made a minute examination of her shoelaces. Bob pointed, gesticulating wildly, and began to shout.

"Wolf! Wolf!" screeched Schoenwald, and all eyes turned in the direction of his flapping arms, expecting to see nothing but woods, and were shocked to observe Leah's little girl, Tiffany, sitting astride a massive, gray wolf. Sheridon's idiot brother, Gideon, stood beside them.

The girl's mouth was slightly ajar, and she stared across the broad expanse of the field.

"Jonathan?" she screamed, hopping from the wolf's back and springing away from it. The wolf leapt, clenching her arms in its huge mouth and dragging her toward the woods.

"JONATHAN-N-N!" The name dwindled and died, and Aggie cast a nervous look at the body crushed between the gears.

The entire crowd fumbled, muttering uncomfortably among themselves. A girl cried weakly in the playground while a little boy sobbed, his mangled arm cradled against his chest.

A siren split the night, as if overloaded with sensory input, and they turned in slow motion to gaze back at Main, where Blount's squad car whizzed past, lights flashing with streaks of red reflecting off the still-green leaves.

No one moved. Time froze, each second trapped like an insect in gooey resin. Except Schoenwald. He took this opportunity to slip, unremarked, into the hedgerow and slink farther into the woods.

And the people came unglued.

Ginny huddled in the passenger seat, knowing better than to speak when Alan was this mad. With Sheridon still hanging around somewhere, Blount sure as shit wasn't going to leave her alone. And he was angry with the Fletchers for calling him—he'd quit, after all—and angrier still at himself for taking the call.

Besides, Alan couldn't believe, wouldn't believe it. He radioed it in, hoping, hoping . . . what?

That Doris Fletcher was so overwrought she had hallucinated her son turned into a jelly stain across the wall and the other twin who clung to his brother's cooling corpse.

Couldn't be. He was just a kid, fer chrissakes.

Blount stormed up the path that led around the side of the Fletcher place toward the barn, determined not to believe it until he saw Doris Fletcher's tear-stained face as she hurried up the winding track toward him.

"Help me, Alan, I can't get Terry to let go of . . ." and she sobbed into her handkerchief, unable to say Eddie's name.

Jimmy's torso inclined toward the woods, as if he could, by stretching far enough, reach out and touch the three shadowy figures. His eyes sparked with the stony glint of hatred, and Aggie looked back in time to see his shining eyes. She recoiled from their glow. They glittered, phosphorescent green like an animal's or a cat's would when pinned under the harsh gleam of a car's headlights.

"Where's Bob?" said Aggie.

"Never mind him," Jimmy snarled. "That beast's got Leah's kid."

"I didn't think you'd care."

"Care? Care! I didn't see you sending old Ditherton off to phone for an ambulance when you first arrived here." He turned from her in disgust and shouted over the lethargic buzz of the assembled townspeople.

"All right, folks, we gotta organize a search. There's a murderer in our midst, and it's got one of our kids."

Aggie did a quick mental double-take, unsure if he was talking about Bob or the wolf. No one else seemed to notice. Gazes turned away from the woods where the animal had escaped, and the group glanced around, looking for Schoenwald.

"Not here anymore, folks. He's gone, and we've got to find him."

His voice rang with an authority that forced people to listen, and the dazed townsfolk rotated to hear what he said, drawn like a sunflower to the sun.

"An ambulance is on the way. We can't do much more to help these." He gestured toward the children. "But we can find the beast that hurt them!"

"Kill the son of a bitch," someone, Aggie thought it was Roger Goodall, yelled, and the group began to break apart —some of them drifting toward the Point and others moving toward the lighthouse.

"No!" Sheridon stopped them. "We've got to get organized. Don't forget there's more than one killer on the prowl tonight, and we must do something about both of them. Go home, arm yourselves, and remember that wolf's got Leah's little girl!" Jimmy bellowed above the crowd's rumble.

No few people coughed and shuffled.

"Well, are you gonna stand there like a bunch of idiots? We must do something!"

They muttered among themselves. A murderer, a killer. Someone to blame for all that had happened to them in the last few weeks.

"Come on, are you gonna stand here like half-wits?"

"No!" the group roared in unison as the turquoise band of the sky overhead darkened to sapphire, and they surged toward Sheridon.

"Or are we going to hunt them down and kill them?"

And Aggie again felt a moment of confusion. *Which "them" did he mean?*

"Are we gonna cower in our homes, or make it safe to walk the streets with pride?"

Time slipped and slithered, a snake eating its tail. And it was fifteen years ago, and a murderer was loose. A younger Jimmy goaded them, fired them to find the man who had so wantonly killed his parents.

A murderer was loose in the town.

"Killer! Wolf!" someone hollered.

"Killer! Wolf!" another voice joined with the first.

And another, until the two words had blurred, becoming one and the same: *killer-wolf.*

Fury welled within Aggie's chest. At last here was something external upon which she could vent her grief and her rage. *Someone she had loved last night. No!*

There had been more bloodshed and destruction than she could stand. All her horror, revulsion, and bewilderment congealed, and she started to shriek along with the rest of the crowd.

"Killerwolf!"

Jimmy took command. "Go and see if you can find that dumb fuck of a cop, maybe he can earn his keep. . . . You, gather branches or limbs to make torches, and you . . ."

He gestured this way and that, giving instructions, and no one thought it odd that the whole town should turn out to hunt a wolf—a species long extinct to the area, driven out years ago by man. No one wondered whether or not the wolf was capable, or culpable, of the crimes which had been visited upon their community. They were united, and even Bob was forgotten. No one questioned as Sheridon took control, apportioning territory and assigning search teams to look for the wolf, with Schoenwald mentioned as something of an afterthought.

Someone thrust a burning brand in Aggie's hand, and the next thing she knew she was being dragged away toward the forest.

19

From his place up in the loft, Blount could see the soft flickering of fairylights as they bobbed through the trees down by the Point. He tore his gaze away from the woods and back to the boy, still clinging to his brother's body. Hidden in shadows, Terry rocked back and forth, whimpering and crying. The only time he roused himself was when Blount attempted to pry Eddie from his grasp. From the boy's hysterical ramblings Blount gathered there'd been some kind of suicide pact over . . . and this puzzled Blount . . . June Gascon.

A suicide pact? Over June?

Only Eddie had lost his nerve and couldn't shoot himself, so Terry had obligingly done the honors for his younger twin, and then he, too, had chickened out.

What a waste!

Alan tried to prod Terry tentatively, but the boy howled, clawing at the man, only to desist when Blount backed away. Terry Fletcher was in a land beyond human contact now.

262

Somewhere with his twin, Blount supposed. It was enough to make you believe the old adage that twins shared a single soul, for truly this young man was lost.

Ginny had taken Doris into the house to make some tea. Poor woman, to lose two sons in one shot, and inwardly, Blount winced at his choice of words.

It would take a while for the State Police to arrive from Bangor. They'd probably just gotten home after filling out the reports from their most recent visit. After the last couple of weeks, Blount wouldn't have been at all surprised if a few weren't sitting around, waiting for something else to happen. They were probably thinking of setting up permanent offices in Stockton Springs. They'd spent enough time here lately.

A flash of red split the night. There was the hum of a car engine as it drew closer, and the crunch of gravel.

Blount rose from his squatting position and lurched forward. His damn feet were asleep. Hanging on to a support, Blount shook one leg and then the other until the pins-and-needles sensation of returning circulation coursed to his legs. He hobbled for the trap door and climbed the ladder down to ground level as a State car thundered past.

Bemused, Blount took his John Deere cap off of his head and scratched his scalp, looking from the State car in the drive to the one that swerved dangerously around the Four Corners and roared up the hill toward town.

"What the hell are you folks doing down here, taking LSD?" the officer said as he got out of his car. "Some guy goes berserk with a snowplow, people dropping like flies, and half the town out hunting for a wolf. You been putting funny stuff in the water or something?"

"What do you mean? What wolf? And what's this about a snowplow?" said Blount.

"Damned if I know. Someone called in saying some jerk decided to plow through a bunch of children down on the playground."

"Son of a bitch," Blount said, sprinting for his car. "Tell my wife where I'm going."

"Hey, I heard you'd quit," the officer said.

"I'm trying, but with all this going on around you, could you?"

The other officer waved him away. "Go ahead, you still got the car, might as well play the part. Go play cops and robbers; maybe you can help Bill and Pete round up the citizens before someone shoots himself in the foot. Quite frankly, I'm sick of this shit. If I never see the inside of this little burg again, it'll be too soon."

Blount ducked into his car just as Ginny came around the corner of the house. He looked from his wife to the officer.

"Stay here, honey, with Doris, and *don't* go into the forest. There's trouble in town."

He started the car.

"Blount!" the other officer shouted.

Alan paused before putting the car into reverse.

"Where's the body?"

Doris's pale white face floated in the living room window, and Blount grimaced apologetically.

"In the loft," he bawled out the window as he backed out the short drive to the street, remembering only after he had turned at the Four Corners that he'd forgotten to warn the cop about the brother.

"Good luck," Blount murmured to the empty car as he pressed on the gas and the car roared up the hill to Highway One.

The voices pursued him. Whispering, relentless voices. At first he hadn't listened, repressing them.

What with the flood and all, he had no time for them, so Bob Schoenwald remained deaf to their dark suggestions. But when he'd lost his job, they grew louder. Now they clamored to be heard, driving him on through the brush.

The man's breathing was labored, and prickers tore at his clothes as Schoenwald plowed through a patch of brambles, slapping them away. The whipping blackberry branches clutched at his pant legs, and something ripped.

Inside his head he heard the metallic clatter of an engine as it tore human sinew from bone. The children's cries still echoed in his ears as they had parted like the sea before the vehicle, diving away from him graceful as porpoises or dolphins. And he hated them even more for that as he brought the blade down to scrape across the ground.

Bob waded on, hands together and arms extended before him, unconsciously imitating the plow with its lethally pointed blade.

The crunch of bone. The smell of diesel, exhaust, and blood.

And his neighbors, friends, standing around him, horror and revulsion in their eyes.

And Aggie!

Bob Schoenwald broke through the briers, fumbling, unable to remember why he ran.

The smell of blood . . . the children.

Schoenwald doubled over as the shock of what he had done hit him. His hands clamped protectively over his abdomen. He had hurt them; he must pay. Bob spun to dive back into the slicing canes, and the voices reasserted control. The half-swing became a complete revolution, and he again faced the sea that was so close that he could hear the breaking of the surf against the rocks. The lighthouse, a refuge from the storm—he was sure he could see its light. A beacon of sanity and a shelter in the fog of confusion.

Behind him little balls of faint illumination bounced up and down. Intermittently someone would let out a whoop or a holler. Farther afield someone else would answer with a whistle.

"Run!" the voice inside his head said, and Bob needed no further urging as brief glimpses of blood and broken bodies surfaced in his consciousness. It took no great intelligence to figure out who they were looking for.

He tottered forward. His feet got tangled in the roots of some tree, and he went facedown. Propping himself against a trunk of a tree, Bob staggered to his feet and propelled himself toward the bay, the lighthouse, and safety.

Fiery brands danced as far as the eye could see. The children had been isolated at the edge of the field. The dead and the injured covered with blankets until the ambulance arrived and someone was assigned to inform their parents.

Sheridon counted noses. Over a hundred people. Their number grew as people came from up and down the street to join the hunt, many toting hunting rifles and guns. They loitered in tight little groups and waited for someone to tell them what to do. He was more than happy to oblige.

The flicker of orange-red torch flames mesmerized Jimmy, reminiscent of the glowing embers of his campfire, and Sheridon shook himself, realizing that this group of dumb fucks would founder without his guidance.

He bent over the ordinance map after allotting leadership to the same old fogeys who had been hanging around Aggie's when this first began. With such leadership, they'd probably shoot each other in a panic, but it would keep them occupied and out of his way.

His generals puffed with self-importance, and converged attentively over the map. Less than a few hours ago, these same men would have quite happily strung him up if they had had the courage.

"You, take a group of"—Jimmy glanced at the crowd— "ten people, and search this area." He stabbed a finger at the map. "And you, get the strip of land near the Retreat." He indicated two members of the group. He went down the list of names. They jostled and jogged, already arguing among themselves for positions of prominence next to their self-appointed leader, and Sheridon had to stop on more than one occasion to suppress the laughter that threatened to bubble to the surface.

Summer hot! Aggie tore at the shirt which clung to her back and neck.

Crickets chirped and cicadas sang. Mosquitoes buzzed around her head, emitting their high-pitched whine, and she swatted at them with her free hand. She thrust the hand holding the torch ahead through the dense growth, trying to get her bearings straight.

She was separated from the rest of the group, and away from the dazzling light of flames, Aggie had time to pause and reconsider what they were doing. This was insane. What the hell was she doing traipsing through the bog around the lighthouse?

The insects around her whirred and clicked. She swore and batted at them.

It wasn't right. Nothing was right anymore. Here it was fricking October already. The bugs should have descended into winter's rigor mortis. The trees should be cloaked in autumnal red rather than this sickly yellow-green.

Mud gripped at her feet, and once already she'd had to stop and extract her shoe from a quagmire.

A flicker appeared in the trees, and she bellowed: "Hey!"

It vanished as if it had never been. Marshlights.

Aggie stopped, scanning the area around her nervously. She was out here looking for a wolf? And what did she propose to do if she found it? Lecture it? Wag a finger at it, call it naughty and send it to bed without its supper? She had no gun.

This was ridiculous; away from Sheridon's spell, the smell of blood, and group hysteria, the whole concept seemed laughable. Only Aggie wasn't laughing. She was fed up. It was time to go home.

With that thought, she spun three hundred and sixty degrees, trying to orient herself or locate some kind of landmark. She reviewed the mental map of the area she was supposed to be searching—with the Penobscot on one side and the long curving road back to town. She had asked for this section of land, for someone said Bob had been headed in this direction when he was last seen disappearing into the brush.

Aggie's step faltered. *That* was why she was out here. Not for some phantom wolf, but Bob. And what would she do if she found *him?* Talk with him? Plead with him? To do what? Give himself up? No, everything inside her protested his surrender to this hysterical mob with a Stand-By-Your-Man fervor. Bob was innocent.

Innocent? How could he be innocent? She had witnessed his guilt with her own eyes, hadn't she?

Aggie swiftly squelched the image of Bob pulling young Jonathan's torn arm from the snowplow.

The insect buzz ceased for a split second, and from her left came the welcome sound of sea and waves. She would head for the water. Once she found the bay, she would know where she was. Like any native, anyone who had grown up in the area, Aggie knew every inch of coastline between here and the Point. As a kid, she had explored it with the other children, during long summer days when the world was fresh and new.

The hum of insects resumed, but not before she had determined the direction of the waves. Holding the torch low, she examined the ground before her and moved on.

Every once in a while she observed the distant flash of neighboring torchlight, but she ignored them. All Aggie wanted to do right now was crawl home, take a bath, and wrap herself around a stiff belt of Scotch. And think.

Screw Bob. Screw the wolf, if indeed it was a wolf. The more Aggie thought about it, the more she was sure that it had probably been a dog—a big dog, some sort of shepherd mix.

What the hell. Leah ran the kennels, didn't she?

Winding her way through tangled undergrowth and boulders, Aggie was almost in the water before she had realized she had reached the shore. She stopped with a small cry. A full moon glinted across the water, silhouetting the lighthouse. A black phallus against a flat, matte background.

A shadow parted from the grove and raced across the field to its base. Aggie bit her lip to stifle her exclamation. Bob!

Schoenwald stopped and turned to examine the area behind him. Aggie dashed out her torch, jamming it into the soft earth as he vanished through the door.

She waited, debating. Reason told her that she should get ahold of Blount to come pick him up. Blount, or somebody else. She should make her way to the nearest road, hitch a ride or walk to the nearest phone so they could take him away. He needed help.

But Aggie couldn't. He had held her; he had loved her.

Maybe if she talked to him. Surely she could discover why he had done what he had done, and she could help him.

So Aggie waited, watching the black, blank edifice, hoping to see him appear at the door.

What the hell was he doing in there?

A pale white smudge appeared in the glass dome of the lighthouse. The apparition floated in the darkness, and Aggie had to squint so she could see. The pale disk of his face detached itself from the building, and she realized that he had somehow managed to get onto the ledge beyond the glass. She dropped the still smoking remains of the torch at her feet and began to run toward the lighthouse as Bob stepped away from the ledge.

The accommodating Jimmy drove his group to the hill between the highway and stony beach. He had deliberately chosen the shell-shocked, the wounded, those people whose children had been hurt or had died, to accompany him. Picking them out easily by their dazed expressions and pain-racked eyes. He *wanted* the most befuddled and inept to be under his command and his control. When they arrived at their location, he parked not in his own driveway, but at the hotel across Highway One, pausing to let people unload.

Standing on the apex of the hill near Highway One like a general with his troops, Jimmy gave his beleaguered corps last-minute instructions. From here he could observe the darting lights as people scoured the surrounding woods. Torches flickered everywhere, and here and there the long pale beam of a flashlight. Jimmy wondered how long before one of these stupid motherfuckers blasted himself in the foot or, better still, his nearest neighbor as he came blundering through the trees.

"Right, everybody fan out. You, go that way, and you, over there, search across the street."

He barked his orders, and they jumped. They followed him like the mindless insects they were, as they had in the past, not knowing this search to be as futile as the last.

Last time the villagers had not even known that the

culprit they sought was, in fact, Jimmy. Unsuspecting, they had followed Sheridon, the object of their hunt. The murderer of his parents who had gotten in his way one time too often. And the idiots never figured it out, never realized that it had been him whose hand had wielded the knife that severed body from head. Jimmy had led them a merry chase, and this time he would do the same.

The last of his helpers vanished into the brush. Alone at last to deal with Leah, and then the kid. Sheridon had apportioned the territory carefully so that the land nearest the mobile home was his. His team ranged elsewhere, stamping loudly through the meadow on the opposite side of the street and crashing drunkenly through the woodland beyond the tracks.

Jimmy dashed across the highway and stared down the tenebrous tunnel of trees to the dooryard. Lights streamed through the windows and the doleful refrain of a Tammy Wynette tune wafted around the small clearing. Tiffany's mother was probably the only person, besides that dumbassed Blount, who wasn't out hunting for the wolf and her own damned daughter.

An unpleasant grin spread across Sheridon's face.

He'd show her what would happen to anyone who was stupid enough to pull a gun on him, and Jimmy stalked down the dark drive to the mobile home.

They nestled in the soft welcoming arms of the thicket. The wolf had not wanted to stop, but the human male had been winded by the chase. The wolf groomed himself, unconcerned. Blackberry canes wove an intricate pattern over their heads. The two humans sat rigid, eyes wide, listening intently to the din beyond the thatchwork of canes and starting at each snap of twig or crackle of leafy bough.

The wolf paused in his grooming to observe the she-cub. He had recognized her easily. The child shone like a jewel, reflecting all that was good or could be good in the human species. Wonder, love, loyalty, and other traits for which lupine sagacity had no name. The beast had felt these things within the human spirit the shaman had planted within his breast, but the concepts were so alien to the animal that they remained identifiable, but undefined.

Had the wolf had human expectations, he would have been disappointed in her. The child was an empty shell, a husk. Something was missing. As if the man who had sired her was already dead, bequeathing to her with his seed nothing but his shell, and not his mortal spark. The seed was damaged, and the girl-child was hollow, an empty vessel waiting to be filled.

The massive head swung to inspect the man. His chest still heaved, and his breath whistled in and out of his chest. Terror shone in the vapid eyes as he stared at the wolf. The man feared for the wolf, and the wolf saw images reflected in the mortal mind. A tiny animal, something the man had once loved, dying in pain. The predator puzzled over this, for the wolf knew he had nothing to fear. As long as the shaman's spirit remained housed within his breast, nothing mortal man could do to him would kill him. The wolf did not fear death. His stay on earth had been overlong, and the beast had come to desire the rest that only death could bring. Even gods got tired of life in a world without worshippers. What need had he for such a place? And what need had it for him? Surely, he would have passed away long before this if the curse hadn't kept him here.

The cub, the wolf had expected, but the man came as a surprise. The man like the child appeared empty, but the wolf sensed he was not. If anything the man was too full, as if life had thrust too much on him and the vessel had broken under the pressure. The seed itself was whole, but the soil upon which it had been planted had been poisoned. So the embryo would lie unable to germinate until the soil was cleansed. Only then would intelligence take root, blossom, and grow.

Now that he had reached his goal, the wolf found that the talisman was lost. He could sense its presence and smell it on the cub and in her clothes, and he wondered how the humans could stand the smell. The great beast nosed at her pocket, pawed at it, but he could not communicate his need. The child looked at him blankly and petted the gray head reassuringly.

Without the bone the evil would continue to run rampant across the land, until the she-cub located it, and the wolf must remain, as trapped by the spell as the human inhabitants of this community. In splitting asunder the body from the finger, the old Indian had severed the man from his malice. The wolf had received the spirit, and the hatred had been buried in an earthen grave. A potential blight upon the land. Centuries later, once unearthed, the curse had been loosed, tainting the town and those who lived in it.

So far the talisman had been kept apart from its human operator by luck and chance, and by the guileless child who knew at least this much instinctively: to isolate evil from its vehicle. But the bone was lost, and the wolf must remain with the child until she found it. Only then would land, beast, and man be free.

The wolf regarded the unlikely pair, wondering how they had survived this long. He should never have let himself be driven away from his onetime home by civilization. His trip from his new territory had taken far too long, and the wolf had almost been too late to help the child.

The girl smiled wanly at the great beast, resting her head against his massive chest. The wolf grinned at her, loving her with the same fierce affection he had once felt for his pups.

For that is what they were, pups, both child and man, helpless in their as yet unformed state. The child, in particular, was vulnerable, by both size and circumstance, and the wolf would defend her in the face of the undying death, the type of extinction that could only be visited upon the immortal. The young man had the size and the bulk to protect himself, and the wolf knew he would come into his own soon.

The great ears moved forward and back. Snuffling and growling, the wolf cocked his head.

The "other" approached. The manifestation of the evil. Hatred's covenant which had found residence within a

corrupt human soul. The massive head swung, following the
sound as the she-cub and man tensed, listening, also. The
man hunkered down, watching intently the movement
between the gaps of branches, and he paled as their adversary passed.

Again the wolf caught echoes from the mortal mind. The
beast perceived a bond that tied the two. Suddenly the
pieces fell into place, and the puzzle presented by man and
child was a puzzle no more.

Unreality heaped upon unreality. Blount emerged from
his car to survey a disaster scene the likes of which he had
seen only on the news. Ambulances were lined up in a neat
row. The medical team moved from child to child, treating
them for mild shock, bandaging a scrape here and there, and
soothing their fears. The ambulance with little Georgie
Wilson, whose injuries were worse than most, screeched
away from the schoolyard. Georgie had a fractured femur
and possibly a fractured fibula, and he—in comparison to
Jonathan, whose body had to be identified in pieces—was
one of the lucky ones.

A police photographer moved furtively around the plow
as if he expected the equipment to wake up any minute and
bite him.

Thunderstruck, Blount leaned against his car, not quite
able to take it all in. Two children killed. Others injured.

By Bob Schoenwald? He wouldn't hurt a fly.

Tragedy heaped on tragedy; oddity upon oddity.

And this was the part Alan couldn't comprehend. The
parents—even the parents of the children who'd been hurt
or killed—were gone following Sheridon. Hunting wolves?
Fucking wolves!

There hadn't been a wolf in the area for decades. Blount
tried to imagine Aggie confronting a wolf with her sharp
tongue, and even sharper temper, and couldn't. But the
undeniable proof darted between the trees. Flitting lights
like fireflies.

Alan had been right in the first place; the whole world had
gone crazy.

". . . they're sending the mortician out for the kids' bodies. If we can ever find the parents, we will have them picked up." The officer nodded toward the bag that shrouded the dead Jonathan.

"I don't know what you've been doing out here lately," he continued. "Acid parties or what? But I sure as shit wish you'd stop it."

"Maybe we should go look for their parents," Blount said.

"Go out in the woods at night, with a bunch of hysterical hicks toting guns? Uh-uh, no, thanks, not me. My bit stops here." He pointed down at the ground below his feet. "Just short of suicide."

"You mean you're not going to do anything?"

"What would you suggest? Arrest the whole town for being a bunch of dumb fucks?" the officer said.

Blount pushed away from the car, angry.

"Well, if you won't, I will," he said.

"Don't get yourself killed," the second officer interjected as Blount slammed the car door and stamped off toward the forest.

20

Leah's head rebounded off the wall with a sharp crack. The force of the next blow drove her teeth through her tongue. She tasted copper, salt, and bitter bile as her stomach tried to erupt into her throat, but Leah would not give Jimmy the satisfaction of making a sound. Not so much as a peep.

Jimmy had snuck up on her. He'd always been a quiet son of a bitch.

Leah grappled with him, trying to extricate herself from Jimmy's rough embrace. Head forward and body bent double, her hands scrabbled to find purchase on the doorframe. He dropped her. Leah's arms pinwheeled and, without Jimmy to support her, she fell face forward, propelled by the momentum of her own struggles.

"Where is she, cunt?" Jimmy said, and she flinched away from his upraised hand, to hold her cheek and wipe blood from her lip.

The muffled shouts of the townspeople rang mockingly

outside the trailer. Help, so close and yet so far away. Leah gazed longingly at the door behind Jimmy. Calculating time and distance and wondering if she were to scream whether or not someone outside would hear and come to her aid.

Sheridon glanced behind him and laughed. "You're not getting out that way."

And he backed to the door, leaned against it and contemplated her with a casual air. Balling his hands into fists, he smiled and advanced upon her again. Leah clambered away from him toward the kitchen door. His hand fell heavily on her shoulder, yanking her around to face him.

"Now, you were gonna tell me about your daughter," he said, the threat implying that a worse beating would follow if she refused.

Sheridon brought the heavy bone handle of his hunting knife crashing down on the base of her skull. Leah crumpled and he stood over her, panting. She had said nothing. Not a word. And his first impulse was to cut her, hurt her, carve her up much like Rich had done to June. He yanked at her hair, lifting her head, and the blade wavered before the hairline. It grazed the skin. Blood beaded along the thin line. It would have taken little more than a flick of the wrist to scalp her, but Sheridon hesitated. He needed Leah as bait to draw the child into the trailer. The hand holding the knife shook with frustrated rage. She could not look too badly used, but he didn't necessarily need her alive. With a snarl he turned loose of her hair. The head rolled limply forward.

Throwing the blade aside, he began to pommel her with both fists. When Jimmy received no reaction, he began to kick her, as if her defenselessness only fueled his fury. The blows were so hard that her flaccid form scooted across the floor away from him, and he felt the crunch of bones as her ribs gave way.

When blood oozed from her mouth, nose, and ears, and he was reasonably sure she would never survive her injuries, he stopped and listened. He heard the ragged bubbling quality to her breath and figured he must have punctured a lung. Jimmy squatted, tucked his forefinger under her chin to gaze upon her face.

"That's what happens when you try to disobey me, babe," he said, and then he stood. With one final glance at her, he muttered, "I'll be back," and moved swiftly to the door.

He had other fish to fry.

Sheridon stomped up the drive to the road. Anger powered his movements, overriding his typically light gait. He scanned the area between trailer and beach, turning first to examine the brier-tangled meadow that led toward the village of Sandypoint and then toward the woods that led to the Point itself, wondering where the girl could have gone. She could be anywhere. Jimmy swore violently. He was stumped by a half-wit child.

Taking a few deep breaths, he calmed himself and then reviewed what areas he had assigned and what areas remained untouched. The meadow was his territory, and unless he searched it no one would. With muttered oath Sheridon jumped over the ditch, diving into the thick growth.

The night had been one of flailing limbs, flashing lights, metallic rumbles, and men's roars.

And blood.

Jonathan, poor Jonathan.

Tiffany tried to put the image out of her mind, ducking to evade another branch as the wolf plunged into the leafy tunnel that led to his adopted bower. She slid from his back, and the wolf hunkered down, tongue hanging from between pointed incisors. Gideon drooped, his breath coming out in a dry, rasping wheeze.

The wolf snarled, and man and child hushed, listening. They could hear the far-off sounds of people. Sometimes one would stray close, breaking like a wave upon the briers and surging to either side of the thicket where man and beast lay hidden. The hunters called back and forth, ignoring the patch of thatch so dense that the branches formed a tent above the heads of the breathless group.

Their sanctuary was some hundred yards away from her home, in the field between trailer and the Sandypoint road. Tiffany had discovered it ages ago and used it as her secret lair. A home away from home. She kept toys here and a blanket, which she had rolled up and set off to the side. The den showed signs of its more recent habitation in the bones and feathers that were strewn about the floor, and Tiffany did not look too closely at the still-wet fragments of tendon and sinew.

The wolf began to growl at the thud of footsteps nearby. Tiffany held her breath, wishing just as hard as she could that the searchers would leave them in peace, and the footsteps went away. She slumped against Gideon, letting the air out with a gentle *whoosh*.

The wolf rose to its feet, sniffed at the air, and plunged for the door. Behind her Gideon moved with such speed that Tiffany collapsed against the branch walls, and the whole thicket shook.

Gideon tried to interpose his body between the wolf and the entrance to the den, blocking the exit, but he wasn't quick enough. His hand snaked out to seize the beast by the scruff of the neck, and the wolf whirled, snapping at the hand. Gideon blanched but did not release his grip. The beast stared at Gideon. When their eyes met, luminous green and empty blue, the man's jaw went slack. Something passed between the two of them, beast and man, for Gideon nodded, releasing his hold on the thick fur.

"Uh-huh," he said, and the wolf turned to leave. Tiffany gave a short cry as the beast slipped away. She slithered upon her tummy through the arch of interwoven branches. Gideon yelped and dragged her back into their protected den.

"Where'd he go?" she said to Gideon, disgruntled. The young man shrugged.

She tugged at the branches and took a halfhearted swipe at the blanket. It rolled away from her to reveal two bones pressed into the soil. Both girl and man gaped at them.

"My lucky piece," Tiffany said, jumping on her prize. Her fingers wrapped around it, and before Gideon could stop her, she bellyflopped, pulling herself through the tunnel into open air.

The gray ears pricked and twitched, zeroing in on the sound. The clumsy human crashed through brush and twig, heedless of the clatter that followed in his wake. Despite the noise, the predator realized that his quarry was traveling with great speed. For the clack of branch and bough was only audible to the wolf's sensitive ears, and already the din was passing beyond the range of the predator's hearing. Still, the wolf could smell the other's darkness and follow it.

The beast shook his head impatiently. The thick mane rippled. The man's actions inside the den had cut vital seconds from the chase, but the wolf was in no hurry. He did not seek confrontation with this dark shade. This human who sheltered the shaman's hatred was irrelevant to the wolf's plan. The man was just another victim of the ancient hex as much as any other member of the accursed village. Perhaps more so. Although the beast had to acknowledge that some quirk within the man himself had caused this. The malice that pulsed through the shaman had found this human a handy domicile because it beat with the same rhythm as his own malignance. The mortal's destruction would not nullify the magic. The evil would only move on to the next most appropriate dwelling. And the next. Until the bitterness was spent or no mortal man survived.

Yet the wolf, who was also a god, had looked into the light one's unshuttered eyes and had seen into his immortal soul. The wolf beheld the human's past, present, and future and could see beyond the vacuous mind into the still, dark places that humans called psyche. The wolf had seen the "other" nestled there. He recognized the vision and understood it. Then the beast had realized that Gideon would never be whole until he could face the darkness within and conquer it. Confronting these shadows meant confronting this other man, whose existence meant nothing to the wolf.

Enough of the god remained, despite his years tied to mortal earth, that the wolf could not let this happen. The light one's soul was worth redeeming. The curse could wait, would have to, since the talisman was lost to him. The human, however, could not. The man had waited far too long already. So the wolf set off at an easy trot, head held high. He did not need to stick his nose to the ground to track this stench.

The creature ran with easy grace, flanks barely touching the branches as he passed. He made no attempt to hide himself. He knew he would pass unseen by man, unless he chose otherwise. Thus, the wolf had shown himself periodically throughout his journey—appearing to a few individuals along the way so they could see and remember that this land once belonged to others. To animals and man, who had lived within its cycles and not tried to reshape it to his liking.

Confident in his pursuit the wolf bounded between leaf and bush to retrieve the man of darkness and present him to the man of light.

When Gideon emerged, Tiffany stood in the open, head tilted to one side. She stuck her hands in her pockets, stared at the stars, and kicked at a branch.

"I'd better go. My mom'll be worried. You wanna come?"

Gideon motioned for her to go on ahead. She slouched away. The young man waited. He turned toward the trailer, and then he swung away to catch a fleeting glimpse of gray as the wolf slunk through the underbrush. Gideon turned a second time, and a third, glancing between girl and beast. His indecision reflected by his action.

Tiffany disappeared from view, and the decision was made. Gideon wheeled, shoving his way through the thick growth, to follow the wolf.

Only when Jimmy reached the other road did he remember the reason he had been stalking through the trees. He paused, turned left to stare at the blacktop which followed the gentle rise of the hill that would eventually dip and lead to the railroad bridge and Sandypoint village beyond. In front of him was a row of houses, and beyond them if he looked hard enough he thought he noted the diamond glint of moonlight upon the water. Chewing on his lip, Sheridon swung to his right where the blacktop stretched to the Four Corners and dwindled to gravel road beyond. Immediately behind him there was a coppice which tapered to brier-laced meadow through which he had already walked.

Where was that damned girl? He didn't even know where to begin looking. She could even be home by now, and Jimmy sneered, thinking of the bloody package that would be there to greet her.

Again Sheridon considered his options—small copse, the village, the Point, or beach. Some sixth sense directed him back the way he came. It could have been the hair creeping up on the back of his neck or simply logic that at this time of night the child would try to find her way home, but Jimmy had learned to trust his instincts. So he rotated smartly upon a booted heel, spinning to confront . . . a wolf.

Sheridon gaped, mouth ajar, while his hair continued its slow dance upon his scalp and a chill raced up his spine. His mind, however, was slower to react. Never in all the scenarios he had planned had he foreseen this. He'd expected triumph, accepted it, and had only spent time and effort deciding what form it would take. Would he tear the child's throat out with his teeth for the trouble she had caused? Or would he tease her, taunt her, *torture* her with her mother's death? Never, though, had he expected to confront a real wolf, in spite of his vision in the flames, for Jimmy, of all men in the area, knew when the last of the species had been seen in Maine, right down to the year and the date.

At the schoolyard Sheridon had caught only a glimpse of the creature as gentle teeth had clamped down on Tiffany's frail arm, causing no pain. Then the girl and beast were gone. Jimmy had noted then the tenderness of the touch and assumed it was the shepherd. What was that damn dog's name? Sheridon did a mental shuffle, brain still unwilling to accept the specter that stood in his path. Belatedly he dismissed the name as trivial, as reason and belief finally collided. The wolf had provided a convenient excuse, fuel to fire the mounting hysteria. He had latched on to it, dismissing all possibility that it was real. A sad lack of forethought on his part, and now it seemed a fatal omission.

All this passed through his mind before his jaw snapped shut. The wolf had not moved, gazing at him with eyes that glowed green in reflected light. It blinked, closing off the lantern glare, and Sheridon ducked into a defensive crouch, hand groping for his knife. Its eyes popped open at the sound of Jimmy's movement. A deep rumbling issued from its throat.

The blade whispered from its sheath, the metal picking up the faint rays of the moon. The huge head swung, luminescent eyes taking in the glint of blade, and the beast's magnificent muscles bunched in preparation for a leap. In another instant it would be aloft, and Jimmy remembered the fight in the distant clearing well enough to not tarry here waiting for the beast to strike.

With a shout he bolted toward the village. Wind brushed his cheek, and the beast stood before him, blocking the road. Sheridon's grip tightened on the knife as he waited for the animal to attack, but it remained still as a statue, an all-too-human grin painted on its lupine features.

Jimmy winced, eyes darting to the woods and then to the nearby houses, ablaze with light. He feinted to his left. Again the beast tensed, ready to jump. And Jimmy changed course, literally falling to his right and rolling back onto his feet, to begin a squatting run toward the house; but the wolf was there before him. Immobile.

With a snarled curse Sheridon shifted his weight, letting his momentum carry him toward the Four Corners, and this time he saw the wolf pounce, in graceful slow motion. It seemed to fly through the air, four paws connecting with Jimmy's back, driving him down to the ground. The animal's weight caused all the air to rush out of him, and Jimmy lay stunned for a minute, not caring what would happen next, but the wolf had bounded past him and was now stationed in the middle of the road beyond, as though guarding the path. Jimmy scrambled to his feet, crouched, pondering the wolf for a minute, thinking that perhaps it meant him no harm—it had had more than ample opportunity to hurt him—when suddenly it moved, diving at him, mouth open. Wicked incisors flashed white, and Jimmy didn't waste any more time on thought or conjecture. He dashed, arms held before him, ready this time to do battle if the beast got in his way, but it did not.

Sheridon rammed through a tangle of branches, bulldozing his way into the coppice. He spared a second for a glance back and wasn't surprised to find the wolf bearing down on him. That was the last time he looked back. Relying on hearing and instinct, he plunged ahead, running like all the hounds of hell were on his heels.

The black nostrils flared, and the wolf was assaulted with a miasma of odors. He caught the stench of malevolence, the pheromones of mortal fear, and beneath it all a faint whiff of the old Indian as he had smelled after death. Beyond that he sensed the man's inherent corruption. The curse had chosen a worthy vessel, for the human had taken all that his Indian ancestors had represented and twisted it, perverted it. The wolf chuffed his abhorrence and gave chase.

Silent and deadly, the wolf zigzagged through the trees behind Jimmy. As if he understood the wolf's intent, the man kept veering, looping off to the right or the left, any way but forward. Circling in either direction would take him sloping back down the hill to the road while the forward thrust was a steep incline, but the beast's wide path thwarted these designs—dodging right and left as the man would attempt to creep on all fours past the hunter.

The predator's heart sang with the thrill of the chase as he drove the man ahead of him. He had not hunted, except to satisfy minimal needs of hunger, since his trek began back in the icy tundra of Canada's Hudson Bay. He missed his pack, then, and he wished them here with him so he could prod the prey into its untender embrace. Something thrashed through the bracken, and the wolf caught a flash of yellow, gold. *The human male. The light one.*

The pack was here.

At that moment the wolf stopped toying with his quarry

and leapt ahead in a flurry of snapping teeth. For the first time a cry escaped the dark one's lips as he broke from the cover of the trees into the thicket beyond—an eerie howl that reverberated throughout the night, competing with the shouts of the human huntsmen far afield.

And the beast knew that he had won. He paused to add his own voice to that of man, the answering cry of the wolf. All voices near and far fell silent. The dark one ducked, diving down to the ground, preferring the scratch of briers to the exposure of the field. Gideon broke into view, heading for a ripple in the long canes, as the wolf vaulted into the meadow behind him.

His eyes bulging with terror and exertion, Jimmy elbowed his way along—scrambling on his stomach, dragging his legs behind him. He moved blindly, following the slant of the hill, trusting the old Indian's spell to guide him. Whipping canes added new lines to his cheeks, and he kept blinking wildly, unable to use his arms to protect his face.

The wolf's wail echoed across the glen, followed by shouts of surprise, but Jimmy didn't take the time to look behind. Each time he did, each time he had tried to double back, he had run into the ghostly gray wolf. Each time the predator had driven him on, as if it had a set path, a set place, in mind. The very fact that the creature didn't finish Jimmy off when it had the opportunity frightened Sheridon more than if the beast had chosen that moment to fight.

Beyond thought Jimmy couldn't decide between stealth or speed, so Sheridon simply continued his slap-dash climb, scrabbling in the dirt like a snake or a worm. The fronds lashed around him, and gnats rose around his head in clouds, maddening him even more. Sweat and blood dripped in his eyes. The salt sting caused his eyes to tear, and he couldn't see where he was going. Stones and dirt made quick work of his shirt, leaving his elbows exposed. Pebbles ground into his flesh, and soon they were abraded and torn.

His belly-scraping pace flagged, and he held his breath,

trying to discern the direction of the beast, but heard nothing beyond the renewed shouting of the huntsmen who scoured the distant woods. Briefly Jimmy considered standing up and calling for help. And he had time to rue his carefully devised scheme which had isolated him upon this hill and placed all help beyond his grasp. Would they even see him? Besides, Jimmy didn't trust his neighbors enough not to shoot him in a panic if he materialized too quickly.

"Over here!" someone yelled, the voice vague and distant. With a sinking heart Jimmy realized just how far away assistance was, and he clambered on.

Wind rushed past his ears as he ran, and Gideon's spirit soared as he kept pace with the wolf. Occasionally he noted the dark shadow which was the object of the wolf's pursuit, and he would swerve, allowing his own light step to thud heavily against the ground, and he delighted when the wraith veered away from him.

Only when Jimmy burst from the clearing did Gideon realize his brother was the quarry. Something hard and brittle glittered in Gideon's eyes. The muscles in his jaw jumped. All joy was lost from the chase, and Gideon redoubled his efforts, arriving at the thicket ahead of the wolf. He surged on through the tangle of blackberries as the wolf hesitated and howled. Gideon recognized the note of triumph, and a thrill shot through him, giving him new strength. His step faltered only long enough to discern his brother's presence in the ripple of the brush, and then he charged on. For the moment the wolf was forgotten, becoming a gray shade in a field of whipping shadows.

Up, up, and up the hill, until his pace slowed—the surge of adrenaline gone. When Gideon reached the short stretch of wood between dooryard and field, he could run no more. He halted as somewhere farther down the hill he observed Jimmy slither from a tunnel of woven cane into the stand of trees. Propped against a poplar, Gideon wheezed, his breath whistling out of him. Then another darker shadow followed Jimmy into the wood. There was a sharp snap, a growl, and an answering expletive as Jimmy met his nemesis yet again, and Gideon levered himself away from the tree and thundered into the wood, ready to give chase once more.

Through the dark woods, stumbling over boulder and stone, Jimmy kept trying to turn west toward the Sandy-point road—heading away from the trailer instinctively. If that was where the wolf wanted Sheridon to go, that was a place to avoid. Each time he did, the beast was there before him as if it divined Jimmy's plan by some sort of clairvoyance or subtle sense of smell, and Sheridon found himself herded back toward the trailer and Leah's body.

And Jimmy gave in, stopped fighting it, allowing himself to be steered. At least there he would have walls, if not stout ones, to guard him, and he had guns. He could shoot the son-of-bitching critter. Blow it to smithereens, and for the first time since this nightmare run had begun, Jimmy started to believe that maybe he could win this one after all.

Gideon raced through the woods, avoiding pitfalls and stones, looping down to where he had last spied his brother and the wolf. Something flitted through the thick underbrush of the ditch, and Gideon hesitated, confused. At that moment the wolf appeared. Gideon grinned at it, but the smile was cold and hard. He plunged ahead. Sharp teeth clamped gently on his wrist.

Gideon glanced down at the beast. It gazed at him, fixing the young man with its green and glowing eyes. Gideon squatted down, mesmerized. The sounds of battle erupted from the trailer, and the wolf loosed him.

Knowing now what he was supposed to do, Gideon slid silently toward the mobile home.

Tiffany meandered up the path, hand still in her pocket. She was glad to have her lucky charm back again. She clenched the twin pieces of white ivory in her fist. Her step faltered as she tried to remember the last time she had seen it. The thought skittered away from her as so many did, and she abandoned it to continue upon the faint trail she had beaten between secret den and trailer dooryard.

She was pleased also with her pet, although she realized somewhere in the back of her mind that the wolf was not a pet and could never be owned by any man. Still, Tiffany had missed Goliath, Bilbo, and all the other dogs, now that vacations were over and the kennel stood empty.

Her path intersected with the drive near the road, and Tiffany turned, shambling on. Her eyes caught the blaze of light that cascaded from the open door, and she halted. Tammy Wynette, her mom's favorite singer, hiccuped as the stereo needle, caught in a scratch, played the same note over and over again. Tiffany gulped, her reluctant gaze sweeping up to the open door and what appeared to be a pile of clothing upon the floor.

"Momma!"

Tiffany raced up to the trailer, rattled up the stairs, and burst into the living room. She stopped to stare at Leah. Blood oozed from her ears, her nose and her mouth. A fine line had been sliced into her forehead near the hairline. Terrified, the girl sunk to her knees, crawling the last few feet to her mother's side. A tremulous hand reached out to grasp Leah's shoulder.

"Momma?" Tiffany shook her mother. Leah rolled onto her back, and Tiffany could see that blood seeped also from underneath her mother's lids as if she cried tears of blood.

"Momma!" She threw herself on her mother, crying, beating futilely on her mother's chest. "Momma, don't die. Please, don't die."

Tiffany pulled away from her mother. "Please, don't go. I need you." She sniffled and pulled her arm across her face to wipe the tears away.

The eyelids fluttered, and the hand flopped loosely on the floor.

"Momma!" And jubilant, Tiffany prepared to throw herself upon the still form and give her a big bear hug when her mother groaned.

"Tiffany?"

"Yes, Momma. I'm here, Momma. I'm here."

Leah coughed, spat out blood and teeth, and struggled to right herself. Tiffany placed her arms under her mother's shoulders and pushed. Leah opened her eyes, and Tiffany recoiled. All that had once been white was bright red where the tiny vessels had burst, spreading blood across the sclera. Tiffany's own eyes glazed as she tried to withdraw to the safety of her mind.

Leah clutched Tiffany's shoulders. "Tiffany, go. Jimmy . . . Jimmy. It's you he wants. Not me. Get out. Get out now before he comes back. Run and hide. Go find Alan Blount. He'll help you."

"No, Momma," and the tears began again when Tiffany realized her mother would send her away alone. "No, I won't leave you. I won't!"

"Please, baby, please," Leah pleaded with her. "I couldn't stand it if he were to hurt you, too." Then she noticed the stubborn set of the girl's chin, and all the arguments died on her lips. "All right, we'll both go then. Help me up."

The two floundered for an instant as Tiffany staggered under Leah's weight. Then the girl locked her knees, allowing her mother to use her shoulder for support as if it were a crutch or a cane, and Leah stood on legs as wobbly as a newborn fawn.

Leah released Tiffany, leaned against the wall and began to propel her body down the long hall to her bedroom. Tiffany trailed behind her mother, hovering like a broody hen over her chicks. Leah brushed her away.

"I'll be all right," she lied. "Go collect the coats and boots. I'm going to pack some clothes."

The hall stretched unendingly before her. Leah had never realized it was this long. Pain thrummed throughout her body. Every step sent agony rocketing up her spine, and each movement tried to dislodge something in her chest. She could feel fluid seeping into her lungs. They bubbled with every breath. It didn't take a medical degree to figure out that one or more of her ribs were broken, and at least one had probably penetrated the vital organs, puncturing a lung.

Leah never knew that there could be such pain, and she had received more than her share of knocks in her life, but every other beating she had endured paled in comparison. The hallway spun around her, and her legs felt like two dead weights, but she forced herself to go on, biting her tongue so that neither moan nor gasp escaped her lips.

Sam, she thought, *we'll go to Sam. He'll help us.* Leah tried to dismiss the image of Sam the last time she had seen him—his eyes glaring in unspoken accusation. *He had to!*

Leah reached the bedroom and stared at the blanket-covered closet. The room dipped crazily as she tried to remember what she was looking for. Her pulse slushed lethargically past her temples. There was a faint footfall behind her, and her mind cleared.

"Momma?"

"Go and find my car keys, honey. I think they're in the kitchen. I'll be with you in a minute."

Again, Leah gathered her dwindling strength around her as she considered the room. She was here to pack. Suddenly her mind was cluttered with things she ought to take, if this was, as she suspected, to be the last time they saw the inside of the trailer. She knew Jimmy. He would not give up easily. If they did manage to escape this time, there wouldn't be a second chance to come and collect their things.

Her shoulders hunched. It was useless. Too much to gather in too little time. Better to flee and trust to blind luck than to wait for Jimmy to return. Leah swung back, using her hands rather than her legs to propel her.

Just then she heard the soft latch of the front door closing.

"Tiffany!"

Jimmy burst through the door. He slumped against the wood, waiting to catch his breath. Fingers made clumsy by fear fiddled ineffectively with the lock. Finally the bolt shot home, and Sheridon grimaced when he realized this flimsy piece of wood was all that stood between himself and that monster. His eyes rolled in his sockets as he sought something to use as a brace for the door.

He grabbed the tattered couch to haul it into position when he heard something stir. He swung as Tiffany rose from where she hid at the other end of the couch to stare at him wide-eyed.

"You!"

21

All thoughts of the wolf faded from his mind, its threat forgotten as he confronted the object of his quest. Leah's shriek echoed from the far end of the trailer, but Jimmy ignored it as if he hadn't heard. Sheridon lunged for the girl, skirting the couch with a graceful animal leap. He landed in a crouch. She sidled away from him toward the darkened hall. He jumped, again using the powerful muscles in his legs to carry him so that he could position himself between Tiffany and the only avenue of escape.

Still in the same half-squatting posture, he swung, rotating on the ball of his foot in response to each feint the child made. Tiffany yielded and pressed herself flat against the wall as if she could dig her way into it.

Sheridon darted forward. His hand snaked out, and he slapped her lightly across the cheek. She slid sideways until she ran into the couch. Jimmy flipped the all-but-forgotten knife from one hand to the other and then hit her again with the hand he had just freed.

Slap . . . flip . . . *slap* . . . flip. He juggled the blade with fluid grace, throwing it from one hand to the other so that the blows came from left and then right. He struck her, not hard enough to bruise, but hard enough to sting. And he toyed with her as the wolf had toyed with him. When Sheridon remembered the ivory teeth, his belly-crawling path through the thicket, fury and rage bounded through him. The child would pay for his humiliation.

Tiffany cradled her head in her arms, attempting to block the blows, and she dodged again for the safety of the hall.

He rocked back and forth—shifting his weight from one leg to the other—and her escape was cut off, his action ensuring that she could bolt neither left nor right. Yet he made no attempt to approach her. She clambered over the arm of the couch and tried to hide underneath the pillows, and he let her. She was his, and he was content to let Tiffany scamper over the sofa's arm and prolong his moment of triumph.

"Got'cha, don't I, little girl?" He spoke for the first time, gloating. "And now you're gonna give me what I want."

Vaguely he heard the *thump-shuffle* of Leah as she made her way awkwardly back toward the living.

"Tiff? Tiff? Answer me, honey, are you all right?"

Jimmy blotted out the hated voice. He would deal with *her* later. Tiffany crab-walked backward across the sofa, crying.

"Wha-wha-what do you want?" she said.

"The bone," he said.

"What bone?"

"You know what bone. An eye for an eye, remember?"

Tiffany eyed the door, and Jimmy laughed. Her gaze flicked out the window.

"Your wolf friend can't help you now unless he's suddenly developed hands, and I'm prepared for that idiot brother of mine," he said, gripping the knife in his hand. "He's something I should have taken care of a long time ago. Now, give it to me before I grow tired of this." Sheridon rose to loom over her.

"What do you want it for?"

Sheridon blinked, taken aback by the question. He cocked his head, considered the child for a bit, and then said: "Because it's special, and it's mine." Jimmy waggled his stump at her. "To replace this."

Out of the corner of his eye he saw the darkness move, and he realized Leah would be with them in a minute. Jimmy launched at Tiffany, his arm lashing out to twist around the child's neck. He held the knife to her throat and spun, dragging her off her feet to face Leah. He let the blade graze the skin, drawing blood, so the stupid bitch would know he meant business.

Suddenly there was a thundering crash behind him, and Jimmy spun again. The door bowed dangerously, and Sheridon backed up a pace while Tiffany's feet kicked weakly in the air.

Another crash and the hinges gave, the cheap wood shattered. Splinters flew as the door hit the floor with a bang, and Gideon landed on all fours on top of it.

Jimmy nearly dropped the girl when he spied the wolf, as big as life, slinking in behind his brother. Sheridon pulled the knife away from her throat and rubbed his eyes with his sleeve. When he looked again it was Gideon who had squatted on the living room floor, glaring up at Jimmy with hatred in his eyes.

The wolf slithered around the man and withdrew into the darkness of the hallway as Gideon rose to his feet. Leah took one look at him and froze. The beast sniffed noncommittally at her, scenting blood and fear, and then turned to watch the battle between darkness and light.

The predator settled on his haunches, regarding the two men as they faced each other, recognizing them for what they were. Two halves of a whole. The man of darkness had stolen something of the other's soul long before he became the instrument of the curse. The beast waited patiently, knowing that it was not his fight. The young man had to reclaim his soul, and the wolf could not help him.

Behind him, the human female mewled and whined like a newborn pup, but the wolf disregarded her, attentive to what the younger man would do next.

Gideon glowered at his sibling through a shock of light hair. His gaze took in the knife, and something niggled at the back of his mind.

Jimmy stood still, Tiffany clutched tightly to his chest. Her feet performed a jerking dance in the air, and she gagged from the pressure of his arm across her windpipe. Sheridon relented slightly and let her rest her feet against an end table.

He put on his best big-brotherly voice and spoke. "Now, Gideon, this is none of your concern. It's between me and them," he said, half-lifting the girl and indicating the shadow in the hall, which he believed to be Leah, with a jig of his elbow. "You just remember, little brother, what I told you a long, long time ago."

It was the wrong thing to say, for Gideon attacked with an animal roar. Startled, Sheridon dropped Tiffany. She rolled and glided agilely across the floor toward the hall and her mother.

Sheridon was torn for a moment between grabbing the child and diving for cover. That second cost him, for Jimmy was hit with 160 pounds of howling hatred. Gideon rammed him, head down, butting him like a bull or a rutting buck. He caught Jimmy in the soft part of the stomach, and all breath rushed out of Sheridon with a gasp.

Gideon ripped into his older brother like a pile driver, pinning him to the wall. He gouged with sharp nails, bit and tore. He used both hands to batter at either side of his head, his fists catching Jimmy against temple or ear. Then Gideon managed to get ahold of Sheridon's throat, and Jimmy did what he had done before to Leah, bringing the butt end of the knife down on Gideon's head—hard—sadly miscalculating the strength of his kid brother's skull. The younger man didn't even blink. And the handle made slick with sweat twisted in his grip, falling from his grasp onto the floor.

The confidence that he had felt when he first faced his brother and not some snarling wolf evaporated. Gideon, whom Jimmy had always been able to intimidate in the past, would not be swayed or threatened. It seemed he was beyond the range of hearing.

Jimmy clawed at the hands that held his throat. His lungs burned, and the world seemed to fade. Stars burst before his eyes, and Sheridon realized if he didn't act soon he was going to pass out.

Powered by fear and rage, he broke his brother's hold, and before the younger man's hands could find purchase again, Sheridon dived for the knife. Gideon followed and the two were rolling across the floor wrestling over the blade. Jimmy, the more practiced fighter, triumphed. He straddled Gideon, Jimmy's knees holding Gideon's arms pinned. With an agile flick of his wrist, Jimmy righted the knife, its blade pointing at Gideon's throat. "I spared you once. I won't do it again."

The young man's face, so animated during the fight, went slack. The jaw drooped and the hint of nascent intelligence retreated as the jagged pieces of shattered memory reformed and reshaped into an ugly image.

And Gideon was a child again, asleep in his room. A dark form hovered above his bed. A glittering blade scraped his throat. A whispered warning, the voice distorted by time.

A shade above his bed. A shade . . . without a face or a name.

The umbra which seemed to surround the face dissipated, and suddenly Gideon saw the features. The tight rictus of a smile, the dark eyes and hair. The image faded, and there was red everywhere. Red on the bed, the walls, and the floor. So much red that he barely noticed his parents' lumpy shapes under the covers. His eyes followed the curve of their bodies until they came to the place where their heads should be. . . .

The picture fractured and reformed.

His mother's head on a platter, eyes protruding in horror. His father's at the head of the table, wearing an expression of shocked betrayal.

And all the pieces fell into place at last.

The shadow's face hovered before Gideon now, the knife nicking his throat. It spoke the fateful words.

". . . I spared you once. . . ."

Sheridon pressed his advantage, ready to drive the point home. Less than an inch separated the blade from his brother's throat. A deep rumble rolled from the tenebrous hallway, and Jimmy swung to search the darkness. He first saw the tall shadow of Leah, silhouetted by the bedroom light. Another growl and he found the deadly wraith of the wolf.

Beneath Sheridon, his brother's body was slack, and Jimmy, seeing this, leaned into the blade just as a howling bundle of gray and silver fur erupted from the doorway.

Jimmy fell away from his brother's inert form as the beast crashed into him. His arms flailed. Sharp teeth chattered inches away from his face, and Jimmy's hand closed upon thin air as the wolf retreated.

Gideon shook himself and stared at his brother—the full light of comprehension dawning in the younger man's eyes. Jimmy blanched as he guessed at its meaning. Caught between man and wolf, Jimmy chose the lesser adversary, but the moment's hesitation gave Gideon the advantage he needed, and he slapped the blade from Jimmy's hand.

Blind with frustration, Jimmy began to pommel Gideon, slamming his fist into the younger man's belly.

"I . . . told . . . you . . . never . . ."

Sheridon punctuated each word with another blow of his fist. The wolf hesitated, indecisively, and Jimmy, keeping it carefully within his sights, grabbed his brother's long hair and slammed his head against the floor as another shape hurdled from the dark hall and Tiffany landed on him, screaming. Sheridon plucked the girl off his back and tossed her lightly away from him. She went sailing across the room to hit the wall with a bang.

Enough of this shit, Jimmy thought.

Their struggles had brought him within reach of the rifle. Before the stunned man or hesitant beast had time to react,

Jimmy's hands closed around the barrel and he was dragging it toward him.

Blount trudged through the trees, bawling as he went, pausing every so often to identify himself before he went blundering through the next clearing. The last thing he wanted was to have some trigger-happy local blow his brains from here to kingdom come.

This was lunacy.

He had to find Sheridon, tell him to call in his human hounds before someone got hurt. Blount was going to Sheridon for help? Things were out of control, and Blount smoldered, fuse almost spent, wondering what price Jimmy would extract for this service. Nothing, as far as Alan was concerned, was beyond the mealymouthed prick. The cop —ex-cop, he reminded himself—in him was sure that Jimmy was responsible for this whole charade somehow. Not just the hunt—the State Police had already disclosed to him that Jimmy Sheridon was their leader—but everything from Defleurieu's stroke to the many deaths that had visited themselves upon the community. He knew that his conclusion defied logic, defied reason, but he was sure of it—knew it with that sixth sense that every police officer developed over a period of years, so akin to an animal's heightened sense of smell—and this stank like a pile of dead fish.

Police officer, hah! His mind jeered. No more. His career was in ruins; his life was in tatters; his code of ethics in shatters; and his belief in himself nonexistent. If nothing else, Sheridon was responsible for this. He had come out the hero, and Blount made to look like the dumb, fat officer. For that reason, if for nothing else, the punk was going to pay.

A wail resounded somewhere up ahead followed by the bone-chilling howl of . . . a wolf? Blount stopped, stunned. Impossible. It had to be a dog somewhere, perhaps in Leah's kennels. He shuffled on.

Someone hailed Blount with a wave of a torch as he stumbled through the trees.

"Hey!" he bellowed. "It's me, Alan Blount, I'm coming through."

"Alan?" another voice, which he recognized as Tom Ditherton's, answered. "Found anything yet?"

"No!"

"Too bad, come on through, I'll hold them back."

"Great," Alan mumbled as he thrust a sapling out of his way and ambled into the clearing, and back out again. He cursed himself roundly for not bringing the car. The State boys had pointed out the path most of the searchers had taken. In his anger Blount had dived into the woods on foot without thinking. Once on the track it hadn't taken a great deal of smarts to figure out just where Sheridon would most likely be heading.

Leah's.

Fuming, Blount clambered up the hill on the south side of the road that led to the Four Corners. Eventually he hit the backyard of the new house—the one that had been brought in and refurbished—just across the blacktop from Leah's trailer.

There was a loud report. Something pinged past his ear, and Alan realized that someone had just shot at him.

"Shit!" He dropped to the earth. "What the fuck are you doing out there?"

"Alan? Alan Blount, is that you?"

"Of course it's me, for chrissake. Who'd you think it was, the Norman Tabernacle Choir?"

"Holy shit, I didn't realize."

Raising himself to his hands and knees, he shouted: "I'm getting up now. For godsake, don't shoot me. Now, you come out where I can see you."

A shadow appeared a few trees away. Blount squinted. Terry Fletcher, Sr., stepped sheepishly into view.

"Fletcher, what the hell are you doing out here? I would think you have your own, ah, troubles to think of."

Fletcher shrugged. "Just trying to help."

"Great, you almost helped me into an early grave," Blount said. "Now give me the gun and you get along home to Doris."

He took the shotgun, and the other man sagged as soon as he was relieved of his burden.

"Don't know what I'm hunting a wolf for anyway," Fletcher said. "That's not what took my son."

"I know, Terry, I know," said Blount, dropping his voice to a low murmur and patting the man awkwardly on the shoulder. "What happened to your torch? Didn't you bring one?"

The bereaved father shook his head no.

"Take my flashlight. I've almost reached my destination." He pointed to the road up ahead. "I'll walk with you."

"Okay," Fletcher said.

"Now stick to the blacktop and make plenty of noise so people know you're coming. Make sure you don't get your ass shot off."

Blount watched the other man as he descended toward the Four Corners. The gun's weight felt reassuring, and he stroked the cool metal. He had come into this foray unarmed, expecting nothing more from this outing than bereaved parents, and *not* a community caught up in some goddamn witch-hunt. Besides, Alan had retired his gun with his career. The service revolver and the badge went hand in glove, and Alan didn't feel he deserved to carry either. But Blount sure as shit wasn't going to let Terry Fletcher run around the woods shooting everything that moved.

Blount peered down the arboreal cave that formed Leah's drive. Limbs cavorted above his head. A distorted rectangle of yellow light splashed across the dooryard. Shouts came from within. Hefting the shotgun so it was cradled in his arms, Blount headed up the drive. The door hung uselessly on its hinges, and Blount adjusted the gun's position slightly so that he could, with a simple movement, swing it up ready for use. Then he yelled before ascending the steps.

Looking inside, he saw Tiffany, bone-white with terror, holding Gideon Sheridon's head on her lap. Leah peered owlishly from the hallway. Darkening bruises on cheek and jowl, blood drying on cheeks, lips, and chin. For a split second Gideon's and Blount's eyes met, and the officer knew something was different about the boy. Intelligence glimmered in normally empty eyes. Then Alan's attention was drawn away to Sheridon, who was staring at him fro behind the service end of a rifle.

"Sheridon!" Blount's bull-bellow alerted Jimmy, and jumped, bringing the rifle with him. Tiffany crawled over Gideon. She lifted his head from her lap, and he opened eyes. Blount clattered up the stairs, but Tiffany didn't noti him. Her gaze was riveted on Gideon. He stared at he smiling benignly, and Tiffany knew—without knowing ho she knew—that he had changed in some inexplicable wa His eyes gleamed lucid and clear, like any grown-up's, full important thoughts and momentous decisions, and when glanced at Jimmy, there was something else again. His ey reflected cold calculation and appraisal that Tiffany ha often seen in her mother's eyes when she juggled th kennel's precarious accounts.

Gideon clambered to his feet, leaning heavily against th small girl. Both were aware of the wolf's presence deep the shadowed hallway.

Blount ambled casually into the room, gun cradled light and ready to swivel into position with the slightest shif Leah peered uncomprehendingly at the pandemonium around her.

The muzzle of Jimmy's rifle wavered back and fort between the three of them. "Stay back. It doesn't matte who I aim at. This sucker will make mincemeat out of all you and probably leave a hole in the side of the trailer, too, said Jimmy.

"Come on, Jimmy, leave 'em alone. Duke's dead, an they say it was a stroke. Ain't no one gonna swear complaint against you. So if you just put the gun down now you've not done anything wrong."

Leah let out a choked protest, and Blount shot her warning glance.

"Just a family squabble, huh?" Jimmy said. "What kin of fool do you think I am?"

The muscles in Blount's face worked up and dow spasmodically as if he swallowed some sharp retort.

Gideon elbowed Tiffany. She glanced up at him.

"The bone," he hissed. For a second she simply stared at him, uncomprehendingly. The young man prodded her, and she dug in her pocket, bringing out the twinned pieces of ivory.

The wolf saw the bones, and had he had human vocal cords, he would have shouted his glee. Instead muscles tensed, and he rushed forward, leaping not at Jimmy, but at Tiffany. The girl didn't appear to notice. She seemed spellbound, staring at the grisly trophy in her upturned palm.

When the predator hit, she felt nothing. A shiver shook her small frame, and she twitched convulsively as the wolf plunged through . . . into her body. Its spirit, the Indian's spirit, filled the empty vessel to overflowing. Images of past, present, and future flashed through her, confusing her, and the next thing she knew she gazed at the scene around her with full comprehension and understanding. She let the bone roll to the floor. The soft thump of its impact drew Jimmy's attention, and he gasped.

His hold on the gun relaxed as he made ready to dive upon the coveted prize, just as Tiffany brought her foot down upon it with as much force as she could muster.

It glanced off the bone, her foot rolling, and she almost toppled and fell. Gideon caught her arm, steadying her. He tousled Tiffany's hair lovingly, and for an instant he looked sad. Then he pushed her gently toward her mother.

"Go," he said. She started to argue, but Jimmy was descending upon them. Tiffany took a couple of trembling paces away and stopped as Gideon brought the heel of his boot down upon the bones hard, and they shattered.

Blount never could completely remember what happened that night, and he never could have explained it to anyone. He never even tried. He couldn't even explain it to himself. The officer would have sworn on any number of Bibles that a wolf had come howling into the room and leapt at the girl. The bewildered man let the muzzle of the gun hover between man and beast as the wolf struck. The force of the impact should have propelled Tiffany through the far window, but didn't. Instead, it looked as though the creature was thrust into her. Not *through,* but *into,* as if she absorbed the other's body, and the two became one. There was a blinding flash, and for a split second Alan thought that both animal and child had exploded. When Blount was able to see again, the animal was gone. Only the girl remained.

Fear flitted across the elder Sheridon's features, to be replaced by incredulity. Tiffany trembled and something rolled out of her small hand. Jimmy's expression changed from bewilderment to victory, and he started to drop to his knees as she stamped on it, whatever it was, losing her balance as it rolled out from under the soft tennis shoe. Gideon grabbed her, and it looked as though he said something before shoving her away from him. Then he brought his heel down hard upon this thing that seemed to be the subject of their dispute.

A second, equally inexplicable light flared between floor, boot, and man. It rocketed up Gideon's body with a strange red glow, rippling through him like electricity. The young man went rigid, surrounded by the brilliant light, and he seemed to soak it up like a sponge. Sheridon, halfway to his knees to retrieve whatever it was Gideon ground beneath his heel, screeched shrilly. The younger brother folded like an empty coat, collapsing in a heap on the floor.

Stunned, Blount lowered the shotgun. Jimmy took this opportunity to act and brought the rifle around, shrieking in rage, and aimed it straight at the girl. Leah, who until this time had remained still as though caught in a thrall, finally moved. Screaming, she threw herself at Tiffany, pushing her daughter toward Blount, and only then did he see her face. Her eyes were bloodred, and it seemed she wept crimson tears. Her nose, or what was left of it, had been pushed to one side of her face.

As she flew across the space that separated her from her daughter, Sheridon squeezed the trigger. The blast reverberated around the small mobile home, and Leah Blair took the bullet meant for her daughter. Its impact changed the course of her body, which was flung against the far wall, and blood, flesh, and bone exploded from her.

Somebody, Sheridon thought it was Tiffany, wailed.

And suddenly the voices roared inside Blount's head. They cried out for justice, and Alan's hatred for Jimmy and his big, smug grin blossomed.

Sheridon leered at him, steadying the butt against his shoulder ready to take aim a second time. What was left of the police officer in Alan died then—the officer who would have cuffed him and read him his rights. Wheeling on Sheridon, Alan shot him right between the eyes.

And Blount released the second barrel. Faces of his friends surfaced in his mind. His neighbors dying, and if he had had the time, he would have discharged a bullet for each one. Suddenly he became conscious of the flames that engulfed the trailer.

Blount acted on reflex, folding his arms around Tiffany and springing for the door. Behind him, the gray form of a wolf shimmered in the flames. The head dipped, and the great beast licked Gideon's face. Then Blount ducked his head, and they somersaulted down to the dooryard. The girl bawled, fighting him, trying to get back to the trailer, crying for her mother.

Distant shouts drew near. The turquoise mobile home burned merrily, blackening and scorching as they watched. Blount turned as all too familiar sirens sounded from the Four Corners.

The child glared at him with eyes that looked old beyond her years. He patted her arm clumsily, dimly recollecting that Tiffany had a brother that lived in Searsport. She wriggled in his grasp. Again Alan looked at her, scrutinizing her face. She didn't have the slightly dull-witted look he remembered in the past. The image of someone who was a few bricks shy, so similar to the soft-focused look he had often seen with Gideon. The gaze that rested on him was intense, anguished. He studied the girl in wonder.

Somewhere on the strip of land between lighthouse and town, Aggie lifted a tear-stained face to stare apathetically at the sky, awash again with perdition's flames. She was slumped against a large boulder, her leg hooked over a natural ledge worn into the rock's granite surface. It began to rumble and shake beneath her.

Dull eyes watched as the cemetery Aggie *knew* couldn't exist began to sink into bubbling, boiling earth. The slanting tombstones and warped wooden crosses shivered as a tremor rattled through them. One fell with a crash, and the graveyard disappeared with a liquid burp.

Fire leapt in a frenzied dance, the curse and its aftermath consumed in the blaze. The wolf stood unaffected. No flames singed his coat, nor did the fierce air currents that whipped around the room ripple his fur. These same flames lapped eagerly up Gideon's pant legs. The wolf whined in the young man's ear. Its long tongue scraped the rough cheek.

Gideon's hair began to sizzle and curl, until it ignited with a *whoosh*, and the young man's spirit separated from the hissing form, rising to hover above the spent body, his purpose fulfilled. The skin on the corpse began to bubble. A wavering image of the young man stepped away from it to stand beside the charring corpse, and a phantom hand went out to stroke the wolf's head.

The spectral eyes sparked with intelligence. In death Gideon was complete and undivided as he had never been in life. Memory—so long denied him—came clearly.

The wolf's lip curled in a canine grin at his new companion and the spirit form smiled back at the wolf. And the two, beast and man, walked through the capering fire together, disappearing into the blaze.

Tiffany and Sam lingered awhile, hand in hand, saying a silent good-bye to the old trailer which they both had called home. Its metal struts stretched to the sky. Twisted and warped by the heat, they curved inward, looking like the blackened ribs of a beached whale. This was only a reflection of the devastation that pockmarked the town. The woods beyond the highway were little more than stubble, and many of the homes were empty, whole families having been wiped out. Those people that remained were leaving in droves. The Fletchers had packed up and moved as soon as they could. Mr. Blisson had already slipped away. Lorraine Garreth and her baby had returned to Vermont to live with her parents.

Autumn, held so long in abeyance, had arrived in a rush, and the trees were stripped of their leaves before they had time to change to fall dress. Skeletal limbs thrashed overhead in a gunmetal sky. Pregnant clouds promised early snows.

Sam and Tiffany were among the last to go, their exit held up by the police investigation. With Leah's and Jimmy's deaths coming on the heels of so many others, the hearing had been a perfunctory affair. It was ruled that Blount had acted in the "line of duty," his abrupt resignation conveniently forgotten, and he was applauded as a hero. Sam tendered his resignation, selling his worldly goods to some fast-talking auctioneer from Bangor. Time to make his dream a reality. With the proceeds from that and the sale of his car, he had scraped together enough money to buy a second-hand Volkswagen camper and still have enough in savings to set themselves up once they had reached their goal.

Sam squeezed Tiffany's hand, still not sure what to make of her yet—this new girl who had been irrevocably altered. The experience had aged her, true, but it had done more than that. She looked at him from eyes grown suddenly wise, and he had discovered in the intervening days that she *could* read—as if she had been storing the knowledge for years and the shock of seeing her mother killed had caused it to surface.

Aggie joined them, taking the girl's other hand. Like Sam, she had sold everything, shop and all, the whole kit'n'kaboodle. She had *had* it. She didn't care what happened to the store now. As far as Aggie was concerned, the whole damned town could survive just as well without her.

Aggie would travel with them—the destination meant little to her now. Any place would do as long as it was away from here.

A horn blared. They turned. Alan Blount's recreational vehicle putted impatiently on the road. Sam dropped his sister's hand and strode to the end of the drive. Aggie glanced down at Tiffany and saw the sorrow etched across her features.

"She's at peace now," Aggie said.

"Uh-huh, I know. They all are," Tiffany replied.

"What's the matter, then?" she said.

"I don't want to go. This is my home." Tiffany looked at Sam. "It isn't a bad place. Just like the people, they aren't bad. They're just . . . hurting, wounded."

"You know you can't stay," Aggie reminded her gently.

Casting a sidelong glance at the "Florida or Bust" sign Sam had spray-painted on the back of the van in one Saturday afternoon's flush of Molson-Golden-inspired enthusiasm, she said, "No, but I can learn. I can become smart, and I can come back. I want to heal things . . . people. Like a doctor or a"—and her eyes sparkled as her mind lit on a thought—"a veterinarian."

Sam, who had come up behind them as they talked, interrupted. "Where'd you learn a big word like that?"

"That's what Dr. Kimball is, isn't he?"

"Sure 'nuff, squirt, you got that right," Sam said in the not-very-convincing southern drawl he had practiced ever since he had decided on this quest.

"Well, that's what I want to be when I grow up. A veterinarian."

He grinned at her. "You know, I think you might just do it."

"And I'll come back."

His face darkened and he scowled. "Well, I can't stop you. By that time you'll be of age. This little scrap of land will still be here, I won't sell it. Who'd buy it? And I most certainly don't want it. But give Florida a chance, won't you?"

"Hey, what'cha waitin' for?" Blount bellowed. Beside

him, Ginny sorted through the ice chest, counting sandwiches and ticking off items against a list. "Aren't you ready yet?"

Sam glanced down at Tiffany, who inclined her head in assent, and he said: "Ayah."

"Meet all of you down at the gas station." Blount thumbed at the basket in Ginny's lap. "All this stuff is for you. I think she brought enough to feed an army." He eyed Sam's dwindling girth. "Maybe it's not such a bad idea after all."

The tires crunched against the gravel as Blount gently eased the RV onto the center of the small road and headed for Highway One, turning south to follow the sun.